IMPACT

DOUGLAS PRESTON

PAN BOOKS

First published 2010 by Forge, Tom Doherty Associates, LLC

First published in Great Britain 2010 by Macmillan

This edition published 2010 by Pan Books
an imprint of Pan Macmillan
20 New Wharf Road, London N1 9RR
Associated companies throughout the world
www.panmacmillan.com

ISBN 978-0-330-50887-2

7 9 8

A CIP catalogue record for this book is available from
the British Library.

Typeset by Intype Libra Ltd, London
Printed in Great Britain by CPI Group (UK) Ltd, Croydon, CR0 4YY

Visit **www.panmacmillan.com** to read more about all our books
and to buy them. You will also find features, author interviews and
news of any author events, and you can sign up for e-newsletters
so that you're always first to hear about our new releases.

To Tony and Petra O'Brien,
Kiera, Liam, and Brenna

Acknowledgements

The author is grateful to Lincoln Child, Eric Simonoff, Bob Gleason, Tom Doherty, Matthew Snyder, Bobby Rotenberg, Claudia Rülke, Jon Couch, Selene Preston, and Isaac Preston for their valuable help.

PART 1

PART 1.

1

APRIL

THE TRICK WOULD be to slip in the side door and get the box up the back stairs without making a sound. The house was two hundred years old and you could hardly take a step without a flurry of creaks and groans. Abbey Straw eased the back door shut and tiptoed across the carpeted hallway to the landing. She could hear her father puttering around the kitchen, Red Sox game low on the radio.

Her arms hugging the box, she set her foot on the first step, eased down her weight, then the next step, and the next. She skipped the fourth step—it shrieked like a banshee—and put her weight on the fifth, the sixth, the seventh. . . . And just as she thought she was home free, the step let out a crack like a gunshot, followed by a long, dying groan.

Damn.

"Abbey, what's in the box?"

Her father stood in the doorway of the kitchen, still

wearing his orange rubber boots, his checked shirt stained with diesel fuel and lobster bait. His windburned brow was creased with suspicion.

"A telescope."

"A telescope? How much did it cost?"

"I bought it with my own money."

"Great," he said, his gravelly voice tense, "if you never want to go back to college and stay a waitress the rest of your life, blow your paycheck on telescopes."

"Maybe I want to be an astronomer."

"Do you know how much I spent on your college education?"

She turned and continued up the stairs. "You mention it only five times a day."

"When are you going to pull yourself together?"

She slammed the door and stood for a moment in her tiny bedroom, breathing hard. With one arm she swept the bedcover free of stuffed animals, set the box down on the bed. She flopped on the bed next to the box. Why had she been adopted by white people in Maine, the whitest state in the union, in a town where everyone was white? Hadn't there been a black hedge-fund manager somewhere looking for kids? "And where do *you* come from?" people would ask her, as if she'd recently arrived from Harlem—or Kenya.

She rolled over in bed, gazing at the box. Sliding out her cell phone, she dialed. "Jackie?" she whispered. "Meet me down at the wharf at nine. I got a surprise."

Fifteen minutes later, cradling the telescope, Abbey cracked the bedroom door and listened. Her father was moving about the kitchen, washing the dishes that she was supposed to have washed that morning. The game was still on, turned up, Dave Goucher's obnoxious voice barking out of the cheap radio. By the sound of her father's occasional swearing she figured it must be a Sox–Yankees game. Good, he'd be distracted. She crept down the stairs, stepping gingerly, trying not to creak the old pine boards, slipped past the open kitchen door and in a moment was out and into the street.

Balancing the tripod over her shoulder, she darted past the Anchor Inn toward the town wharf. The harbor was as calm as a millpond, a great sheet of black water stretching to the dim silhouette of Louds Island, the boats lined up by the tide like white ghosts. The peppercan buoy marking the channel at the mouth of the narrow harbor blinked its light, blink, blink, blink. Above, the heavens swirled with phosphorescence.

She angled across the parking lot, past the lobster co-op, and headed onto the wharf. The strong smell of herring bait and seaweed drifted on the damp night air from a stack of old lobster traps at one end of the pier. The lobster joint hadn't opened yet for the summer season and the outdoor picnic tables were still turned up and chained to the railings. Back up the hill she could see the lights of the town and the steeple of the Methodist Church, a black spire against the Milky Way.

"Hey." Jackie stepped out of the shadows, the red glow of a joint bobbing in the dark. "What's that?"

"A telescope." Abbey took the joint and inhaled sharply, with a crackle of burning seeds. She exhaled and handed it back.

"A telescope?" asked Jackie. "What for?"

"What else is there to do around here but look at the stars?"

Jackie grunted. "How much was it?"

"Seven hundred bucks. Got it on eBay, a Celestron six-inch Cassegrain, automatic tracking, a camera and everything."

A low whistle. "You must be getting some good tips over at the Landing."

"They love me over there. I couldn't get bigger tips if I was giving out blow jobs."

Jackie burst out laughing, wheezing smoke and coughing. She passed the joint back and Abbey took another long hit.

"Randy's getting out of Maine State," said Jackie, lowering her voice.

"Oh God. Randy can sit on a lobster buoy and rotate five times."

Jackie muffled a laugh.

"What a night," Abbey said, staring at the immense bowl of stars. "Let's take some pictures."

"In the dark?"

Abbey looked over to see if she was kidding, but there was no wry smile on those lips. She felt a wave of affection for her dim, lovable friend. "Believe it or not," Abbey said, "telescopes work better in the dark."

"Right. That was stupid." Jackie knocked on her own head. "Hello?"

They walked out to the end of the pier. Abbey set up the tripod, making sure it was anchored on the wood planking. She could see Orion hanging low in the sky and aimed the telescope in that direction. Using the computer starfinder attached to the telescope, she punched in a preset location.

With a whirring of worm-gears, the telescope slewed around to point at a patch at the bottom of Orion's sword.

"What're we going to look at?"

"The Andromeda Galaxy."

Abbey peered into the eyepiece and the galaxy sprang into view, a glowing maelstrom of five hundred billion stars. She felt her throat constricting with the thought of the immensity of it, and her own smallness.

"Lemme see," said Jackie, sweeping back her long, unruly hair.

Abbey stepped back and silently offered her the eyepiece. Jackie fitted her eye to it. "How far away is it?"

"Two and a quarter million light-years."

Jackie stared for a while in silence, then stood up. "Think there's life out there?"

"Of course."

Abbey adjusted the telescope, zooming out, increasing its field of view, until most of Orion's sword was visible. Andromeda had shrunk into a little fuzz-ball. She pressed the cable release and heard the faint click as the shutter opened. It would be a twenty-minute time exposure.

A faint breeze came from the ocean, clanking the rigging of a fishing boat, and all the boats in the harbor swung in unison. It felt like the first breath of a storm, despite the dead calm. An invisible loon called from the water and was answered by another one, far away.

"Time for another doobie." Jackie began rolling a joint, licked it, and put it in her mouth. A click and flare of the lighter illuminated her face, her pale, freckled skin, green Irish eyes, and black hair.

Abbey saw the sudden light before she saw the thing itself.

It came from behind the church, the harbor instantly as bright as day; it streaked across the sky in utter silence, like a ghost, and then an immense sonic boom shook the pier, followed by a blast-furnace roar as the thing blazed over the ocean at incredible speed, disappearing behind Louds Island. There was a final flash of light followed by a cannonade of thunder, rolling away over the ocean distances into silence.

Behind her, up in the town, dogs began barking hysterically.

"What the *fuck*?" Jackie said.

Abbey could see the whole town coming out of their houses and gathering in the streets. "Get rid of the pot," she hissed.

The road up the hill was filling with people, jabbering away, voices raised in excitement and alarm. They began moving down toward the piers, flashlights flickering, arms pointing skyward. This was the biggest thing that had happened in Round Pond, Maine, since a stray cannonball went through the roof of the Congregational Church in the War of 1812.

Suddenly Abbey remembered her telescope. The shutter was open and still taking a picture. With a trembling hand she found the shutter release and clicked it off. A moment later the image popped up on the telescope's small LCD screen.

"Oh my God." The thing had streaked through the center of the image, a brilliant slash of white among a scattering of stars.

"It ruined your picture," said Jackie, peering over her shoulder.

"Are you kidding? It *made* the picture!"

2

THE NEXT MORNING, Abbey shoved through the door of the Cupboard Café with a stack of newspapers under her arm. The cheerful log-cabin diner with its checkered curtains and marble tables was almost empty, but she found Jackie sitting in her usual place in the corner, drinking coffee. A damp morning fog pressed against the windowpanes.

She hustled over and slapped *The New York Times* down on the table, exposing the front-page article below the fold.

Meteor Lights up Maine Coast

Portland, Maine—At 9:44 p.m. a large meteor streaked across the skies of Maine, creating one of the most brilliant meteor displays seen over New England in decades. Witnesses from as far as Boston and Nova Scotia reported seeing the spectacular fireball. Residents of Midcoast Maine heard sonic booms.

Data from a meteoroid tracking system at the University of Maine, Orono, indicated that the meteor was several times brighter than the full moon and may have weighed as much as fifty tons when it entered the Earth's atmosphere. The single track reported by witnesses suggests the meteorite was of the iron-nickel type, as those are the least likely to break up in flight, rather than the more common stony-iron or chondritic type. Its speed, tracking scientists estimated, was 48 kilometers per second or about 100,000 miles per hour—thirty times faster than a typical rifle bullet.

Dr. Stephen Chickering, professor of planetary geology at Boston University, said: "This isn't a typical fireball. It's the brightest and biggest meteor seen on the East Coast in decades. The trajectory took it out to sea, where it landed in the ocean."

He also explained that its journey through the atmosphere would have vaporized most of its mass. The final object that struck the ocean, he said, probably weighed less than a hundred pounds.

Abbey broke off and grinned at Jackie. "You read that? *It landed in the ocean.* That's what all the papers are saying." She settled back and crossed her arms, enjoying Jackie's wondering look.

"Okay," said Jackie, "I can see you've got something on your mind."

Abbey lowered her voice. "*We're going to be rich.*"

Jackie rolled her eyes theatrically. "I've heard that before."

"This time I'm not kidding." Abbey looked around. She slid a piece of paper out of her pocket and unfolded it on the table.

"What's that?"

"It's the data printout of GoMOOS Weather Buoy 44032, between 4:40 and 5:40 GMT. That's the instrument buoy out beyond Weber Sunken Ledge."

Jackie stared at it, crunching her freckled brow. "I know it."

"Look at the wave heights. Dead calm. No change."

"So?"

"A hundred-pound meteorite slams into the ocean at a hundred thousand miles an hour and doesn't make waves?"

Jackie shrugged. "So if it didn't land in the ocean, where did it land?"

Abbey leaned forward, clasped her hands, her voice dropping to a hiss, her face flushing with triumph. "On an *island.*"

"So?"

"So, we borrow my father's boat, search those islands, and get that meteorite."

"Borrow? You mean steal. Your father would never let you *borrow* his boat."

"Borrow, steal, expropriate, whatever."

Jackie's face darkened. "Please, not another wild-goose chase. Remember when we went looking for Dixie Bull's treasure? And how we got in trouble digging in the Indian mounds?"

"We were just kids then."

"There are dozens of islands out there in Muscongus Bay, tens of thousands of acres to cover. You'd never search them all."

"We don't have to. Because I've got *this.*" She pulled out the photograph of the meteor and laid it on top of a chart of Muscongus Bay. "With the photo, you can extrapolate a line to the horizon and then draw a second line from that point to where the photo was taken. The meteorite must have landed somewhere along that second line."

"I'll take your word for it."

Abbey pushed the chart toward her. "There's the line." Her finger stabbed a line she had penciled across the chart. "Look. It intersects just *five* islands."

The waitress approached with two enormous pecan sticky buns. Abbey quickly covered up the chart and photograph and sat back with a smile. "Hey, thanks."

When the waitress had gone, Abbey uncovered the chart. "That's it. The meteorite is on one of these islands." Her finger thumped on each one in turn as she named it: "Louds, Marsh, Ripp, Egg Rock, and Shark. We could search them in less than a week."

"When? Now?"

"We have to wait til the end of May, when my father'll be out of town."

Jackie crossed her arms. "What the hell we gonna do with a meteorite?"

"Sell it."

Jackie stared. "It's worth something?"

"Quarter million, half a million. That's all."

"You're shitting me."

Abbey shook her head. "I checked prices on eBay, talked to a meteorite dealer."

Jackie leaned back, a grin slowly spreading over her freckled face. "I'm in."

3

MAY

DOLORES MUÑOZ CLIMBED the stone steps to the professor's bungalow in Glendale, California, and rested a moment on the porch, her large bosom heaving, before inserting the key. The scrape of the key sounding in the lock, she knew, would trigger an explosion of yapping as Stamp, the professor's Jack Russell terrier, went berserk at her arrival. As soon as she opened the door the ball of fur would shoot out like a bullet, barking furiously, whirling about the tiny lawn as if to clear it of wild beasts and criminals. And then he would make his rounds, lifting his little leg on each sad bush and dead flower. Finally, his duty done, he would rush over, lie down in front of her, and roll on his back, paws folded, tongue hanging out, ready for his morning scratch.

Dolores Muñoz loved that dog.

With a faint smile of anticipation she inserted the key in

the lock, giving it a little rattle and waiting for the eruption of excitement.

Nothing.

She paused, listening, and then turned the key, expecting joyful barking at any moment. Still it did not come. Puzzled, she stepped into a small entryway. The first thing she noticed was that the side-table drawer was open, envelopes scattered on the floor.

"Professor?" she called out, her voice hollow, and then, "Stamp?"

No answer. Lately the professor had been a later and later riser. He was one of those types who drank a lot of wine with dinner and snifters of brandy afterward and it had been getting worse, especially after he stopped going to work. And then there were the women. Dolores was no prude and she wouldn't have minded if it was the same girl. But it never was, and sometimes they were ten, twenty years younger than he was. Still, the professor was a fine, fit man in the prime of life who spoke excellent Spanish to her using the Usted form, which she appreciated.

"Stamp?"

Maybe they had gone out for a walk. She moved into the front hall and peered toward the living room, suddenly drawing in her breath. Papers and books were scattered over the floor, a lamp was overturned, and the far set of bookshelves had been swept free, the books lying in jumbled heaps below.

"Professor!"

The full horror of it sank in. The professor's car was in the driveway and he must be at home—why didn't he answer? And where was Stamp? Almost without thinking, her plump hand fumbled the cell phone out of her green housedress to dial 911. She stared at the keypad, unable to press in the numbers. Was this really the kind of thing she should get involved in? They would come and take down her name and address and check her out and the next thing she knew, she would be deported to El Salvador. Even if she called anonymously from her cell, they would still track her down as a witness to . . . she refused to complete the thought.

A feeling of terror and uncertainty seized her. The professor could be upstairs, robbed, beaten, injured, maybe dying. And Stamp, what did they do to Stamp?

Panic took hold. She stared about wildly, breathing heavily, her large bosom heaving. She felt tears spring into her eyes. She had to do something, she had to call the police, she couldn't just walk out—what was she thinking? He might be hurt, dying. She had to at least look around, see if he needed help, try to figure out what to do.

Moving toward the living room, she saw something on the floor, like a crumpled pillow. Unbearable dread in her heart, she took a step forward, then another, placing her feet with infinite care on the soft carpet, and gave a low moan. It was Stamp, lying on the Persian rug with his back to her. He could have been sleeping, with his little pink tongue lolling out, except that his eyes were wide open and clouded over and there was a dark stain on the rug underneath him.

"*Ohhh ooohh,*" she said, the involuntary sound coming out of her open mouth. Beyond the little dog lay the professor, on his knees, kneeling almost as if praying, almost as if he were still alive, oddly balanced so it looked like he should topple over, except that his head was hanging to one side, halfway off, like a broken doll's head, and a coil of wire wrapped around two dowels of wood dangled from the half-severed neck. Blood had sprayed like a hose over the walls and ceiling.

Dolores Muñoz screamed, and screamed again, knowing vaguely that deportation lay in those screams but somehow unable to stop and no longer caring.

4

WYMAN FORD ENTERED the elegant confines of the Seventeenth Street office of Stanton Lockwood III, science advisor to the president of the United States. He remembered the room from his previous assignment: the power wall, the pictures of the wife and towheaded children, the Important Washington Power Broker antique furnishings.

Lockwood came around the desk, silver haired, his blue eyes crinkling, footfalls hushed on the Sultanabad carpet. He grasped Ford's hand in a politician's shake. "Nice to see you again, Wyman." He reminded Ford of Peter Graves, the white-haired man who played the leader of the Mission Impossible force on the old television series.

"Good to see you, too, Stan," Ford said.

"We'll be more comfortable over here," he said, gesturing toward a brace of leather wing chairs flanking a Louis XIV coffee table. As Ford settled in, Lockwood seated himself opposite, giving the knife-edge in his gabardine slacks a little tug. "What's it been, a year?"

"More or less."

"Coffee? Pellegrino?"

"Coffee, thanks."

Lockwood signaled his secretary and leaned back in the chair. The old trilobite worry stone appeared in his hand and Ford watched him roll it about pensively between thumb and forefinger. He bestowed a professional Washington smile on Ford. "Any interesting cases lately?"

"A few."

"Time for a new one?"

"If it's anything like the last one, no thanks."

"Trust me, you'll like this assignment." He nodded to a small metal box on the table. "They call them 'honeys.' You heard of them?"

Ford leaned over and peered through a thick glass window in the top of the box. Inside winked a number of deep orange gemstones. "Can't say I have."

"They appeared on the Bangkok wholesale market about two weeks ago. Going for big money—a thousand dollars for the cut carat."

A serving man came in wheeling a fussy little sideboard with silver coffeepot, lump raw sugar, cream and milk in separate silver pitchers, and china cups. The little tray rattled and squeaked as it was pushed along. He parked it next to Ford.

"Sir?"

"Black, no sugar, please."

The man poured. Ford sat back with the steaming cup and took a sip.

"I'll leave the pot here in case the gentleman wants another."

The gentleman would want another, thought Ford, draining the tiny china cup with one gulp and refilling it.

Lockwood worried the stone in his hands. "I've got a team of geophysicists at Lamont-Doherty in New York working on what they are. The stones are unusual in composition, with an index of refraction higher than a diamond, specific gravity thirteen point-two, hardness nine. The deep honey color is almost unique. A beautiful stone—with a twist. They're laced with Americium-241."

"Which is radioactive."

"Yes, with a half-life of four hundred thirty-three years. Not enough radiation to kill you right away but enough to create long-term exposure problems. Wear a string of these around your neck and you're liable to lose your hair after a few weeks. Carry a pocketful of these around for a couple of months and you might sire the monster from the black lagoon."

"Lovely."

"The stones are hard but brittle and easily pulverized. You could take a few pounds of these gems, grind them up, pack them in C-4 in a suicide belt, detonate it in Battery Park when the wind is from the south, and you could loft a nice radioactive cloud over the financial district, wipe out a few trillion dollars of U.S. market capitalization in half an hour and render lower Manhattan uninhabitable for a couple of centuries."

"Nice work if you can get it."

"Homeland Security is freaking out."

"Do the Bangkok dealers know they're hot?"

"The reputable wholesalers won't touch 'em. They're being funneled through the dregs of the gem market."

"Any idea how these gems formed?"

"We're working on it. Americium-241 is not an element that exists naturally on Earth. The only known way it can be made is as a by-product of a nuclear reactor producing weapons-grade plutonium. These 'honeys' might well be evidence of illicit nuclear activity."

Ford finished his second cup and poured himself a third.

"All indications are that the stones are coming out of a single source in Southeast Asia, most likely Cambodia," said Lockwood.

Draining the third cup, Ford leaned back. "So what's the assignment?"

"I want you to go undercover to Bangkok, follow the trail of these radioactive honeys back to the source, locate it, document it, and come back out."

"And then?"

"We make the problem go away."

"Why me? Why not CIA?"

"This is sensitive stuff—Cambodia is an ally. You get caught, we need deniability. It's not the kind of operation the CIA does well—small and quick, in and out. A one-man job. I'm afraid you won't have Agency backup on this one."

"Thanks for the offer." Ford set down his cup and rose to leave.

"The president's approved the op personally."

"Excellent coffee." He headed for the door.

"I promise, we won't hang you out to dry."

He paused.

"It's simple: go in, find the mine, get out. Do absolutely nothing. Don't touch the mine. We're still analyzing those gemstones—they might be extremely important."

"I have no interest in going back to Cambodia," said Ford, his hand resting on the doorknob.

"It does no service to your wife's memory to keep running from your past."

Ford was startled at this unexpected and painful insight from Lockwood. He sighed and folded his arms.

"The money's good," said Lockwood, "the CIA won't interfere, you'll be in control, in charge of your own people. You have the backing of the Oval Office—what more could you want?"

"What's my cover?"

"Crooked American black-market gem wholesaler."

Ford shook his head. "Won't work. A wholesaler wouldn't care about finding the source—he'd be content to buy from middlemen. I'll be a get-rich-quick schemer looking for a one-time killing—the kind of guy who thinks he'll get a better price by bypassing the wholesalers and going directly to the source."

"Is that a yes?"

"Give me a rap sheet with an arrest for smuggling cocaine, dismissed on a technicality."

"You want to get killed?"

"And two brutal murder charges, acquitted. That'll make 'em think twice."

"If that's the way you want to play it, fine."

"I'll need some gold to throw around. American eagles."

"Will do."

"I want translators standing by, twenty-four/seven, fluent in the common Southeast Asian languages, especially Thai. There are a couple of high-tech devices I'll need."

"No problem."

"If I fail, bury me in Arlington Cemetery, twenty-one-gun salute, the works."

"I'm sure that won't be necessary," said Lockwood, his thin lips tightening into a mirthless smile. "Does this mean you're in?"

"What's the compensation?"

"A hundred thousand. Same as last time."

"Make it two, so I can pay my secretary's health insurance."

Lockwood extended his hand. "Two."

They shook. As Ford left the office, he noticed the worry stone going a mile a minute in Lockwood's manicured hand.

5

MARK CORSO ENTERED his modest apartment and shut the door. He stood there for a moment, as if seeing it for the first time. The crying of a baby came through the walls and a heavy smell of fried bacon permeated the stale air. The air-conditioner unit, which took up a third of the window, thumped and shuddered, issuing a feeble current. The faint sound of sirens penetrated from outside. In front of him, the picture window looked out over a busy intersection with a car wash, drive-thru burger joint, and a used-car lot.

For the first time, Corso took a grim satisfaction in the general seediness of the apartment, the paper-thin walls, the stains on the rug, the dead ficus in the corner, the soul-crushing view. A year ago he had rented the apartment long-distance, suckered by the glowing description on a Web site and a raft of artfully shot photographs. From Green-point, Brooklyn, it had seemed like pure California dream-ing, a large one-bedroom "drenched" with light, with a private garden, swimming pool, palm trees, and (best of all) a parking garage with his very own assigned space.

Now, finally, he could say good-bye to this dump.

The past few months at NPF had been crazy, with his old professor and mentor Jason Freeman getting canned— followed by his freakish murder in a home invasion and robbery. That had shaken Corso up like nothing since the death of his father. Freeman had been going downhill for a while, coming in late to work, blowing off staff meetings, arguing with colleagues. Corso had heard rumors of women and heavy drinking. It distressed him deeply because Freeman, his undergraduate thesis advisor back at MIT, had been the one who brought him into the Mars mission at NPF.

That morning, Corso had learned he was going to be promoted to Freeman's place. It was an enormous step forward, with a new title, more money, and prestige. He wasn't even thirty yet, younger than most of his colleagues, a rising star. Nevertheless, his good fortune built on the back of his beloved teacher's failure filled him with conflicting feelings.

He turned from the window and pushed the sting of guilt out of his mind. What happened to Freeman was tragic, but it was random, like being struck by lightning, and Corso had done all he could. He'd supported Freeman among his colleagues and had tried to warn him about what was happening. Freeman seemed in the grip of some reckless obsession or force larger than life that was dragging him down, despite all Corso could do.

The promotion meant he'd finally have the money to break his lease, kiss his security deposit good-bye, and find something better. No problem there; Pasadena wasn't like Brooklyn and there were thousands of other apartments for rent. Having been there a year, he was familiar enough with the area to know where to look and which areas to avoid.

In the middle of these thoughts a timid knock came on the door. Corso turned from the window, peeked through the eyehole to see the building super standing with something in his hand. He opened the door and the rotund little man stuck out a hairy arm with a small cardboard box. "Package."

He took it, thanked the man, shut the door. Something from Amazon, it seemed . . . but then he looked more closely and felt a sudden freezing of his spine. The box had been reused; the package was from Jason J. Freeman.

For a crazy moment Corso thought maybe Freeman wasn't dead after all, that the old reprobate had gone to Mexico or something, but then he noted the cancellation date, which was ten days old, and the MEDIA MAIL stamp on the box. Ten days . . . Freeman had mailed the package two days before his murder and it had been in transit ever since.

His heart racing, Corso took a paring knife from the kitchen and slit open the box. He removed wadded newspaper to expose a letter and, nesting underneath, a high-density hard drive stenciled with the Mars mission logo. As he lifted it out, he saw, with a sudden feeling not unlike nausea, that it was classified.

#785A56H6T 160Tb

CLASSIFIED: DO NOT DUPLICATE

Property of NPF

California Institute of Technology

National Aeronautics and Space Administration

With a trembling hand Corso placed it on the coffee table and slit open the envelope with his fingernail. Inside was a handwritten letter.

Dear Mark,

I'm sorry to burden you but there's no other way. I don't have much time to write, so I'll be blunt. Chaudry and Derkweiler are arrant fools, they are political animals through and through, and they're incapable of understanding the significance of what I've discovered. This is huge, unbelievable. I'm not about to hand it to those bastards, especially after the way they've treated me. It's a serpent's den over there at NPF with all those self-important hemorrhoidal shit-encrusted assholes. Everything is political and nothing's about science. I just couldn't take it any longer. It's impossible to work there.

To make a long story short, I saw the writing on the wall, so before I was fired I smuggled out this drive.

Someday I'll tell you all about it over a brace of martinis but that's not why I need your help now. My last week at NPF I did something really stupid, really compromising, and because of that I've got to park this drive with you. Just for a while, as a precaution, until things cool off. Do this for me, Mark, please. You're the only one I can trust.

Don't contact me, don't call, just sit tight. You'll hear from me sooner rather than later. In the meantime, I'd love to have your thoughts on the gamma ray data in here, if you get a chance to look at it.

Jason

And then, scrawled at the bottom almost as an afterthought, was the password to the drive.

For a moment Corso couldn't even think as he stared at the letter, until he realized it was rattling in his trembling hand.

This was a disaster. A catastrophe beyond belief. A breach of security that would stain everyone involved. This would fuck up everything. Not only was it highly illegal for the classified hard drive to be outside the building, but the fact that Freeman had even managed to smuggle it out would cause an uproar. Security of classified information had been drummed into them from day one. Zero tolerance. He remembered the scandal back at Los Alamos in the nineties when a single classified hard drive went missing. The news made the front page of *The New York Times*, the director was forced out, and dozens of scientists fired. It was a bloodbath.

He sat down, his head in his hands, clutching his hair. How did Freeman get it out? These drives had to be wrapped with a security seal every night, logged, and locked in a safe. They were encrypted up the wazoo and physically alarmed. Every use of the drive was recorded on the user's permanent security record. If the drive were moved more than a certain distance from its approved server, alarms would go off.

Freeman had somehow evaded all that.

Corso rubbed his eyes with the palms of his hands, tried to calm himself down. If he brought this to the attention of NPF, it would cause a scandal, cast a dark cloud over the whole Mars mission, and taint everyone—especially him. Freeman and he went back years. Freeman had brought him in, mentored him; he was known as Freeman's protégé. He had tried to help Freeman during his free fall over the past few months.

But of course he had to do the right thing and report it. No choice. He had to.

Or did he? Was it better to do the right thing or the smart thing?

He began to understand why Freeman had sent it to him via media mail instead of by some other means. Untraceable. Nothing to sign for and no tracking number.

If Corso destroyed the drive and pretended he never received it, nobody would be the wiser. Eventually they might discover the drive was missing and that Freeman took it, but Freeman was dead and that's where it would end. They'd never trace the drive to him.

Corso began to feel calmer. This was a manageable problem. He would do the smart thing, destroy the drive, pretend he'd never gotten it. Tomorrow, he'd drive up into the mountains, go for a hike, bust it up into pieces, burn, scatter, and bury them.

He immediately felt a wash of relief. Clearly that was the correct way to handle this problem.

Standing up, he went into the kitchen and got himself a beer, took a frosty pull, came back into the living room. He stared at the drive, sitting on his coffee table. Freeman was excitable, a bit crazy, but he was also brilliant. What was this big thing, this gamma ray thing? Corso found his curiosity aroused.

Before he got rid of the drive, he'd just take a quick look at it—see what the hell Freeman was talking about.

6

AT THE WHEEL, Abbey guided the lobster boat toward the floating dock, tossed out a fender, and neatly brought it alongside. *See that, Dad?* she thought, *I'm perfectly capable of piloting your boat.* Her father had gone to California on his annual visit to his widowed older sister and would be gone for a week. She'd promised to take care of the boat, check up on it, look into the bilges every day.

That's what she planned to do—on the water.

She remembered those summers when she was thirteen, fourteen—when her mother was still alive—the mornings she had set off with her father to go lobstering. She worked as his "stern man," baiting the traps, measuring and sorting the lobsters, tossing back the shorts. It galled her that he had never let her take the wheel—ever. And then, after her mother died and she'd gone off to college, he'd hired a new stern man and refused to take her back on when she'd returned. "It wouldn't be fair to Jake," he said. "He's working for a living. You're going to college."

She shook off these thoughts. The pre-dawn ocean was as still as a mirror, and since it was a Sunday, when it was illegal to fish, there were no lobster boats out. The harbor was quiet, the town silent.

She threw a couple of dock lines to Jackie, who cleated the boat. Their supplies were piled on the dock: ice chests, a small propane tank, a couple of bottles of Jim Beam, two duffel bags, boxes of dry food, foul weather gear, sleeping bags, and pillows. They began stowing the gear in the cabin. As they worked, the sun rose over the sea horizon, throwing gold bullion across the water.

As Abbey exited the pilothouse, she heard the backfiring of a car engine and the grinding of gears from the pier above. A moment later a figure appeared at the top of the ramp.

"Oh no, look who's here," said Jackie.

Randall Worth came strolling down the ramp, wearing a tank top despite the fifty-degree temperature, showing off his crappy jailhouse tats. "Well lookee here. If it ain't Thelma and Louise."

He was tall and ropy with greasy hair to his shoulders, scabs on his face, stubble sprouting from his chin. He wore shitkicker leather motorcycle boots with dangling chains, even though he'd never been on a real motorcycle in his life. He grinned, showing two rows of brown, rotting teeth.

Abbey continued to load the boat, ignoring him. She had known him almost all her life and she still couldn't believe the self-induced catastrophe that had befallen the cheerful, dumb, freckled kid who was always the worst player at the Little League games but who never stopped trying. Maybe it was the inevitable nickname they coined from his last name, chanting it at the baseball games. *Worthless. Worthless.*

"Going on vacation?" Worth asked.

Abbey swung a duffle up on the gunwale and Jackie shoved it in the corner of the cockpit.

"You haven't visited me since I got out of Maine State. My feelings are hurt."

Abbey swung up the second duffel. They were almost done. She couldn't wait to get away from him.

"I'm talking to you."

"Jackie," said Abbey, "grab the other handle of the ice chest."

"Sure thing."

They lifted the ice chest and were about to heft it over the gunwale when Worth stepped around, blocking them. "I said, I'm *talking* to you." He flexed his muscles, but the effect on his wasted body was ridiculous. Abbey put the chest down and stared at him. She felt a sudden, huge sadness.

"Oh, am I in your way?" said Worth, smirking.

Abbey crossed her arms and waited, looking away.

Worth stepped right up to her, leaning over, his face close to hers, the fetid B.O. smell enveloping her. He stretched his chapped lips in a crooked smile. "You think you're going to dump me?"

"I didn't dump you, because there never was a relationship to begin with," said Abbey.

"Oh yeah? Well, what did you call this?" He wiggled his hips obscenely, moving them in and out and moaning in falsetto, "*Deeper, deeper.*"

"Yeah, right. Should've saved my breath for all the good it did me."

Jackie burst out laughing.

A silence. "What's that supposed to mean?"

Abbey turned away, all sympathy gone. "Nothing. Just get out of my way."

"When I fuck a girl, I own her. You didn't know that, nigger?"

"Hey, shut your fucking face, you racist asshole," said Jackie.

Why, *why* had she been so stupid to get involved with him? Abbey grasped the handle and lifted the cooler. "Are you going to move or do I have to call the police? If you violate parole, you're back in Maine State."

Worth didn't move.

"Jackie, get on the VHF. Channel sixteen. Call the cops."

Jackie jumped into the boat, ducked in the pilothouse, and pulled down the mike.

"Fuck you," Worth said, stepping aside. "Forget the cops. Go ahead, I ain't stopping you. I just got one thing to say: you don't dump me." His arm held high, he stabbed a finger down at her. "'Cause you're dark oak. And you know the saying, *If you're looking to split wood, go for the dark oak.*"

"Get a life." Abbey, her face on fire, brushed past him and heaved the last ice chest up on the gunwale, stowing it in the cockpit. She took the wheel and laid her hand on the shift lever.

"Cast off, Jackie."

Jackie uncleated the lines, tossed them in, and hopped aboard. Abbey threw the boat into forward, kicked out the stern, reversed, and backed it away.

Worth stood on the dock, small, skinny as a scarecrow, trying to sound tough. "I know what you're up to," he called. "Everybody knows you're looking for that old pirate treasure again. You're not fooling anyone."

As soon as *Marea* cleared the peppercan buoy at the head of the harbor, Abbey swung to starboard, gunned the engine, and headed out to sea.

"What an *asshole*," said Jackie. "You see that meth mouth on him?"

Abbey said nothing.

"Racist jerk. I can't believe he called you a nigger. White trash honky motherfucker."

"I wish . . . I was a nigger."

"What shit are you talking now?"

"I don't know. I feel so . . . *white*."

"Well, you are sort of white. I mean, you can't dance worth shit." Jackie laughed awkwardly.

Abbey rolled her eyes.

"Seriously, nothing about you seems black, really, not the way you talk, not your background or friends . . . no offense, but . . ." Her voice trailed off.

"That's the problem," said Abbey. "Nothing about me really seems like me. I'm phenotypically black but white every other way."

"Who cares? You are what you are, fuck the rest." After an awkward silence, Jackie asked, "Did you really sleep with him?"

"Don't remind me."

"When?"

"At that going-away party at the Lawlers', two years ago. Before he got into meth."

"Why?"

"I was drunk."

"Yeah, but *him*?"

Abbey shrugged. "He was the first boy I kissed, back in

sixth grade . . ." She looked at Jackie's smirk. "All right, I'm stupid."

"Nah, you just have bad taste in men. I mean, *really* bad taste."

"Thanks." Abbey opened the pilothouse window and the sea air poured in over her face. The boat split the glassy ocean. After a while she felt her spirits returning. This was an adventure—and they were going to be rich. "Hey, first mate!" She held up a hand. "High fives!"

They smacked hands and Abbey gave a whoop. "Romeo Foxtrot, shall we *dance?*" She stuck her iPod into the dock of her father's Bose stereo and dialed in the "Ride of the Valkyries," cranking it up to full volume. The boat roared down Muscongus Sound, Wagner booming over the water.

"First mate?" she said, "Make an entry in the log. *Marea,* May 15, 6:25 A.M., fuel 100 percent, water 100 percent, bourbon 100 percent, weed 100 percent, engine hours 9114.4, wind negligible, sea state one, all systems go, heading sixty degrees true at twelve knots for Louds Island in search of the Muscongus Bay meteorite!"

"Aye aye, captain. Shall I roll a blunt first?"

"Capital idea, first mate!" Abbey whooped again, all thoughts of Worth vanquished. "It doesn't get any better than this."

7

FORD PAID THE cab driver and strolled down the sidewalk. The Bangkok gem district lay in a warren of side streets off Silom Road, not far from the river, a mixture of giant, warehouse-like wholesalers mingled with the ugly shop fronts of the gem-scam operations. The street was choked with traffic, the narrow sidewalks blocked by illegally parked cars, the buildings on either side cheap, modern, and tawdry. Bangkok was one of Ford's least favorite cities.

At the corner of Bamroonmuang Road he came to a low building in dark gray brick. A sign above the door read PIYAMANEE LTD. and the smoked windows reflected his image.

With a quick comb-through Ford slicked back his hair and adjusted the raw silk jacket. He had dressed like a drug dealer, silk shirt unbuttoned to the sternum, gold chains, Bollé shades, three-day stubble. Shoving his hands into his pockets, he sauntered in the open door and stood looking around. The interior was dim so the gems couldn't be examined too well, and the air smelled faintly of Clorox. Glass counters with anemic lighting formed a giant open square. A young American couple, evidently honeymooners, was looking at a spread of muddy star sapphires laid out on black velvet.

He was immediately rushed by two salesgirls, neither of whom could have been more than sixteen years old.

"*Sawasdee!* Welcome, special friend!" One of them held out a mango drink, with a flower and umbrella. "You come for last-day Thai government export special to buy gems, sir?"

Ford ignored them.

"Sir?"

"I want to see the owner." He spoke to the air about a foot above their heads, hands in his pockets, shades still on.

"Gentleman wish welcome drink?"

"Gentleman not wish welcome drink."

The girls went off, disappointed, and a moment later a man appeared from the back room, dressed in an impeccable black suit with a white shirt and gray tie, hands clasped together, making several obsequious half-bows as he approached. "Welcome, special friend! Welcome! Where do you come from? America?"

Ford gave him a hard stare. "I'm here to see the *owner.*"

"Thaksin, Thaksin, at your service, sir!"

"Fuck this. I ain't talking to a lackey." Ford turned to leave.

"Just a moment, sir." A few minutes passed and a very small, tired man came out from the back. He was dressed in a track suit and he walked stooped, with none of the hurry of the others, bags under his eyes. When he reached Ford, he paused, looked him up and down with an inscrutable calmness. "Your name, please?"

Without answering, Ford removed an orange stone from his pocket and showed it to the man.

The man took a casual step back. "Let us go back into my office."

The office was small and covered in fake wood paneling that had warped and detached in the humidity. It stank of cigarettes. Ford had done business in Southeast Asia before and knew that the shabbiness of an office, or the poor cut of a man's clothes, was no guide to who that person was; the most dilapidated office might be the den of a billionaire.

"I am Adirake Boonmee." The man extended a small hand and gave Ford's a neat little shake.

"Kirk Mandrake."

"May I see that stone again, Mr. Mandrake, sir?"

Ford removed the stone but the man did not take it.

"You may place it on the table."

Ford put it down. Boonmee eyed it for a long moment, moved closer, then grasped it, held it up to a strong point light shining from a corner of the room.

"It's a fake," he said. "A coated topaz."

Ford feigned a moment of confusion, recovering quickly. "Naturally, I'm aware of that," he said.

"Naturally." Boonmee placed it down on a felt board on his desk. "What can I do for you?"

"I have a big client who wants a lot of these stones. Honeys. Real ones. And he's willing to pay top price. In gold bullion."

"What has led you to think we sell this kind of stone?"

Ford reached into his pocket and pulled out a stack of

American gold eagles and let them fall to the felt, one by one, with a dull clinking. Boonmee didn't even appear to look at the coins. But Ford could see the pulse in his neck quicken. Funny how the sight of gold did that.

"That's to open the conversation."

Boonmee smiled, a curiously innocent, sweet expression that lit up his small face. His hand closed over the coins and slipped them into his pocket. He leaned back in his chair. "I think, Mr. Mandrake, that we will have a good conversation."

"My client is a wholesaler in the U.S. looking for at least ten thousand carats of raw stone to cut and sell. I myself am not a gem dealer; I wouldn't know a diamond from a piece of glass. I'm what you might call an 'import facilitator' when it comes to, ah, getting shipments through U.S. Customs." Ford allowed a certain braggadoccio to creep into his voice.

"I see. But ten thousand carats is impossible. At least, right away."

"Why's that?"

"The stones are rare. They're coming out slowly. And I'm not the only gem dealer in Bangkok. I can start you off with a few hundred carats. We can work up from there."

Ford shifted in his seat, frowned. "You aren't going to 'start me off' at all, Mr. Boonmee. This is a one-shot deal. Ten thousand carats or I walk down the street."

"What is your price, Mr. Mandrake?"

"Twenty percent higher than the going rate: six hundred American dollars an uncut carat. That's six million dollars, in case math isn't your strong suit." Ford gave an appropriately stupid grin.

"I will make a call. Do you have a card, Mr. Mandrake?"

Ford produced an impressive, Asian-style card on heavy card stock with stamped gold embossing, English on the front, Thai on the back. He handed it to Boonmee with a flourish. "One hour, Mr. Boonmee."

Boonmee inclined his head.

With a final handshake, Ford walked out of the shop and stood on the corner, looking for a cab, waving off the tuk-tuks. Two illegal cabs came by but he waved those off as well. After ten minutes of pacing about in frustration, he took out his wallet, looked through it, and went back inside.

He was immediately rushed by the salesgirls. Bypassing them, he went to the back of the shop. He rapped on the door. After a moment, the little man appeared.

"Mr. Boonmee?"

He looked at him, surprised. "A problem?"

Ford smiled sheepishly. "I gave you the wrong card. An old one. May I—?"

Boonmee went to his desk, picked up the old card, handed it to him.

"My apologies." Ford proffered the new card, slipped the old one into his shirt pocket, and hustled back out into the hot sun.

This time he found a cab right away.

8

AMAZING HOW PLACES *like this always look the same,* thought Mark Corso as he walked down the long polished halls of the National Propulsion Facility. Even though he was on the other side of the continent, the halls of NPF smelled just like those at MIT—or Los Alamos or Fermilab for that matter—the same mixture of floor wax, warm electronics, and dusty textbooks. And they looked the same, too, the rippled linoleum, the cheap blond-wood paneling, the humming fluorescent panels spaced among acoustic tiles.

Corso touched the shiny new identity badge hanging on a plastic cord around his neck almost as if it were a talisman. As a kid he'd wanted to be an astronaut. The Moon was taken but there was Mars. And Mars was even better. Now, here he was, thirty years old, the youngest senior technician in the entire Mars mission, at a moment in human history like no other. In less than two decades—before he was fifty—he would be part of the greatest event in the annals of exploration: putting the first human beings on another planet.

And if he played his cards right, he might even be mission director.

Corso paused at an empty glass case in the hall to check his reflection: spotless lab coat casually unbuttoned, pressed white cotton shirt and silk foulard tie, gabardine slacks. He was punctilious with his dress and careful to avoid any suggestion of the nerd. Gazing at his reflection, he pretended to be seeing himself for the first time. His hair was short (read: reliable), beard (unconventional), but neatly trimmed (not too unconventional), his frame thin and athletic (not effete). He was a good-looking guy, dark in the Italian way, chiseled face, big brown eyes. The expensive Armani glasses and tailored clothes reinforced the impression: no geek here.

Corso took a deep breath and knocked confidently on the closed office door.

"*Entrez*," came the voice.

Corso pushed open the door and entered the office, standing in front of the desk. There was no place to sit; the office of his new supervisor, Winston Derkweiler, was small and cramped, even though the team leader could have gotten himself a much bigger office. But Derkweiler was one of those scientists who affected a disdain for perquisites and appearances, his blunt manner and sloppy look broadcasting his pure dedication to science.

Derkweiler eased himself back in the office chair, where his soft corpulance settled in, conforming to the chair's contours. "Adjusting to the asylum, Corso? You got a big new title now, new responsibilities."

He didn't like being called Corso, but he'd gotten used to it. "Pretty well."

"Good. What can I do for you?"

Corso took a deep breath. "I've been going over some of the Martian gamma ray data—"

Derkweiler suddenly frowned. "Gamma ray data?"

"Well, yes. I've been familiarizing myself with my new responsibilities and as I was going through all the old data . . ." He paused as Derkweiler continued to frown ostentatiously. "Excuse me, Dr. Derkweiler, is something wrong?"

The project manager was looking at him instead of the data printout that Corso had laid in front of him. His hands were folded pensively. "How long have you been looking at old gamma ray data?"

"This past week." Corso suddenly felt apprehensive; maybe Derkweiler and Freeman had had a run-in over the data.

"Every week we have half a terabyte of radar and visual data coming in here, piling up, unlooked at. The gamma ray data is the least important."

"I understand that, but here's the thing." Corso felt flustered. "Dr. Freeman, before he, ah, left NPF, was working on an analysis of the gamma ray data. I inherited his work in the area and in going over it, I noted some anomalous results . . ."

Derkweiler clasped his hands and leaned forward on the desk. "Corso, do you know what our mission is here?"

"Mission? You mean . . . ?" Corso found himself flushing like a schoolboy who'd forgotten his lesson. This was ridiculous, a senior technician being treated this way. Freeman had complained to him repeatedly about Derkweiler.

"I mean—" Derkweiler spread his arms with a big smile and looked around his office. "Here we are in beautiful suburban Pasadena, California, at the lovely National Propulsion Facility. Are we on vacation? No, we are not on vacation. So what are we doing here, Corso? What's the mission?"

"Of the Mars Mapping Orbiter or NPF in general?" Corso tried to keep his face neutral.

"Of the MMO! We're not raising organic fryers here, Corso!" Derkweiler chuckled at his bon mot.

"To observe the surface of Mars, looking for subsurface water, analyzing minerals, mapping terrain—"

"Excellent. In preparation for future landing missions. Perhaps you haven't heard yet that we're in a new space race—this time with the Chinese?"

Corso was surprised to see it put in such stark, cold-war terms. "The Chinese aren't anywhere near the starting line."

"Not at the starting line?" Derkweiler almost hopped out of his seat. "Their Hu Jintao satellite is a few weeks from Mars orbit!"

"We've had orbiters around Mars for decades, we've landed probes, we've been exploring the surface with rovers—"

Derkweiler waved him silent. "I'm talking about the long-range picture. The Chinese have leapfrogged the Moon and are going straight to Mars. Don't underestimate what they can do—especially with the U.S. dithering around with its space program."

Corso nodded agreeably.

"And here you are messing around with gamma rays. What do stray gamma rays have to do with the Mars mission?"

"There's a gamma ray detector on the MMO," Corso said. "Analysis of that data is part of my job description."

"That detector was stuck on at the last minute," Derkweiler said, "by Dr. Freeman, over my objections, for no discernable reason. Gamma rays were Dr. Freeman's little hobbyhorse. Look—I don't fault you. You're trying to straighten out the mess Freeman left behind and you haven't learned the priorities. May I therefore suggest that you stick to the mission—the SHARAD mapping data?"

Struggling to maintain his best ass-kissing smile, Corso picked up the gamma ray plots and slid them back into the manila envelope. He would get along with Derkweiler come hell or high water. "I'll get to work on that right away," he said crisply.

"Excellent. Your first presentation as senior staff is in a week—I want you to do well. First impressions and all. You understand?"

"I do. Thank you."

"Don't thank me. It's my job to be a pain in the ass." Another chuckle.

"Right."

As Corso turned to go, Derkweiler said, "One other thing."

He turned.

"You'll probably be interested in this." He tossed over a stapled sheaf of papers that landed on the desk in front of Corso. "That's the final police report on Dr. Freeman's murder. It was a robbery—looks like Dr. Freeman came home at the wrong time. Bunch of stuff stolen, a Rolex, jewelry, computers . . . I thought you might like to see it. I know you were close to him."

"Thank you." Corso took it.

He walked back to his office, slipped behind his desk, and

shoved Freeman's old gamma ray plots into a drawer and slammed it. Freeman had been right, Derkweiler was the boss from hell. Still, the gamma ray anomalies that he'd seen on Freeman's hard drive—and that he'd followed up on at work—were startling. More than startling. Freeman was right: it could be a major discovery, potentially explosive. The more he thought about the implications, the more frightened he became. He just had to keep his head down, work up the data, and present it in a cool, objective manner. Derkweiler might not like it, but what counted was the opinion of the mission director, Charles Chaudry, who was everything Derkweiler was not.

He took up the report on Freeman's death and flipped through it. It was written in cop-speak, using phrases like "the perpetrator committed aggression on the victim with a piano-wire garrote" and "the perpetrator searched the premises and effected rapid egress from the scene of the homicide on foot." As he read, he felt his sorrow and horror at Freeman's murder mingling with a feeling of relief at the random nature of the crime. And they'd caught the guy—a drug addict looking for money. The usual sad and senseless story. He closed the report with a shiver of mortality. He had been shocked that only about twenty people had come to Freeman's funeral, and that he was the only one from NPF. It had been one of the saddest experiences of his life.

Shucking off these morbid thoughts, Corso turned his attention to his workstation and pulled up the SHARAD data, the shallow-ground-penetrating radar which the MMO was using to map the subsurface features of Mars. He worked on it uninterrupted until the close of day, processing the data and fine-tuning the resulting imagery. He still had the hard drive back at his apartment and he could continue to work on the gamma ray data at home. Despite two security audits, still no one realized the hard drive was missing; Freeman had somehow bypassed all security checks and procedures. If the missing drive ever were noted, Corso had a plan to get rid of it immediately. But until then, it was exceedingly useful to have it at home, where he could work on it uninterrupted until late in the night.

This discovery, he reflected, was going to make his career.

9

WYMAN FORD ENTERED his suite in the Royal Orchid and stood gratefully in the blast of air-conditioning coming from a vent in the ceiling in the middle of the room. Through the giant picture window covering one end of the room, he could see the longtail boats coming and going on the Chao Phraya River. At noon, the sun was at its zenith and a brown pall lay over the burning city, the color washed out of everything. Even by Bangkok standards it was a scorcher.

The last time he had been in Bangkok was four years ago, with his wife, just before she was murdered. They had stayed at the Mandarin Oriental, in a wildly extravagant suite, with strategically placed mirrors—he stamped down hard on the memory, forcing his thoughts into another channel. His eye roved the cityscape below and settled on the spires of the Temple of the Dawn, which in the dead, polluted air looked like a cluster of gilded toothpicks rising from a sea of brown.

With a long sigh, he went to the hotel safe, unlocked it, and withdrew his laptop and an unusual USB card reader.

When the computer had booted up, he took the original business card, the one he had retrieved from Boonmee, and inserted it into the reader. A window opened on his computer screen, and he downloaded the contents of the microchip embedded in the thick paper of the card. He packaged it as an audio file and e-mailed it to Washington.

Fifteen minutes later his account chimed and he downloaded the return e-mail.

Call to cell phone number: 855-0369-67985
Location of receiving phone: Sisophon, Cambodia
Registered owner of receiving phone: Prum Forgang
Transcription of conversation (translated from Thai):
A: Hello?
B: This is Boonmee Adirake. Much health and prosperity to you, Prum Forgang.
A: I am honored to receive your call, Boonmee Adirake.
B: I have an American looking to buy ten thousand carats of honey stones.
A: You know very well I can't get that much.
B: Let me explain. This man was carrying a colored topaz, not even in a lead box. He knows nothing. He has rich backers and it's a one-time deal. He's an idiot. We could sell him anything.
A: What do you suggest?
B: An assortment of raw, low-grade honey stones, mixed in with enhanced topaz or heat-treated citrine.
A: That I can do.
B: I need them within twenty-four hours. The man is in a hurry.
A: Good for you that he is in a hurry. And?

B: I will get the highest possible price and you will get forty percent of it.

A: Forty percent? My dear friend! Why this lack of fairness? I'm the one supplying the goods at my own expense. Make it fifty.

B: Forty-five. I found the customer.

A: Forty-five is a most awkward number. I'm hurt you would nickel and dime me like some cheap hustler and not an old and trusted associate.

B: You're the one arguing over five percent.

A: I have four children to think about, Adirake, and a wife who is like a bird with her beak open all the time. No, I will not do it for forty-five. I insist on fifty.

B: By the testicles of Yaksha! All right, I will make it fifty—this time. Forty for the next deal.

A: Accepted. You will of course look carefully into the background of this American before you deal with him. And you will get a suitable down payment.

B: You can be sure I will.

A: Excellent. I'll assemble the shipment and send it off by my courier this evening. You'll have it tomorrow morning.

Ford closed the computer and leaned back in the chair, thinking. Sisophon was a chaotic, medium-sized city on the main road from Thailand to Siem Reap, Cambodia, a haven for smuggling, forgery, and counterfeiting. He flicked open his cell, dredged up a number from memory, and punched it in. He wasn't sure if the number would still be working— or if the man at the other end would even be alive.

A cheerful voice answered immediately, speaking English

in a lilting accent that was a cross between upper-crust British and Chinese. "Hello, Khon speaking!"

Ford felt a flood of relief to hear the man's voice again. He was alive and, by the sound of it, very well indeed. "Khon? It's Wyman Ford."

"Ford? You old dog! Where the hell have you been and what the damn brings you back to the Royaume du Cambodge?" Khon loved to swear in English but never quite managed to pull it off.

"I've got an assignment for you."

A groan came over the crackling lines. "Oh no."

"Oh yes," said Ford, "and it's a good one."

10

THE *MAREA* GLIDED into the passage between Marsh Island and
Louds Island, the water green and calm, reflecting the dark
trees of both shores. Abbey Straw steered into an isolated
cove, pulled the throttle back into neutral, and reversed it
briefly, bringing the boat to a halt.

"First mate, drop anchor!"

Jackie bounded forward, pulled the pin on the anchor,
and played the chain out of the locker. "We're all alone," she
called back. "No boats around."

"Perfect." Abbey glanced at her watch. "Six hours of day-
light to look for the meteorite."

"I'm famished."

"We'll pack lunch."

They climbed in the dingy and rowed the hundred yards
to the pebbly beach. Pulling the rowboat above the high-tide
mark, they stood on the deserted beach, looking around.
They were at the wild end of the island, the beach strewn
with the detritus of winter, broken lobster traps, buoys,

driftwood, and rope. The tide was ebbing, exposing seaweed-covered rocks in the cove, which humped out of the water like the hairy heads of sea monsters. A smell of salt mingled with evergreens hung in the damp, cold air. Where the beach ended a dense forest of black spruce rose up. Louds was all but deserted this time of year, the island's few seasonal summer camps shuttered. Nobody would bother them.

"Man, it's thick," said Jackie, contemplating the wall of forest. "How're we gonna find a meteorite in there?"

"By the crater and smashed trees. Believe me, a hundred-pound rock going a hundred thousand miles an hour is going to leave a mess." Abbey got out her chart and spread it on the sand, weighing down the corners with stones. The line she had drawn sliced across the island at an angle, intersecting the beach they'd landed at. She laid her compass on the map and adjusted the bearing, stood up, and took a heading.

"We go this way," she said, pointing.

"You bet."

Abbey led the way into the deep spruce forest. She remembered a poem she'd had to memorize in school and recite one evening in front of the school and her parents. She'd choked up and forgotten it completely—stood there on stage for one long, agonizing minute before rushing off in tears—but now it sprang into her head unbidden.

This is the forest primeval. The murmuring pines and the
   hemlocks,
Bearded with moss, and in garments green, indistinct in the
   twilight,
Stand like Druids of eld, with voices sad and prophetic.

That was sort of the story of her life: bad timing.

She ventured deeper into the woods, following the compass bearing. A dim, greenish light penetrated through the tall trees, and the wind sighed through the distant treetops. It was like walking up the aisle of a vast green cathedral, the trees like massive columns, the ground springy and carpeted in moss. Abbey inhaled the rich piney scent, recalling the many times she had camped on the island as a little girl with her mother and father, in the meadow on the north end. They lay in their sleeping bags under the night sky, counting the shooting stars. Back then the island was completely abandoned, the old farmhouses sagging and falling into ruin. Now retired people had started buying them up for cottages and the island was changing. Soon, she thought, all the wildness, the atmosphere of desertion and desuetude would be gone, replaced by cute summer cottages, lace curtains, and gangster grandmas shooing kids off their property.

The forest grew thicker, and they had to crawl on hands and knees underneath a series of fallen tree trunks.

"I don't see any craters," said Jackie.

"We've hardly begun."

They soon broke into a clearing, a stone wall enclosing a huddle of tombstones. The old island cemetery.

"Lunchtime!" cried Jackie, climbing over the wall, shucking her pack and flopping herself down. With her back against a tombstone, she began rolling a joint.

Abbey walked around the old cemetery, reading the tombstones. The funny old Maine names were like the muster roll to a lost world: Zebediah Loud, Hiram Carter, Ora May Poland, Nehemiah Swett. Her thoughts drifted back to her mother's funeral. Abbey remembered escaping the crowd around the open grave and climbing a hill, reading the tombstones as a way to keep herself together. At the top she looked back down on the huddled mass of people around the black hole, the leafless trees, the icy grass, the bright green Astroturf laid around the grave.

It still didn't seem possible, her mother gone. She could never forget that day in the clinic when she asked the doctor: How did it happen? He looked at her so sorrowfully, a good man defeated by science. "We really don't know," he said, "but for some reason, five or ten years ago, a cell split the wrong way and that started it . . ."

A cell split the wrong way. Strange how such a tiny thing could have such a gigantic effect.

"Yo Mama!" Jackie called, her voice rising from the forest of stones. "Will you quit genuflecting to your ancestors and get back here and share this blunt with me?"

Abbey walked back to where Jackie was sitting against a tombstone. "*My* ancestors? Speak for yourself, white girl."

"Don't give me that shit, you're as much a Mainer as I am. No offense."

She sat down cross-legged, took the joint, inhaled, handed it back. As the burning sensation spread from her lungs to her head, she unwrapped her sandwich and bit into it. They ate in silence and then Abbey lay back in the grass, tucked her hands behind her head, and looked up into the sky. "Did you notice?" she asked. "At least half the people buried here are younger than we are."

"You always get so morbid."

"I'll be less morbid after I find the meteorite."

They both laughed, lying in the grass, faces to the sky.

11

RANDALL WORTH CAME around Thrumcap Island in his twenty-four-foot PC-6, the *Old Salt*, diesel engine hammering away, laying a bourbon-colored cloud of exhaust on the water. The FM radio was tuned to TOS and it blasted static with just enough definition for Worth to guess which tune might be playing.

Worth lobstered alone, without a stern man, because no one would work for him. So much the better, he didn't have to split his profits. A while ago some bastard had cut half his string because he was caught taking shorts. *Fuck 'em, fuck 'em all.*

He threw over the last trap and brought the boat into a tight idle, wheel hard to starboard. The line zinged out, the float popping into the water, followed by the buoy. For a moment Worth let the boat drift while he pounded down the last half of a Coors Light and threw the can overboard. He wiped his mouth and eyed the engine panel. The engine was running cold, the injectors were shot, there was fuel coming out the wet exhaust and spreading rainbows over the water. Every few minutes the bilge pumps would kick in, vomiting oily water over the side. He spat again, the gobbet lying on the deck like a shucked oyster. He kicked the raw water hose and washed the lougey out the scuppers.

He hoped his piece-of-shit boat would last the season. Then he'd buy insurance and sink it. All he had to do was stick a bad fuse into the bilge pump, moor his boat, and wait two days.

As Thrumcap Island passed to starboard the distant outline of Crow Island came into view, the huge white dome of the old Earth Station rising up like a bubble. The Crow Island ferry was just coming out of the harbor, churning away as it rounded the point and headed for Friendship. As he glanced back toward the mainland he was surprised to see a boat anchored in a quiet corner of Marsh Island Passage. He squinted.

The *Marea*. Abbey Straw's boat.

He immediately throttled down, staring. A feeling of rage crawled up his spine and spread through his brain like water into a sponge. Fucking jungle bunny, he couldn't forget what she'd said about that *deeper, deeper* shit. Right in front of that cunt Jackie Spann, somebody should whack her upside the head. There they were, on Louds Island, looking for the treasure of Dixie Bull. The rumor going around town was that Abbey had gotten her hands on a map.

As the boat drifted in the tidal current, Worth pulled the last can of Coors out of the plastic rings and tossed the plastic overboard. *Maybe it'll strangle a few seals.*

He hammered down the beer and stuck the can in the beer holder screwed to the side of the engine panel. He was starting to feel edgy, tense, his skin crawling. The crank bugs. He began itching nervously at the skin of his cheek, inadvertently breaking off a scab, feeling the wetness of blood on his fingertips.

He swore. Ducking into the tiny cuddy, he removed a glass bulb pipe from behind some gear, dropped in a rock, and with a shaking hand lit a Bic and directed the flame down into the bulb. There was a sudden cooking noise and he drew in hard, filling the bulb with smoke, then taking it into his lungs. Leaning back against the hull, he closed his eyes and let the rush happen, a sense of elation so strong it made him feel, for a moment, almost like a real human being.

He stuffed the pipe and crank back behind the fishing gear and bounded into the wheelhouse, feeling on top of the world. Once again he saw the *Marea* casting a long shadow on the water, and a black rage seized his heart. They were digging for treasure and with a map they might even find it.

Suddenly, he had an idea. A good idea. In fact, it was the best idea he had ever had.

Worth checked his watch: four o'clock. The girls were obviously going to spend the night on the boat. This would give him time to go into Round Pond, fuel up, load up on beer and beef jerky from King Ro. He could pay a visit to his connection and score some more crank and collect the money he was owed for the stuff he'd boosted out of that mansion on Ripp Island. He could be back out at Louds at dawn.

With an out-loud laugh he goosed the throttle to 3000 rpms, spun the wheel, and headed back out past Thrumcap

Island and around the southern end of Louds toward Round
Pond Harbor.

With the money from the treasure, he'd buy himself a new
boat—and he'd name it the *Skull and Crossbones*.

12

"HE LOOKS LIKE Squealer, the Beanie Baby pig," said Mark Corso. "You ever see that pig? Big, soft, fat, and pink."

Marjory Leung leaned back on the stool and laughed, her long black hair swaying, then lifted the martini to her pursed lips. Corso watched her abdomen stretching, her apple-shaped breasts sliding under the thin stretchy cotton of her top. They were in one of those California theme bars, done up in bamboo and teak, with corrugated tin roofing and colored floor lights, tarted up like some watering hole on the beach in Jamaica. Reggae music throbbed in the background. Why was it in California that everything had to look like somewhere else? He remembered what Gertrude Stein had said about California. *There is no there there.* How true it was.

"Freeman warned me about him," he added. "How the hell did a guy like that get to be second in command?"

Leung set the drink down and leaned toward him, conspiratorially, her thin, athletic body like a bent spring. "You know why he keeps his door shut?"

"I've often wondered about that."

"He's surfing for porn."

"You think so?"

"The other day I knocked on the door and I heard this sudden movement inside, like he was startled. And then when I came in he was hastily tucking in his shirt and his computer screen was blank."

"Putting away his schlong, I bet. The very thought makes me want to puke."

Leung issued a bell-like laugh, twisting on her stool, her hair swinging again, her knee touching Corso's. Her drink was almost empty.

He polished off his own drink and waved his hand for another round. The knee remained in contact with his. Leung worked at the Mars mission down the hall as a Mars meteorology specialist. She was funny and irreverent, a refreshing change from the nerds who swarmed that end of the building. And she was smart. First-generation Chinese, she'd grown up in the back of a Chinese laundry run by her parents. They didn't speak English and she went to Harvard. Corso liked that kind of story. She was like his own grandfather, running away from home in Sicily and getting to America, all by himself, at the age of fourteen. Corso felt a kind of kinship with her.

"You read that report on Freeman?" he asked her.

"Yeah." The bartender slid the drinks over and she took hers. "So *creepy*. We used to come here for drinks once in a while."

Corso had heard about something brief between Leung and Freeman. He hoped it wasn't true.

"It's just awful, him getting murdered like that." She shook her head, sending ripples through that hair.

Corso took a chance, pressing his knee against the side of hers with a little more pressure. There was an answering pressure. He could feel the flush of the martinis traveling through his capillaries.

"You must have taken it hard," she said.

"I did. He was a really good guy. A little crazy."

"You know why he got fired?" she asked.

"Not specifically. Other than a sort of general deterioration. He might have had a run-in with Derkweiler over data issues."

"Data issues?"

"Gamma ray data." Corso realized he was approaching a security compartment line, talking about data outside of the building with a person in another section. He sipped his drink; fuck the rules.

"Oh yeah," she said. "He was talking about that but I didn't really get it. What about gamma rays?"

"Seems to be a gamma ray source somewhere on Mars. A point source. At least, that's what I get when I subtract the overall background noise—a faint periodicity."

She leaned forward. "Wait a minute. You're kidding."

She got it right away, thought Corso. "No, no kidding. The period is somewhere around twenty-five to thirty hours. Which is pretty close to the Martian day."

"What the heck in the solar system could be producing gamma rays? Not even the sun has enough energy."

"Cosmic rays."

"Yeah, but cosmic rays produce a weak, diffuse glow from every body in the solar system. You say this signal has periodicity. That implies a point source on the planet's surface."

Corso was even more taken aback by how fast she was figuring it out.

"Right. Problem is, the Compton detector on MMO isn't directional—no way to tell where the gamma rays are coming from. It could be anywhere on the planet's surface."

"You have any ideas what it might be?" Leung asked.

"At first I thought it might be from a nuclear reactor that crashed on the planet's surface—maybe from a secret government project. But I ran the calculations and it would have to be, like, a reactor the size of a mountain."

"What else?"

Corso took another swig. He could feel his heart pounding from the pressure of his knee, now on her inner thigh. She was returning the pressure. "I've been wracking my brains. I mean, high energy gamma rays are usually only produced by big-time astrophysical processes—supernovae, black holes, neutron stars—stuff like that. Or in a nuclear reactor or atomic bomb."

"This is incredible. You're on to something big."

He turned to her. "I think it could be a miniature black hole, or a very small neutron body, somehow caught on the surface of Mars or orbiting around it."

"You're shitting me."

He gazed steadily into her lively, black eyes. "No. I'm not. *When you've eliminated the impossible . . .*"

"*. . . whatever remains, however improbable, must be the truth.*" She finished the familiar aphorism for him, punctuating it with a bright smile on her red lips.

He lowered his voice. "If this is a miniature black hole or

tiny neutron star, it could grow, eat Mars—and sterilize the Earth with killing gamma rays—or even explode. This isn't some academic exercise. This is *real.*"

Leung breathed out. "Jesus."

He put his hand on her leg, gave it a squeeze. "Yes. It is real."

She leaned forward, her face closer to his. He could smell her shampoo. "What are you going to do about it?"

"It's going to be the subject of my presentation." He slid his hand just a bit under her skirt, which was riding up on her thigh as she sat on the stool. After a moment she flexed her hips forward, causing the hand to slide up farther. He could feel the hotness of her thighs.

She leaned closer to him and said, "Mmmmm," into his ear, her peppermint breath tickling his face.

"Another drink?" he asked.

She adjusted herself on the stool, sliding her hips even farther forward so that his fingers came in contact with the hot curve of her panties. She pressed her thighs together on his hand. "Do you want to come back to my place?" she whispered, her lips brushing his ear.

"Yes," he said. "Yes, I do."

13

SISOPHON WAS AS ugly as Ford remembered it, whitewashed cement buildings scattered among tattered palms and sickly banyan trees. The streets were dirt and many of the building facades were still pecked with shrapnel from the war. As Ford's driver entered town, a UN Land Cruiser, stuffed with blue-helmeted men, careened past, its sides emblazoned with UNDP MINE ACTION SERVICE logos.

The Tourist A-1 Hotel was right where it had always been, more rundown than ever, the street outside thronging with child vendors. The cinder block building mostly hosted NGOs and had probably never seen a real tourist in all its shabby days. Ford booked a room and left his suitcase with the manager, giving him a ten-thousand riel note with a promise of fifty thousand more if the case was intact on his return.

Leaving the hotel on foot, Ford directed his steps toward an open-area antiquity workshop on the outskirts of town. As he walked, cement buildings gave way to wood-and-thatch huts on stilts, small rice paddies, and water buffalo hauling wooden carts. The antiquity workshop, sprawling over a vast field, was a scene of bustle and activity. Open-sided tents were set up in long rows, inside of which stonemasons labored to the merry clink of steel chisels on stone. It was one of the more famous antiquity workshops in Cambodia, where a battalion of talented artisans turned piles of broken sandstone rocks into fake Angkorian antiquities to be sold in Bangkok and around the world.

Strolling through the cheerful outdoor workshop, Ford watched stoneworkers chiseling away at chunks of stone propped on sandbags, from which emerged eleventh-century dancing apsaras, devatas, buddhas, lingams, and nagas. In a nearby metal shed, powered by its own generator, the hum of high-tech printing could be heard, as forgers created the documents necessary to authenticate an antiquity and give it a convincing provenance. To one side the fresh sculptures were being subjected to acid sprays, mud baths, tea stainings, egg-white coatings, and even burial to make them look old.

Ford scanned the crowds of workmen, buyers, and sellers, looking for the figure of his old friend Khon. And there he was, impossible to miss, the rotund figure and polished head moving among the artisans, chatting with everyone, rapping on various pieces with his walking stick, laughing loudly, and enjoying himself immensely.

"Khon!" Ford strode over and clasped the man's hand warmly.

"Wyman, my good friend! How fucking delightful to see you!"

"The name's Kirk," Ford said, with a wink.

Without a beat, Khon declaimed, "Kirk, my good friend!"

He laughed, a bell-like laugh, his head thrown back, then composed himself, his face becoming serious. "I never thought I'd see you again, after . . ." His voice trailed off.

"Here I am."

"Kirk, you're damned thin! And so much gray hair! There's an ancient Cambodian saying: 'Just because there's snow on the roof doesn't mean there isn't a fire in the fireplace!' " He laughed again.

"Somehow I doubt that's an ancient Cambodian saying."

Khon waved his hand. "I brought you a present." He dipped into his pocket, removing a small stone head of Garuda, the mythical birdlike creature. "It's a fake of course. Welcome back."

Ford was glad he had remembered the Cambodian way of exchanging gifts. "Here's something for you."

Khon stared at the carved green stone through his round spectacles. "Don't tell me you've been buying gems in Bangkok!"

"It's an emerald, and it's real. Lousy quality, mind you, but I liked the carving. And trust me, I didn't get taken."

Khon squinted at the small stone, took off his glasses, wiped them on his shirttail, and put them back on. "Why, it's Garuda again!"

"Great minds think alike." Ford gestured with his head toward an empty area of the field. "Let's take a walk."

They strolled along. Khon said, "I never had the chance to tell you how very, *very* sorry—"

Ford stopped him with a light touch to his arm. "Please don't."

Khon nodded and they walked across the field. He waved his hand. "Good business, this, eh what?"

"An excellent business," said Ford. "Now they aren't tearing down temples to steal the real thing. I heartily approve."

"Welcome to the new Cambodia!"

As they strolled along, Ford took the opportunity to examine his old friend out of the corner of his eye. He hadn't changed in the slightest; although Khon had to be at least fifty, he seemed ageless. Neatly dressed in an olive canvas jacket, white shirt, loose cravat, khaki pants, and walking stick, he could have been an extra from an Indiana Jones film. Appearances were deceiving; he was a man of rare courage, placid and unflappable. *That's what happens*, Ford thought, *when you grow up under the Khmer Rouge.*

"Well, Kirk, what's the assignment?"

"Honeys."

"Girls or stones?"

"Stones. I'm here to track down the source. The mine."

Khon halted, turned. "You back at the CIA?"

Ford shook his head. "Freelance job."

Khon's hand relaxed on his walking stick. "For who?"

"Never mind for whom. My job is to get the GPS coordinates, document the mine, photograph and videotape it, and pass on the information."

"And what will 'they' do with it?"

"Don't know, don't care."

Khon wagged his head thoughtfully, thumbing an ear.

"There's a middleman honey dealer here by the name of Prum Forgang," said Ford. "Know him?"

Khon nodded his rotund head. "Oh yes. He's one of the top gem brokers in town. Antiquities, gems, and rice—the three pillars of our economy."

"Any family?"

"A son. Eighteen. Bright lad. Going to university in Phnom Penh."

"Does Prum live alone?"

"Yes."

"We'll pay him a visit tonight."

Khon's eyes lit up. "Will there be violence?"

"No."

Khon's face fell. "How are you going to get what you want?"

Ford squinted at the metal building on the other side of the field, where the hum of printing could be heard. "You say he has a son in university? Maybe all it will take is a few pieces of paper."

He broke into a fast walk, heading for the printing building.

14

RANDALL WORTH TIED up his dinghy at the town floating dock, slung on his backpack, and stomped up the ramp to the wharf, keeping his head down. It was five o'clock—maybe he wouldn't run into anyone. He could feel the heavy lump of the old RG .44, the gun he carried on his boat, tucked in his belt.

"Hey, Worth."

Fuckin' A. Worth looked up to see the last man he wanted to see—Ernie Jura, owner of the lobsterman's co-op, six foot four, two hundred twenty pounds, standing there in foul-weather gear and rubber boots. Jura'd tormented him in high school and never stopped.

"I'm going to need that money you owe for diesel, three hundred and twelve bucks. I can't fuel you up again until I get it."

"I told you I'll *pay* you." Worth felt his limbs trembling with anger. Jura, he was sure, was one of the bastards who had cut his traps.

Jura looked at him hard, his eyes narrow. "I hope you do."

Worth brushed past him, and then, on impulse, gave him a little shove with his shoulder as he went by. Jura seized his collar and hauled him around, pushing his beefy face into Worth's, breathing beer breath over him.

"Listen, punk. You lied when you bought that diesel, said you had the cash on you. So you *pay* me, cocksucker, or I'm gonna make a bow tie of your balls, hang them round your neck, and send you off to dancing school." He pushed Worth away, turned his back, and said over his shoulder, "I want the money. Before noon tomorrow. You got that, *Worthless*?"

Worth reached in, hand closed around the grip of the RG. Keeping his back turned, Jura began working on one of the swivel lifts, hunching over it, unscrewing a bolt.

"*Asshole*," Worth said.

Jura ignored him. Worth began to ease out the gun, then thought better of it. He would get Jura later. Now he had bigger fish to fry. And he needed more diesel, somewhere, somehow.

He walked down the pier to his truck parked in the lot, felt in his pocket for the keys. They'd already cut him off in New Harbor and Muscongus. To get fuel he'd have to drive his boat all the way to Boothbay and even then he probably wouldn't get credit. He needed to get the diesel here, now, right away, if his plan was to succeed.

He shoved the key into the ignition and turned, the engine wheezing, grinding, and finally starting. He checked the gas gauge; enough to get him to Waldoboro.

Easing it into drive, he heard the clunk of the transmission as it shifted. He lurched out of the lot and took a right on Route 32, heading for Waldoboro.

*

THE WHITE CLAPBOARD house stood on the main road, porch sagging, paint peeling, dead car on blocks on the lawn. Dusk was falling and the lights were on in the attached barn. Worth parked in the driveway, got out, and went to the side barn door. He gave it a double rap. He felt a lot better since he'd smoked a little crank on the way over. That shaky feeling had left his legs and his mind felt clearer, stronger.

"Who is it?" came a voice.

"Worth."

The sound of a lock being turned. The door opened and Devin Doyle stood there, in painter's overalls, holding a beer and a cigarette. His hair stuck out, he hadn't shaved; he was one of those thirty-year-olds who looked eighteen. And acted it.

"Hey, Randy, you fucking ape, whassup?"

Worth came in and Doyle shut the door behind him, turning all the locks. The back of the barn was piled high with stolen furniture, covered with dirty tarps.

"Beer?"

Worth grabbed a Bud Light and threw himself down on a ratty sofa. He took a long pull, draining half the can. He put it on the table and closed his eyes.

Doyle collapsed in a sofa chair. "Hey, Randy, you seen those new Britney photos with the shaved pussy? I got 'em on my computer, you won't believe—"

"I've come for my cut," said Worth.

"Hey, man, what's this shit? Your *cut?*"

"You heard me." He slowly opened his eyes and stared.

"I told you: when I get paid, you get paid." Doyle sucked in a last lungful, blew it back out, stubbed the cigarette in a clamshell sitting by his chair. He hunted around with his hand for the beer, found it, picked it up.

"I boosted that crap off Ripp Island a week ago," said Worth. "I took a risk. I did my job. Now I want my cut." He could feel a muscle in his neck beginning to twitch.

"We don't even know what your cut is until I move the shit. Antiques aren't like flat-screens. I told you this would take time, and you agreed."

Closing his eyes again, playing it cool, Worth said: "Sorry. Don't got no stinkin' time. I brought you a hundred thousand dollars' worth of antiques and I want my money." He popped open his eyes, dropped his booted leg to the floor. "*Capisce?*"

"Hey, Randy, don't talk shit to me. I'll be lucky to get ten—and you'll get half, like we agreed. When I get *paid*. Okay?"

"*Not* okay, dickweed."

Doyle fell silent. Randy picked up the beer, drained it, crushed the can in his hand, and tossed it at Doyle like a Frisbee. It bounced off his shoulder. "You listening?"

The muscle in his neck was jumping like a kangaroo.

"Look, Randy," said Doyle, "we had an agreement. I'm working on it. By Monday, I'll have something for you."

Worth could see that Doyle was sweating. He was scared.

"You say ten thousand? Cool. I want my half. Now. As a down payment."

Doyle spread his hands. "I don't *have* five thousand, for fuck's sake."

Worth rose from the sofa, swelling with confidence in the effect he was having on Doyle. His neck was now twitching, jerk, jerk, jerk, scaring the mortal shit out of Doyle. He could see the man's eyes darting around, looking for a weapon. "Don't even think about it," Worth said, pushing up close, crowding him in the chair.

"Give me til Monday."

"I want my five grand. Now." He pushed himself at Doyle even closer, shoving his dick practically into Doyle's face.

"I don't have it." Doyle crowded back in the chair.

Worth slapped him hard across the top of the head, once, twice.

"Fuck! Randy, what the fuck are you doing?" He tried to stand up but Worth shoved him back down. He stood over him with his legs spread, straddling him, trapping him in the seat. God *damn*, he was starting to feel like Tony Soprano. He reached around and pulled the .44 from under his belt, shoving the barrel in Doyle's ear. "Get me the fucking money."

"Randy, you crazy? You're all fucked up on meth—"

Worth whapped him again, this time across the face, back and forth.

"Stop it!" Doyle tried to fend him off, his skinny arms held up in front of his face, ducking and dodging. "Please!"

"Where's your wallet? Gimme your wallet." He smacked at him again.

With a shaking hand, still fending him off with the other, Doyle groped in his overalls and pulled out his wallet. The faggot was actually crying. Worth took it, opened it up, and fished out a wad of money. It was a bunch of fifties. He let the wallet fall to the floor, counted out the bills. "Lookee here. Eight hundred bucks."

He feigned a sudden lunge at Doyle and the man cringed, his hands flying up. Worth laughed. "Cocksucker." He folded up the money, stuffed it into his back pocket. He poked the gun barrel into Doyle's forehead, gave it a little push. "Listen, fuck-face. I'm coming back Monday. I want four thousand two hundred waiting for me, with a card."

"We had an agreement," said Doyle miserably. His face was streaked like a snot-nosed kid.

"Now we have a *new* agreement."

15

FORD WAITED FOR Khon to come out of the bar and fell into step beside him as he walked down the muddy street.

"Prum's a man of regular habits," said Khon. "He'll leave the bar at one sharp, get in his new Mercedes, and drive the three hundred yards back to his house, arriving at one-oh-five."

"Is he a tough customer?"

"Mentally, yes."

"Will he be drunk?"

"No. He drinks two beers a night, no more, no less."

They approached Prum Forgang's house, a new white-washed cinder block construction erected next to what was evidently his original home, a traditional Cambodian *dnmak* on stilts, with a water buffalo sleeping underneath. Rice paddies surrounded the house on three sides, with a front yard full of coconut palms.

"We'll approach from the back," said Ford. They left the road and took a path that ran along the top of a dike between rice paddies. It was a warm, clear night, a full moon just rising in the east, coming up blood red. Ford inhaled deeply the smell of Cambodia: mud, vegetation, humidity.

"Lovely night for a stroll," said Khon, breathing deeply and stretching out his arms.

Keeping on top of the dikes, they circled back and around. The whitewashed back of Prum Forgang's house loomed out of the darkness, a ghostly rectangle set against the dark. They came up to the back door and Ford quickly picked the simple lock. They let themselves in.

The interior of Prum's house smelled of sandalwood. Keeping the lights off, they made their way to the front sitting room. Ford occupied an overstuffed sofa chair at a strategic position to the left of the door, while Khon settled himself on a sofa on the right.

"Twelve forty," said Ford, in a whisper. He removed his .32 Walther PPK from his pocket and rested it in his lap.

At the appointed time, exactly 1:05 A.M., the headlights of Prum's new Mercedes swept through the curtained windows and a moment later Ford heard his key in the lock. The door opened, a match flared—there was no electricity at that time of night—and Prum stood there, staring at them.

He instantly tried to duck back out the door, but quick as a flash Ford leapt up and slammed his foot into the door, blocking it from being reopened. He pressed the gun to the man's head and held his finger to his lips. *Sssshhhhh.*

Prum merely stared.

Ford gently closed the door and gestured at Prum with the gun. "*Suor sdei*, Mr. Prum. Shall we sit down?"

Prum remained standing, very tense. Khon appeared

from the shadows and lit a single lantern, filling the room with a feeble yellow light.

"I said sit down."

Prum took a seat warily, like an animal ready to spring. "What do you want?"

"We come to you in friendship and trust, with an excellent business proposition."

"You break into my house in friendship?"

"We let ourselves in the back for your own protection, not ours."

Prum shifted uncomfortably. Ford studied the man. He was middle-aged, skinny and small with a potbelly and a restless manner. He wore a Hawaiian shirt, untucked, baggy pants, and flip-flops, and he smelled faintly of beer and cheap perfume. His large, liquid eyes were very alert. He remained silent.

Ford smiled. "Mr. Prum, we are here to learn the location of the honey gemstone mine."

Prum said nothing.

"We are willing to pay handsomely for the information."

"I don't know what you're talking about."

"You don't want to hear our proposal?"

"There's nothing you could offer me—not money, not women—that would make me change my mind." Prum smiled. "Look around: I have all I need. A nice car, a beautiful house, flat-panel television, computer. Nice things. And I know nothing about any mine."

"They'll never know you gave us the information."

"I don't know anything."

"Not the slightest bit curious to hear our proposal?"

Prum said nothing.

Ford rose, walked over to Prum, flipped the gun around, and handed it to him butt first. "Take it."

After a hesitation, Prum snatched it. He popped out the magazine, slipped it back in. "It's loaded," he said, pointing the gun at Ford. "I could kill you right now. I suggest you leave."

"That wouldn't be a good idea."

Prum smiled broadly. It was as Ford hoped: with the gun in his hand he was feeling secure. Little did he know Ford had taken apart the rounds, poured out the powder, and fitted them back together.

"Here's the proposition." Ford slowly reached into his pocket and removed a small document. He laid it down in the yellow pool of light. It was a student visa to attend university in America.

Prum snorted. "I have no need of that. I'm fifty years old! I'm a rich man, respected. I'm in business and everything I do is legal. I break no laws and steal nothing from anyone."

"The visa isn't for you."

Prum looked puzzled.

"Go ahead . . . take a look."

Prum hesitated, then reached out and took it. He opened it up and stared at the photograph on the front.

Ford slipped an envelope out of his pocket, and laid it next to the visa. The envelope had a crimson logo on it with a single word, *Veritas*, and a Cambridge, Massachusetts, return address.

"Read the letter."

Prum laid down the passport and took up the envelope. He slipped out the letter on heavy cream paper and squinted, reading it in the dim light, the paper shaking slightly.

"It's an acceptance letter to Harvard University for your son, signed by the Dean of Admissions."

A long silence ensued. Prum slowly laid the letter down, an unreadable look in his eyes. "This is the carrot, I see. And what is the stick?"

"I'll get to that in a moment."

"I can't rely on your promises. These are meaningless pieces of paper. Anyone could have forged these."

"True. You'll have to judge my sincerity. Right here, right now. The opportunity will pass, never to come again."

"Why do you want to know the location of the mine?"

"That gets us to the stick. Where do you think these honeys are ending up, Mr. Prum? On ladies' necks."

"So?"

"One of the biggest honeys ended up on one of the biggest ladies' necks, the wife of a very important United States senator. She was the admiration of all of Georgetown until she lost her hair and got weeping sores on her breasts from radiation poisoning. We traced those stones to *you*."

A silence, and then Prum exhaled. "*Mhn sruel kluen tee!*"

Ford recognized the vulgar Khmer expression. "This is some serious shit, as we say in English."

Prum wiped his face with a handkerchief. "I never knew this. I never even imagined. I am a businessman."

"You know they're radioactive."

Silence.

"The stick is the senator is told you're the one who did this to his wife. What do you think will happen to you then?"

"If I tell you about the mine, they'll kill me."

"The CIA'll kill you if you don't."

"Please, don't do this to me."

"Look, the mine owners won't know you told us. That's why we came at night through the back door."

Prum shook his head vigorously. The gun, all but forgotten, rested in his limp hand. "I need time to think."

"Sorry. Decision time, Mr. Prum."

He mopped his face again. "This mine, it's my livelihood."

"You've had a good run."

"In addition to Harvard for my son, I want money."

"You're really pushing it."

"A hundred thousand dollars."

Ford glanced at Khon. The Cambodian love of bargaining never ceased to amaze him. He rose, swiped up the visa and letter. "The CIA will take care of you." He turned to go.

"Wait! Fifty thousand."

Ford didn't even pause as he headed for the door.

"Ten thousand."

Ford was almost out the door.

"Five thousand."

Ford paused, turned. "You get the money *if* and *when* the mine is successfully located." He came back in. "Now give me back my gun."

Prum handed it over. He rose shakily to his feet, went to a wooden chest in the corner, unlocked it, and took out a map. He unrolled it on a table, placing the oil lamp on it. "This," he said, "is a map of Cambodia. We are here, and the mine is . . . *here*." A tiny finger fell with a thump on a wild, mountainous area in the far northwest. The Cambodian turned his liquid eyes on Ford. "But I tell you this for your own good: if you go there, you'll never come back alive."

16

MARK CORSO FELT a presence in the doorway of his cubicle, and as he straightened up from his work he surreptitiously used his elbow to shove some papers over the gamma ray plots he'd been working on. "Hello, Dr. Derkweiler," he said, forcing his features into a semblance of respect.

Derkweiler entered. "Just checking up on that SHARAD image processing."

"Almost done."

The supervisor leaned over his shoulder, humming, and peering at the papers and printouts neatly squared off on his desk. "Where is it?"

"Right here." Corso wasn't exactly sure where it was, somewhere in the stack of printouts, but he didn't dare sort through them for fear of exposing the gamma ray plots. "I'll have it on your desk by the end of the day."

Derkweiler reached out with one of his trotters, pushed a few papers around. "Desk nice and neat. Not like the rest of us slobs around here. Good for you." His breath smelled of orange Tic Tacs.

Another push of the papers. "What's this?" He reached down, slid a computer printout clear from the stack—a gamma ray plot. "If I didn't know better, I'd say you were still working on that gamma ray data. You promised the SHARAD images to me yesterday."

"I'm still working on them. They'll be on your desk before five. Dr. Derkweiler, for the record, my assignment here is to analyze all the E.M. data and that includes gamma rays."

More sucking on the Tic Tac. "Mr. Corso, I think we might have a fundamental misunderstanding here about how this department is run. We work as a team and I'm the team leader. I'm sorry, but I thought I made it clear that the SHARAD images were your first priority. I want it all done—*all* of it—and presented at the meeting next week."

Corso said nothing.

"Do you understand, Mr. Corso?"

"I do," he said.

Corso waited until Derkweiler had left, and then he sank into his chair, trembling. The man was intolerable, a mediocrity who somehow rose into a supervisory position and was now relishing every moment. He cast a sour eye over the gamma ray plots, sitting on top of the other papers. He would have to bust ass to finish crunching all that SHARAD image data by five. Why was he so insistent on the SHARAD images? It wasn't like Mars was going anywhere soon. At the same time, the gamma ray data was truly bizarre. He had taken it a step beyond what Freeman had done. If Derkweiler didn't see the value of it, surely Chaudry would.

A soft knock came at the open door and he turned to see

Marjory Leung standing in the doorway like a gazelle, one leg straight, the other cocked, leaning on the door with a smile on her face, her long torso flexed like a bow.

"Hey," she said.

Corso smiled and shook his head. "Is he gone?"

"Turning the corner now."

He passed his hand through his hair. "Come on in."

She flopped herself down in the chair in the corner and leaned her head back, her hair spreading on the seat back. "Lunch?"

He shook his head. "I've got to finish this data."

"How's it going?"

"It's a number grind. I've been spending all my time on gamma rays."

"Progress?"

Corso glanced at the open door and she got the message, reached out and closed it.

"A little. I'm pretty sure whatever it is is on the surface somewhere. The periodicity is just too close to the planet's rotation to be otherwise. I've been combing through the images, trying to find some visual artifact that might correspond to the gamma ray emitter. Mars is a big place and we've got over four hundred thousand high-res photos. Needle in a haystack."

She heaved herself up and Corso watched her stretch, her shirt riding up, exposing her flat belly. A very graphic memory of their night together flashed into his mind.

"If not lunch," she said, tossing her hair, "then how about dinner?"

"With pleasure."

"The pleasure will be mine," she said.

17

FORD PULLED THE Land Cruiser up next to a row of battered motorbikes and eyed the hand-painted sign above the door of the small government office. In French and Khmer, the sign identified it as the Office of the Sub-Councilman of the District of Kampong Krabey, Commune of Svay Por. Ford stepped out into the heat, so great it rose in sheets around him, distorting the air.

"God help us," said Khon, squinting at the shabby, cinder block building. "I hope you brought a lot of dollars."

Ford patted his pocket.

They knocked on the wooden door. A voice called them in. The sub-councilman's office consisted of a single room, with cement walls and floor, freshly whitewashed, with a desk in the middle, facing the door, and two secretaries' desks flanking either side. Two metal chairs were placed in rigid formality in front of the desk. A back door led to an out-house behind. The room stank of cigarettes.

The sub-councilman, a handsome man with a scar on his

face, rose with a huge smile, displaying the biggest, whitest rack of teeth Ford had ever seen, which contrasted sharply with the man's olive drab shirt, sagging blue pants, and flip-flops. His neck was thick and fleshy, his face a shining mask of good cheer.

"Welcome! Welcome!" the councilman cried in English, his arms extended. His face wore an expression that would not have been out of place on someone who had just won the lottery. *And maybe he had*, thought Ford, thinking of the inevitable bribes to come.

Khon made an elaborate greeting in Khmer. Ford remained silent, thinking it best, as he usually did, to disguise his knowledge of the language.

"We speak English!" the man cried. "Sit down, please, my special friends!"

Ford and Khon seated themselves in the hard metal chairs.

"*Hre min gnam sa!*" The man screeched at one of his secretaries, who leapt up and rushed out, bowing twice as she passed.

"It is nice day, yes?" said the man, with another smile, folding his hands in front of him. Ford noticed he was missing both his thumbs.

"Very," said Khon.

"Very health here, in Kampong Krabey."

"It's quite healthy here," said Khon. "I noticed right away that you have fucking good air."

"Good air! Kampong Krabey District, good!"

Ford and Khon smiled, nodded agreeably.

The secretary came back, carrying three coconuts, their tops lopped off by a machete, straws stuck in them.

"Please!" said the official. They drank the coconut milk, which was still warm from hanging on the tree. Ford thought he had never tasted anything quite so good.

"Excellent," said Khon. "What fine hospitality you offer us in the Kampong Krabey District."

"Best coconut!" the man cried, sucking his so vigorously the straw made a gurgling sound. He thumped the empty husk down on the desk and belched. "What you need, friend?" the man asked, spreading his hands. "I give you anything."

"This is Mr. Kirk Mandrake," Khon said, "and he is an adventure tourist. I am Khon, his interpreter."

"Aveentah touist!" the official repeated, with a vigorous nod, clearly having no idea what it meant. "Good!"

"He wants to visit a ruined temple known as Nokor Pheas."

"I not know this temple."

"It's very deep in the jungle."

"Where is temple? In Kampong Krabey District?"

"No. It's beyond the district. We have to travel northeast through your district to get there."

The smile on his face cooled. "Beyond my district, nothing! Nobody! No temple!"

Khon rose and unrolled a map on the official's desk. "The temple is here, in the Phnom Ngue hills."

Now the smile vanished completely. "That is bad area. Very bad."

"My client, Mr. Mandrake, wishes to see the temple."

"You cannot go there. Too dangerous."

Khon went on as if he hadn't heard the official. "Mr. Mandrake will pay well for the permit. He also needs your help in marking the trails on our map. And of course we would wish to avoid land mines. You know the district and you have the land mine clearance maps."

"Too dangerous. I speak Khmer, so you understand. That okay, Mr. Mandrake, if I speak Khmer now?" Another brilliant smile.

"Of course."

He began speaking in Khmer and Ford listened closely. "Are you crazy?" the official said. "That area is infested with Khmer Rouge. They're just bandits now, gem smuggling and kidnapping for ransom. If they got their hands on your client, it would be a *huge* problem for me. You understand?"

"I understand," said Khon, responding in Khmer. "But my client is very anxious to see this ruin. He came all the way to Cambodia just for this. We'll be in and out—no lingering. Believe me, I know what I'm doing. I've guided people like him before. Just last month, I took some Americans to Banteay Chhmar."

"I cannot allow it."

"He will pay you well."

The official spread his hands. "What good is his money if I have to deal with a kidnapping? Of an American, no less? What would happen to my position here? The district is peaceful now, no problems, everyone's happy. It wasn't always like this, you know."

"Perhaps a large amount of money will compensate for the inconvenience."

There was a pause. "How much?"

"A hundred dollars."

The official threw up his hands. "Are you joking? Make it a thousand."

"A thousand? I will consult with my client."

Khon turned to Ford and said in English, "The permit is a thousand dollars."

Ford frowned. "That's a lot of money."

"Yes, but . . ." Khon shrugged.

Ford frowned, screwed up his brow, then nodded sharply. "All right. I'll pay."

The official piped up in Khmer, "And then one hundred dollars for access to the land mine clearance maps!"

Khon turned. "One hundred dollars more? Now you're the one who's joking!"

"Fifty then."

Khon spoke to Ford. "And another fifty dollars for the maps."

"What about the motorbikes? We need motorbikes," Ford said, feigning anger. "How much more is this going to cost?"

The haggling went on for another fifteen minutes, and finally it was done. One thousand, one hundred and forty dollars for the permit, maps, the rental of two motorbikes, gas, a few provisions, and safekeeping of the Land Cruiser while they were gone. Ford removed the money and gave it to the councilman, who took it with both hands, reverently, smiling whitely, and locked it in his desk.

Ford and Khon went outside and sat down in the shade of a jackfruit tree, awaiting the arrival of the rental motorbikes from a nearby village.

"You told me to bring five thousand dollars," said Ford. "That poor fellow had no idea what we were willing to pay."

"That man just earned two years' salary. He's happy, we're happy—why question the generosity of the gods?"

With a blatting sound, two motorbikes ridden by skinny teenagers arrived and wheezed and coughed to a stop.

Ford stared at the ancient bikes, held together with gaffing tape and baling wire. One had a bamboo cage rack strapped to the back, fouled with clots and streaks of dried pig's blood. "You've got to be kidding me."

Khon laughed. "What were you expecting, Harleys?"

18

THE BLUE HILLS in the distance were the first thing Ford noticed as the trail opened into a small clearing. For the past five hours, they had been threading a web of jungle trails and he was exhausted, his bones rattled loose. He halted his bike and shut off the engine as Khon pulled up alongside. He watched the Cambodian gingerly remove the map from his backpack and unfold it, but despite all his care it was beginning to fall apart at the seams from humidity and use. Khon squinted at the map through his thick glasses, then looked up. "Those are the Phnom Ngue hills, and behind them the mountains along the Thai frontier."

"Man, it's hot. How do you do it, Khon?"

"Do what?"

"Stay so cool, so well-pressed."

"One must keep up appearances," he said, folding up the map with his plump, manicured fingers. "The village of Trey Nhor lies at the base of those hills. That's the final outpost of Cambodian sovereignty. After that—no-man's-land."

Ford nodded. He dabbed the sweat off his face and wiped his hands, threw his leg over the bike, fired up the tinny engine, goosed the throttle, and they set off once again, slowly bumping and weaving along the rutted trail. Over the next few kilometers they passed through several hamlets—a cluster of thatched houses on stilts, a water buffalo pulling a cart, children reciting loudly in unison in a thatched school hut—and then the trail rose to higher ground. A ridge loomed in the distance, smoke filtering up through the tree-tops.

"Trey Nhor," said Khon.

They drove through the forest, the whining sound of the motorbike engines like a swarm of mosquitoes. Ford felt grateful for the breeze, even if it was hardly cooling. In a few kilometers the huts of the village appeared, scattered among giant fromager trees with ribbed trunks and roots that crawled over the ground like snakes. A moment later they came into a dirt plaza, surrounded by bamboo shelters with thatched roofs. A cluster of ancestor poles stood in the center of the plaza, like a group of skinny demons. Ford gazed around; the village appeared to be empty.

They parked their bikes, kicked down the stands, and dismounted. All around the tiny clearing stood the immense, sighing forest, the human presence almost lost among the trees.

"Where is everybody?" Ford asked.

"Looks like they ran away. All but one." Khon nodded toward a shelter, and Ford could make out a wizened woman inside, sitting on a woven mat. Khon pulled a bag of candy out of his pack and they walked over. "This area was hit pretty hard during the Killing Fields," Khon said, "and they're still afraid of strangers."

"Ask her about trails into the Phnom Ngue hills."

She seemed more ancient than a person could be and still be alive, a rack of bones covered with loose, wrinkled skin. And yet she was remarkably vivacious. Sitting cross-legged on a mat, she smoked the bitter end of a cheroot and grinned at Ford, exposing a single tooth. Khon offered her the open bag of candy and she dipped her hand in, removing at least half of it in a massive, clawlike grip.

Khon spoke to the woman in dialect. She answered animatedly, her head nodding vigorously, boney fingers gesturing and pointing.

"She says we better not go in there."

"Tell her we're going and we need her help."

Khon spoke to the woman at length. "She says there's a Buddhist monastery about two kilometers north of here, reachable on foot only. The monks, she says, are the eyes and ears of the forest. We should go there first, and they'll show us the way. She'll take care of our motorbikes for the rest of that candy."

THE TRAIL ASCENDED THROUGH A GROVE of crooked jackfruit trees and climbed a heavily forested ridge. The heat was so intense Ford could feel it entering his lungs with every breath. After half an hour they came to a ruined wall of giant laterite blocks, tangled with lianas, with an ancient staircase leading up the side of a hill. They climbed it and at the top arrived at a grassy area littered with half-buried blocks; beyond, a quincunx of broken towers pushed up from the clinging jungle, each tower displaying the four faces of Vishnu gazing in the cardinal directions. An ancient Khmer temple.

In the middle of the ruins, in a grassy clearing, stood the bombed-out shell of a much more recent Buddhist monastery. Roofless, its ragged stone walls were silhouetted against the sky. Beyond, Ford could see the gilded towers of stupas, or tombs, rising above the foliage. Bees droned in the heavy air and there was the scent of burning sandalwood.

At the front of the monastery, standing in the doorless entryway, was a monk wrapped in saffron robes with a shaved head. Small and wizened, he peered at them with a lively face and a pair of sparkling black eyes tucked among a thousand wrinkles. Two tiny hands clutched the edges of his robe.

Khon bowed and the monk bowed. They spoke, but once again Ford couldn't follow the dialect. The monk gestured Ford over. "You are welcome here," he said in Khmer. "Come."

They entered the roofless temple. The floor was of close-cut grass, as smooth and tended as a golf green. At one end stood a gilded statue of the Buddha, in the lotus position with half-closed eyes, almost buried under offerings of fresh flowers. Joss sticks burned in clusters around the statue, perfuming the air with sandalwood and merintane. A dozen robed monks stood behind the Buddha, almost defensively in a tight cluster, some hardly in their teens. The temple walls were made of stone recycled from the older ruin, and Ford could see pieces of sculpture peeking out of the broken, mortared blocks—a hand, a torso, half a face, the wildly gyrating limb of a dancing apsara. Along one wall ran two ragged lines of bullet pits made from a spray of automatic weapons fire. It looked to Ford like the site of an old execution.

"Please, sit down," the monk said, gesturing at some reed mats spread on the grass. The afternoon sun slanted in the broken roof, painting the eastern wall gold, incense smoke drifting in and out of the bars of light. After some minutes of silence a monk came in with an old cast-iron pot of tea and some chipped cups, placed them on the mat, and poured. They drank the strong green tea. When they had finished, the abbot rose.

"Do you speak Khmer?" he asked Ford in a birdlike voice.

Ford nodded.

"What brings you to the end of the world?"

Ford dipped into his pocket and took out the fake honey stone. With a gasp, the abbot rose quickly and stepped back in one fluid motion, and the other monks shuffled away. "Get that devil stone out of here."

"It's a fake," said Ford smoothly.

"You're gem traders?"

"No," said Ford. "We're looking for the mine producing the honey stones."

For the first time, a flicker of emotion passed across the monk's face. He seemed to hesitate, running a hand over his dry, shaven scalp. His fingers made a slight bristling noise as they ran over the stubble. "Why?"

"I come from the U.S. government. We want to know where it is and shut it down."

"There are many ex–Khmer Rouge soldiers there, armed with guns, mortars, and RPGs. Violent people. How do you expect to go there and survive?"

"Will you help us?"

The monk spoke without hesitation. "Yes."

"What do you know about the mine?"

"There was a big explosion in the forest about a month ago. And then, a little while later, they came. They raided mountain villages to get people to mine the devil stones. They work them to death and then go out and capture more."

"Can you tell us anything about the layout of the mine, the number of soldiers, who's running the place?"

The abbot made a gesture and a monk on the other side of the room rose and went out. A moment later he came back leading a blind child of about ten in monk's garb. His face and scalp were a web of shiny scars, his nose and one ear gone, his two eye sockets knots of fiery scar tissue. The body under his robes was small, thin, and crooked.

"This one escaped to us from the mine," said the abbot.

Ford looked at the child more closely, and realized she was a girl, dressed as a boy.

The monk said, "If they knew we were hiding her, we would all die." He turned to her. "Come here, my child, and tell the American everything you know, even the worst parts."

The child spoke in a flat, emotionless voice, as if reciting in a schoolroom. She told of an explosion in the mountains, the coming of ex–Khmer Rouge soldiers; how they attacked her village, murdered her mother and father, and force-marched the survivors through the jungle to the mine. She described how she slowly went blind sorting through piles of broken rock for the gems. Then, in clear, precise language, she described in detail the layout of the mine, where the soldiers patrolled, where the boss man lived, and how the mine operated. When she was done, she bowed and stepped back.

Ford laid down his notebook and took a long breath. "Tell me about the explosion. What kind of explosion?"

"Like a bomb," she said. "The cloud went way up into the sky and a dirty rain fell for days afterward. It knocked down many trees."

Ford turned to the monk. "Did you see the explosion? What was it?"

The abbot looked at him with penetrating eyes. "A demon from the deepest regions of hell."

19

ABBEY JAMMED THE pin into the anchor stay and came aft, hopping down into the wheelhouse. "We're outta here," she said, grabbing the wheel and revving the engine, swinging the prow away from Marsh Island, which they had just searched.

"That was a bust," Jackie said crossly.

"Two down, three more to go," said Abbey, trying to put a little cheer into her voice. "Don't worry—we'll find it."

"We better. Crawling through that brush just about did me in. I feel like I was tied up in a sack full of wildcats. Look at all these scratches!" She stuck her arm in front of Abbey's face.

"War wounds. You can brag to your grandchildren about them." She guided the *Marea* around the northern end of Marsh Island. The sinking sun blazed blood-orange over the distant mainland, a soft haze drifting in the air. She checked the chartplotter and set a course for the next island on her list: Ripp. She could see it on the sea horizon, several miles beyond the old Earth Station complex on Crow. The station always looked so out of place, a huge white bubble rising from the rugged islands like a giant puffball mushroom. A small cluster of lights floated on the water, the Crow Island ferry heading for Tenants Harbor.

"Remember when we went out there on a field trip?" Jackie said, following her gaze. "Those three freaks living on the island, tending the station 'round the clock?"

"That was when they were using it to send signals to the Saturn probe."

"You have to wonder what kind of crazy-ass person would take a job like that on an island in the middle of nowhere. Remember the guy with the buck teeth leering at us? Ew. What do you think they do all day long?"

"Maybe they're busy calling E.T."

"Yo, E, got any more of that Martian bud?" Jackie said.

Abbey laughed. "Speaking of mind-altering substances, I note the sun's below the yardarm." She held up a bottle of Jim Beam.

"Roger that."

Abbey took a pull and handed the bottle over. Jackie took her own swig. The sun winked out on the horizon and a slow twilight spread across the glassy bay.

"Uh oh," said Abbey, peering ahead. She picked up the binoculars from the dashboard and glassed the island ahead. "The lights are on in the house on Ripp. Looks like the admiral's already up from Jersey for his summer vacation."

"Shit."

As they neared the island, a shingled mansion hove into view, all turrets and gables, lit up by exterior floods.

"That admiral, he's one crazy motherfucker," said Jackie.

"They say he was in the Korean War, killed a bunch of women and children."

"Urban legend."

"What I'm saying is, maybe we should forget Ripp."

"Jackie, the line runs right across the middle of the island. We'll search it at night—tonight."

Jackie groaned. "If the meteorite landed on Ripp, the admiral would have already found it."

"He wasn't around when it fell. And it's a big island."

"They say he has security guards."

"Yeah, right, a couple of donut-eaters parked on their fat asses in the kitchen watching *American Idol*."

Abbey scanned the harbor and house with the binoculars. The admiral's launch, a Crownline outboard, was tied up to a floating dock while a large motor yacht was anchored in the cove. She could see activity in the windows of the house.

"We'll anchor on the other side."

"Watch out for the riptide running along the western side," said Jackie. "It's pretty vicious. The best approach is from the south-southwest at a bearing of twenty degrees."

"All right." Abbey turned the wheel, altering their course to approach the island from the far end. They halted about a hundred feet offshore and anchored. The stars were coming out. Dousing the anchor lights and electronics, she left the boat dark, while Jackie stuffed a small backpack with the essentials: Jim Beam in a metal flask, scuba knife, binoculars, canteen, matches, flashlights, batteries, and a can of Mace.

They climbed in the dinghy. The water lay glossy and dark, the island looming ahead, swallowed in blackness. Abbey rowed toward shore, feathering her oars to reduce the splash of water. The boat crunched on the sand and they hopped out. Through the trees Abbey could just see the glimmer of light from the house.

"Now what?" Jackie whispered.

"Follow me." Abbey took a heading with her compass, crossed the beach, and bulled her way through a thicket of beach roses, finally breaking into the forest. She could hear Jackie's breathing behind her. In the trees it was as black as a cave. Turning on her flashlight, she kept it hooded with her hand as they moved through the mossy woods, casting right and left with the light, looking for a crater. Once in a while Abbey stopped to check their bearing on the compass.

Ten minutes passed but they found nothing. Toward the far end of the island, they slogged through a swamp and waded across a sluggish stream, water up to their chests, Abbey holding the backpack over her head. The swamp gave way to an open field. Crouching in the trees, Abbey scouted it with the binoculars while Jackie took off her shoes and dumped out muddy water.

"I'm freezing."

The field sloped up a hill to a manicured lawn and tennis court, beyond which stood the giant house. She saw a movement in one of the windows: a moving shadow.

"We've got to cross that field," whispered Abbey. "Could be a crater there."

"Maybe we should go around."

"No way. We do this right."

Neither one moved.

Abbey nudged her. "Scared?"

"Yes. And wet."

Abbey slipped the hip flask out of her pack and handed

it to her friend. Jackie took a shot and Abbey followed with a slug of her own.

"Fortified?"

"No."

"Let's get this over with." Abbey could feel the warmth creeping through her belly and she headed into the field. The glow from the house was all the light they needed and she shoved her flashlight into the backpack. Moving slowly on hands and knees, keeping low, they crept across the dead, matted grass.

About halfway across, a dog barked in the distance. They both instinctively flattened themselves in the grass. The faint sound of Frank Sinatra came from the house and then faded—someone had opened and closed a door. They waited.

Another distant yelp. Abbey could feel icy water trickling down her back and she shivered.

"Abbey, please. Let's get out of here."

"Shhh."

As Abbey was about to rise, she saw two fleet shadows come tearing around the corner of the house and hurtling across the top of the lawn, weaving back and forth, noses down.

"Dogs," she said.

"Jesus, no."

"We gotta get the fuck out of here. On three, we break for the stream."

Jackie whimpered.

"One, two, *three*." Abbey leapt up and tore across the field, Jackie following. A furious barking erupted behind them. They dove into the stream, the sluggish but powerful current pulling them along, swirling them toward the woods. Abbey immersed all but her face, trying to breathe through her pursed lips. The barking got closer, and now she could see flashlights bobbing at the top of the hill, two men running down the field toward them.

More barking sounded, now upstream, where they'd entered the water. Shouts from the approaching men, a gun-shot.

The dark trees closed around her as the current swept her into the forest. She tried to look for Jackie but it was too dark. The current was getting swifter as the water ran between polished boulders and thick-rooted spruce trees. She heard a sound—the roar of water—as the current sucked her along, ever faster.

Waterfall. She struck out for shore, grasped a boulder, but it was slippery with algae and she was pulled away. The roar got louder. Looking downstream, she saw a thin white line in the darkness. Scrabbling at another rock, she clung for a moment, but the current swung her body around and it, too, was torn from her grasp.

"Jackie!" she spluttered, and felt a sucking current, a sudden weightlessness, a white roar all about her, and then a sudden plunge into cold, tumbling darkness. For a moment she didn't know which way was up, and she swam wildly, kicking and stroking, trying to establish equilibrium—and then her head broke the surface. Gasping for breath, flailing and trying to keep her head above the pounding rush of water, she cast around, stroked away from the turbulence, and a moment later found herself in a calm, sluggish pool. The night sky, the ocean—she was at the margin of the shore. The current carried her between bars of gravel and she kicked for the embankment, her feet digging into the loose shingle below. Hauling herself up the gravel bar, she coughed and spat water. She looked around but all was quiet. The men and dogs were nowhere to be seen.

"Jackie?" she hissed.

A moment later Jackie heaved herself out of the water, rising to her knees, spluttering.

"Jackie? You okay?"

After a moment a hoarse voice answered, "Fuck yeah."

Keeping to the edge of the trees, they followed the shore around to the dinghy, hauled it down to the waterline, climbed in, and pushed off. A moment later they were back on the *Marea*. After a brief silence, they both dissolved into raucous laughter.

"All right," said Abbey, recovering her breath. "Let's haul anchor and get the hell out of here, before they come looking for us in that big yacht of theirs."

They both stripped off their wet clothes and hung them on the rails. Buck naked, they drove the boat off into the ocean night, swapping a pint of Jim Beam.

20

FORD CONSIDERED HIMSELF a fast hiker, but the Buddhist monk moved through the forest with the swiftness of a bat, swooping along the trails in his flip-flops, his saffron robes flapping behind him. For hours they walked in silence without resting, until they came to a boulder at the mouth of a steep ravine. Here the monk stopped abruptly and, with a flouncing of his robes, seated himself, bowing his head in prayer.

After a silence he looked up and pointed up the gorge. "Six kilometers. Follow the main canyon to the hill, and climb it. You'll find yourself above the mine, looking down into the valley. But watch out—there's a patrol that passes along the flanks of that hill."

Khon put his hands together and bowed in thanks.

"Bless the Buddha on the trail," said the monk. "Now go."

Khon bowed again.

They left him there, sitting on the rock, head bowed in meditation. Ford led the way up the gorge, threading between many huge boulders rolled and polished by ancient floods. As the canyon narrowed into a ravine, the trees on the steep hillsides leaned over them, forming a tunnel. Insects droned in the heavy air and the air smelled of sweet-fern.

"Awfully quiet around here," said Ford, huffing.

Khon wagged his round head.

Here and there, Ford noticed Buddhist prayers carved into the boulders, the script almost obliterated by time. At one point they passed an entire reclining Buddha, forty feet long, carved from a natural outcrop in the side of the canyon. Khon paused to make a silent offering, casting flowers on it.

At the head of the ravine a trail began to climb a steep hill. As they neared the top, sunlight loomed up through the trees. A broken wall encircled the summit, and through its ramparts Ford could see the ruins of a modest temple rising from the tangling vines. A burned and twisted anti-aircraft gun, dating back to the Vietnam War, occupied one end of the temple, a second gun emplacement at the other.

Gesturing for Khon to stay back, Ford crept through the foliage and climbed over the broken wall. He heard a rustle and spun, drawing his Walther, but it was only a monitor lizard crawling away into a pile of dead leaves. Keeping his pistol unholstered, he proceeded into the clearing, looked around, and gestured for Khon to come up. They worked their way up the trail to the second gun emplacement, which had been set up at the very brow of the hill, affording a view into the valley beyond.

Ford crept to the edge of the stone platform and peered down.

The sight was so strange he couldn't comprehend at first

what he was seeing. The trees in the center of the valley had been flattened in a perfect radial pattern, pointing away from a central crater like the spokes of a giant wheel. A pall of smoke lay over a scene of incessant activity. Lines of ragged people moved to and from the central crater, carrying burden baskets filled with rocks on their backs, tumplines stretched across their foreheads. They dumped the bluish rocks on a huge pile fifty yards distant and shuffled back to the mine, backs bent, to refill the baskets. The rock pile in turn swarmed with emaciated children and old women, who split the rocks with small hammers and sorted through the pieces, searching for gems.

The central crater was, quite evidently, the mine itself.

In the valley above the mine, an area had been cleared in the fallen timber and a crude village erected, crooked wattle huts with thatched roofs standing in rows, the encampment enclosed by rolls of concertina wire lying on the ground. It was not unlike a concentration camp. Plumes of smoke rose from dozens of cooking fires. A pair of old tanks were parked at either end of the camp and soldiers carrying heavy weapons patrolled the perimeter of the valley. More soldiers kept the lines of miners moving, prodding the slow and weak with long, sharpened sticks—but always keeping their distance.

Ford reached into his pack and slipped out a pair of binoculars to take a closer look. The crater leapt into view— a deep, vertical shaft, showing unmistakable evidence of having been created by a powerful meteoritic impact. He examined the line of miners; they were in hideous physical condition—hair falling out, ragged bodies covered with open sores, skin dark and shriveled, backs bowed, bones prominent. Many people were so eaten up by radiation poisoning—bald, toothless, and emaciated—that Ford couldn't tell the men from the women. Even the soldiers guarding them looked listless and ill.

"What do you see?" Khon whispered from behind.

"Things. Terrible things."

Khon came crawling up with his own binocs. He stared for a long time, in silence.

While they watched, one of the miners carrying ore staggered and fell, the basket spilling to the ground. He was small and slight, and, Ford guessed, no more than a teenager. A soldier dragged the boy out of the line and kicked him, trying to get him to rise. The boy struggled but was too weak. Finally the soldier placed a pistol against the boy's head and fired. Nobody even so much as turned a head. The soldier waved over a donkey cart, the corpse was swung in, and Ford watched as the donkey was driven to the edge of the valley. There the body was dumped into a trench cut like a raw wound into the red soil of the rainforest—a mass grave.

"You see that?" Khon said quietly.

"Yes."

Ford glassed the soldiers on patrol and was shocked to see that most of them, too, looked like teenagers and some were clearly children.

"Take a look up the valley," murmured Khon, "where those big trees are still standing."

Ford swung the glasses up and immediately spied a wooden house tucked in amongst the trees at the head of the valley. Built in classic French colonial style, with a pitched tin roof, dormer windows, and walls of whitewashed boards and batten. The roof sloped down to a broad verandah, shaded by tall flowering heliconias in vivid orange and red. As he watched, he could see an old, birdlike man moving around the verandah, pacing back and forth, holding a drink in his fist. His hair was snow white, his back bowed almost to a hunchback position, but his face appeared unlined and alert. As the man paced, he was talking to two other men, making chopping gestures with his free hand. Teen soldiers with AK-47s guarded both sides of the house.

"You see him?"

Ford nodded.

"I'm pretty sure that man is Brother Number Six."

"Brother Number Six?"

"Pol Pot's right-hand man. Rumors had it the bastard was controlling an area somewhere along the Thai–Cambodian border. Looks like we just found his little fiefdom." Khon slipped his binoculars back into his pack. "Well, I guess that wraps it up."

Ford said nothing. He could feel Khon's eyes on him.

"Let's take some pictures, roll videotape, get a GPS reading, and get the damn out of here."

Ford lowered his binoculars and did not respond.

Suddenly, Khon frowned. He spied something in the weeds at his feet; reaching out, he plucked it up and showed it to Ford. It was a hand-rolled cigarette butt, fresh and dry.

"Uh oh," said Ford.

"We must get off this hill."

They crept back from the edge and scurried at a crouch past the gun emplacements. Ford spied a movement in the forest below and pitched himself to the ground, Khon following.

He gestured to Khon. "Patrol."

"They're surely coming up this way."

"Then we go down the other side."

Ford crawled on his belly toward the encircling wall and crouched below it, Khon following.

"Can't stay here. Got to get over that wall."

Khon nodded.

Ford found a good handhold, hauled himself up to just below the broken edge, then threw himself over and down. He lay there, breathing hard. He hadn't been seen. A moment later Khon appeared at the top. A deafening burst of automatic weapons fire ripped out of the jungle to their left, spraying across the wall, sending chips of stone flying like shrapnel.

"*Hon chun gnay!*" Khon cried, launching himself from the top and landing heavily next to Ford and rolling. The gunfire swung around and tore into the vegetation over their heads, spraying them with shredded leaves and twigs.

The firing stopped as abruptly as it had started and Ford could hear shouts as hidden soldiers ran through the trees below them. Trying to keep himself as flat as possible, he aimed his Walther in the direction of the voices and fired a single shot. The response was a torrent of more gunfire, still coming in high. A second spray of rounds snicked off the upper stones of the wall.

"Let's get out of here," said Ford.

Khon pulled out his 9mm Beretta. "No shit, Yanqui."

An RPG overshot their position and detonated on the hilltop above them, the concussion bucking Ford over. His ears ringing, he struggled to clear his head. "Run down that draw while I cover you. Then take cover and do the same for me."

"Right."

Ford fired the .32 in the general direction of the soldiers, and a moment later Khon leapt up and tore down the hill. Ford kept up a slow, irregular suppressing fire as Khon dodged down the hill and disappeared.

A minute later Ford heard the *pop pop* of Khon's covering fire for him. He scrambled to his feet and tore downhill, into the draw. An RPG went off behind him, throwing him forward—and a good thing, as the vegetation where he had just been was chopped into bits by a discharge of automatic weapons fire.

He crawled down the draw as twigs and wet flecks of vegetation rained down on him. They were still firing high, raking the understory, unable to get the right angle from their position. A moment later he saw Khon ahead.

"Run!"

They both pounded downhill, crashing their way through bushes and vines. Bursts of fire ripped through the vegetation around them, but gradually it became more distant and sporadic.

Ten minutes later they hit the upper part of the ravine, and paused at the banks of the stream to catch their breaths. Ford knelt and threw water into his face and neck, trying to cool himself off.

"They're tracking us," said Khon. "We've got to keep moving."

Ford nodded. "Upstream. They won't expect it."

Wading in the water, stepping from pool to rushing pool, Ford climbed up the loose boulders of the steep streambed. A half hour of grueling climbing brought them to a spring, where water poured from a fissure. A ridgeline lay a hundred yards above and a dry gully went off to the right.

They crossed the gully and climbed the ridge, down the other side, and up the next one, bulling through dense thickets of brush. A couple of hours passed and twilight began to fall. The forest sank into green gloaming.

Khon threw himself down on a bed of small ferns, rolled on his back, tucked his hands behind his head. A big smile spread over his placid features. "Lovely. Let's make camp."

Ford sank onto a fallen log, breathing hard. He took out his canteen, handed it to Khon, who drank deeply. He then drank himself, the water warm and fetid.

"You verified the mine," said Khon, sitting up and examining his fingernails. He took out a nail file and began to clean and sand them. "You have the location. We can go back now."

Ford said nothing.

"Right, Mr. Mandrake? We go back now?"

Still no answer.

"No more saving the world, please!"

Ford rubbed his neck. "Khon, you *know* we've got a problem."

"Which is?"

"Why did they send me here?"

"To locate the mine. You said so yourself."

"You saw it. Are you trying to tell me the CIA didn't already know exactly where it was? No way could our spy satellites have missed that place."

"Hmmm," mumbled Khon. "You have a fucking point."

"So why the charade of sending me in?"

Khon shrugged. "The CIA moves in mysterious ways."

Ford rubbed his face, smoothed back his hair, breathed out. "There's another problem."

"Which is?"

"Are we going to leave those people to die?"

"Those people are already dead. And you told me you were ordered to do nothing. No touchee mine. Right, Mr. Mandrake?"

"There were children there, *kids*." Ford raised his head. "Did you see them blow that teenager away, just like that? And the mass grave? There must be a couple of hundred bodies in there already and the trench wasn't even a quarter full. This is genocide."

Khon was shaking his head. "Welcome to the land of genocide. Leave it."

"No. I'm not going to just walk away."

"What can we do?"

"Blow the mine up."

21

MARK CORSO CLUTCHED the CD-ROM in his hand, feeling the sweat from his fingers sticking to the plastic case. It was his first time in the MMO conference room, the sanctum sanctorum of the Mars mission. It was disappointing. The stale air smelled of coffee, carpeting, and Pledge. The walls were done up in fake paneling, some of which had buckled. Plastic tables against the walls were loaded with flat-screen computer monitors, oscilloscopes, consoles, and other random electronic equipment. A screen lowered from the ceiling covered one end of the room, and the ugliest conference table he had ever seen, in brown Formica with stamped aluminum edges and metal legs, dominated the center.

Corso took his seat in front of a little plastic sign sporting his name. He slipped his laptop out, plugged it into a dock, jacked it in, and booted up. Meanwhile the other technicians were trickling in, chatting, joking, and tanking up on weak California coffee from an ancient Sunbeam in the corner.

Marjory Leung sat down beside him, plugged her own computer in. A fragrance of jasmine drifted over him. She was unexpectedly well dressed in a sleek black suit and Corso was glad he had donned his best jacket that morning with one of his most expensive silk ties. The white lab coats were nowhere to be seen.

"Nervous?" she asked.

"A little." It was Corso's first senior staff meeting, and he was third in line out of ten presenters, each with five minutes and questions.

"Pretty soon it'll seem routine."

The room fell silent as the MMO mission director, Charles Chaudry, rose from his seat at the far end of the table. Corso liked Chaudry—he was young, hip, with premature gray hair pulled back into a tight ponytail, utterly brilliant and yet down to earth. Everyone knew his story: born in Kashmir, India, he came to the U.S. as a baby in the wave of refugees fleeing the Second Kashmir War of 1965. He'd worked his way up from nothing, a classic immigrant success story, to earn a Ph.D. in planetary geology from Berkeley, his dissertation winning the Stockton Award. As if to make up for his foreign birth, Chaudry was quintessentially American—Californian even—a rock-climber, mountain biker, and avid surfer who tackled the winter waves at Mavericks, said to be the most dangerous break in the world. There were rumors he came from a rich Brahmin family of obscure nobility and sported a title back in the home country, a pasha or nabob, or so the jokes went, but nobody really knew. He was somewhat vain but that was a fault common among NPF staff.

"Welcome," he said, in an offhand way, flashing a white

smile at the group. "The mission's making great progress." He ran through some of their recent successes, noted a glowing article in the science section of *The New York Times*, quoted another piece in the British publication *New Scientist*, mentioned with a certain schadenfreude suspected problems with the Chinese Hu Jintao orbiter, and cracked a few jokes.

"Now," he said, "let's get to the data presentations." He glanced at a piece of paper. "Five minutes for each, followed by questions. We'll start with the weather report. Marjory?"

Leung rose and launched into her talk, a PowerPoint presentation on Mars weather, showing infrared images of equatorial ice clouds recently photographed by the MMO. Corso tried to concentrate, but he was too distracted. His moment was fast approaching—five minutes to make his first impression as a senior technician. He was about to make a high-risk move, uncharacteristic of him, but he felt secure with it. He'd gone over it a hundred times. It might be unorthodox but it would blow them away. How could it be otherwise? Here was a stunning mystery, apparently uncovered by Dr. Freeman shortly before his death which he hadn't had the time to analyze. Corso had carried the torch. It was, he felt, a way to honor his professor's memory while at the same time advancing his own career.

He slid his eyes toward the far end of the conference table and took in Derkweiler, sitting at the foot, fat leather portfolio in front of him. Derkweiler would come around when he saw which way the wind was blowing.

Corso listened to the first reports but hardly heard them. He felt a flurry in his gut as the presentation before his drew to a close.

"Mark?" said Chaudry, glancing over at him. "You're up."
He smiled encouragingly.

Corso slid the CD into the computer drive. It took a
moment to load, and then the first image in the PowerPoint
presentation popped up on the project.

The MMO Compton Gamma Ray Scintillator:
An Analysis of Anomalous High-Energy
Gamma Ray Emission Data
Mark Corso, Senior Data Analysis Technician

"Thank you, Dr. Chaudry," said Corso. "I have a bit of a surprise for you all—a discovery that I believe has some
significance."

Derkweiler's face darkened. Corso tried not to look at it.
He didn't want to be thrown off his game.

"Instead of the SHARAD data, I would like to focus on
the data gathered by the MMO's Compton Gamma Ray
Scintillator."

The room had fallen very, very silent. He risked a glance
at Chaudry. The man looked interested.

He went to the next image, showing Mars with many
orbital trajectories drawn around it. "This is the trajectory of
the Mars Orbiter over the past month, collecting data in an
almost polar orbit . . ." He rushed through familiar information, punching through several screens in quick
succession until he got to the money shot. It showed a graph
with periodic spikes. "If there were a gamma ray source on
Mars, this is the *theoretical* signature as seen from the Mars
Orbiter."

Nods, murmurs, exchanged glances.

He went to the next image, two graphs, one on top of the other, with the spikes almost coinciding.

"And this, ladies and gentlemen, is the *actual* gamma ray data from the orbiter, laid over the theoretical graph." He waited for the reaction.

Silence.

"I would call your attention to what appears to be a fairly significant match," he said, trying to maintain a modest, neutral tone.

Chaudry squinted, leaning forward. The others just stared.

"I know the error bars are somewhat large," said Corso, "and I'm well aware that the background noise is high. And, of course, the scintillator is nondirectional. It can't focus on the exact source. But I've run a statistical analysis and determined that there's only one chance out of four that this match is a coincidence."

More silence. A kind of nervous shuffling in the room.

"Your conclusion, Dr. Corso?" came Chaudry's question, in a studiously neutral tone of voice.

"That there is a gamma ray source on Mars. A *point* source."

A shocked silence. "And what might this gamma ray source be?" asked Chaudry.

"That is the very question that needs to be answered. I believe the next step is to examine the visual and radar images and try to find a corresponding artifact."

"Artifact?" Chaudry asked.

"Feature, I mean. Artifact was a rather poor choice of words; thank you for the correction. I don't mean to imply we're looking for something unnatural."

"Any theories?"

Corso took a breath. He had debated whether to offer his thoughts. *In for a penny, in for a pound.* "This is sheer speculation, of course, but I have several conjectures."

"Let's hear them."

"It could be a natural geological reactor, as has been discovered on Earth. In which the movement of rock or water concentrates a mass of uranium to create a subcritical mass, which would decay, emitting gamma rays."

A nod.

"But that theory has significant problems. Unlike Earth, Mars has no plate tectonics, no faulting or large-scale water movement that could do this. A meteorite impact would spread, not concentrate material."

"What else might it be?"

Corso took a deep breath. "A miniature black hole or a large piece of neutron-degenerate matter would emit copious high-energy gamma rays. Such an object might have arrived on Mars through an impact event and somehow lodged or been trapped close enough to the surface to emit gamma rays into space. In fact, such an object might still be active, eating up the planet so to speak—hence the gamma rays. This could be . . ." He paused, then forged ahead, ". . . a possible crisis situation. If Mars were swallowed by a black hole or crushed down to neutron matter, the gamma ray flux would sterilize the Earth. Completely."

He stopped. He had said it. As he looked around, he saw incredulity staring back at him. No problem—the data didn't lie.

"And the SHARAD data?" asked Chaudry.

Corso stared at him, disbelieving. "I'll have it ready in a

few days. I felt, and I hope you'll agree, that the gamma ray data was more important."

Derkweiler spoke up, his voice surprisingly friendly and well-modulated. "Dr. Corso, I'm sorry, I was under the impression that you would be presenting the *SHARAD* data at the meeting today."

Corso looked from Derkweiler to Chaudry and back. Everyone would now see what a putz Derkweiler was. "I felt this was more important," he finally said. He looked at Chaudry, hoping for, praying for, encouragement.

Chaudry cleared his throat. "Dr. Corso, at first glance I'm not sure I share your enthusiasm for these data. The error bars render a lot of this 'match' meaningless. A one in four departure from noise is not exactly definitive."

"A lot of cosmological data are barely above noise level, Dr. Chaudry," said Corso, quietly.

"True. But for the life of me, I can't even *begin* to imagine what could be emitting gamma rays on the surface of a dead planet with no current tectonic activity and no magnetic field. This business of a black hole or . . ." his skeptical voice trailed off.

Corso cleared his throat and plowed ahead. "I would recommend we search the planet's surface for a visual feature corresponding to the gamma ray emitter. If we could pinpoint the gamma ray source on the planet's surface, we could photograph it with the HiRISE camera. Or, what's more likely, we've probably *already* photographed it and haven't recognized the significance."

Chaudry seemed to collect himself. He stared for a long time at the image on the screen, everyone waiting for him to speak. "I see a problem."

Corso waited, his heart in his mouth.

"The periodicity of the gamma ray source of yours is allegedly about thirty hours—according to your plot. But Mars rotates once every twenty-five hours. How do you account for the discrepancy?"

Corso had noted the difference, but it seemed small. "Five hours is within the margins of error."

"Excuse me, Dr. Corso, but if you extrapolate along your graph, the two periodicities get out of phase. Wildly out of phase. *That's* no margin of error."

Corso stared at the graph. Chaudry was right—he saw it instantly. An elementary, stupid, unforgivable mistake.

There was a dead silence. "I see your point," Corso said, his face burning. "I'll go back over the data and see if I can't clear that up. But the periodicity is there. It could be in orbit about the planet."

Derkweiler spoke up. "Dr. Corso, even if this were accurate, which I doubt, this is still an irrelevant diversion from our current mission. I'd rather you turned your efforts to the SHARAD polar data—which is very late."

"But . . . surely we should investigate this gamma ray anomaly," Corso said weakly. "This could pose a significant risk to life on Earth."

"I'm not sure there *is* an anomaly," said Chaudry. "And I do *not* appreciate the alarmist sentiment built on such wobbly data. We've got to be very careful around here."

"Even if there's a small chance of—"

Chaudry interrupted. "When you stare at noise too long, you start seeing things that aren't there. The human mind often tries to impose patterns where none exist." He spoke calmly, almost compassionately. "The SHARAD data is what's important. The late Dr. Freeman made a mistake in focusing so much of his time on the gamma ray data. I'd hate to see you fall into the same error."

Derkweiler turned to Chaudry. "Chuck, I'll finish the SHARAD analysis myself and have it on your desk tomorrow by five. My apologies."

Chaudry nodded. "Tomorrow at five, then. Appreciate it, Winston."

Corso sat through the rest of the presentations with his hands folded, an attentive expression fixed on his face, seeing nothing, hearing nothing, feeling like he was dying inside. Even Marjory Leung's comforting pat on his shoulder as he rose to leave didn't help. How could he have made such an elementary mistake?

Freeman had been right: Chaudry was in fact as big an idiot as Derkweiler. But where did that leave him? Totally fucked.

22

FORD SAT CROSS-LEGGED on the ground, staring at the fire and listening to the sounds of the jungle night. The dark forest enclosed them like a humid dungeon.

Khon reached over, raised the lid of the pot cooking on the fire, and stirred the contents with a stick. He said, his voice laden with skepticism, "So—what's next? How are you going to blow up the mine?"

Ford sighed.

"During the Killing Fields," Khon said, "I saw my uncle shot in the head. You know what his crime was? He owned a cooking pot."

"Why was that a capital offense?"

"That's the Khmer Rouge. That's how they think. Owning a cooking pot meant he hadn't gotten into the collective spirit, the communist spirit. It didn't matter he had a five-year-old boy who was starving. So they executed his boy in front of him, and then killed him. These are the men you're up against, Wyman."

Ford broke a stick, tossed the pieces in the fire. "Tell me about Brother Number Six."

"He was part of Pol Pot's student group in Paris in the fifties. He became a member of the Central Committee during the Killing Fields, went by the name of Ta Prak."

"Background?"

"Educated family from Phnom Penh. The bugger ordered the killing of his own family—brothers, sisters, mother, father, grandparents. He held it up as a badge of honor to show the purity of his ideals."

"Nice guy."

"After the death of Pol Pot in '98, he disappeared in the north and started smuggling drugs and gems. His 'revolutionary ideals' degenerated into criminality."

"What motivates him now?"

"Survival. Pure and simple."

"Not money?"

"You need money to survive. What does fucking Brother Number Six want? I tell you what he wants: to live out the last of his days in peace and quiet and die a natural death. This is what the mass murderer wants: to die of old age, surrounded by his children and grandchildren. He's almost eighty, but he clings to life like a young man. All that horror in that valley, the mine, the enslavement—it's all about squeezing out those last years of life. You see, if the bastard relaxes his grip, even for a second, he's a dead man and he knows it. Not even his soldiers will back him up."

"And then an asteroid falls into his lap."

Khon stared at him across the fire. "Asteroid?"

Ford nodded. "The explosion that the monks talked

about, the crater, the flattened trees, the radioactive gemstones—everything points to an asteroid impact."

Khon shrugged, tossed a stick in the fire. "Let your government take care of it."

"Did you see the kids picking through that pile of rocks? It's killing them. If we don't destroy the mine, they'll die."

After a silence, Khon rummaged in his pack and removed a pint bottle. "Johnnie Walker Black," he said. "Clears the mind." He tossed it over.

Ford cracked and unscrewed the cap, raised the bottle. "Prost." He took a sip, then another, and passed it back. Khon helped himself, placed the bottle between them. He lifted the lid on the rice, nodded, took the pot from the fire, and scooped out steaming rice onto tin plates.

Ford accepted the plate and they ate in silence as the fire died down into ashy coals.

To live out the last of his days and die a natural death. If that's all that motivated him now, perhaps dealing with Brother Number Six wouldn't be so difficult after all.

"Khon, I have the glimmer of an idea."

23

RANDALL WORTH HOOKED his boat up to a disused mooring in the Harbor Island anchorage and doused his lights. The girls had left the admiral's island in a big hurry and gone to ground in a cove on Otter Island. They'd be there for the rest of the night.

Fucking insane, landing on the island when the admiral was home—especially after the old fart had discovered half his antiques gone. Worth wheezed with laughter, thinking of the admiral finding his house stripped, a shit deposited on his floor.

Worth pulled a Bud out of the cooler, popped it, and took a good pull. They must have a hot lead on the treasure to take a risk like that. He got a knob thinking about how he'd do those two bitches, pirate style, first one, then the other. After he got the treasure.

His mind circled back to his encounter on the dock with Abbey. *Deeper, deeper.* What a slut, saying that right in front of big-mouth Jackie Spann. Jackie would laugh it all over town. He felt a burning rage take hold, like crank fumes in his head. He hated the whole town. The kids who had pushed him around in school and called him "Worthless" were now coaches, insurance salesmen, mechanics, fishermen, accountants—the same bastards, only grown up. He would fuck 'em all, starting with Abbey and Jackie, and then kill them. Abbey reminded him of his mother who had screwed every big-gut in town, groaning and humping, while he was forced to listen through the paper walls of the trailer. The best day of his life was when she wrapped her rice-burner around a tree and had to be cut out in sections.

He tossed the beer can overboard and cracked another, his fingers trembling. He gave a long pull, then another, draining it in less than a minute, tossed it. Cracked a third, belched, sucked it down. He could feel the creep of the alcohol in his brain, but it wasn't helping with the crank bugs. It wasn't tamping down that twitchy feeling of ants and worms. A sour taste of nausea burbled upward into his gullet and a muscle began twitching in his neck. One of his scabs was bleeding again.

His eye fell on the RG .44, sitting on the console. He picked it up, flipped open the cylinder. Might be a good idea to fire it a couple of times, make sure it still worked. He ejected the unfired rounds, looked them over. They were a bit mottled but still looked tight. He shoved them back in, closed the cylinder, and went out on deck. Taking a few deep breaths, he looked around. With the money from the treasure, he wouldn't have to deal with dickheads like Doyle anymore. No more B&Es, no more risking prison. He'd open that pub he'd always thought about, with the widescreen TV, wood paneling, pool table, English ale on tap. In prison he'd spent hours in his cell constructing it in his mind's eye, the sawdust-covered floor, the smell of beer and fries, the wrap-around oak bar, the waitresses in miniskirts waggling their pert asses.

Another shiver in his spine, an unpleasant creeping sensation, destroyed the daydream. He wouldn't yield to the sensation. Not yet. He would never let the meth take control.

What could he shoot at? A slice of Moon was up and he could see a lobster buoy about seventy-five feet away, rising and falling with the gentle swell. He had once been a decent shot, but the gun, he knew, was a piece of crap and seventy-five feet was a long distance for a .44.

His hands were dirty and he wiped them down on his shirt, feeling the bony ribs underneath. Jesus, he was getting thin. He felt that itching sensation again, like hookworms wriggling under his skin.

He raised the revolver with both hands, aimed at the buoy, thumbed back the hammer, and fired.

A deafening boom sounded and the gun kicked back. Three feet to the right of the buoy a jet of water shot up.

"Fuck," Worth said out loud. He aimed again, relaxed, tried to control the tremor in his hands, fired. This time a gout went up to the left. He paused, waited until his irritation had passed, then aimed a third time, controlling his breathing, steadying himself, squeezing slowly. This time, the lobster buoy jumped up in the air with a snap, Styrofoam pieces flying.

He lowered the gun, flush with satisfaction. This called for a celebration. He fumbled around in the cuddy, moving aside the fishing gear, retrieving his pipe and stash. With trembling fingers he prepared the hit. Like a drowning man coming up for air, he sucked it in hard, filling every lobe and air sac of his lungs with hot crank.

He sagged back against the wheel, feeling the rush radiate outward from his lungs to his reptilian brain stem and up into his higher brain, and he groaned out loud with the sheer pleasure of it, the absolute bliss, the fucked-up world softening and melting away into a lake of smooth uncaring contentment.

ABBEY KICKED BACK in the canvas deck chair, her feet propped on the gunwale, looking skyward. Midnight. The *Marea* rode at anchor in a deep cove on the south side of Otter Island. The night blazed with stars, the Milky Way arching overhead. Water lapped against the hull, and a steak sizzled on the grill.

"What about the meteorite?" said Jackie. "We didn't finish searching the island. Maybe we missed the crater."

"I'm not going back there." Abbey took a swig from the only bottle of real wine she had brought, a Brunello from Il Marroneto, vintage 2000. A magnificent wine. She didn't dare tell Jackie she'd spent almost a hundred dollars on it.

"Lemme have a sip." Jackie's voice was temporarily interrupted by the bottle. "That's kind of dry for my taste. Mind if I mix it with a cooler?"

Abbey smiled. "Be my guest." She turned back to the night sky. Whenever she looked at it, she felt strangely elated and a feeling that could only be called religious stole over her. "That's a big place up there," she said.

"Where?"

Abbey pointed up.

"I can't even imagine it."

"The human *brain* can't imagine it. The numbers are too large. The universe is a hundred and fifty-six billion light-years in diameter—and that's just our part of it. The part we can see."

"Hmmm."

"A few years ago the Hubble Space Telescope stared for eleven days at an empty spot of night sky no bigger than a dust speck. Night after night it collected the faintest light from that pinpoint of sky. It was an experiment to see what might be there. You know what it saw?"

"God's left nostril?"

Abbey laughed. "Ten thousand galaxies. Galaxies never seen before. Each one with five hundred billion stars. And that was just *one* pinprick of sky, chosen at random."

"You really believe there's intelligent life elsewhere in the universe?"

"The math requires it."

"What about God?"

"If there is a God—a *real* God—it wouldn't be anything like the lame-ass Jehovah dreamed up by shepherds tending their flocks. The God who made this would be . . . magnificent beyond all comprehension." Abbey took another sip. The wine was opening up. She could really get used to drinking fine wine. Maybe she should go back to college and become a doctor after all. The thought immediately soured her mood.

"So what are we going to do with this meteorite if we find it?"

"Sell it on eBay. Don't overcook that meat."

Jackie took the steaks off, put them on paper plates, passed one to Abbey. They ate for a few minutes in silence.

"Come on, Abbey. Stop kidding yourself. You really think we're going to find it? It's a wild-goose chase, like when we went looking for Dixie Bull's treasure."

"What's the matter—not having any fun?"

Jackie took a small sip of wine and cooler. "All we've been doing is dragging our asses through the woods. And that chase on Ripp Island scared the crap out of me. This isn't the adventure I thought it would be."

"We can't give up now."

Jackie shook her head. "Your father's going to have a shit-fit about you stealing his boat."

"*Borrowing.*"

"He'll kick you out of the house and you can forget going back to college."

"Who said I want to go back to college?" Abbey said hotly.

"Come on, Abbey, of *course* you have to go back to college. You're like the smartest person I know."

"I get enough of this shit from my father without you piling it on."

"There's no meteorite," said Jackie defiantly.

Abbey tipped up the bottle, finished the wine, and ended up with a mouthful of sediment. She spat it over the side. "There is a meteorite and we're going to find it."

The sound of three measured gunshots came rolling across the water and all was silent again.

"Sounds like the yahoos are out tonight," said Abbey.

24

FORD NOTICED A strange silence in the jungle as they approached the edge of the valley. The forest at the margins of the blow-down zone had been abandoned by life. A light smoky haze drifted through the trees, bringing with it the smell of burning gasoline, dynamite, and rotting human flesh. The heat grew as they approached the clearing, and Ford could hear but not yet see the activity ahead: the clank of iron on stone, the shouts of soldiers, the occasional gunshot and cry.

The tree trunks thinned and light loomed up beyond. They had reached the clearing. Beyond, hundreds of trees lay on the ground, flattened from the explosion, torn and shattered, stripped of leaves. The mine area itself was a scene out of the busiest and lowest circle of hell . . . a hive of monstrous activity.

Ford turned to Khon and looked him over one last time. The Cambodian looked the part of a miner—filthy face, ragged clothes, the scabs and sores they had doctored on his arms using mud and red dye from tree bark. He was still fat but it now looked more like the product of disease.

"You look good," said Ford, adopting a light tone.

Khon's grim face softened. Ford held out his hand, grasped Khon's. "Take care. And . . . thanks."

"I survived the Khmer Rouge once," said Khon cheerfully. "I can do it again."

The little round man made his way through the fallen timber and out into the cleared area, limping toward the line of miners. A soldier shouted at him and shoved him into line, gesturing with his weapon. Khon stumbled forward, as if drugged, and vanished into the shuffling masses.

Ford checked his watch: six hours before he made his move.

OVER THE NEXT hours, Ford circled around the camp observing the routine. As noon approached, he moved carefully to the head of the valley, avoiding the patrols, and from a small hill observed the white house where Brother Number Six held court. The man had spent the entire morning on the verandah in a rocking chair, smoking a pipe and gazing on the scene below with a smile of contentment, like an old grandpa watching his grandchildren play in the backyard. Various soldiers came and went, bringing reports, taking orders, and taking turns standing guard. Ford's attention was drawn to a skinny, gloomy-looking man with bags under his eyes, a bent frame, and hangdog face who never seemed to leave Six's side. He seemed to be an amanuensis of some kind, leaning over and speaking into the man's ear, listening and taking notes.

At noon, a manservant in white came out of the house

and passed around drinks. Ford watched the two men, Six and his advisor, sipping and chatting like guests at a garden party. The time passed slowly. Lunchtime at the mine arrived, and the ragged lines of humans gathered around the cooking fires, each receiving a ball of rice in a banana leaf. Five minutes, and then back to work.

As Ford watched the camp, he realized that an elite group of guards in pressed uniforms seemed to be guarding the rest of the soldiers. There were about two dozen of them patrolling the perimeter of the camp, heavily armed with Chinese-made AK-47 knockoffs, RPGs, M16s, and Vietnam War–era 60mm light mortars. Guards guarding guards. Maybe, Ford thought, it would be like the *Wizard of Oz*: all you had to do was kill a few—or one—and everyone else would fall into line.

At one o'clock sharp, Ford rose from his hiding place and walked toward the valley on an open trail, making noise and whistling. When he came within a few hundred yards of the white house, a burst of gunfire shredded the leaves above his head and sent him to the ground. A moment later three soldiers converged, yelling in a hill language. One held a gun to his head while the others roughly searched his clothing. Finding him unarmed, they jerked him to his feet, pulling his hands behind him and tying them, and pushing him forward along the trail. In a few minutes he was standing on the verandah, in front of Brother Number Six.

If Six was surprised to see him, he didn't show it. He rose from his rocking chair and strolled over, examining Ford as if he were a piece of interesting sculpture, his birdlike head bobbing up and down. Ford examined his captor in turn. The man was dressed like a French colonial official in an embroidered white silk shirt, khaki shorts, knee-high black socks, and wingtips. He was smoking latakia in an expensive English Comoy pipe, generating fragrant blue clouds of smoke. His face was delicate, almost feminine, a puckered scar above his left eyebrow. As he circled Ford, he smacked his red, girlish lips, his white hair slicked back with Vitalis.

Inspection complete, Six walked over to a verandah post, knocked the dottle out of his pipe, reamed it, and then, while leaning on the post, repacked and lit it. The process took a long five minutes.

"*Tu parles français?*" he finally said, his voice unexpectedly smooth, buttery, his French elegant.

"*Oui, mais je préfère* to speak English."

A smile. "You not carry identification." His English was much cruder, with a nasal Khmer accent.

Ford said nothing. In the door of the house, the stooped figure appeared, the advisor that Ford had earlier noted. He was dressed in loose khakis, his thinning gray hair hanging limply over his forehead, dark circles under his eyes, perhaps fifty years old.

Six spoke to the arrival in standard Khmer. "We found an American, Tuk."

Tuk peered at Ford with his drooping, sleepy eyes.

"Your name?" Six asked.

"Wyman Ford."

"What you doing here, Wyman Ford?"

"Looking for you."

"Why?"

"To have a conversation."

Six slid a knife out of his pocket and said quietly, "I cut your testicle off. Then we have conversation."

Tuk held up a restraining hand and turned to Ford, speaking in a much more practiced, British-accented English. "You are from where, exactly, in America?" The lidded eyes closed, remained closed for a moment, then opened.

"Washington, D.C."

Six gestured lightly with the knife toward Tuk and spoke in Khmer. "You're wasting time. Let me work on him with the knife."

Tuk ignored him and turned to Ford. "You are in the government, then?"

"Excellent guess."

"Who did you come here to have a conversation with?"

"Him. Brother Number Six."

There was a sudden, freezing silence. After a moment, Six waved the knife in his face. "Why you want meet me?"

"To accept your terms of surrender."

"Surrender?" Six pushed his face in close. "To who?"

Ford looked up into the sky. "Them."

Both men looked into the empty sky.

"You have . . ." Ford smiled and glanced at his watch, ". . . about a hundred and twenty minutes before the Predator drones and cruise missiles arrive."

Six stared.

"Do you want to hear the terms?" Ford asked.

Six pressed the flat of the knife blade into Ford's throat, giving it just a slight turn. He could feel it begin to bite into his flesh. "I cut your throat!"

Tuk laid a light hand on Six's arm. "Yes," he said easily. "We want to hear the terms."

The knife blade relaxed and Six stepped back.

"You have two options. Option A: you don't surrender. In

two hours, your mine will be flattened by cruise missiles and Predator drones. Then the CIA will come in to clean up—to clean *you* up. Maybe you die, maybe you escape. Either way, you'll be hunted to the end of your days by the CIA. You will have no rest in your old age."

A pause.

"Option B: you surrender to me, abandon the mine, and walk away. In two hours it is flattened by American bombs. The CIA pays you one million dollars for your cooperation. You live the rest of your life in peace, a friend of the CIA. Your old age is calm, restful, and financially secure."

"Why CIA not like this mine?" Six asked. "All legal here."

"You don't know who's buying your gemstones?"

"I sell gemstone to Thailand, all legal."

Tuk nodded slowly, as if in agreement, his eyes half-closed.

"Right. All legal. You're selling honey stones to wholesalers like Piyamanee Limited."

"All legal!" Six said.

"Do you know who the wholesalers in Bangkok are selling to?"

"Why I care? I not break law."

"Just because you're not breaking the law doesn't mean you aren't pissing us off."

Six fell silent.

"Let me explain something," Ford went on. "The Bangkok wholesalers are selling to gemstone brokers in various countries in the Middle East, who are fronting for a Saudi dealer who sells in bulk to buyers in Quetta, Pakistan, who are hiring mules to transport the gems to Al Qaeda in

South Waziristan. Do you know what Al Qaeda is doing with the gemstones?"

Six stared. This was clearly a new thought to him.

"Al Qaeda is grinding up the gems, concentrating the radioactivity in them, and is using them to make dirty bombs."

"I know nothing. Nothing!" shrilled Six angrily.

Ford smiled. "Yeah, you and Sergeant Schultz."

"Who is Sergeant Schultz?"

Ford waited, letting the silence build. "So: option A, or option B?"

"You are man who walk in here with stupid story, no more." Six spat.

"Ask yourself, Brother Number Six: would I walk in here without backup?"

"You bring no evidence, no proof, not even ID!"

"You want proof?"

Six narrowed his eyes.

Ford nodded toward the hills. "I'll show you proof. I'll order a Predator drone to fire a missile into the top of one of those hills over there. That good enough for you?"

Six swallowed, his big ugly Adam's apple bobbing. He said nothing. Tuk's eyes remained lidded.

"Untie my hands," said Ford.

Six muttered an order, and Ford's hands were untied.

"Put the knife away."

The Cambodian put the knife back into its sheath.

Ford pointed west. "See that far hill, the one with the double top? We'll hit that one with a small missile."

"How you give order?"

Ford smiled. He knew that most older Cambodians had

an almost supernatural dread of the CIA and he was hoping to capitalize on that fear. "We have our ways."

Six was now sweating.

"Within half an hour, you will have your proof. In the meantime, I wish to be treated as an honored guest, not like a criminal." He gestured to the men with the guns.

Six said something and the guns lowered.

"There's a lot of hardware above your heads that you can't see. You do anything to me and it'll rain death and destruction down on you so fast you won't even have time to take a piss."

Six's face remained impassive. He leaned over and spat on the verandah. "You have half-hour. Then you die." He shuffled back over to his rocking chair, sat down, and began rocking.

25

EGG ROCK WAS just about the most desolate island Abbey had ever seen, little more than a pile of sea-battered boulders in the Atlantic Ocean. It took less than five minutes to determine that the island had no crater. After wandering about disconsolately, they rested on the highest boulder at the top of the island. Seagulls wheeled overhead, crying out. The ocean thundered on the encircling rocks.

"Well?" said Jackie, sitting beside her. "That was a bust."

Abbey swallowed. "We still have Shark."

"Yeah, right."

"Fog's coming in," said Abbey. The fog bank was rolling in from the south, a low, gray line on the horizon. Even as she watched, the bank began swallowing Monhegan Island, which grayed out and disappeared, and a moment later it ate up the smaller island, Manana, next to it. She could hear the lonely moan of the Manana Island foghorn every few seconds.

Her eyes moved across the water to Shark Island, a speck

of land about eight miles offshore, no more than two acres in extent, treeless and desolate. It was the last island on their list. If the meteorite wasn't there . . . she tossed a pebble, musing gloomily about their odds of finding a crater on Shark. The clouds above began to roll in and a shadow fell across them, the light leaving the air, enveloping them in a cold seaweed smell.

"Gonna rain," said Jackie. "Let's go back to the boat."

Abbey nodded. They picked their way down through the rocks and the sea wrack to the dinghy and launched it into the light swell. The ocean was calm and it seemed to be settling down, as it often did in a fog. Abbey rowed back to the *Marea*, pulling hard, and in a moment they climbed over the stern. Back in the pilothouse, Abbey ran through a mental list, checking the fuel level, batteries, and bilge. She started the engine, the Yanmar rumbling to life. As she was switching on the electronics, Jackie came in.

"Let's find a nice gunkhole somewhere, drop anchor, and get stoned."

"We're going to Shark Island."

Jackie groaned. "Not in the fog, please. My head aches from that wine last night."

"Fresh air will do you good." Abbey hunched over the chart. Shark Island was exposed to the wild Atlantic, surrounded by sunken ledges and reefs, and swept by dangerous currents. It was going to be a bitch to get on it. She tuned the VHF to the weather channel and the strangely flat computer voice began reciting the report.

"Let's just park here for a while, wait for the fog to blow over," Jackie said.

"This is our chance. The sea's relatively calm."

"But the *fog*."

"We've got radar and a chartplotter."

As the fog bank rolled toward them, an eerie half-light fell on the sea.

Jackie flopped into the seat next to the helm. "Come on, Abbey, can't we just chill for a while? I've got a hangover."

"Weather's coming in. If we don't take advantage of the calm sea now, we may be waiting for days. Look—once we land, it'll take us five minutes to explore that rock."

"No, please."

Abbey laid a hand on her friend's shoulder. "Jackie, the meteorite is waiting."

Jackie snorted sarcastically.

"Haul anchor, first mate."

As Jackie stumbled forward, the fog bank swallowed the boat, shrinking the world into a few yards of gray twilight.

Jackie slotted the anchor into its stay and smacked in the anchor pin. "You're a Captain Bligh—you know that?"

With her eye on the chartplotter, Abbey eased the boat into forward, and swung the bow of the *Marea* toward Shark Island. "EBay, here we come."

26

FORD WAITED ON the verandah as the minutes passed. The soldiers stood around, weapons at the ready. Six sat in the rocking chair, gazing down the valley, the chair making a faint creaking sound as it rocked back and forth, back and forth. Brutally hot even in the shade of the verandah, the air was dead. A cacophony of sounds reverberated from the mine, where ragged lines of workers labored in an endless loop of horror, an occasional gunshot marking the unceremonious end of another life. Children swarmed over the rock pile and the smoke from cooking fires rose into the white-hot sky. Tuk stood unmoving, his eyes closed as if in sleep. The soldiers shifted nervously, their eyes darting into the sky or over at the double-topped hill.

The slow rocking creaked to a halt. Six checked the fat Rolex watch on his wrist, and lifted his binoculars to examine the hill. "Forty minute. Nothing. I give you ten minute free."

Ford shrugged.

"We go in house," Six said to Ford, rising from the chair. "Cooler in there."

The gunmen pushed Ford through the house to the back. A shedlike extension had been built out behind the kitchen, next to a pigpen. The room, made of raw lumber, was empty except for a wooden table and chair. As soon as they entered the room, the pigs outside began squealing and snorting with anticipation.

Ford noted dried blood on the chair and in several large smears on the floor that had been halfheartedly mopped up. Flies roared in the stinking heat. A streak of blood led to a door in the back, which opened directly into the pigpen.

The soldiers pushed Ford into the chair and tied his hands behind his back and to the chair rails. They duct-taped his ankles to the chair legs and wound an old chainsaw chain around his waist and the chair, padlocking it behind, the teeth biting into his skin.

The soldiers worked with an efficiency borne of practice. Tuk entered the room and stood in one corner, long arms folded in front.

Outside, the pigs began to scream.

"Well, well," said Six, positioning himself in front of Ford. He slid an old Ka-Bar knife out from under his shirt, and smiled. Standing in front of Ford, he hooked the knife under the top button of his shirt, and gave it a little flick. The button popped off. He positioned it under the next button, popped it off, and the next, until the shirt was open.

"You a big liar," he said.

The knife flicked off the last button, and then he hooked it under Ford's tank top, blade out, and made a neat slice upward, cutting it open. He raised the tip of the blade to

Ford's chin, paused, and gave it a little flick. Ford felt a sting-
ing sensation and the gathering of blood on his chin,
dripping down to his lap.

"Oops," said Six.

The knife flashed, making a little cut across Ford's chest,
flashed back, making another. Ford stiffened as he felt the
warm blood running down. The knife was extremely sharp
and so far he felt very little pain.

"X mark spot," said Six.

"You really enjoy this sort of thing, don't you?" said Ford.

Tuk watched from the doorway.

The point of the knife gently traced a line down his chest
toward his abdomen. The point hooked in his trouser
button.

A deep *boom* rumbled across the valley and echoed among
the hills. Six and Tuk seemed to freeze.

"Oops," said Ford.

Six sheathed the knife and exchanged a rapid glance with
Tuk. The tall man, with no sense of hurry, strolled out of the
room toward the front of the house. A moment later he
returned and nodded to Six. The Cambodian barked an
order at the soldiers, who untied Ford from the chair, gave
him a rag to mop his cuts, and led him back through the
house and onto the verandah. A crooked, snakelike cloud of
smoke and dust was just dissipating over the summit of a
nearby hill.

"Wrong hill," said Six, parsing the cloud and sky with his
binoculars.

Ford shrugged. "Those hills all look alike."

"I not see drone."

"Of course you don't see it."

Ford noted that Six, who up until now had appeared impervious to the heat, was badly sweating.

Ford said, "You now have sixty minutes before this camp is destroyed and all of you hunted down and shot like dogs. You better make up your mind soon."

Six stared at him, his small black eyes tight and hard. "How I get this million dollar money?"

"Get my backpack."

Six yelled an order and a soldier disappeared, returning with Ford's pack, which had been taken from him on his capture.

"Give it to me," Ford said.

Ford took the pack and removed an envelope. It had already been torn open and examined. He handed it to Six.

"What this?"

"That's the letterhead of Atlantic Vermögensverwaltungs-bank, in Switzerland. It contains a numbered back account and authorization code. Please note the amount on deposit: one-point-two million Swiss francs, or about one million dollars. With that money, you'll be able to settle down some-where, safe from harm, and live the rest of your days in comfort and ease, surrounded by your children and grand-children."

Six removed a linen cloth from a pocket and slowly passed it across his brow.

"All you have to do," Ford said, "is present this letter and the code to collect your money. The bearer of the letter and code gets the money—do you understand? *Whoever* it is. But there's a catch."

"Yes?"

"If I don't show up in Siem Reap within forty-eight hours and report in, the money vanishes from the account."

Six mopped his brow again. Ford glanced at Tuk. He wasn't sweating; he was frowning and staring at the spindly cloud disappearing in the sky above the hill.

Tuk spoke: "That was a small missile. I think maybe we should send a man up the hill to check it out." He turned to Ford and smiled broadly.

Ford checked his watch. "Be my guest. You've got fifty minutes left."

Tuk regarded him through the slits of his eyes. "That's enough time." He turned and said something to Six in dialect, who gave orders in dialect to one of the soldiers, a small, wiry boy of no more than eighteen. The boy put down his gun, took off his ammo belt, and stripped down to black pajama pants and a loose shirt. Six pulled a 9mm out of his belt, checked the magazine, and gave it to the boy, along with a walkie-talkie. The boy disappeared like a flash into the jungle.

"He will reach the hill in fifteen minutes," said Tuk. "And then we will see if that was a missile strike—or a fake." He smiled and stared at Ford, his eyes opening all the way for the first time, giving him a comic, surprised look that was even more creepy.

They waited. Outwardly Ford remained calm. Khon, apparently, had not had time to reach the double-topped hill. And it seemed he hadn't been able to lay his hand on much explosives—it had been a rather anemic explosion.

The tension on the verandah increased.

"Ten minutes," said Tuk, with another rotten smile.

The shoulders shifted uneasily. Six sweated. He read

through the letter again, folded it up, put it in the envelope, and slipped it inside his shirt.

"Five minutes," said Tuk.

Another *boom* echoed across the valley and a fiery cloud rose above the jungle trees, billowing upward. Six fumbled a walkie-talkie off his belt and yelled into it, trying to make contact with the soldier. Nothing but static. He tossed it aside and scanned the empty sky with his binoculars. "I not see drone!" he screamed.

Ford kept his attention on Tuk. The old man had shifted his attention from the hill to Ford and was staring at him with canny brown eyes. A long, hard stare.

"Whoever presents the letter, you or your proxy," Ford repeated slowly, "gets the money." He looked at Tuk as he said this, and saw understanding in the man's wickedly intelligent eyes.

With a single smooth motion, Tuk removed a 9mm pistol from his belt, aimed it at Six's head, and fired. The white-haired man's head jerked to one side, his face a mask of pure astonishment, his brains splattering loudly across the veran-dah floor. He crumpled with a soft flop and lay still, his eyes remaining wide open.

The soldiers jumped as if shot themselves, swinging their weapons wildly around toward Tuk, their eyes bugging out.

Speaking calmly in Khmer, Tuk said, "I am in charge now. You work for me. Do you understand? Each of you gets a bonus of one hundred American dollars for your coopera-tion, payable right now."

A moment of confusion and it was over. Each soldier pressed his hands together and bowed toward Tuk.

The tall Cambodian bent down and neatly slid the letter

from Six's jacket pocket, rescuing it just before the soaking puddle of blood overran the floor. He slipped it into his pocket and turned to Ford with a faint smile. "What now?"

"Order your soldiers to clear the camp. Of everyone: guards, prisoners, miners. If the CIA finds itself bombing workers remaining in the camp you won't get your money. The bombs will begin dropping in . . ." he checked his watch, "thirty minutes."

Quietly, Tuk went into the house and a minute later returned carrying a bundle of twenties wrapped in plastic. He counted out five twenties for each soldier, then gave each one an extra twenty and told them to clear the camp and drive everyone into the jungle—the Americans would begin bombing in thirty minutes.

As they ran down the trail, firing their weapons into the air, Tuk held out his hand to Ford. "I always liked doing business with the Americans," he said, with a faint smile.

Ford managed, with some effort, to smile in return.

27

ABBEY STARED AT the green sweep of the radar scope as the *Marea* chugged along in the heavy fog at five knots, condensation streaming off the windows of the pilothouse.

"My poor aching head," said Jackie. "Don't make me do this."

"We're almost there."

"You're a regular Bligh." Jackie popped the top off a Tylenol bottle and shook out two pills, then cracked a beer and took a pull. She held it toward Abbey. "Little hair of the dog?"

Abbey shook her head, still staring at the radar. "There's that boat again."

"Boat? What boat?"

"There." She pointed to a green blob on the radar screen, about half a nautical mile behind them.

"What kind of boat?"

"I dunno. A smallish one. I think it's been following us."

"How do you know it's not some lobsterman?"

"Who'd be lobstering in this fog?" Abbey fiddled with the gain on the radar. "I can't see shit."

"Cut the engine," said Jackie.

She did and they drifted, listening. "You hear that?"

"Yeah," Jackie said.

"That boat's been hanging on our ass for a couple of hours now."

"Why would someone be following us?"

Abbey restarted the engine. "To steal our treasure?"

Jackie laughed. "Maybe your cover story was too good."

Abbey throttled up, keeping an eye on the little green blob of the boat, waiting for it to move. But it didn't. It just stayed where it was.

She made a course for the lee end of Shark Island, going slow. It wouldn't take long to explore. It was basically a treeless hump in the middle of the ocean, with a gradual slope at one end and a steep bluff at the other, which, from a distance, gave it the appearance of a shark fin. She had never been on the island and didn't know anyone who had. The fog was so thick Abbey could barely see the bow rail.

"Damn, Abbey, you really think we'll find that meteorite?"

Abbey shrugged.

"When in doubt," said Jackie, "smoke some reefer."

"No thanks."

She went to roll one.

"We have work to do," Abbey said in irritation. "Can't you wait?"

"All work and no play makes Jackie a dull girl."

Abbey sighed while Jackie scratched away at the lighter, which refused to operate in the damp air. "I'm going below."

They were now about half a mile from Shark. Abbey throttled down, keeping her eye on the chartplotter and sonar. There were reefs and ledges all around the island and, with a falling tide, Abbey didn't want to risk getting too close. She throttled into neutral.

"Jackie, drop anchor."

Jackie came up, joint in hand, and looked around. "Thickafog, as my grandfather would say." She stuffed the roach into her pot tin, went forward, and pulled the anchor pin. "Ready?"

"Let 'er go."

Jackie shoved the anchor over and let it run out to the bottom. Abbey reversed the boat while Jackie played out the rode, set the anchor, and cleated it off.

Jackie came back. "So where's the island?"

"Due south about two hundred yards. I didn't dare go in closer."

"Two hundred yards? I ain't rowing."

"I'll row."

Abbey tossed into the dinghy a pick, shovel, bucket, coil of rope, a backpack with sandwiches and Cokes, as well as the usual matches, Mace, flashlights, and a canteen of water.

"What's with the pick and shovel?" asked Jackie.

"Because the meteorite's got to be here." She tried to put some conviction into her voice. Who was she fooling? This was the story of her life, one dumb-ass idea after another.

Balancing on the gunwale, Abbey scrambled into the dinghy and set the oars in the oarlocks, while Jackie settled herself in the stern. "You hold the compass and point," Abbey said.

Jackie cast off and Abbey began to row. The *Marea*

vanished in the mist. Pretty soon they passed a rock sticking above the water like a black tooth, ringed with seaweed. Another rock and another. The sea rose and fell in an oily swell. There wasn't a breath of wind. Abbey could feel the wetness of the fog collecting in her hair, on her face, running down into her clothes.

"I can see why you didn't want to bring the boat in here," Jackie said, peering around at the rocks looming out of the fog, some standing six feet high, looking almost like human figures rising from the water. "Creepy."

Abbey pulled.

"We could be the first people to land on Shark Island ever," said Jackie. "We should plant a flag."

Abbey kept pulling. Her heart was sinking. It was pretty much over. There wasn't going to be any meteorite.

"Hey, Abbey, I'm sorry I bitched at you back there. Even if we don't find a meteorite, we had an adventure."

Abbey shook her head. "I just keep thinking about what you said, how I've fucked up my life, dropping out of college. My father saved up for years to pay my tuition. Here I am, twenty years old, living at home and waitressing in Damariscotta. Loser."

"Cut it out, Abbey."

"I owe eight thousand dollars, and my father *still* has to pay."

"Eight thousand? Wow. I didn't know that."

"My father gets up at three thirty to set his traps, works like a dog. He raised me himself after Mom died. And here I am, stealing his boat. Why am I such a despicable daughter?"

"Parents are supposed to work their fingers to the bone

for their kids. That's their job." Jackie tried to laugh. "Whoops, here we are."

Abbey looked over her shoulder. The dark shape of the island rose up behind them. There was no beach, just seaweed-covered rocks in the mist.

"Prepare to get wet," said Abbey.

The boat bumped into the closest flat rock and Abbey maneuvered it around sideways, got out, and held the painter. The swell swirled up around her legs and fell while she braced herself. Jackie tossed out the pick, shovel, and backpack and climbed out. They pulled the boat up and looked around.

It was a wild scene of desolation. A massive jumble of split granite boulders rose up before them, jammed with shattered tree trunks, wrecked fishing gear, broken buoys, and frayed rope. The rocks were white with seagull guano and above them, invisible birds wheeled and cried in angry protest.

Abbey shouldered the pack. They scrambled over the fringing scree of flotsam and climbed up the sloping rocks, finally reaching the edge of a saw grass meadow. The island angled upward toward the tip of the bluff, capped by a giant wedge of broken granite like a dolmen, deposited by the glaciers. The saw grass gave way to gooseberry bushes and wind-screwed bayberry. They reached the granite slab and walked past it, toward the bluff end of the island.

On the far side of the slab, Abbey halted, staring. "Oh my God."

In front of her was a fresh crater, five feet in diameter.

28

FORD FOLLOWED THE soldiers down the trail and found the mining camp a scene of chaos, the dust rising, soldiers fleeing and miners milling about, shocked and confused, unable to comprehend what was happening. Others, including entire families, were running, hobbling, or limping away into the forest, some carrying or helping along their sick.

Looking about for Khon, he finally spied the familiar round figure jogging down from the edge of the forest, carrying a pack. He caught up to Ford, heaving, his face coated with sweat. "Mr. Mandrake! Greetings."

"Nice work, Khon." Ford unzipped the pack, pulled out a handheld RadMeter. He switched it on, took a reading. "Forty millirems per hour. Not bad."

Khon looked at the bloodstains on Ford's shirt. "What'd they do to you?"

"You were a little late with the fireworks, my friend. Almost too late."

"I had a bit of trouble stealing the dynamite from the shed. I only had time to reach the closest hill."

"How'd you handle the soldier who came to inspect?"

"I figured they might do that. I divided the charge and set a second one as a booby trap. Poor fellow."

"Clever." Ford pulled a digital camera and GPS out of the pack. He tossed the GPS to Khon. "You mark waypoints. I'm taking pictures."

"Right, boss."

Ford approached the mouth of the mine shaft, holding out the RadMeter. It was a clearly an impact crater, layers of ejecta sprayed out in a radial pattern, all brecciated rock and shatter cones.

"Eighty millirems," Ford said. "It's still fairly low up here. We can stand an hour of this at least before we have to worry."

He cautiously peered into the pit. The crater sloped inward ever steeper, turning into a vertical shaft of about ten feet in diameter with walls of fused glasslike material. Lights were strung on wires attached to the sides of the shaft, with two sets of bamboo ladders going down to what appeared to be a gem-bearing layer. The generator powering the electricity was still running in a nearby shed. A massive scaffolding of bamboo above the pit supported a winch and cargo net for raising and lowering equipment.

Ford stared into the hole, increasingly mystified. It was an incredibly deep crater—bottomless, it seemed—as if the impactor had just kept right on going. He took some pictures of the shaft, then finished up with a panoramic set of pictures all around, three hundred and sixty degrees. He took a set of readings from the RadMeter at fixed distances.

Khon soon returned with the GPS. "All done."

The camp was now almost completely deserted, except dead bodies scattered about.

"Let's blow up this pop stand before our friends realize they've been conned," said Ford. "Because if we don't, they'll be back. And *this* will start over again." He felt sick with anger looking at the dead bodies strewn about. Some were not even dead, trying to crawl away.

Ford and Khon busted open the doors of the dynamite shed and loaded crates of dynamite onto the abandoned mule cart, along with detonators, timers, and wire. They hauled the dynamite to the mine and stacked the crates onto the cargo net, spread on the ground. Ford plugged each crate with a detonator and wired them all to a timer and a backup.

Ford set the timer. "Thirty minutes."

Working the electric winch, they lifted the net, swung it out over the mouth of the pit, and lowered it down about a hundred feet, playing out the detonator wires as it went. They rested the improvised bomb on the bamboo platform. Ford disabled the motorized winch by knocking off the terminal with a metal bar and ripping out some wires.

"Twenty-five minutes," Ford said, checking his watch. "Let's get the hell out of here."

They jogged toward the wall of jungle and kept going, soon picking up the old trail they had come in on. As they ran, they passed ragged groups of slow-moving villagers. Nobody paid any attention to them. The soldiers had vanished.

"It's close," said Ford, feeling an almost unbearable knot in his stomach. He had never in his life experienced a more hellish scene of human misery, cruelty, and exploitation.

What was it in the Cambodian national character that allowed a genuinely kind, gentle, and considerate people, of strong Buddhist faith, to descend to these depths?

They paused, resting on a boulder in the dry streambed. The explosion came right on schedule.

29

RANDALL WORTH CUT the engine and drifted in the fog, staring at his radar. The bright blob on the screen, a few hundred yards due south, must be the *Marea*. Beyond it a smear of green represented Shark Island.

Shark Island. Eight miles out to sea, no harbor, surrounded by reefs, impossible to land on except in a dead calm. *A perfect treasure island*. Why hadn't he thought of it himself?

He dropped anchor, taking care not to rattle the chain. When it was set, he began loading up his backpack. In went a small portable toolbox, wire cutters, baling wire, duct tape, a knife, the RG .44 Mag, and a box of Winchester hollowpoints.

He settled back to wait, listening into the fog. The island was about four hundred yards off and the fog dampened any sound. He could hear nothing. He felt his heart pounding and he tried to ignore that crawling sensation under the surface of his skin, the crank bugs. Not yet, not now. He had to keep his head clear.

Then he heard something: a faint shout. He leaned forward. The shout was followed by a faint but distinct series of whoops, then cheering. *Cheering.*

He sat up, his heart pounding. Those were the sounds of triumph. They'd found it. *Unfuckingbelievable.* He grabbed the backpack, tossed it in the dinghy, leapt in after it, pushed off, and began rowing like hell for the *Marea*. There was almost no sea and the fog was a lucky break.

After a few minutes, the outline of the *Marea* loomed up. He raised his oars and listened intently. Closer to the island, he could now hear their disembodied voices more distinctly, excited talk, the unmistakable sounds of digging, the clank of a shovel and the ring of a pick on stone. He pulled up to the stern of the *Marea*, tied off the dinghy, hauled in his pack, and hopped aboard.

Standing in the wheelhouse, Worth made an effort to get his breathing under control, stop the trembling of his hands. That meth was really fucking him up, making him jumpy. After this he'd be set for life and then he'd quit. He wouldn't need it anymore. He could hear his heart banging away, feel the blood rushing through his ears. A bottle of Jim Beam stood on the console in the wheelhouse, and he seized it, taking a good swig, then another. Slowly he came down.

Keeping his mind focused, he checked the battery switch and made sure it was off. Pulling the portable toolbox out of his pack, he took out a screwdriver and unscrewed the electrical panel, setting it aside. A mass of wires greeted his eyes, all neatly color coded and bundled.

He knew exactly what he had to do.

30

BY THREE O'CLOCK that afternoon, Mark Corso was starting to breathe easier. When he'd arrived in his office that morning, the day after the disastrous staff meeting, he was relieved to find no pink slip on his desk. All day he had worked like crazy on the SHARAD data and now it was done. And very well done, he had to say so himself: the charts and everything neatly organized, bound, pouched, and slipcased, the images crisp and clear, cleaned of noise, and digitally processed.

There had been no nasty visit from Derkweiler, no warning memo or call. He hadn't even seen the man. He had made a mistake with the periodicity but he was sure he'd made no mistake with the gamma ray data. It was real, he knew it was real, and just maybe Chaudry would think about it and realize it was worth investigating.

Mark Corso tucked the package under his arm, swallowed hard, and set off down the hall toward Derkweiler's office. A quick knock, a "come in," and he eased open the door with trepidation. There was Derkweiler, sitting behind his desk, incipient sweat moons under his arms. "So it's you, Corso."

"I've got the SHARAD data," Corso said, with as much cool dignity as he could muster. He patted the folder under his arm and swallowed hard, speaking the lines he'd rehearsed to himself earlier. "I want to apologize for yesterday's presentation. I got carried away by the gamma ray data. I can assure you it won't happen again."

Derkweiler was looking at him. Not exactly staring, but looking steadily, his eyes rimmed in red. He looked like he'd been up all night.

"Mr. Corso. . . . Well, I'm sorry to have to say this to you." Derkweiler sighed, placed his hands on the desk. "Yesterday, I did the paperwork to . . . terminate your employment here. I'm very sorry."

Thunderstruck, Corso could find no response.

"We're a quasi-government bureaucracy and it takes a while for a termination to work its way through the system. I regret you've had to wait. But I think we both know this isn't going to work out." His gaze remained on Corso, steady and cool.

"But Dr. Chaudry . . . ?"

"Dr. Chaudry and I are in full agreement on this."

Again, Corso tried to swallow. Physically, he couldn't seem to get himself going. He was like the tin woodsman, all frozen up.

"Well," said Derkweiler, giving the table a final pat. "That's all. You've got until the end of the day. I'm terribly sorry but I think it'll be for the best."

"But . . . do you still want the SHARAD data?" Corso said, before realizing just how inane he sounded.

A look of irritation crossed Derkweiler's features as he reached out and took the folder. "I guess you didn't hear what I said at the meeting: that I'd prepare the SHARAD data myself. I was up *all night* doing it." He extended his arm over the wastebasket and dropped the folder in. "I don't need it or want it now."

Corso felt himself flushing deeply at the gratuitous gesture. Derkweiler continued staring at him. "Is there something else, or are we done here?"

Corso turned stiffly and walked out.

"Please shut the door behind you."

Corso shut the door and stood in the hall, trembling. His shock and disbelief turned to a feeling of physical sickness, and then to anger. This was wrong. This was unjust. Throwing his work in the wastebasket . . . That was unwarranted. He couldn't let this happen.

He turned back and opened the door—and caught Derkweiler in the act of bending over the wastebasket, fishing his packet out of the trash.

That did it. Corso found his mouth opening, words coming up almost as if someone else were saying them. "You . . . you fat-ass piece of shit."

"Excuse me?"

"You heard me." Who was speaking here? What was he even saying? Corso had never been so angry in his life.

Derkweiler reddened and let the folder drop back into the trash, and then he leaned back in his chair and put his hands behind his head, exposing the full extent of his underarm wetness. "Going out with a bang, I see. Anything else you want to add?"

"In fact, there is. I'm amazed to find you here at NPF at

all, let alone in a supervisory position. You are mediocrity incarnate. You and Chaudry both. I handed you evidence that something dangerous, possibly catastrophic, might be occurring on or near Mars. It's staring you in the face and you don't see it. You're no different from the Inquisition that convicted Galileo."

"Ah, so now you're Galileo?" A cold hard smile creased Derkweiler's face, suddenly disappearing. "Well, Corso, now that you've vented, please go straight to your office and remain there. You've got fifteen minutes to clear out your desk. At that time, security will escort you from the premises. Understood?"

He swiveled his chair around and turned his fat back to Corso and began typing on his computer keyboard.

Fifteen minutes later Corso was heading out the front lobby of NPF, escorted by two security guards. He carried a small cardboard box of his meager possessions: his framed diplomas from Brown and MIT, a geode paperweight, and a picture of his mother.

As he stepped into the hot sunlight, walking into a sea of shining cars in the gigantic parking lot, Mark Corso had a revelation. He halted, almost dropping his box. He recalled a small, seemingly insignificant fact: Deimos, one of the tiny moons of Mars, orbited the planet every thirty hours. That explained the periodicity anomaly.

The gamma ray source was not on Mars—*it was on Deimos.*

31

THE FOG TURNED to a drizzle as Abbey feverishly cleared rocks from the crater, prying them out with a pick and tossing them over the rim. The meteorite had punched through about a foot of soil into the bedrock below, spewing out dirt and leaving behind a fractured mass of stones and mud. She was surprised at how small the crater was, only about three feet deep and five feet wide. The rain was now drizzling steadily and the bottom of the crater was turning into a churned-up mess, a pool of muck mingled with broken rocks.

Abbey pried out a particularly large fragment and rolled it up to the crater's rim, Jackie grabbing it and dragging it out.

"There are a lot of damn rocks in here," said Jackie. "How're we going to know which is the meteorite?"

"Believe me, you'll know. It's made of metal—nickel iron."

"What if it's too heavy to lift?"

Abbey pried another rock out of the bottom, hefted it, dumped it over the rim. "We'll figure out something. The paper said it was a hundred pounds."

"The paper said that it might be *as small as* a hundred pounds."

"The bigger the better." Abbey cleared some smaller rocks and tossed out a few shovelfuls of viscous mud. As they worked, the drizzle became a steady rain. Even with her slicker she was soon soaked. Cold mud kept slopping over the tops of her boots until her feet were slushing and sucking with every movement.

"Get the bucket and rope out of the dinghy."

Jackie disappeared in the mist, returning five minutes later. Abbey tied the rope to the bucket handle and scooped up mud, which Jackie hauled out and dumped, handing it back for another load.

Abbey grunted as she hoisted up another bucket of mud. She took the shovel and began probing down into the muck with it, the tip clinking on rock. "That's bedrock, right there." More probing. "The meteorite's got to be down there, right among those busted-up rocks."

"So how big is it?"

Abbey thought for a moment, did a mental calculation. What was the specific gravity of iron? Seven and change. "A hundred-pound meteorite," she said, "would be about ten, twelve inches in diameter."

"That all?"

"That's plenty big enough." Abbey inserted the tip of the pick between two broken rocks and pried them apart with a sucking sound of mud, and wrestled them up the slope. She was getting coated with mud and the rain was trickling down her neck, but she didn't care. She was about to make the discovery of a lifetime.

RANDY WORTH SCREWED the *Marea*'s engine panel back on and wiped off his greasy fingerprints. He shifted position and shined the light down into the engine compartment—everything looked normal, no sign of his work. He set the hatch back in place and dogged it down tight, again wiping it clean of greasy marks.

The tools went back into the backpack, which he zipped up and slung over his shoulder. He stood up and looked around, his eye traveling over every surface, seeking any inadvertent sign of his presence. All clean. He checked the engine settings, circuit breakers, and battery dial to make sure they were all in the position he had found them.

He ducked out of the pilothouse and listened toward the island. The rain was now drumming on the roof and pecking the surrounding ocean, but he could still hear the sounds of digging, the ring of iron against rock, the babble of excited conversation. It sounded like they'd be at it for a while yet.

He moved to the stern, untied his dinghy, and climbed in. His skin itched, his scalp crawled, and something funny was going on behind his eyeballs. Crank was what he needed, and fast. He'd worked hard—he'd earned it. He pulled hard with the oars, so hard that one jumped out of its oarlock. With a curse, his hands trembling, he refitted it and rowed on. Soon the *Marea* had disappeared in the mist and a few minutes later his own scow loomed up, streaked with rust and oil.

He climbed into his boat and retreated into the cuddy, where he fumbled around for the stash and pipe. He took out a rock with trembling fingers, tried to put it in the bowl, dropped it, swore, hunted it down, managed to get it in, and fired it up.

Oh motherfuck, that was *good.* He lay back with a groan, feeling his cock go hard with the rush, his thoughts turning to what he would do to those bitches when he got them.

ABBEY CONTINUED SHOVELING mud into the bucket and prying out rocks, gradually clearing out the bottom of the crater where the bedrock had fractured. The rain continued, getting harder, and she could begin to hear surf on the invisible rocks below. A swell was making—they had better finish soon.

She pried out an exceptionally big rock and Jackie climbed down to help her manhandle it out of the hole. She probed some more with the shovel, then got on her hands and knees and felt about in the chilly muck with her hands. "It really busted things up down here. But I think we're getting close."

"You look a fright," said Jackie, with a laugh.

"You don't look like a debutante at the cotillion either."

More rocks, more mud came out of the hole. She stopped to feel around the muck with her hands.

"Abbey, we're not finding any meteorite."

"It's here. It's got to be."

She got on her knees and scooped mud off the granite bedrock below. The rain began washing the bedrock clean. Abbey could see, with mounting excitement, a radiative pattern of cracks in the bedrock, but the mud kept flowing in. "It's got to be right here," she said loudly, as if to make it so. She scooped more mud and rocks into the bucket.

"It wasn't one of the rocks we tossed out, was it?" Jackie asked.

"I told you, it's nickel iron!"

"Whoa, just asking."

Exasperated, her heart sinking, Abbey felt all over the bottom of the depression. Perhaps the meteorite was wedged so firmly it felt like part of the bedrock. She scooped as much of the mud and gravel up with her hands as she could, filling the bucket a few more times.

"Jackie, fill that bucket with seawater and we'll wash this clean."

Jackie disappeared down the hill with the bucket, and returned a few minutes later. Abbey dashed it over the muddy, broken layer of bedrock.

There was a gurgling sound and the water ran down a hole in the bedrock, just like going down the drain of a sink.

"What the fuck?" She stuck her fingers in the hole.

"I'll get some more water."

Jackie jogged back up the hill with the bucket slopping water over the side. Abbey snatched the bucket and poured it into the pit. Once again the water disappeared, as if down a drain, this time exposing a perfectly round hole in the bedrock, about four inches in diameter, going straight down into the Earth. A web of cracks radiated from it.

Abbey removed her glove and stuck her hand in the hole, feeling down as far as she could. The sides were as smooth as glass, a cylindrical hole so perfect it could have been drilled.

She seized a pebble and dropped it into the center of the hole. After a moment, she heard a faint splash from below.

Abbey stared up at Jackie. "It's not here. The meteorite isn't here."

"Where is it?"

"*It just kept going.*" And, despite all her efforts to stifle it, she began to sob.

32

THE RUINED MONASTERY was crowded with fleeing villagers, the monks laying out sick people in the bombed-out sanctuary and bringing them food and water. The sound of crying children and weeping mothers mingled with the babble of confused and terrified voices. As Ford looked around for the abbot, he was startled to see orange-robed monks carrying heavy weapons, bandoliers of ammunition slung over their shoulders, evidently patrolling the trails coming in from the mountains. In the distance, over the hilltops, he could see a black column of smoke rotating into the hot sky.

He finally found the abbot, kneeling over a sick boy, comforting him and giving him sips of water from an old Coke bottle. The abbot looked up at him. "How did you do it?"

"Long story."

He nodded and said, simply, "Thank you."

"I need a private place to make a satellite call," said Ford.

"The cemetery." He gestured toward a mossy trail.

Leaving the chaotic scene at the monastery behind, Ford

made his way into a thinned area of forest. Scattered among the trees were dozens of stupas, small towers, each containing the ashes of a revered monk. The stupas had once been gilded and painted but now they were faded by time, some broken and tumbling to the ground. Ford found a quiet spot among the tombs, took out his satellite phone, plugged it into a handheld computer, and dialed.

A moment later Lockwood's thick voice came on. It was 2 A.M. in D.C. "Wyman? Did you succeed?"

"You're a damned liar, Lockwood."

"Just hold on. What do you mean?"

"You knew all along where the mine was. The damn thing's huge, you couldn't miss it from space. Why did you lie to me? What was the purpose of this charade?"

"There are reasons for everything—excellent reasons. Now: do you have the readings I asked for?"

Ford controlled his anger. "Yes. Everything. Photographs, radiation measurements, GPS coordinates."

"Excellent. Can you upload them to me?"

"You'll get your data when I get my explanation."

"Don't play games with me."

"No games. Just an exchange of information. In your office."

A long silence. "It's foolish of you to take that line with us."

"I'm a foolish man. You already knew that. Oh, and by the way, I blew up the mine."

"You *what?*"

"Blown. Gone. Sayonara."

"Are you crazy? I told you not to touch it!"

Ford made a huge attempt to control his boiling anger.

He took a deep breath, swallowed. "They'd enslaved whole villages, women and children. Hundreds of people were dying. They were filling up a mass grave with the dead. I *couldn't* let it continue."

There was a silence. "What's done is done," said Lockwood finally. "I'll see you in my office as soon as you can get here."

Ford killed the call, unplugged the phone, and powered it down. He took a few deep breaths, trying to regain his equilibrium. It was quiet in the cemetery; twilight was falling and the last glimmer of light clipped the treetops, sprinkling the cemetery in flecks of green-gold light. Gradually he felt a bit of sanity returning. What he had seen would never leave him, as long as he lived.

And then there was the problem about the mine itself—something he had not mentioned to Lockwood. It was a realization so strange, so utterly bizarre, that it defied analysis. But the implications were terrifying.

33

BACK AT THE wheel of his own boat, Worth cracked a beer and watched the rain running in ever-changing curves down the windows. The girls had been on the island for two hours at least. *Must be a big fucking treasure*, he thought.

He checked the RG .44 Mag again, the gun he'd used to rob Harrison's Grocery when he was fifteen, holding it up, sighting down the barrel, balancing it in his hand. He'd recently tried to pawn it to get money for crank but no one would take it. Said it was a piece of shit. What did they know? It had worked just fine the other night, and he smiled at the thought of all the frogs he and his uncle had turned into little pink clouds with the gun.

He sighted down the barrel, pretending to aim at a gull bobbing in the water behind the stern rail. He wished he could pot it—it would raise a nice cloud of feathers—but he couldn't risk the noise. "Bang bang," he said. The gull flew away.

He placed the gun on the dashboard, next to four boxes

of bullets, a fixed-blade Bowie knife, baling wire, cutters, rope, and duct tape. He didn't think he was going to need the latter, but it was there just in case. He took another swig of beer and listened. Beyond the hiss of the rain it had become silent out there, in the fog, with only the intermittent cry of an invisible gull. He could feel the early stirrings of the crank bugs, but he ignored them. No way could he be high when it came time to pull this off.

He felt the boat move a little, the stern swinging in the freshening breeze. In the past half hour the swells had started to come in, long and low, signaling the approach of weather. He checked his watch. Five o'clock. It was getting late. With the rising sea he knew they couldn't anchor off Shark Island for the night—too exposed. They'd get the treasure on board and run for the inner islands, probably back to the cove on Otter where they had gone to ground after that business on the admiral's island.

He heard something and listened. Faint voices coming across the water, the rattle of oars in oarlocks. They were rowing back. He could hear them shipping the oars and unloading stuff into the boat, the thump of gear, the clanging of a shovel. Their voices were low, very low. With the coming of the rain the fog had thinned, but visibility was still less than a hundred yards.

Worth gave everything a quick check. All was ready.

He heard the engine on the *Marea* fire up. It idled for a while as they raised anchor. They were probably messing around with the VHF radio and radar, wondering why they weren't working. If they were smart, they'd have brought a handheld radio and GPS as backup, but his search of the *Marea* hadn't turned up either one.

The *Marea*'s engine revved and Worth watched the green blob of the boat move on his radar. He glanced at his watch, marked the time. Five-oh-nine.

He reset his radar's range to two miles, turned up the gain, and watched the *Marea* moving westward, toward the inner islands, just as he expected. When the *Marea* crossed the one nautical mile line on his radar, Worth started his own engine, hauled anchor, and began following them at a distance. It was a six-mile stretch of open water to reach the shelter of the inner islands and they were cruising at six knots. The sea was getting rougher by the minute.

After about a mile, he slowed. The *Marea* had stopped. He quickly shut down his own engine and drifted, listening. Nothing. The *Marea*'s engine had definitely quit: it was dead in the water, shrouded in fog, seven miles offshore, communications down.

He restarted his engine and throttled up full, heading straight for the *Marea*. The image loomed on the radar, getting closer, half a mile, quarter mile, three hundred yards . . .

At a hundred yards he made visual contact, the *Marea* materializing out of the fog. One of the girls was messing with the VHF radio, the other had the engine hatch open and was peering inside with a flashlight. They both turned and stared at him.

Hello, bitches.

Twenty feet from the *Marea* he swung his boat ninety degrees to starboard, shifted into neutral, and reversed hard, bringing the boat to a sudden halt. Then he grasped the handle of the RG with both hands, took aim at the two girls, and opened fire.

34

MARK CORSO SLAMMED and locked the door to his apartment, dropped the box on the kitchen table, and rummaged frantically under the sink for a screwdriver. The baby was crying again, the air-conditioner still groaned, and sirens wailed on the boulevards, but it was all background noise to Corso, who was intent on the task at hand. Shoving the screwdriver in his back pocket, he picked up a kitchen chair and moved it into the center of the living room, climbed up, and unscrewed the light fixture in the ceiling. He pulled it down and reached up into the hole, retrieving the hard drive.

In a moment he had his desktop booted up and plugged into the drive. With a feverish intensity he typed in the password, getting it wrong three times in a row before he calmed himself. He quickly looked up Deimos's actual orbital period—which was 30.4 hours, as compared to 24.7 hours in the Martian day. Then he called up the gamma ray data and examined the periodicity: 30.4 hours.

He had spent hundreds of hours looking at high-res

pictures of the Martian surface, looking for something different, something odd, something that might be a gamma ray source. But the orbiter had taken pictures of four hundred thousand square kilometers of the Martian surface at the highest resolution, and looking through the images was like looking for a needle in a haystack in a field of haystacks. Deimos was different. Deimos was tiny—a potato-shaped rock only fifteen by twelve kilometers. Whatever was generating gamma rays on Deimos would be easily found.

Hardly able to breathe, he searched the folders and files on the 160-terabyte drive and located the small one labeled DEIMOS. About three or four months before, he now recalled, the MMO had made a close pass of Deimos, hitting it with ground-penetrating radar and taking extremely high-resolution pictures. It was the first time Deimos had been imaged since *Viking I* in 1977.

He opened the file and saw that there were only thirty visible-light images and twelve radar images of Deimos.

Calling up the first image, he enlarged it to the highest resolution, laid a grid over it, and visually inspected each square, one at a time, for anything that looked funny. Deimos had a largely smooth, featureless surface, mostly covered with a thick gray blanket of dust, only lightly held in place by the moon's feeble gravity. There were half a dozen craters, of which only two had been named, Swift and Voltaire.

Trying to slow himself down, to be methodical, he eyeballed each grid in turn. The resolution was good enough to show individual boulders on the surface, some as small as three feet across.

Finishing up with that photograph, he went on to the

next, and the next. An hour passed, and then two, and finally Corso was finished. He had found nothing: just a few large, deep craters, rocks, fragments of ejecta, and endless fields and drifts of regolith.

He rose, suddenly feeling utterly exhausted and deflated. It occurred to him he might have been pursuing a will-o'-the-wisp: perhaps all he was seeing was the cosmic-ray-induced glow from the entire moon, which was so small as to appear to be a point source in the data.

With this discouraging thought in mind, he put on a pot of coffee. While it was percolating, he thought about his own situation. It was a disaster. He was fucked financially. He had already broken the lease on this apartment, losing his deposit and last month's rent; he'd put down first, last, and a deposit on a more expensive apartment that he now couldn't afford. He didn't have enough money left to move his shit from one apartment to the next, let alone move back to Brooklyn. And yet that's what he'd have to do. He couldn't afford to stay here while looking for a new job, keeping up with his student loans, and paying off his maxed-out credit cards. He didn't want to stay in Southern California anyway; he loathed everything about the place—except Marjory. *Marjory.* They'd given him such a bum's rush out of NPF that he hadn't even had time to say good-bye to her, to explain, to be cheered up by her wisecracks and off-color comments.

The only thing that would save him at all was the eight thousand dollars he had coming in severance and vacation pay.

He poured a cup of coffee, dumped in an excess of cream and sugar, and sipped it. He still had the radar images of Deimos to look at but he doubted they would reveal anything, since the radar resolution was thirty meters, as opposed to one meter for the photographs. At least there were fewer images to look through.

Reluctantly, he went back to the hard drive and called up the radar images. They had been computer processed into long vertical slices through Deimos's surface, the radar penetrating as much as a hundred meters deep. The images came up as long, black strips, like ribbons, with the surface and subsurface features outlined in red and orange.

Almost immediately, he saw something odd. Under Voltaire crater, a dense, symmetrical knot of material reflected back a bright orange. He squinted, trying to make it out. Then he leaned back: of course, it was merely the meteoritic body which had gouged the crater in the first place. No mystery there. NPF scientists had probably already examined it and come to the same conclusion.

Nevertheless, he called up the visual image of Voltaire crater and examined it again. It was the deepest and freshest crater on Deimos, so deep that part of the crater bottom was in shadow.

He leaned forward, squinting. There was something in that shadow.

Using the proprietary image enhancement software loaded on the drive, Corso worked on pulling the image out of the darkness. He increased contrast, painted it in false colors, sharpened edge transitions, and manipulated almost every pixel to extract the maximum visual information from the faintest and most ambiguous data. Corso had been doing this very thing for almost a year and he knew exactly how to tease the image into life—if it was a real image and not a glitch. It was a difficult and subtle process which took almost an hour. With each pass, his surprise turned to astonishment, amazement, and finally stupefaction. Because what he saw, deep in the shadows of Voltaire crater, was not a natural object. There could be no doubt. It was not a glitch, a software artifact.

It was a construction, an artificial object, a *machine.*

Breathing hard, he stood up and went to the window, leaning on the sill and sticking his head into the feeble stream of cool air coming from the AC, sucking it in, trying to get his breathing under control. The sun was setting over the intersection, casting a brownish light over the wastescape of cars, traffic lights, power lines, and tawdry businesses, all dotted about with limp palm trees.

A machine. An *alien* machine.

Mark Corso suddenly felt calm. Amazingly calm. This was far bigger than his petty personal problems. He reminded himself why he had gone into science to begin with. This was why.

Now that he was out of work, he had time to think things through and decide what to do. The data was classified and his possession of it a felony, so he couldn't just announce his discovery. If he reported it back to NPF, they would surely find a way to deprive him of credit and perhaps even send him to prison. For that reason, he had to move carefully, think things through, not do anything rash. He needed space and time and calm to make the right decisions. Because what he did next would not only determine his future, but it might well affect the future of the planet.

He took another deep breath, rose, and began to pack up his apartment for his move back to Brooklyn.

35

A THUNDEROUS ROAR sounded, once, twice, the rounds punching through the fiberglass walls of the wheelhouse, spraying Abbey with sharp slivers. With a yell she threw herself to the deck, her mind in a blank panic. The boat had suddenly materialized out of the fog, bearing down on them at full speed, and as it swung sideways and reversed with a huge roar, she had found herself staring at Randall Worth with a massive handgun, pointing it at them and firing.

"What the fuck?" Jackie screamed, huddled on the deck.

Boom! Boom! Two more bullets crashed through the windows and another blew out a hole the size of a tennis ball near her head.

"Jackie!" she screamed. "Jackie!"

"I'm here," came her choked voice.

Abbey turned to see her friend cowering in the corner, hands over her head. "*Get below!*" she yelled, crawling toward the companionway. "Below the waterline!" She reached the companionway and tumbled headfirst down it, spilling onto the floor of the cabin. Jackie arrived a moment later, screaming and covering her head.

"Jackie, are you hurt?" Abbey yelled.

"I don't *know*," Jackie sobbed.

Abbey checked Jackie all around, but could find no blood beyond cuts from fiberglass shrapnel.

"What the fuck?" Jackie screamed, her hands over her head. "What the *fuck*?"

"It's Worth. He's shooting at us."

"*Why*?" she wailed.

Abbey shook her again. "Hey! *Listen—to—me*."

Jackie gulped.

Another round of gunfire smashed through the superstructure, ripping through the hull and portholes above the V-berths. One of the shots blasted a hole at the waterline and the sea came gushing in.

Jackie screamed, covering her head.

"Listen to me, God damn it!" Abbey reached over and tried to pull Jackie's hands away from her head. "We're below the waterline. He can't hit us here. But he's going to board. We've got to defend ourselves. Do you understand?"

Jackie nodded, swallowing.

Abbey looked around. The V-berths were a mess, the sleeping bags rumpled up, dirty dishes in the sink, everything covered with shredded fiberglass powder. The water was gushing in through the hole and she could hear the automatic bilge pumps running.

The toolbox under the sink. Staying low, she reached across and yanked opened the cabinet.

A voice sounded across the water. "Hey, girls! Daddy's home!" Another six blasts from the gun followed, ripping through the cabin over their heads. Keeping low, Abbey dragged the toolbox out and unlatched it, the tools spilling to the floor. She sorted through them, grabbing a fish knife and a hammer. "The Mace. Where is it?"

Jackie gasped. "In the backpack in the stern compartment."

"Shit." Sticking the knife in her belt, Abbey handed the hammer to Jackie. "Take this."

Jackie took the hammer.

Boom! Boom! Boom! Boom! Boom! Boom! Another set of shots from the gun. The splinters of fiberglass ricocheted around the cabin, filling the air with choking, resinous dust. Abbey crawled up to the companionway door, turned the lock, and crawled back.

"We're sinking," Jackie said.

"That's the least of our problems."

She heard the sound of Worth's engine rumbling as he came up alongside their boat. The engine sound went into neutral, then a quick reverse, and a moment later she felt the boat bump up against theirs. His feet landed on their deck with a thump.

"Fuck, *fuck*," said Jackie, heaving. "He's boarding."

Abbey tried to stop herself from hyperventilating. They needed a plan. "You lie on the floor," she said. "In the middle. Pretend to be shot. I'll hide in the head. When he busts through that door, I'll jump out and stab him with the knife."

"Are you crazy? He's got a *gun!*"

"He's all fucked up on drugs. Do as I say and lie down."

Jackie curled up on the floor, helpless and sobbing.

Ducking into the head, Abbey closed the door so that

only the barest crack remained, through which she could see the stairs of the companionway. She tensed, ready to spring.

She heard the *tump tump* of Worth's boots over the deck. "Daddy's home!"

Abbey clutched the knife, peering through the crack.

Slow footfalls moved around the deck and into the pilot-house. He tried the door into the cabin with a shake. "Now you're gonna learn the meaning of *deeper*, you coon bitch! You and your butch friend. I'm taking your treasure and I'm going to teach you a lesson you'll never forget!"

Treasure? The moron had believed their story. She could hear his ragged, labored breathing, the unsteady tremor in his voice. It scared her even more than the gunshots.

"We . . . don't *have* any treasure," Jackie said, curled up on the floor and choking in fear.

A raucous laugh. "You think I'm stupid, you little cunt? Don't fucking lie to me. I'm here to get the treasure—and teach you two a lesson in *respect*."

"I *swear* we don't have—"

She was interrupted by a kick to the flimsy door, which cracked it almost in half. Jackie gave a scream. "No! Don't!"

Abbey tensed.

Another kick and the door parted, hanging in two pieces from the frame. Worth appeared at the top of the stairs, bending over, peering down, a big gun in his hand. "*Wendy, I'm home!*" He kicked away the two pieces of door and placed a big boot on the top step, another step, and another, until he stood at the bottom of the little stair. Jackie was curled up on the floor, sobbing, He aimed the gun at her, holding it sideways.

"Where's the treasure?"

"Please, I swear it . . . *There isn't any treasure . . .*" Jackie sobbed, covering her head, curling up. "No treasure . . . please . . . just a crater . . ."

"Bullshit!" he screamed, shaking the gun. "Don't fuck with me!"

One more step.

He took another step.

Abbey burst out of the head and brought the knife down toward his back with all her might. But he heard her and flung up his free arm, smacking her away. The knife flew out of her hand and he fired the gun at her, wildly, the round blasting another hole in the hull well below the waterline.

A jet of seawater came gushing in.

Abbey threw herself at him but he slugged her in the stomach and she fell to her knees, wind knocked out, choking and gasping, trying to get her breath back, icy seawater pouring over her.

"Where's the treasure, bitch!" He grabbed her hair, jerked her head around, and jammed the gun into her ear.

She managed to suck in air, heaving. He pulled her head around, pushed the gun barrel into her mouth. "Hey, Jackie! Tell me where the treasure is or I pull the trigger!"

"The treasure was a lie," gasped Jackie. "Please believe me, just a cover story—"

He thumbed back the action. "Stop lying, bitch, or she's dead! Now where the fuck is it? Go get it, now!"

Abbey tried to say something, but couldn't. The water was coming up fast.

"Last chance!"

"Okay, all right, I'll tell you!" Jackie screamed. "Stop and I'll tell you!"

"*Where?*" Worth shrieked, his voice cracking into the high register.

"In the stern cockpit under the rear hatch. Taped up underneath the deck, above the rudder box."

"Hurry, go get it! The boat's sinking!"

Jackie climbed to her feet. She was dripping wet. The water was six inches deep already.

"You! Abbey! Go with her." He yanked the gun out of her mouth, breaking one of her teeth, and jerked her up, shoving her up the ladder and manhandling her through the pilothouse to the stern.

"Open it!" Worth yelled at Jackie, still holding Abbey with the gun at her head.

Jackie tried to open the hatch, lifting the lever and twisting it.

"Hurry up or I shoot her!"

She heaved on it, heaved again. "I can't! It's stuck, I need help!"

Worth thrust Abbey to the deck. "Go help her!" His face was contorted, blazing red, the cords in his neck standing out, his greasy hair matted on his skull, mouthful of rotten teeth stinking.

Abbey scrambled across the deck and grabbed one side of the lever, Jackie the other. Their eyes met, and they both made a show of trying to twist open the lever. It still wouldn't release.

"Harder!"

More struggling.

"Get on the other side of the boat," Worth said. "Both of you. Over there." He waggled the gun.

Abbey and Jackie moved to the other side of the boat.

They huddled together, and Abbey nudged Jackie, making a movement with her eyes toward the hammer she still had. Jackie slipped the hammer into her hand.

Slowly, keeping an eye on them, Worth laid down the gun, grabbed the handles, and wrenched them around. The hatch unlocked easily.

"Weak-ass bitches," he said, sliding the hatch aside. He hesitated, staring eagerly at the dark opening. He just couldn't help himself: he stuck his head down to peer below the deck.

Abbey leapt across the deck and brought the hammer down with both hands just as he was pulling his head back out. It hit the top of his skull with a sickening sound, like a bat hitting a hollow log. Worth slumped forward. Blood welled from the depressed fracture, gushing onto the deck, running and mingling with the rainwater. Worth's little finger twitched grotesquely and went still. Jackie leapt on the backpack and pulled out the Mace, spraying it on his inert form.

There was a long silence and then Jackie said, her voice full of awe, "Oh my God, he's dead."

Abbey stared. It seemed unreal, like a movie. She couldn't move, she couldn't breathe.

"Abbey?" said Jackie. "We're sinking."

Her father's boat was sinking. She dropped the hammer and ran to the engine panel. Both bilge pumps were going full bore, but even as she checked for damage, there was a sizzling sound as the rising water topped the battery cases and shorted them out. The electrical systems went dead, the bilge pumps humming down to silence.

Jackie went into action. She charged down into the cabin,

sloshing through the rising water, examined the holes. Then she grabbed a blanket and some loose rope and hauled it on deck. "Abbey! Help me!" She tossed her rope. "Cut the line into four pieces and tie them onto the corners of the blanket!"

Abbey obeyed while Jackie pulled off her shoes, held her breath, and jumped in the water. She surfaced.

"Hand me one end of the blanket! We'll tie it around the boat, cover these holes!"

Abbey tossed the blanket overboard, and Jackie grabbed one end and swam under the boat, wrapping the blanket over the holes, and then came up the other side with the lines in hand. She surfaced, gasping. "Take these!"

Abbey tied the lines to the rails and hauled Jackie back on board. The *Marea* was beginning to list.

"Is that going to work?" Abbey said.

"Might buy us time. We'll use Worth's boat to tow and beach her on the nearest island," said Jackie. "Follow me." She leapt from the *Marea* to the *Old Salt*, which was still tied up, engine idling, and took the helm, Abbey following. Jackie thrust it into full throttle. The engine roared, the boat straining forward, pulling the nine-ton *Marea* alongside it, Jackie adjusting the rudder to compensate for the dead weight.

"Where are we going?" Abbey cried.

"Franklin. We're going to run both boats right up on the beach. It's the only way. Abbey, check those cleats—make sure they hold."

While Abbey checked, Jackie pulled down the VHF and began broadcasting a mayday. "This is the *Marea*, *Marea*, *Marea*, position 43 50 north 69 23 west. My boat is sinking, we have a severely injured passenger. A second boat is on scene and towing. I require immediate assistance. Over."

She stopped broadcasting and waited. A minute later the response came.

"*Marea*, this is the Coast Guard station Tenants Harbor, responding. The closest boat to your position is the lobster boat *Misty Sue*, south of Friendship Long Island, coming to your assistance at ten knots. The *Misty Sue* will communicate with you on channel six. Over."

"There's nobody closer?" Jackie screamed. "We're sinking!"

"There aren't many vessels out there, *Marea*. We're sending out the Coast Guard RB-M *Admiral Fitch* from Tenants Harbor with a paramedic, over."

"I'm going to try to beach it on Franklin," Jackie said.

"*Marea*, what's the nature of the injury?"

"He's dead, I think. Head bashed in with a hammer."

A silence. "Repeat that, please."

"I said he's *dead*. Randall Worth. He shot up our boat and boarded. Attempted robbery. So we killed him."

A pause. "Is anyone else hurt?"

"Not really."

"This is a crime scene, then, and should be treated as such. Please be advised . . ." The voice droned on. They were barely crawling along at three knots and slowing down as the *Marea* continued to take on water. Abbey checked below; the blanket had slowed the flow of water but hadn't stopped it. Franklin was four miles away—at this speed more than an hour of travel time.

"Fuck!" Jackie said out loud, cutting off the Coast Guard

and tuning to channel 6. "This is *Marea*, calling *Misty Sue*, what's your position?"

"Just coming through the Allen Island passage. What's happening?"

"I'm towing a sinking boat. I need more towing power. I'm looking to beach it on Franklin."

"I should be there in . . . forty minutes."

Worth's boat struggled to make headway, hauling the sinking *Marea* alongside of it. The *Marea* was now listing badly and their boat was losing steerage due to the deadweight.

"We've got to cut it loose," said Jackie. "When it sinks, it'll capsize us, pull us under."

"No!" Abbey said. "Please. We'll uncleat it from the side and retie it to the stern—and drag it behind us. We'll go faster that way."

"Give it a try."

Abbey untied the *Marea* and pulled ahead, attaching a cable from the anchor post to a stern cleat on Worth's boat.

"That cleat's not going to hold," said Jackie.

"Better than the other one."

Jackie eased up the throttle, letting the strain build gradually. The *Marea* was now listing so hard to port that water began pouring in one of the stern scuppers. Worth's boat roared and strained, the cable taut as a violin string, but still they were barely moving.

"Abbey, for God's sake it's sinking! It's going to pull us under!"

"No, please, it's my father's only boat! Just keep going!"

Jackie pushed the throttle all the way forward. The engine screamed with the strain, there was a crack like a shotgun blast and the cleat snapped out, taking a piece of the stern with it. Worth's boat leapt forward, the strain gone. Jackie threw the helm hard aport and brought the boat back around toward the *Marea*. But it was too late. With a sigh, the lobster boat settled onto its side, air rushing out. Then it slipped under the waves and vanished, leaving an oil slick behind.

"Oh my God," said Jackie. "Worth was still on board."

Abbey stared in horror, not quite able to grasp the awfulness of what had just happened. "My father's boat . . . it just *sank*."

36

THE PEPPERCAN BUOY at the mouth of Round Pond Harbor loomed out of the drizzle, rolling back and forth in the rising swell. Abbey stood at the wheel of Worth's boat, following the Coast Guard boat *Admiral Fitch* into the harbor. It had caught up with them about a mile out—too late to be of any use—and the Coast Guard were now having a grand time "escorting" them back in. The fog had mostly lifted, leaving the world in a damp, depressing twilight. As the piers loomed into view, Abbey could see a mass of flashing lights in the parking lot above the waterfront.

"Looks like we've got a welcoming committee."

Inside the harbor, she throttled down and glanced over at Jackie. She looked terrible, her damp hair hanging down limp and dirty, dark circles under her eyes, her hands, face, and clothes covered with mud.

"What do we tell them?" Jackie asked.

"Everything except the meteorite. We were looking for Dixie Bull's treasure. Just like they think."

"Um, why not tell them about the meteorite?"

"There still may be a way to make money on this."

"How?"

"I don't know. Gimme time to work it out."

A long silence. "Maybe they can raise my father's boat," said Abbey, "and get it running again."

"Of course they'll raise it," Jackie said. "It's a crime scene and there's a body on board. But it's totaled, Abbey. It sank in a hundred feet of water. I'm sorry."

Abbey glanced at her friend and saw she was crying. "Hey, Jackie. Hey . . . You tried your best to save it." She put her arm around her. "God, I'm sorry I dragged you out on this wild-goose chase. It's like all the other crazy things I've gotten you into. I don't know why you stay my friend."

"I don't either," said Jackie.

"I love you, Jackie. You saved my life."

"And you saved mine and I love you, too."

Abbey wiped away a tear herself. "Aw, fuck it, we'll get through this."

As the docks loomed into view, Abbey could see at least a dozen cop cars had converged in the parking lot, parked willy-nilly, their light bars going. And behind them, on the lawn of the Anchor Inn, it seemed like half the town had turned out to watch them come in. Along with news crews and television cameras.

"Oh my God, will you look at all those people?" said Jackie, wiping her face and blowing her nose. "I look like shit."

"Get ready for your fifteen minutes of fame."

She could now hear the hubbub coming over the water, the murmuring crowd, the shouting cops, the hiss of police radios. Even the volunteer fire department was there, Samoset No. 1, with their brand-new fire truck. They were all decked out in slickers and carrying Pulaskis. Everyone was having a grand old time.

"RBM *Fitch* to *Old Salt*, come in," the officious voice hissed over the VHF.

"*Old Salt* here." It made Abbey almost sick to even speak the name of Worth's shit-can of a boat.

"*Old Salt*, the state police have requested you berth in position one at the commercial dock and immediately leave the boat, taking nothing. Don't shut off the engine or tie up. Law enforcement will board and take over."

"Got it."

"RBM *Fitch* over."

The *Fitch* eased up to the public dock, the Coast Guard fellows hopping out in their crisp uniforms and tying up with drill-like efficiency. Abbey brought the *Old Salt* up behind it. The state police were swarming the dock and they immediately hopped aboard, securing the boat. Abbey stepped off, Jackie by her side. An officer came up, holding a clipboard. "Miss Abbey Straw and Miss Jacqueline Spann?"

"That's us."

Abbey glanced across the parking lot. It seemed like the entire town was staring down at her from behind a cordon of police. And to one side, cameras were rolling. She heard a shout, a struggle. "That's my daughter, you idiot! Abbey! *Abbey!*"

It was her father. Home early.

"Let go of me!"

He came running down the grassy hill, checked shirt untucked, beard flapping, pounded down the wooden stairs, past the bait shed, and down the pier. He got to the top of the ramp and, gripping both rails, came charging down at her, hair wild.

"Dad—"

The officer stepped back as he ran to her. He wrapped her in his arms, a big sob wrenched from his broad chest. "Abbey! They say he tried to kill you!"

"Dad . . ." She wiggled a little but he wasn't letting go. He hugged her again, and then again, while she stood there, feeling awkward, mortified. *What a show in front of the whole town.*

He held her by her shoulders and stood back. "I was so *worried*. Look—your tooth! And your lip is cut. Did that scumbag—?"

"Dad . . . *Forget* the tooth . . . Your boat sank."

He stared at her, thunderstruck.

She hung her head and began to cry. "I'm sorry."

A long silence, and then he swallowed, or at least tried to, his Adam's apple bobbing. After a moment he put his arms around her again. "Ah, well. A boat's just a boat."

A ragged cheer went up from the town.

PART 2

PART 2

37

FORD ENTERED THE office to find Lockwood seated at his desk. A brigadier general with grizzled hair in a rumpled field uniform stood next to him, whom Ford recognized as the Pentagon liaison to the Office of Science and Technology Policy.

"Wyman," Lockwood said rising, "you know Lieutenant General Jack Mickelson, USAF, deputy director of the National Geospatial-Intelligence Agency. He's in charge of all GEOINT."

Ford extended his hand to the general, who rose as well. "Good to see you again, sir," he said, with a certain amount of coldness.

"Very good to see you, too, Mr. Ford."

He shook the general's hand, which was soft, not the usual rock-hard grip of the military man forever seeking to prove his manhood. Ford remembered liking that about Mickelson. He wasn't so sure he liked the man now.

Lockwood came around his desk and gestured toward the sitting area of his office. "Shall we?"

Ford sat down; the general took the seat opposite and Lockwood took the sofa.

"I asked General Mickelson to join us because I know you respect him, Wyman, and I was hoping we could resolve these issues quickly."

"Good. Then let's cut to the chase," said Ford, facing Lockwood. "You lied to me, Stanton. You sent me on a dangerous mission, you misled me as to the purpose of that mission, and you withheld information."

"What we're about to discuss is classified," said Lockwood.

"You know damn well you don't need to tell me that."

Mickelson leaned forward on his elbows. "Wyman . . . if I may? You can call me Jack."

"With all due respect, General, no apologies and no chitchat. Just explanations."

"Very well." His voice had just the right note of gravel, his blue eyes friendly, his excellent sense of self-possession softened by the casual uniform and easy manner. Ford felt a rising irritation at the snow job to come.

"As you may know, we maintain a network of seismic sensors around the world for the purpose of detecting clandestine nuclear tests. On April fourteenth, at nine-forty-four P.M., our network detected a possible underground nuclear test in the mountains of Cambodia. So we investigated. We quickly proved the event was a meteoroid impact, and we found the crater. At about the same time, a meteor was seen over the coast of Maine, falling in the ocean. Two simultaneous strikes. Our scientists explained that it was most likely a small asteroid that had broken into two pieces in space and drifted far enough apart that they landed in widely separate locations. I'm told it's a common occurrence."

He stopped as a soft alarm chime went off on Lockwood's desk, and a moment later the coffee came in, the steward pushing the little coffee cart with the silver pot, tiny cups, and sugar lumps in a blue glass dish. Ford poured a cup and drank it black. Dark, powerful, fresh-brewed. Mickelson abstained.

When the steward left, Mickelson went on. "Meteoroid strikes aren't part of our mission, so we simply filed away the information. That would have been the end of it. But—"

At this the general took a slim blue folder out of his briefcase, laid it down, and opened it. Inside was an image from space of what Ford immediately recognized as the honey mine in Cambodia.

"Then the radioactive gemstones began appearing on the market. This became a top concern of our antiterrorist people, who worried they might become source material for a dirty bomb. Anyone with a high school chemistry lab setup could concentrate the Americium-241 from these stones."

"What about the impact in Maine? Did you investigate that?"

"Yes, but the meteorite fell into the Atlantic half a dozen miles offshore. Unrecoverable, and impossible to pinpoint the impact location."

"I see."

"Anyway, we knew about the impact crater in Cambodia, we knew the gemstones were coming from that general area, but we couldn't confirm the link. That could only be proven on the ground."

"And that's where I came in."

Mickelson nodded. "You were told all you needed to know."

"General, with all due respect, you should have given me more backup, I should have been briefed, shown the satellite images. That's what you would have done for a CIA operative."

"Frankly, that's why we reached beyond the CIA for this mission. All we wanted was a pair of eyes on-site. On the ground. Independent confirmation. We didn't expect. . . ." He cleared his throat and leaned back, "that you would actually *destroy* the mine."

"I still don't believe you're telling me the entire truth."

Lockwood leaned forward. "Of course we're not telling you the entire truth. For chrissakes, Wyman, when is anyone told the entire truth in this business? We wanted to examine that mine intact. You've created a *huge* problem for us."

"There's another drawback with hiring a freelancer," said Ford coldly.

Lockwood sighed in irritation.

"Why was the mine so important?" Ford asked. "Can you tell me that, at least?"

"The meteoroid appears to have been highly unusual, judging from our analysis of the gemstones."

"Such as?"

"Even if we knew, which we don't yet, we couldn't tell you. Suffice to say it wasn't anything we've seen before. And now, Wyman, the data? Please."

Ford had already noted the soldiers outside Lockwood's office, and he knew well what would happen to him if he didn't comply. No matter: he had gotten what he came for. He slipped a flash drive out of his pocket and tossed it on the table. "It's all there, encrypted: pictures, GPS coordinates, video." He gave them the password.

"Thank you." Lockwood smiled grimly and took the flash drive. He slipped a white envelope out of his pocket and placed it on the table. "The second installment of your compensation. You're expected at a full debriefing at Langley this afternoon at two o'clock. In the DCI conference room. Your assignment will then be most decidedly over." Lockwood smoothed a hand down his red silk tie, adjusted his blue suit, touched his gray hair above his ears. "The president wanted to convey his thanks for your effort, despite, ah, your failure to follow instructions."

"I'll second that," said Mickelson. "Wyman, you did well."

"Glad to be of service," said Ford, with a touch of irony. Then he added, casually, "One thing I almost forgot."

"Yes?"

"You mentioned that the asteroid broke in two and that the two pieces struck the Earth."

"Correct."

"That's wrong. There was only one object involved."

"Impossible," said Mickelson. "Our scientists are certain there were two strikes, one in the Atlantic, one in Cambodia."

"No. The mine in Cambodia wasn't an impact crater."

"What was it then?"

"An *exit* hole."

Lockwood stared, while Mickelson rose from his chair. "Are you suggesting—?"

"That's right. The meteorite that struck in Maine passed

through the Earth and exited in Cambodia. The data on that flash drive should confirm it."

"How can you tell the difference between an entrance and exit hole?"

"It's not unlike entrance and exit wounds caused by a bullet: the former is neat and symmetrical, the latter a God-awful mess. You'll see what I mean."

"What on God's name could go *through* the Earth?" Mickelson said.

"That," said Ford, picking up his check, "is a damn good question."

38

ABBEY HAD PREPARED cheeseburgers for dinner but they were overcooked and dry, the cheese had burned in the pan, and the buns were soggy. Her father sat across the table, chewing silently, eyes downcast, his jaw muscles working slowly. He had been ominously silent all evening.

He laid the half-eaten burger down on his plate, gave the plate a token push, and finally looked at Abbey. His eyes were bloodshot. She thought for a moment he might have started drinking again, which he'd done pretty hard after her mother's death. But, no, that wasn't it. He didn't smell of beer.

"Abbey?" His voice was hoarse.

"Yes, Dad?"

"I heard from the insurance company."

She felt the lump of burger in her mouth sort of stick. She made an effort to swallow it down.

"They're not covering the loss."

A long silence.

"Why not?"

"It was a commercial policy. You weren't lobstering. What you were doing they consider recreation."

"But . . . you could always *say* I was lobstering."

"There's a Coast Guard report, police reports, newspaper articles. You weren't fishing. End of story."

Abbey's mouth had gone dry. She tried to think of something to say and couldn't.

"I still owe on the boat, and until it's paid off there's no way I can get a loan for another. I'm paying on a mortgage that's worth more than the house. What little savings I had went to your year-and-a-half messing around in college."

Abbey swallowed again, staring at the plate. Her mouth was dry as ashes. "I'll give you my waitressing money. And I'll sell the telescope."

"Thank you. I'll accept the help. Jim Clayton's offered me a position as stern man this season. With what you make and I make, if it's a good season, we might just keep the house."

Abbey felt a giant tear creep out of her eye and roll down the side of her nose, hang there, and fall on the plate. Then came another, and another. "I'm really sorry, Dad."

She felt his rough hand seek hers, close around it. "I know."

She hung her head, the tears dropping on her burger bun, making it soggy. After a moment her father released her hand and rose from his place. He went over to his old Black Watch tartan chair by the woodstove, settled into it, and picked up *The Lincoln County News*.

Abbey cleared the plates, scraped the uneaten burgers into the bin for the chickens, and washed the dishes in the sink, stacking them on the side. Her father had talked about getting a dishwasher someday, but that day was never going to come.

Well, Abbey thought, with a curious sense of numb detachment, she had pretty much ruined her father's life.

39

"YOU HAVE ARRIVED at your destination," said the smooth female voice from the GPS. Wyman Ford parked the car in the apron of dirt in front of the country store and got out, looking around. The field opposite the store was swaying with lupines ready to burst into flower. At the top of the hill behind him were two churches flanking the street, one a brown Congregationalist church and the other a white Methodist "house of worship." A dozen clapboard houses lined the road and a small grocery occupied a listing, shingled building.

That was the extent of the town.

Ford consulted his notebook. The towns of New Harbor, Pemaquid, Chamberlain, and Muscongus had been crossed out, leaving one left.

Round Pond.

The road ran past the store and dead-ended at the harbor. He could just see, beyond a cluster of pine trees, a harbor full of fishing boats and a small sliver of ocean beyond.

He went into the country store and found it noisy with kids buying penny candy. He walked around, looking at the items for sale: the candy, postcards, knives, boat models, toys, puppets, kites, CDs of local musical groups, calendars, jams and jellies, and a stack of newspapers. It was like walking back in time to his own childhood.

He picked up the newspaper, called *The Lincoln County News*, and got in line with the kids. A few minutes later they had banged out the door with their brown paper bags of candy. A high school girl was manning the counter. He laid down the paper on the counter and smiled. "I think I'd like some candy."

She nodded.

"I'll take a . . . let's see . . . a fireball—haven't had one of those in years—some malted milk balls, a rope of licorice, and a peppermint stick."

She collected the candy in a bag, laid it on the paper. "Two dollars ten cents."

He fished in his pocket, took out his wallet. "I heard a meteor came over here a few months back."

"That's right," the girl said.

He thumbed through the bills in the wallet. "You see it?"

"I saw the light out the window. Everybody did. And then there was a sound like thunder. When we went outside there was a glowing trail in the sky."

"Did anyone find the meteorite?"

"Oh no, it hit out to sea."

"How do they know?"

"That's what all the papers said."

Ford nodded, finally getting the money out.

"Is the harbor down there?"

She nodded. "Take the right past the store—dead-ends at the wharves."

"Any place to buy live lobster?"

"The co-op."

He took the bag of candy and the paper and went back to his car. Popping the fireball in his mouth, he looked at the front page of *The Lincoln County News*. Plastered at the top was a headline:

Body, Gun Recovered from Sunken Boat

There was a blurry photograph of a Coast Guard vessel at sea hauling a body on board with grappling hooks. Ford read the article, his interest piqued. Turning to the inside, he saw a picture of the two girls who'd been attacked, a high school yearbook picture of the dead attacker, and several photographs of the ruined boat hauled into dry dock. This was big news in Round Pond—a high-seas robbery attempt, complete with a boarding, attempted murder, and a sunken boat. Something to do with a legendary treasure. It aroused his investigative instincts: the story had gaps, inconsistencies, which cried out for explanation.

He turned the page, read about the bean supper at the Seaside Grange, complaints about a new traffic light, an article about a soldier returning from the Middle East. He scanned the police notes, read a scolding editorial about a poorly attended school board meeting, looked through the real estate and employment ads, read the letters to the editor.

Finally he folded up the paper, charmed by the picture he had acquired of the town. A quiet little New England fishing village, impossibly picturesque, economically stagnant.

Someday the real estate developers would get their hooks in a town like this and it would be all over. He hoped that someday never arrived.

He started the car and drove down the road toward the harbor. Almost immediately it came into view—lobsterman's co-op on his right, piers, a dockside restaurant, a harbor full of fishing boats, the heady smell of salted fishing bait.

He parked and went over to the co-op, a wooden shack sitting above a pier, wooden flaps opened, tanks of water brimming with lobsters. A chalkboard gave the day's prices. A bald man in orange waders came to the window.

"What can I do for you?"

"Do you lobster these waters?"

"No, but my daughter does. I just sell 'em."

Ford could see a young woman in the back, manning the lobster cookers.

"You see the meteor?"

"No. I'd gone to bed."

"Did she? I'm interested in it."

He turned. "Martha, fellow here wants to know if you saw the meteor."

She came over, drying her hands. "Sure did. Came right over us. I saw it through the window while I was washing dishes."

"Where'd it go?"

"Straight past Louds Island and out to sea."

Ford held out his hand. "Wyman Ford."

The woman took it. "Martha Malone."

"I'm hoping to find that meteorite. I'm a scientist."

"They say it fell in the ocean."

"You're a lobsterwoman?"

She laughed. "You must be from out of town. I'm a lobster fisherman."

"Here's the problem." Ford decided to get right to the point. "That night, the ocean was dead calm. The GoMOOS weather buoy out there didn't register even the slightest ripple at the time of the impact. How do you explain that?"

"There's a lot of sea out there, Mr. Ford. It could have landed a hundred miles offshore."

"You haven't heard of anyone around here talking about finding a crater or seeing any evidence of blown-down trees?"

A shake of the head.

Ford thanked her and walked back to his car. He popped a malted milk ball in his mouth and sucked on it thoughtfully. Once in the car, he flipped open the glove compartment, removed the notebook, and crossed out "Round Pond."

And that was it. It had been the wildest of wild-goose chases.

40

ABBEY STRAW CARRIED two baskets of fried clams and a brace of margaritas to the table where the couple from Boston were seated. She set down the food and drink. "Can I get you folks anything else?"

The woman examined her drink, her long fingernails clicking irritably on the glass. "I said no salt." She had a heavy Boston accent.

"My apologies, I'll bring you another." Abbey swept up the drink.

"And don't think you can just wipe off the salt, I'll still taste it," said the woman. "I need a *fresh* drink."

"Of course."

As she was about to leave, the man said, gesturing at his plate, "Is this all you get for fourteen bucks?"

Abbey turned. The man weighed at least two hundred and fifty pounds, wearing a double-knit golf shirt stretched to the theoretical limit, green slacks, bald with a fat-dimple right in the center of the bald area. Thick black hair grew out of his ear holes.

"Is everything all right?"

"Fourteen bucks for ten clams? What a rip-off."

"I'll get you some more."

As she headed toward the kitchen, she heard the man speak again, loudly, to his wife. "I hate these places where they think they can hose the tourists."

Abbey went back into the kitchen. "I need more clams for table five."

"What, they complaining?"

"Just give me the clams."

The chef chucked three small clams on a side plate.

"More."

"That's all they get. Tell 'em to go fuck themselves."

"I said *more*."

The chef dropped another two on the plate. "Fuck 'em."

Abbey reached over, scooped out another half-dozen, heaped them on the plate, and turned to go.

"I tole you before, don't touch my stove."

"Fuck you, Charlie." She went back out, placed the plate in front of the man. He had already finished the ten clams and tucked into the new plate without pause. "More tartar sauce, too."

"Coming right up."

A tall man was just being seated in her section. On her way to get the tartar sauce, she stopped by, gave him a menu. "Coffee?"

"Yes, please."

As she poured the cup, she heard the querulous voice of the man from Boston rising above the general conversation.

"Problem is, they think we're all rich. You can just hear them licking their chops when summer arrives and people start coming up from Boston."

Abbey was momentarily distracted and the coffee she was pouring slopped over the edge of the cup.

"Oh, I'm *sorry*."

"Don't worry about it," said the tall man. "Really."

She looked at the man for the first time. Angular, large hooked nose, jutting jaw—lean and strong in a curiously pleasing way. When he smiled, his face changed dramatically.

"Hello? The *tartar sauce?*" came a loud voice from the next table.

The tall man nodded, winked. "Better take care of them first."

She hurried off and returned with tartar sauce.

"AFT," the man said, snatching it up and spooning it onto the clams.

She went back to the tall man, ticket in hand. "What can I get for you?"

"I'll take the haddock sandwich, please."

"Anything to drink besides coffee?"

"Water's fine."

She hesitated, glanced over at the Boston table to see if there was anything else, but they were busy eating. He followed her glance. "Sorry about them."

"Not your fault."

"You live around here?"

Lately this had been happening a little too frequently. "No," she said, "I live out on the peninsula."

He nodded thoughtfully. "I see. Then you must've gotten a good view of the meteorite a few months ago?"

Abbey was instantly wary, taken aback by the unexpected question. "No."

"You didn't see the meteorite's trail or hear the sonic booms?"

"Not at all, no, I didn't." Feeling that her denial had been too emphatic, she cast about, trying to cover up her reaction. "That's *meteor*, not meteorite."

The man smiled again. "I always get those two terms mixed up."

She quickly went on. "Anything on the side? Salad? Fries?"

"I'm fine."

She put in the order and hurried back to the table with the two people from Boston, who had finished eating. "Can I get you anything else?"

"What, you need the table already?"

The wife said, "I think it's inexcusable when they try to hustle you out."

She checked her other tables, picked up the haddock sandwich, brought it over.

"Hey, where's our check?" came a cry from the Boston table. "Can't you see we're done?"

She pulled out the ticket, went to the cash register, rang it up, printed it out, and came back and laid it on the table. "Have a nice day."

The man flipped open the check, ostentatiously examining the total. "What a rip-off." He counted out some money on the table, a lot of change and crumpled bills, and left it in a heap on the check.

The tall man left a while later, leaving a tip so large it made up for what she had been stiffed by the Boston table.

As she cleared his table, she wondered why he asked pointed questions about the meteor. The man seemed nice but there was something shifty about him—distinctly shifty.

41

WYMAN FORD HAD crossed the Wiscasset Bridge when he finally pulled off the road in front of an antique shop. He threw the car into park and sat there, thinking. He couldn't put his finger on it, but something wasn't adding up. It had to do with the odd behavior of the girl in the restaurant and this crazy story in the local paper. He picked up the paper, which he'd tossed on the passenger's seat. The girl in the restaurant was definitely the girl in the news story, the one searching for the pirate treasure. When he'd asked her about the meteorite, she'd suddenly become nervous. Why? And how many small-town waitresses knew the difference between the terms meteor and meteorite?

He pulled out and headed back the way he had come. Ten minutes later he walked into the restaurant. The girl was still there, bustling around, and he watched her from the maître d's station at the door. She was definitely the one from the story in the papers—in fact, she was the only African-American he'd seen on his entire trip to Maine. Short black hair that curled around her face, bright black eyes, slender and tall, with an athletic frame. Walking around with a sardonic, even ironic expression on her face. No makeup at all. A stunningly beautiful girl. Twenty-one, maybe?

As soon as he stepped into the dining room she saw him, and a guarded look came into her face. He nodded at her, smiled.

"Forget something?" she asked.

"No."

Her face frosted up. "What do you want?"

"I'm sorry, I don't mean to pry, but aren't you the girl who was involved in that incident I read about in the paper?"

Now her face became positively cold. She crossed her arms. "If you don't mean to pry, then don't." She turned to leave.

"Wait. Give me a minute. This is important."

She waited.

"You corrected me on my use of the word *meteor* versus *meteorite.*"

"So?"

"How'd you know the difference?"

She shrugged, folded her arms, glanced back at her section.

Ford wasn't even sure where he was heading with this, what he hoped to find out. "It must have been exciting when that meteor streaked overhead."

"Look, I have to get back to work."

Ford looked at her steadily. She was oddly nervous. "You sure you didn't see it? Not even the trail? It persisted in the sky more than half an hour."

"I already told you, I didn't see it at all."

Her eyes were tense. Why would she lie? He pressed ahead, still unsure of where this was going. Clearly she wasn't used to lying, and her face betrayed confusion and alarm. "Where were you when it fell?"

"Sleeping."

"At nine-forty-four P.M., a girl your age?"

She faced him directly, crossing her arms. "You're really interested in that meteorite, aren't you?"

"In a way."

She narrowed her eyes. "You *looking* for it?"

"As a matter of fact, I am."

She seemed to consider this, then she smiled. "You want to find it?"

"That would interest me very much."

She stepped closer and spoke in a low voice. "I get off in half an hour. Meet me in the bookstore café down the street."

A HALF-HOUR LATER, the girl arrived. She had changed from her waitressing uniform into jeans and a plaid shirt.

Ford rose and offered her a seat.

"Coffee?"

"Triple shot of espresso, two shots of cream, four sugars."

Ford ordered coffees and carried them to the table. She looked at him directly, her brown eyes disconcertingly alert. "You start first. Tell me who you are and why you're looking for the meteor."

"I'm a planetary geologist—"

She gave a sarcastic snort. "Cut the bullshit."

"What makes you think I'm not?"

"No planetary geologist would have mixed up the words

meteor and *meteorite.* A real planetary geologist would have used the scientific term, *meteoroid.*"

Ford stared at her, flabbergasted at being smoked out so easily—by a small-town waitress no less. He quickly covered up his confusion with a smile. "You're a bright girl."

She continued to look at him steadily, her arms folded in front of her on the table.

Ford extended his hand. "Let's start with an introduction. I'm Wyman Ford."

"Abbey Straw." The cool hand slipped into his and he gave it a shake.

"I'm sort of a private investigator. That *meteoroid* interests me. I'm trying to track it down."

"Why?"

He thought of lying again, decided on a half-truth instead. "I'm working for the government."

"Really?" She leaned forward. "Why's the government interested?"

"There were certain . . . *anomalies* about the fall that make it interesting. I hasten to say I'm not here in any official capacity—you might say I'm freelancing."

Abbey seemed to be thinking, and then she spoke slowly. "I know a lot about that meteoroid. What's it worth to you?"

"Excuse me." Ford was nonplussed. "You want me to *pay* you for the information?"

Abbey reddened. "I need money."

"What kind of information do you have?"

"I know where it landed. I've seen the crater."

Ford could hardly believe his ears. Was she lying? "Care to tell me about it?"

"Like I said, I need money."

"How much?"

A hesitation. "One hundred thousand dollars."

Ford stared at her, and then started to laugh. "Are you crazy?"

Her face faltered. "I only ask because . . . well . . . that's what it cost me to find the crater."

"For a hundred thousand dollars, I could find the crater five times over."

"Trust me, Mr. Ford, you could search that bay a hundred years and not find it—unless you knew exactly where to look. It's small and unrecognizable from the air."

Ford leaned back, sipped his coffee. "Perhaps you might tell me how you made this discovery and why it cost you a hundred thousand dollars."

The girl took a long sip of her coffee. "I will. Back on April fourteenth, I had just bought a telescope and I was taking a time exposure of the constellation Orion. Wide field. The meteor passed through and I got the streak on film. Or rather digitally."

"You *photographed* it?" Ford could hardly believe his luck.

"Then I had an idea—I checked the GoMOOS weather buoy data on the Internet. No waves. I figured it must have hit an island instead of the water. So, by angulating from the photograph, I was able to identify a line along which it must have fallen. I borrowed my father's lobster boat, took a friend, and went out looking for it."

"Why so interested in meteorites?"

"Meteorites are worth a lot of money."

"You're quite the entrepreneur."

"To cover our tracks we circulated a phony story about looking for a pirate treasure."

"I'm beginning to see the real story," said Ford.

"Yeah. Our meth-addicted stalker was addled enough to believe it and attacked us, sinking my father's lobster boat. The insurance company wouldn't pay."

"I'm sorry."

"My father's making payments on a boat that doesn't exist. We might lose our house. So you see why I need money—to get him a new boat."

Emotion welled up in her eyes. Ford pretended not to notice. "You found the crater," Ford said easily. "So what did the meteorite look like?"

"Did I say I found a meteorite?"

Ford felt his heart quicken. He knew instinctively the girl was telling the truth. "You didn't find a meteorite in the crater?"

"Now we're getting into the information that's going to cost you."

Ford looked at her steadily for a long time. Finally he spoke. "May I ask what a girl with your brains is doing waitressing in Damariscotta, Maine?"

"I dropped out of college."

"What college?"

"Princeton."

"Princeton? Isn't that somewhere in Jersey?"

"Very funny."

"What'd you major in?"

"I was supposedly pre-med but I took a lot of physics and astronomy courses. Too many. I flunked organic chem, lost my financial aid."

Ford thought for a while. What the hell. "It just so happens a hundred thousand dropped in my lap the other day which I don't really need. It's yours—to buy a new boat. But it comes with conditions. You're working for me, now. You'll be absolutely quiet, tell nothing to no one, not even your friend. And the first thing we're going to do in this new boat is visit the crater. Agreed?"

The girl surprised Ford by the sheer wattage of her smile. She stuck out her hand. "Agreed."

42

MARK CORSO TOSSED the mail on a table and threw himself into an armchair in his friend's basement apartment on the Upper West Side. His head dropped back against the cushion and he closed his eyes. He felt logy, an incipient hangover creeping up behind his eyeballs. For the last three nights he had worked double shifts at Moto's, one to one, and to get through them he'd been nursing screwdrivers under the bar. Even with the long hours he still wasn't making enough to pay his overdue share of the rent. He needed that severance check from NPF and he needed it fast. In what little free time he had, he'd been job hunting and obsessively going over the images on the hard drive, refining and polishing them. He'd hardly slept. And on top of it, he missed Marjory Leung awfully, fantasized about her long, nude, springy body day and night. He'd talked to her a half a dozen times but it was clear the relationship wasn't going to continue—although they remained good buddies.

Fighting the urge to sleep, he roused himself and eyed the

mail. Depressingly slim responses to his job queries and applications. With an effort of will he scooped up the pile, tore open the first letter, and read the first line. Crumpling it into a ball he dropped it, opened the second, the third, the fourth.

The pile of paper at his feet grew.

The sixth and last letter stopped him dead. It was from the personnel office at CalTech, which administered NPF. At first he thought it might be his severance check, but when he opened it all he found was a letter. He scanned it in disbelief, his eye fixing on the first paragraph.

"After reviewing your employment records and the notice of termination for cause from your former supervisor at NPF, we have determined that you do not qualify for the severance package or unused leave compensation as outlined in your employment contract. We refer you to regulations 4.5.1 through 6 in the *Handbook for Employees* . . ."

He read it twice and tossed it on the table. This wasn't happening to him. They owed him two weeks' severance and two weeks' unused vacation: over eight grand. After six years of graduate school and eighty thousand dollars in student loans, here he was, crashing in a friend's basement apartment with less than five hundred dollars in his bank account, no job, no prospects, and a brick of maxed-out credit cards so thick he couldn't fit them all in his wallet. And now he couldn't even pay the back rent.

Slowly, inexorably, his anger built. Those bastards at NPF would pay. They owed him eight thousand dollars and he would get his money, one way or another. There had to be a way to get back at them.

The door opened and his roommate stood in the doorway. "Hey, Mark, I hate to be a jerk about that back rent, but I need the money. Like now."

MARK CORSO ARRIVED on the doorstep of his mother's old brownstone in Greenpoint, suitcases in hand, and rang the bell. The hangover was now full-blown, his eyeballs throbbed and he had a mouthful of paste. He hadn't been able to bring himself to call ahead. Inside, he could hear the shuffling of feet, the sound of locks being turned, and then his mother's quavering, uncertain voice.

"Who is it?"

"Me. Mark."

The final lock was turned and there was his mother—short, plump, iron-gray hair—her face lighting up. "Mark!" The arms went around him in a suffocating embrace, once, twice. She smelled of fresh pasta and her arms were patched with flour. "What have you got here, suitcases? Are you moving back in? Don't stand outside in the cold, come in! Are you here to stay or just a visit? You look so tired!" Another embrace, this one with a hint of tears.

She led her son, unresisting, into the parlor, and sat him down on the sofa.

"I'll make you your favorite, a Fluffernutter, you just stay right there and relax. You're so thin!"

"I'm fine, Mom."

Corso kicked off his shoes, stretched out on the sofa, clasped his hands behind his head, and stared up at the swirls of brushed stucco on the ceiling of his childhood home, thinking about the money NPF owed him. They couldn't deny him two weeks' severance just like that, without due process. And vacation time? He'd earned that. This was not right. He wondered if Derkweiler wasn't actively interfering with his efforts to find a new job—he hadn't even had a nibble. Incredible: here he was, sitting on the scientific discovery of a lifetime, unable to do anything with it, and being treated like shit by the establishment.

He had an ace in the hole: the hard drive. He wondered when they would miss it. An idea began to form. Years back, he recalled, a classified hard drive was misplaced at Los Alamos National Labs. It made the front page of *The New York Times* and led to the canning of the director and a bunch of scientists. Maybe the NPF drive needed to show up in some FBI office. The very fact it was outside the fence would cause a scandal. And who would get blamed? The mission director.

He sat up. *That was it.* Chaudry's career would be ruined if it became known someone in his unit had walked out with a classified hard drive. And Derkweiler would also be toast. He had them both by the short hairs. But there was no point in taking them down just for revenge. No . . . The threat of going to the FBI would only be his leverage. The stick, so to speak. The carrot was that he had a discovery that would make both of them famous, as well as himself—if they had the wisdom to reinstate him.

Now this was a plan. A quick phone call, nothing in writing. He would ask for nothing more than he deserved, something that Chaudry could do for him with the mere stroke of a pen—rehire him. With his discovery, all would be forgiven. He felt a mounting excitement. If Chaudry rejected his overture and reported the stolen drive, the man's career would be ruined. He'd never work with classified material again. Chaudry was smart, he was cool-headed, and above all he was ambitious. He would see the lay of the land.

Corso looked at his watch. Ten A.M. in New York, seven A.M. in California; Chaudry would still be at home. Perfect.

It was a matter of thirty seconds to get the home phone number off the Internet. Corso dialed it with slow deliberation, his heart hammering in his chest, while rehearsing his message. *I have a classified NPF hard drive which contains all the high-res pictures of the planet. Freeman sent it to me before he was murdered. And on this drive is an image of an alien artifact. A machine. Trust me, you won't find it. But I did.*

So here's the deal. Rehire me, you get the hard drive back, no one will know about the security breach—and we'll share credit for the greatest scientific discovery of all time. Refuse and I mail this drive to the FBI anonymously and your career is over. Finished. Nada. Remember what happened at Los Alamos?

The choice is yours. Think it over before doing anything stupid.

The phone began to ring. "Hello?" came Chaudry's cool voice.

43

FORD STEPPED OUT of the dinghy onto the rocks of Shark Island and breathed deeply of the salt air. He was glad to be on solid ground—the boat ride off shore, even in a calm ocean, had left him queasy. He was not, it must be admitted, a sailor. The brilliant summer day bathed the island in warm sunlight and the ocean lay shimmering from mainland to sea horizon. Seagulls cried and wheeled about above their heads, irritated at being disturbed from their habitual resting places on the shore rocks.

"Don't soil your Guccis," Abbey said.

He followed her to the top of the island, picking his way among rocks and bayberry bushes, and in a moment found himself at the edge of a small crater. The recent rains had washed clean the fractured bedrock at the bottom of the crater. In the middle of the bedrock, surrounded by cracks, Ford could see a perfect hole, about three inches in diameter.

He took a deep breath. What could have made an entry

hole of three inches, pass through eight thousand miles of planet, and exit, making a hole ten feet across?

"We went to find a meteorite," said Abbey, "and that's what we found: a hole." She laughed ruefully.

Ford slipped a handheld radiation meter out of his gear bag. It registered normal background radiation only, about 0.05 millirem per hour. He took some pictures and got a GPS fix on the hole. Then he crouched and took a reading inside the hole itself, passing the RadMeter back and forth. It finally registered a slight uptick, to 0.1 millirem/hr.

"Am I going to have two-headed children?"

"Hardly."

He slipped into the crater and knelt, reaching inside the hole with his fingers and feeling around. The walls were smooth and glassy, just like the walls of the bigger hole in Cambodia. The extraterrestrial object—whatever it was—had bored a round cylinder in the rock as perfect as if it had been drilled. Cracks radiated outward, but there was little sign of violence and almost none of the usual explosive contact that occurs on impact—the hole was amazingly clean, the ground hardly disturbed. It was as if some unusual force had absorbed or canceled out the energy of the impact. The same thing must have happened at the far side of the Earth, in Cambodia. The exit hole should have been enormous, like that made by a bullet passing through a pumpkin, the shock wave alone blowing debris out the far end and leaving an active volcano or eruption of magma. But no. Both holes had somehow sealed themselves up at both ends. No magma, no eruption, just residual radiation. It made no sense. Anything large and fast enough to vaporize a hole in rock and actually drill through the Earth would have blown the island to smithereens.

Ford peered down the hole with a flashlight; it went straight down as far as the beam could reach. He shivered. Something about this business frightened him; he wasn't sure why. He measured the hole, recorded the entry angle on it, took some pictures. Getting his rock hammer out of his pack, he chipped a few fragments from the lip of the hole, some displaying the glassy inner wall, and sealed them in ziplock bags. He also took samples of dirt and plants.

"How the heck," said Abbey, "could a meteor big enough to light up the Maine coast only leave a tiny hole like that?"

"A damn good question." Ford rose to his feet, brushed the dirt off his knees.

"How deep do you think it went before it finally stopped?"

Ford cleared his throat and looked at her. "It didn't stop."

"What do you mean?"

"It went all the way through the Earth."

She stared at him. "You're kidding me, right?"

"No joke. It came out in northwestern Cambodia. Only it was a lot bigger when it exited—the hole wasn't three inches in diameter, it was ten feet."

"Holy shit."

"It blew out of the ground with such force that it flattened a square mile of jungle."

"Any idea what it was?"

Ford began packing up his gear and samples. "Not a clue."

"Sounds like a miniature black hole to me. Goes all the way through the Earth, getting bigger as it goes, leaves behind traces of radiation."

"That's an intriguing hypothesis."

"Have you figured out where it came from?"

Ford hefted the bag. "No."

"Why not?"

Ford sighed. "And how would one do that?"

"You've got a photograph of it coming in, you've got the entry point and angle, exact time of impact, exit point and angle—heck, with that information I'm pretty sure you could extrapolate its orbital trajectory backward. They do it all the time with ECOs."

"ECOs?"

"Earth Crossing Objects. It's a classic problem of orbital dynamics."

Ford stared at her. "Could *you* do it?"

"Gimme an hour and a MacBook running Mathematica."

44

CORSO LET HIMSELF into the brownstone, moving slowly, trying not to wake his mother. He stumbled over the rug in the front hall, cursed, and went into the parlor, shutting the pocket door to keep down the noise. He had just finished up the shift at Moto's, although he had stayed on to have a drink or two of his own. It was now two A.M. Eleven P.M. in California.

Eleven. He sank down on the sofa, feeling flushed. He had talked to Marjory earlier that day, a very unsatisfying call, cut short because she was at work. They'd only been going out a week when he left; what they had together was wild and erotic but it wasn't going to work long-distance.

God, it was awful. He'd never had so much fun with a girl. And he desperately needed to talk to someone else, get a second opinion from someone who knew the players, knew the place.

He picked up the phone, dialed the number. It rang four times before her voice answered, small and far away.

"Mark?"

"Yeah, hi, it's me."

"Are you all right?"

"I'm fine, no problem. Listen, I have to talk to you about something . . . something at work. Really important."

A silence. "What about work?" Her voice sounded wary. She'd made it pretty clear she didn't want to get involved in his travails or endanger her own career because of him.

"I've got a hard drive from NPF. One of the classified ones. It's got all the high-res imagery on it."

"Oh, shit, Mark, don't tell me this. I don't want to hear it."

"You've got to hear me. I found something on it. Something incredible."

"I *really* don't want to hear any more. I'm hanging up now."

"No, wait! I found an image of an alien . . . machine or artifact on . . ." He paused. *Don't tell her the real location.* "On Mars."

A silence. "Wait a minute. What'd you just say?"

"I found an image. A very, very clear image of a very, *very* old construction on the surface of Mars. Unmistakable."

"You've been drinking."

"Yes, but I made these discoveries when I was sober. Marjory, you *know* I'm not an idiot, you know I graduated first in my class at MIT, and you know I was the youngest technician in the entire Mars mission. You know that when I tell you this is real, it's *real.* I think this machine is the source of the gamma rays."

He could hear her breathing on the other end of the phone. "A lot of geological formations can look artificial."

"This is no formation. It's about six meters in diameter, consisting of a perfectly cylindrical tube with a rim projecting from the surface about two meters in diameter, surrounded by five perfectly spherical projections, the entire thing mounted on a pentagonal platform, partially drifted over with regolith."

"How do you know it's old?"

"The regolith. And you can see pitting and erosion from micrometeoroids. It's got to be many *millions* of years old."

Another silence. "Where on Mars is it? I want to see the images."

"Sorry, I'm not going to tell you that."

"Why not?"

"Because I found it, I'm getting the credit. Surely you understand."

"I do. But . . . What are you going to do about this? *How* are you going to get credit?"

"I called Chaudry."

"*Jesus.* You *told* him you stole a classified drive?"

"I didn't actually steal it, but yes, I told him. I said if he rehired me, I'd come back with the drive, all would be forgotten, and we'd share in the discovery. If not, I'd send the hard drive to the FBI and his career would be fucked."

"Oh my God. And?"

"The asshole didn't believe me about the alien machine. He said I was a psychopathic liar. He didn't even believe I had a classified hard drive. So I e-mailed him a detail from a high-res image—to prove it. Not a picture of the machine, of course, because he'd then find it using the data file. But I did send him a super-high-res of another image. The fucker called me back so fast."

"You're crazy."

"This is a high-stakes game."

"And?"

"It sort of backfired. He said he wouldn't do shit for me. And now I couldn't do shit to him. Because if I mailed the drive anonymously to the FBI, and he got nailed, he'd point the finger at me. '*I go down, you go down,*' he said. It's a Mexican standoff."

A long pause. "He's right, you know."

"I realize that now. The fucker stalemated me."

"Now what?"

"This isn't over by a long shot. I'm thinking of taking the drive to the *Times*. I swear to God I'm getting the credit for this if it's the last thing I do." He hesitated. "I need a second opinion. I need to hear what you think. I've been thinking about this so much I'm about to explode."

He could hear the long-distance hiss on the line for a long time, the faint sound of music in the background. "Don't do anything right away," Leung said slowly. "I'm not sure going to the *Times* is the best idea. Give me a few days to think about it, okay? Just sit tight and don't do anything."

"Hurry up. I'm a desperate man."

45

ABBEY HADN'T BEEN able to figure out what to say to her father at dinner, and now, at six A.M., as she lugged her suitcase down the stairs, she still had no idea how she was going to break the news.

She found him sitting at the kitchen table drinking coffee and reading the *Portland Press Herald*. She was shocked at how tired he looked. His light brown hair lay in straggly locks plastered to his forehead, he hadn't shaved, and his shoulders were stooped. He was not tall but he had always been straight, stocky, and muscular. Now he looked half-collapsed. Since she had sunk his boat and wrecked his livelihood, he had quit bugging her about college and her future, stopped complaining about all the money he'd spent. It was almost like he'd given up on her—and his own life. He couldn't have made her feel worse if he'd tried.

As she set her suitcase by the door he looked up in surprise. "What's this? You going somewhere?"

She struggled to smile brightly. "I got a new job."

His eyebrows went up. "Sit down, have a cup of coffee, and tell me about it."

The sun streamed in the window, and she could see the blue of the distant harbor beyond, dotted with fishing boats, and, through the opposite window, the big meadow behind the house, the grass long and green. Half an hour until the car arrived. Taking a mug out of the cupboard, she poured herself a cup, added her usual four teaspoons of sugar and a good pour of heavy cream, stirred it up, and sat down.

"No more waitressing?"

"No more. I got a real job."

"At Reilly's Market? I saw they'd posted a notice looking for summer help."

"I'm going to Washington."

"Washington? As in D.C.?"

"For a week or two, and then maybe I'll be back. The position involves a certain amount of travel."

Her father leaned forward, an uncertain look on his face. "Travel? What in the world will you be doing?"

She swallowed. "I'm working for a planetary geologist. I'm his assistant."

Her father stared at her with narrowed eyes. "What do you know about geology?"

"It's not geology. It's *planetary* geology. Planets, Dad. It's more like astronomy. This scientist runs a consulting firm for the government." She paused, remembering what they'd discussed. "He was in the restaurant a couple of days ago, and we got to talking, and he offered to hire me as his assistant." She took a slug of coffee and smiled nervously.

"Why, Abbey, that's great. If you don't mind me asking, what's the pay?"

"It's excellent. In fact, there was a signing bonus . . ."

"A what?"

"A signing bonus. You know, when you take a new job, you sometimes get a bonus for accepting."

The eyes got narrower. "That's for highly skilled people. What skills do you have?"

Abbey just hated lying. "I took astronomy and physics courses at Princeton."

He looked at her steadily. "Are you sure this is legit?"

"Of course! Look, there's a car coming for me in fifteen minutes, so I gotta say good-bye. But there's something I want to tell you first—"

"A *car*? For you?"

"Right. Car service. To the airport. I'm flying to Washington."

"I want to meet your employer. I want to talk to him."

"Dad, I'm a big girl. I can take care of myself." She swallowed, glanced out the window.

Her father, frowning, set his coffee cup down. "I want to meet him."

"You will, I promise." She pointed out the window. "Look at the harbor."

"What?" Her father's face was all red with worry.

Now or never, Abbey thought. "Hey, look at your mooring!"

He turned and squinted out the kitchen window, then scraped back his chair in irritation. "Agh, for chrissakes, some jackass is hanging on my mooring."

"Those damn summer people," said Abbey. It was a familiar refrain, the summer cruising folk snagging the empty moorings of fishermen.

"They come up from Massachusetts, think they own the harbor."

"Better get the name of the boat and tell the harbor-master."

"I certainly will." He rummaged in the magazine basket and pulled out a set of binoculars. He squinted, staring through them. "What the hell?"

"What's the name of the boat?"

"Is this some kind of joke?"

Abbey couldn't hold it in any longer. "Dad, it's the *Marea II.* A thirty-six-foot Willis Beal, two hundred fifteen horse-power Volvo engine with less than two thousand hours, pot hauler, raw water, tanks, the works. Built in 2002 by RP Boatworks. Ready to fish. It isn't new but all I had was a hundred grand."

The binoculars began to shake. "What . . . the *hell*?"

A honk came from the driveway.

"Oops, there's my ride."

"I can't possibly afford the payments . . ."

"It's free and clear. I bought it for you with my signing bonus. All the papers are on board. Gotta go."

"Abbey . . . wait, you *bought* me a *new boat*? Wait, for God's sakes . . ."

"Got my cell, I'll call you from the road."

She rushed out of the house, tossed her suitcase in the back of the black SUV, and jumped in after it. Her father came to the door, still confused. She waved as the car scurried off down the graveled driveway and onto the main road.

46

AS FORD ENTERED the glass-and-chrome lobby of the Watergate Hotel, the assistant manager, who must have been lying in wait, came whisking around from behind his desk, hands clasped in front. He was a small man dressed in hotel black with a pinched, obsequious expression on his face. "Mr. Ford?"

"Yes?"

"Please excuse my concern, but it's about the girl in the room you booked."

Ford detected a note of disapproval in the man's anxious voice. Perhaps it had been a mistake to book her at the Watergate. There were plenty of quieter and cheaper hotels in Washington. He raised his eyebrows. "What's the problem?"

"She hasn't left the room in two days, she won't let the staff in to clean or stock the minibar, she's been getting food deliveries at all hours of the night, and she won't answer the room phone." A literal wringing of the hands. "And, well, an hour ago there were complaints of noise."

"Noise?"

"Yelling. Whooping. It sounded like some sort of . . . party."

Ford tried to maintain the serious expression on his face. "I'll look into it."

"We're concerned. We just renovated the hotel. Guests are responsible for any damage to rooms . . ." The disapproving voice trailed off into a significant silence.

Ford dipped into his pocket and pressed a twenty into the man's hand. "Trust me, everything's going to be fine."

The man gave the bill a disdainful look as he pocketed it, retreating back to his station. Ford moved toward the elevators, considering that this was turning out to be a more expensive proposition than he had imagined.

He knocked and Abbey opened the door. The room was a mess, dirty dishes, pizza boxes, and empty Chinese food cartons piled up in the entryway, emitting a smell of stale food. The trash can was overflowing with Diet Coke cans, papers were scattered about the floor, and the bed was wrecked.

She saw him looking around.

"What?"

"They have a quaint custom in large hotels like this called maid service. Ever heard of it?"

"I can't concentrate when someone's cleaning around me."

"You said this would take an hour."

"So I was wrong."

"You? Wrong?"

"Hey, maybe you better sit down and take a look at what I found."

He looked at her closely; she was haggard, her hair knotty and in disarray, eyes bloodshot, clothes with a slept-in look. But the expression on her face was one of pure triumph. "Don't tell me you solved the problem?"

"Does a toilet seat get ass?"

He winced. "You should publish a dictionary of your expressions."

Reaching into the minifridge, she pulled out a Diet Coke. "Want one?"

He shuddered. "No thanks."

She settled into the chair in front of the computer and he took the one beside it. "The problem was a little more difficult than I thought." She took a long pull on the Coke, stretching out the moment. "Any object in the solar system traces out a curve—either an ellipse or a hyperbola. A hyperbolic orbit means it came from outside the solar system and is going back out again—moving at faster than escape velocity. But our Object X was moving in an elliptical orbit."

"Object X?"

"Gotta call it something."

Ford leaned forward. "So you're saying it originated inside the solar system?"

"Exactly. I had the angle of entry into the Earth and a picture of Object X coming in. But what I didn't have was its velocity. Turns out the University of Maine at Orono has a meteoroid tracking station. They didn't get a picture of X but they got the acoustical signature on tape—the sonic booms—and got a precise velocity of twenty-point-nine kilometers per second. A lot slower than the hundred thousand miles an hour first reported in the papers."

Ford nodded. "Following you so far."

"So it was in an elliptical orbit. The apogee, the farthest point from the sun, is where it probably started its journey."

"I see."

She hit a few keys, and a schematic of the solar system came into view. She typed in a command and an ellipsis appeared. "Here's the orbit of Object X. Please note: the apogee is right at the orbit of Mars. And here's the kicker: if you extrapolate backward, you find that Mars itself was right at that point in its orbit when X began its journey toward Earth."

She sat back. "Object X," she said, "came from Mars."

A long silence enveloped the hotel room. Ford stared at the screen. It seemed incredible. "You're sure about this?"

"Triple-checked it."

Ford rubbed his chin and sat back. "Looks like we need to go where they know about Mars."

"And where's that?"

Ford thought for a moment. "Right now they're mapping Mars. Over at NPF, the National Propulsion Facility in Pasadena, California. We should head over there, poke around, see if they've found anything unusual."

Abbey cocked her head and looked at him. "You know, Wyman, there's one thing I don't get. Why are you doing this? What's in it for you? Nobody's paying you, right?"

"I'm deeply concerned. I'm not sure why, but my internal alarms are going off like crazy and I can't rest until I figure this out."

"Concerned about what, exactly?"

"If that was a mini–black hole, the planet was just kissed by the Grim Reaper. We came *this* close to extinction. What if there are more where that came from?"

47

HARRY BURR WAITED in the car park of the upscale Connecticut mall, leaning on the fender of his yellow VW New Beetle, smoking an American Spirit cigarette. The message had come in the night before, *urgent*. Burr had never had an assignment that wasn't urgent. When somebody wanted somebody else dead, it was never "take your time, no rush."

He rolled the cigarette thoughtfully between thumb and forefinger, feeling the sponginess of the filter, watching the smoke curl up from the glowing ash. A foul habit, bad for his health, unattractive, working-class. Tweedy professors didn't smoke, or if they did, it was a briar pipe. He tossed the butt on the cement floor of the parking garage and ground it up with a dozen twists of the sole of his penny loafer until it was a shredded tuft. He would quit, but not right now.

A few cars passed and then one slowed as it approached him. It was an ugly American car, a late-model Crown Victoria, black, naturally. His employers, whoever they were, watched too many movies. He loved his New Beetle and it was perfect for his work. No one expected a contract killer to arrive in a Beetle. Or wear a tweed jacket with leather elbow patches from L.L. Bean with chinos and argyle socks.

As he watched the black car ooze up, Burr didn't know and didn't want to know who was hiring him, but he was pretty sure it was quasi-official. He'd had a fair amount of that kind of work lately.

The Crown Vic stopped and the smoked window—smoked window!—rolled down. It was the same Asian man he had dealt with before, in a blue suit and sunglasses. Still, he went through the little password charade. "You leaving this space?" he asked.

"Not for another six minutes."

They loved that kind of stuff. In response, a hand extended with a fat manila envelope. Burr took it, opened it, riffled the brick of money, tossed it onto the passenger seat.

"Above all, we want that hard drive," said the man. "We're raising the bonus to two hundred thousand dollars for the drive, intact. You got that?"

"I got it." Burr smiled blandly and waved the car away. The Crown Vic departed with an ostentatious squeal of rubber. *Nice*, he thought, *draw a little attention to yourself, why dontcha?*

He slid back into his car and opened the envelope, pouring out its contents: fact sheet, photographs, and money. A lot of it. With far more to come. This was a good job, even an excellent one.

Shoving the money into the glove compartment, he scanned the photographs and perused the assignment letter. He whistled. This was going to be easy. Get a hard drive and kill a geek. There must be something pretty sweet on that hard drive.

He plucked a glossy product photograph of a hard drive out of the batch and gazed at it, shoved it back, sorted through the others, and then scanned the fact sheet. He'd review it more thoroughly tonight, do the research, make the hit tomorrow. He could hardly imagine now what it was like in the days before Google Earth, MapQuest, Facebook, YouTube, reverse white pages, people search, and all the other privacy-busting tools on the Internet. In half an hour he could do what was once a week's worth of research.

Harry Burr laid the papers aside and indulged in a little self-reflection. He was good, and not just because he was prep-school educated and could recite the Latin first declension. He was good because he didn't like killing. It gave him no pleasure. He didn't need to do it, he didn't have to do it, it wasn't like eating or sex. He was good because he felt for his victims. Knowing they were real people, he could put himself in their shoes, look out at the world through their eyes. That made it so much easier to kill them.

And finally, Harry Burr was efficient. Back when he was another person, a snot-nosed, prepped-out prick in Greenwich named Gordie Hill, his father had taught him all about efficiency. He had a storehouse of quotations he would roll out: if you're going to do it, do it; if you make a lot of money, no one will care how you did it; if you intend to win, one way is as good as another. "The victor will never be asked if he told the truth," was what the old man said when he walked out of the kitchen after shooting his mother. Never to be seen again. A few years later Harry learned his father had been quoting Hitler. Now that was funny.

Harry Burr smiled. He was "damaged," or so he was led to believe by the parade of school psychologists, social workers, counselors, and all the other professional advice-giving-for-one-hundred-dollars-an-hour folks after his mother's murder. So why not make a career of being damaged? He plucked the crumpled cigarette pack out of his shirt pocket. Fishing the last one out, he lit it and put the empty pack back in his pocket. What was it St. Augustine said? "God give me chastity, but not right now." One of these days he'd quit, but not right now.

48

ABBEY WAITED BEHIND Ford as he knocked on the open door of the office of Dr. Charles Chaudry, director of the Mars mission. She felt itchy and hot in the new suit Ford had made her wear, especially in California in June.

The director rose and came around his desk, hand extended.

"My assistant, Abbey Straw."

Abbey shook the cool hand. Chaudry was a handsome man with a lean, chiseled face, dark brown eyes, springy on his feet, athletic, personable. He sported one of those tight little ponytails that seemed endemic to Californians of a certain age.

"Come in, please," said the man, his tenor voice almost musical.

Ford eased his frame into a chair and Abbey followed suit. She tried to hide her nervousness. Part of her was thrilled at the cloak-and-dagger business, the pretense with which they'd gained access. This Ford fellow, who looked so buttoned down and mainstream, was actually a subversive at heart. She liked that.

The office was pleasantly large and spare, with windows looking out over gray-brown mountains that rose abruptly behind the giant parking lot. Two walls of books added to the comfortable, scholarly atmosphere. Everything was as neat as a pin.

"Well now," said Chaudry, folding his hands. "So you're writing a book on our Mars mission."

"That's right," said Ford. "A big, beautiful photography book. They tell me you're the man in charge of mapping and photographing the surface."

Chaudry nodded.

Ford went on to describe the book in enthusiastic detail, the layout, what it would cover, and of course all the beautiful photographs it would contain. Abbey was amazed at the transformation from his usual dry and cool manner to a bubbling enthusiasm. Chaudry listened politely, hands tented in front.

Ford finished up. "I understand that because this is a NASA project, the photographs are in the public domain. I'd like access to all your images, at the highest resolution."

Chaudry unclasped his hands and leaned forward. "You're right that the images are in the public domain—but not at the highest resolution."

"We're going to be running double trucks and gatefolds and we'll need the best resolution we can get."

The director leaned back. "The high-res images are strictly classified, I'm afraid. Don't be concerned—we can get you all the images you need at a resolution more than adequate for a book."

"Why classified?"

"Standard operating procedure. The imaging technology is highly classified and we don't want our enemies knowing just how good that technology is."

"Just how high is the highest resolution?"

"Again, I can't talk about specifics. Generally, from orbit, we can see something on the ground as small as fifty centimeters. And with our SHARAD radar we can look as much as a hundred meters under the surface, too."

Ford whistled. "Seen anything unusual?"

Chaudry smiled, showing very white teeth. "Just about everything we see is unusual. We're like Columbus setting foot in America."

"Anything . . . not strictly natural?"

The smile faded. "And what do you mean by that?" he asked coolly.

"Let's say you were to see something on the surface that wasn't natural—say, an alien spaceship." Ford chuckled lightly. "What would you do then?"

Now the smile was completely gone. "Mr. Ford, please don't even joke about that. We get a lot—and I mean a *lot*—of nuts in here pushing crazy theories. We've actually had demonstrations in front of the buildings by groups demanding we release pictures of the alien civilizations we've discovered." He paused, and then added: "You *are* joking, Mr. Ford? Or do you have some specific reason for asking the question?"

"Yes," said Ford. "I was joking."

Abbey spoke. "You're right, Dr. Chaudry. I read somewhere that almost forty percent of Americans believe in the existence of intelligent life somewhere else in the universe. Imagine being that dumb!"

Chaudry shifted uncomfortably.

"Well," said Ford briskly, casting a sharp eye on Abbey. "You've been most helpful, Dr. Chaudry."

Chaudry rose with evident relief. "Mr. Ford, we'd be glad to cooperate with your book. All the pictures are online at our Web site. Just pick out the ones you want and my press office will be glad to get you a DVD of the images at the highest *legal* resolution." He gave a rather forced smile and eased them out of the office with a practiced hand.

"That was a waste of time," muttered Abbey, as they walked down the long halls.

Ford rubbed his chin and looked about, then turned a corner and headed down a wrong hall.

"Yo, Einstein," Abbey said. "You're going the wrong way."

A smile crept onto Ford's face. "Darn. This is such a big, confusing place. Easy to get lost." He continued on, turning another corner, going down another hallway.

Abbey tried to keep up with his long strides.

"Just follow my lead," said Ford. He turned another corner and Abbey realized he already seemed to know the layout of the place. They came to an office door, which was shut. Ford knocked and a rather irritated voice sounded within, "Come in."

Ford opened and door and entered. Abbey saw a large man with an unpleasantly fleshy face, wearing a short-sleeved shirt with hammy arms. It was hot and the place smelled of sweat.

"Dr. Winston Derkweiler?" Ford rapped out.

"Yes?"

"I'm with the Agency," Ford said, then nodded toward Abbey. "My assistant."

Derkweiler looked at her, then back at him. "Agency? Which agency?"

"About a month ago," Ford continued as if he hadn't heard, "one of your scientists was murdered."

Abbey was surprised. This was all new to her. Ford played his cards close.

"That's right," said Derkweiler, "but I understood the case was closed."

Ford turned to Abbey. "Ms. Straw, would you please shut the door?"

"Yes, sir." Abbey shut the door, and then turned the lock for good measure.

"The case may be closed, but the security breach is still under investigation."

Derkweiler nodded. "Security breach? I'm not sure I understand."

"Let us just say Dr. Freeman was indiscreet."

"It doesn't surprise me."

"I'm glad you understand the problem, Dr. Derkweiler."

"Thank you."

Ford smiled. "I was told I could count on you for help. Now then, I'd like a list of the staff in your department."

Derkweiler hesitated. "Well, speaking of security, I . . . I'd need to see your pass or ID or something."

"Naturally! My apologies." Ford removed a well-worn badge, on which Abbey could see a blue, white, and gold seal with the legend, Central Intelligence Agency.

"Oh, *that* agency," said Derkweiler.

The badge swiftly disappeared back into Ford's suit. "This is just between us—understood?"

"Absolutely." Derkweiler delved into his files and removed a piece of paper, handing it to Ford. "There it is: personnel in my department—names, titles, contact info."

"And ex-personnel?"

Derkweiler frowned, rummaged through some files. "Here's a list as of last quarter. If you want to go further back, I'd suggest checking with the personnel office directly."

They were out of the building in five minutes, in the vast parking lot to the side of the building. It was brutally hot in their rental car, the seat like a skillet. Abbey had never been to Southern California before and she hoped never to return. How could people stand the weather? Give her Maine in January.

Ford started the car and the AC came on in a blast of hot air. Abbey looked at him with narrowed eyes. "Good job, Special Agent Ford."

"Thank you." Ford slipped the lists Derkweiler had given him out of his pocket and handed them to her. "Find me a disgruntled former employee, preferably someone who was fired."

"You think they're covering something up?"

"A place like that is *always* covering something up. That's the nature of the beast. All large bureaucracies, no matter what they do, are dedicated to controlling information, expanding their budgets, and self-perpetuation. If they've found anything unusual about Mars, you can bet it's been hidden. God bless the disgruntled employee—no one does more to bring openness to government."

49

MARK CORSO LET himself into the dingy brownstone, riffled through the stack of mail on the side table, tossed it back in disgust, and went into the parlor. He flopped down on the sofa and fired up the Xbox running Resident Evil 5. He had to go to work at Moto's in another hour and he wanted to kill some time.

As the game started, the small parlor shook with the sounds of weapons fire, explosions, and ripping meat. He played for ten minutes but it wasn't any good. He paused the game and set the console aside, silence descending. It just wasn't fun anymore, he couldn't get back in the groove. Not with this discovery still up in the air, waiting for Marjory to call, waiting, waiting, waiting. He was taking the drive to the *Times* first thing tomorrow morning.

It had been only two days since his call to Marjory but she was still cautioning him to keep quiet about it. Maybe she was buying time while looking for the machine herself. Good luck—she'd never find it on the surface of Mars.

He thought back to the journalist who'd called him that morning. He'd been cautious, circumspect, but he gave her enough information, he hoped, to light a fire under Chaudry's ass. Give him a scare when the piece came out. Although, in thinking back over the conversation, he felt a little uneasy, wondering if he should have been a little less forthcoming. But she had assured him it was off the record, background only—his name would never come up.

Passing by the side table, he went through the mail again irritably, pointlessly. No job offers, nothing. He swelled with anger at the idea that they had cheated him out of eight thousand dollars and he recalled Chaudry's cool contempt as he repulsed his offer and threatened him back.

Feeling all nerves, he went into the bathroom and splashed some water on his face, toweling it dry. The cold water did nothing to help. He couldn't wait to get to Moto's, to be distracted, calm down with a stiff drink. Moping about the house all day long was killing him.

He would definitely talk to the *Times*. The government wouldn't dare arrest him after that. He'd be a hero. A Daniel Ellsberg.

In the middle of these ruminations, the deep electronic gong of the doorbell rang.

"Mark?" He heard his mother's timid voice from the kitchen. "Would you get that?"

Corso went to the door and looked through the peephole. A man in a tweed jacket stood there, looking uncomfortably hot in the gray, muggy morning air.

"Yes?" Corso asked through the door.

The man didn't respond, instead holding up a battered

leather wallet which fell open, displaying a police badge. "Lieutenant Moore."

Oh shit. Corso peered intently through the peephole. The officer continued to hold up the badge, almost as a challenge. The photo seemed right. But it was the Washington, D.C. Police. What did that mean? Corso felt an overwhelming panic. Chaudry *had* turned him in.

"What's it about?" Corso tried to say, almost choking on the words.

"May I come in, please?"

Corso swallowed. Did he have a right to refuse entry? Did the man have to show a warrant? Maybe it was better not to piss him off. He unshot the bolt, unhooked the chain, turned the lock, and opened the door.

Officer Moore slipped inside and Corso quickly shut the door behind him. "What's it about?" Corso said, standing in the hall.

The man smiled. "Nothing serious. Now—is there anyone else in the house?"

He did not want his mother hearing any of this. "Uh, no. Nobody." He'd better get the cop out of sight, quick. "In here," he said, gesturing to the parlor. They went in, Corso quietly shutting the door. Maybe he should be calling a lawyer. That's what everyone said you should do. Never talk to the cops without one. "Please sit down," he said, trying to keep his voice relaxed, as he took a seat on the sofa.

The cop, however, remained standing.

"I think I need to talk to a lawyer," Corso said, "as a matter of course. Whatever this might be about."

The man reached into his jacket and removed a large

black handgun. Corso stared at it. "Look, officer, you don't need that."

"I think I do." He removed a long cylinder and affixed it to the end of the gun. And now Corso noticed he was wearing black gloves.

"What are you doing?" Corso asked. This wasn't normal. His mind was boiling with confusion and conjecture.

"Don't lose it. No screaming, no weeping, stay in control. Everything's going to work out if you do what I say."

Corso fell silent. The man's soothing voice reassured him but nothing else made any sense. His mind was racing.

The man reached over and picked up the Xbox. The image was still frozen on the screen. "You play, Mark?"

Corso tried to answer, but it came out a gurgle.

The man flicked the switch and the game resumed. He turned up the sound until it was just about deafening.

"Now, Mark," said the man, speaking over the noise and pointing the gun at him. "I'm looking for a hard drive you took from NPF. That's all I want and when I get it I'll leave. Where is it?"

"I said I want a lawyer." Corso choked on his own words, swallowed, trying to recover his breath.

"You don't get it, shithead. I'm not a cop. I want the hard drive. Give it to me or I'll kill you."

Corso's mind reeled. Not a cop? Had Chaudry sent a hit man? This was crazy. "The drive?" he stammered. "All right, yes, yes. I'll tell you exactly where it is—I'll take you there—no problem. . . ."

The door to the parlor burst open. "What in the *world*?" shrilled his mother, standing there in her apron, dishrag in her hands, her eyes widening as she saw the gun. "*Aiiii!*" she shrieked, taking a step backward. "A gun! Help! Police! *Police!*"

The man pivoted and Corso leapt up to protect his mother but it was too late. The gun went off with a muffled sound and he saw, with utter disbelief and horror, his mother punched back by the round, blood spraying on the wall behind her. Eyes wide open, she stumbled back into the wall, losing one of her shoes, and toppled awkwardly to the ground.

With an inarticulate cry of existential rage Corso swept up the first weapon that came to hand, a lamp from the table, and swung it at the man. He ducked, the lamp shattering against his shoulder. The man staggered back, gun raised.

"No!" he cried. "Just tell me where the drive—"

Roaring like a bear Corso rushed him, seizing his neck in his hands and trying to crush the life out. He felt the gun shoved into his gut; there was a sudden raw punch, once, twice, which drove him back into the wall and then he was somehow on the floor curled up with his mother and all became peace.

50

WHEN SHE WAS going to Princeton, Abbey had made several trips to New York City with her friends, but they had never strayed from Manhattan. As she stood at the edge of Monsignor McGolrick Park in Brooklyn, rain dripping from the rim of her umbrella, she realized this was a New York she had never seen, a real working-class neighborhood of modest apartment buildings, vinyl-sided row houses, keys-made-here shops, dry cleaners, and neighborhood eateries.

"Number eighty-seven Driggs Avenue," Abbey said, consulting a damp street map. "Must be that street across the park."

"Let's go."

Two days before, Abbey's calls to ex-NPF employees had hit paydirt with a technician named Mark Corso. Posing as a journalist doing an exposé on unfair personnel practices at NPF, she had really gotten him going. Not only was he pissed off about being fired, but he was eager to spill NPF's darkest secrets—or so he claimed. And he hinted at having some really hot information that would "blow NPF out of the water."

They headed across the park and crossed the street toward one house in an identical row, streaked with damp, curtains drawn. They walked up the steps and Ford rang the doorbell. Abbey could hear it ringing forlornly within. A long wait. He rang again.

"You sure he said four o'clock?"

"Positive," said Abbey.

"He might have had second thoughts."

Abbey dipped in her pocket for the cell phone Ford had given her, and dialed Corso's cell.

"You hear that?" She could hear at the edge of audibility a sound of music inside the house.

Ford leaned toward the door. "Hang up and call again," he said.

She did so.

The music stopped, then a moment later it started again.

"It's got to be his," said Abbey. "Only a NASA engineer would have the theme of *Serenity* as his ringtone."

There was no way to see in; the drapes were firmly pulled—even the ones on the second floor. The house looked shut up tight. The door had three little windows, arranged diagonally, but they were of rippled, opaque colored glass.

Ford knelt and examined the doorjamb and lock. "No sign of a break-in."

"What do we do?"

"Call the police anonymously," he said, "and watch."

They cut across the park to an old phone booth sitting on the corner. Ford lifted the receiver with a handkerchief and dialed 911. "Eighty-seven Driggs Avenue," he said, in a rough voice. "Emergency. Go there. Now." He hung up. As he came out, Abbey was alarmed by the grim look on Ford's craggy face. She had been going to say something funny but decided against it.

Ford drifted back into the park, hands shoved into his pockets, Abbey at his side. They took shelter from the drizzle in a pseudo-classical outdoor pavilion and waited for the police to arrive. Within a few minutes two cop cars came cruising down Driggs Avenue, lights flashing but sirens off. They stopped. A pair of officers from the first vehicle went up the stairs and knocked on the front door. No answer.

"Let's get a little closer," Ford said, drifting over. Three police officers were now at the door, knocking persistently, while a fourth remained in the squad car, talking into the radio. One of the cops fetched a wrecking bar out of his car and poked it through a door window. He picked out the glass, reached in, and unlatched the door.

The two cops disappeared into the house, one with a handheld radio.

Ford quickly crossed the street and leaned in the window of the second squad car. "There a problem?"

"Routine check," said the cop, waving them along.

All of a sudden his radio burst to life. "We have a ten–twenty-nine double homicide at Eighty-seven Driggs; two squad cars on scene, sealing the premises." Then another burst, "Two ambulances and CS team dispatched and en route; ten-thirteen homicide division . . ." The radio went on in this fashion and almost immediately sirens could be heard approaching. From her vantage point across the street

Abbey could just see through the door into the interior of the parlor: a wall, with a starburst of blood on it, and below a woman's bare foot.

51

IT AMAZED ABBEY how quickly the deserted, rain-drenched park filled with people. They came out of the town houses and apartments, white-haired ladies speaking Polish, middle-aged men with bratwurst guts, young professionals, hip-hop kids, junkies, drunks, shopkeepers, and yuppies, forming a loose crowd in front of the small three-story row house. Ford and Abbey mingled with the crowd while the police pushed everyone back, set up barricades, and blocked off the street. Two ambulances arrived, followed by unmarked cars packed with homicide detectives in brown suits, ambulances, a crime-scene van, and finally the local news vans.

Abbey crowded forward with the others, listening to the babble of voices. Somehow, as if by osmosis, the crowd knew everything: two bodies found in the front hall, shot at point-blank range, house tossed. No one had heard anything, no one had noticed strange people, no one had seen cars parked in front.

As the cops bawled at the growing crowd, Ford nodded to Abbey and they pushed toward a gaggle of local women.

"Excuse me," said Ford, "but I'm new to the neighborhood. What happened?"

They turned to him eagerly, all speaking at once, interrupting each other, while Ford encouraged them with wide-eyed interest, adding interjections and expostulations. Once again she was amazed at Ford's chameleon-like ability to play a part and extract information.

"It's Mrs. Corso and her son Mark . . . He'd just come back from California . . . A lovely woman, husband died of a heart attack several years ago . . . Been a struggle since . . . Lived here all their lives . . . A good boy, studied hard, went to Brown University . . . Working at Moto's to earn pocket money . . . Seems like yesterday he was playing stickball in the park . . . A tragedy . . ."

When the information from the ladies had been exhausted, they retreated to the edge of the crowd. Ford's face was dark. "What was his title in the personnel file?" he asked Abbey.

"Senior data analysis technician."

Without another word, Ford flipped open his cell phone and called the NPF switchboard, and in a moment was connected to Derkweiler.

"This is Ford from the Agency," he said in a clipped voice. "This fellow Corso who was working for you—what exactly did he do and why was he fired?"

There was a long silence as Ford listened into his phone. Abbey could just hear the squawk of Derkweiler's voice on the other end. Ford thanked him and hung up.

"Yeah?" Abbey asked.

"He was in charge of processing radar and visual data from the Mars Mapping Orbiter."

"And?"

"He was fired for cause. Derkweiler said he didn't have 'adequate prioritization skills,' became 'obsessed with irrelevant gamma ray data,' refused to follow instructions, and caused a scene at a scientific meeting."

Abbey thought for a moment. "*Obsessed*, huh?"

Ford cleared his throat. "What do you know about gamma rays?"

"That there shouldn't be any from Mars."

52

HARRY BURR SAT in a Greek diner opposite McGolrick Park with a cheeseburger, coffee, and the *Post*, watching the rain run down the plate glass window in ever-changing rivulets. There were mathematical rules in the rivulets, rules that described chaos. It was sort of like the rules that described a hit. Controlled chaos. Because you could never anticipate everything. There was always a surprise: like dear old mother being in the house after Corso told him he was alone. Or being forced to kill Corso.

Always a little surprise.

He refocused his eyes farther away and had a clear view across the corner of McGolrick Park to the row house where he'd done Corso and his mother. The geek had been about to tell him where the drive was, he was pissing his pants with eagerness to tell him—and then the old lady walks in.

He nursed the strong coffee, leafed through the *Post*, and watched the show. He hadn't found the hard drive but he knew the bar where Corso worked and he knew his ex-roommate's address. The hard drive would be at the bar or the friend's place. He'd check out the bar first. If Corso were really smart he might have mailed it back to himself or even stuck it in a safe-deposit box. But he was pretty sure he'd have kept it close by.

He took another sip of coffee, turned the pages of the paper, pretending to read. It had been slow in the restaurant and now it was empty, most of the customers having finished up quickly and gone into the park to check out the show. He kept an eye on the crowd, looking for anyone who might be a relative, a friend—a girlfriend—to whom Corso might also have given the drive.

Two people in the park began attracting his attention, a black girl and a tall, craggy man. They seemed just a little too alert, a little too detached from the rest, to be neighborhood rubberneckers. They were watching, observing. They were involved.

He marked them in his memory in case he saw them again.

53

ABBEY SLID ONTO the bar stool at Moto's, Ford taking the stool beside her. It was an ultra-hip New York bar along the waterfront in Williamsburg, done up in black and white, with faux zebra-striped shoji screens and lots of black-and-white enamel, frosted glass, and chrome. Behind the bar stood a wall of liquor bottles, gleaming in a cool white lighting. The place was empty at four o'clock on a rainy weekday afternoon.

As they took their seats, a bald Japanese man with a brick-like physique and black-rimmed glasses, dressed in traditional garb, came over. He slid his hand along the bar holding a small napkin by the corner, which stopped in front of Abbey. "Lady?"

Abbey hesitated. "Pellegrino."

The hand slid down in front of Ford with another napkin tweaked between thumb and forefinger. "Gentleman?"

"Beefeater martini," said Ford. "Straight up with a twist. Dry."

Sharp nod, and the man began making the drinks with virtuosic efficiency.

"You must be Mr. Moto," Ford said.

"That's me!" Moto's face broke into a dazzling smile as he shook the drink and poured it out with a flourish.

"Name's Wyman Ford. Friend of Mark Corso."

"Welcome! But Mark isn't here. He'll be in tonight. Seven." He poured the drink out with a flourish, flipping the shaker in the air, catching it, rinsing it, and sliding it into a holder.

"I've just come from McGolrick Park," said Ford. "I'm afraid I've got some bad news."

"Yes?" Moto paused, stopped by Ford's look.

"Mark and his mother were killed sometime last night or this morning. Break-in and robbery."

Moto stood immobile, thunderstruck.

"The police are there now."

Moto slapped the bar and slumped, put a hand to his head. "My God, oh my God, this is terrible."

"I'm sorry."

Moto remained silent for a moment, his face covered. "The things these punks do. His mother, too?"

Ford nodded.

"Punks. He was a good kid. Smart. Oh my God." He was deeply shaken.

Ford nodded sympathetically. "Did he bartend for you?"

"Every night since he came back."

"What happened, he lose his job in California?"

Moto waved his hand. "He worked for the National Propulsion Facility. Got laid off. Punks, they catch them?"

"Not yet."

Abbey said, "I hope they fry 'em."

Moto nodded vigorously. His eyes were red.

"Mark was an old friend of mine," said Abbey. "Changed my life."

Ford turned to look at her rather sharply.

"Tutored me in math when I was a freshman in high school, kept my ass from failing. I can't believe it, I saw him just yesterday. He was telling me he'd discovered something important out there, at NPF. Something about gamma rays."

Moto nodded again. "They wouldn't pay his severance so he was going to get back at them. Broke him up, getting fired. I never seen him so broken up."

"How was he going to get back?"

"Said he found something and they were ignoring it. He was going to make them pay. Ah, the poor kid, started to take a few at work. When a bartender starts getting into the sauce . . ." His voice trailed off, the man unwilling to speak against the dead.

"What did he find?" Abbey said.

Moto wiped his leaking eyes. "Jesus. These punks."

"What did he find?" Abbey repeated gently.

"I don't remember. No, wait—he said he found something on Mars. Something emitting rays."

"Rays? Were they gamma rays?"

"I think that's what he said."

"How, exactly, was he going to make them pay?"

"One night, he'd been dipping into the sauce pretty bad, he showed me a hard drive he got from NPF."

"How? What was on it?"

"Said a professor friend of his had stolen it, given it to him. There was something on the drive going to make him famous, change the world, but he wouldn't say what. He wasn't making a lot of sense."

"Where's the drive now?"

Moto shook his head. "No idea. What does it matter? The punks—killed his mother, too . . . Too many punks in this crappy world." A tear trembled on the end of Moto's nose.

There was a rattle and the door chimed. Moto quickly wiped his eyes, blew his nose, and composed himself. A man walked in wearing a gray turtleneck with a tweed jacket and khaki pants, and took a seat at the far end of the bar. Abbey narrowed her eyes; he looked just like her old calculus professor at Princeton.

Moto ducked his head. "Excuse me," he said softly, "got customer." He walked down the bar.

Abbey turned to Ford. "There are those gamma rays again."

"The hard drive is what the killer was looking for when he tossed the house."

"Yeah, and I bet the gamma ray data is *on* that hard drive."

Ford didn't answer. Abbey saw his gaze flicker over to the man at the end of the bar, the new customer, who was leaning over the bar and talking to Moto in a low voice.

The conversation went on for a while and Moto's voice started rising, taking on a querulous tone, still not loud enough to make out individual words. Abbey tried to ignore it, pondering instead the problem of gamma rays from Mars, but she noticed that Ford was staring intently at the man and she wondered what he found so interesting.

"I tell you nothing, you punk!" Moto cried out suddenly.

The stranger said something in a low voice.

"I not answer your questions! Get out or I call police!"

Moto pulled a cell phone out of his pocket and started punching in a number. "I dial nine-one-one!"

The man lashed out at Moto, knocking the cell phone from his hand, at the same time reaching into his jacket and pulling out a large handgun.

"Get your hands above the bar," he said, and then as Moto raised his hands, he swung the gun toward them. "You two— I know your game. Get the fuck over here."

Before Abbey could respond, Ford leapt up and tackled Abbey off her stool, flinging her to the floor behind the curve of the bar. A moment later the man began firing, a strangely high-pitched *kwang!* sound shaking the bar, *kwang! kwang!* and the glass wall behind the bar exploded into fragments. Ford dragged her along the floor. "Get moving! Crawl!"

Kwang! Broken glass and liquor cascaded down around them. Abbey could hear Moto screaming obscenities in the background, the word *punk* rising above all others, and then a series of shots from another gun, much louder. *Boom-boom-boom-boom!* followed by the word, "*Punk!*"

She frantically crawled behind Ford toward the back.

Kwang! Kwang! More glass and bottles came crashing down, with splinters of wood and pieces of insulation and wallboard whirling through the air. Moto roared something in Japanese.

Kwang! Kwang! The bar above their heads exploded into splintered wood, pieces of metal, and chunks of drywall and insulation.

"Get back here!" the man screamed.

Suddenly Moto was staggering along beside them, wheezing and coughing, blood spraying from his mouth. He clutched an enormous revolver in his hands and turned to fire two more shots, which went wild.

Kwang! Kwang! came the response and Moto, struck in the chest, was thrown backward into the shattered wall, one hand clawing away at the shower of broken glass, before crashing to the floor.

Kwang! Kwang! A small bar refrigerator tumbled to the floor in front of her, several bullet holes in it, spraying Freon in a cloud of condensates—and there, duct-taped to the back of it, was a slender, brushed-aluminum case with a stenciled logo of which Abbey saw only the initials NPF.

Almost without thinking she ripped it off, stuffed it into her belt.

"Run!" Ford said, turning around and seizing her by the arm; they bolted through the door, into a little stockroom filled with boxes. Another door stood in the back of the stockroom and Ford slammed through it and they tore down a narrow flight of stairs into a basement corridor, turned a corner, sprinted up another set of stairs, busted through a pair of metal crash doors into a back alley. Still gripping her arm, he hauled her along the street and around the corner to a busy intersection. They paused, gasping for air.

"You all right?" Ford asked.

"I don't know." She gasped, sucking in air, her heart galloping in her chest. "You're bleeding."

He pulled out a handkerchief, wiped his face. "It's nothing. We've got to get out of here." He raised his hand, whistled for a cab.

She shook glass out of her hair, trying to get herself under control. Her hands were trembling. It was horrible to see a man killed in front of her; it reminded her all over again of

Worth lying on the deck, blood welling up from his caved-in head. She leaned over and vomited on the sidewalk.

"Taxi!" Ford yelled, handing her a handkerchief.

She gasped, tried to straighten up, wiped her mouth with the handkerchief.

"Taxi!"

"Aren't we waiting for the police?"

"Absolutely not." He flagged down a cab, opened the door, and shoved her in. "La Guardia," he said to the driver. "Take Grand to Flushing. Stay off the expressway."

"Your call, man. Gonna add ten minutes."

The cab lurched forward into the rush of traffic. "Why are we running?" Abbey almost shouted.

Ford leaned back, his face covered with sweat. A cut on the bridge of his nose was welling blood. "Because we don't know who just tried to kill us."

"Kill *us*? Why?"

Ford shook his head. "I don't know. He was a professional. If our late, brave friend didn't have that cannon behind the bar, we'd all be dead. I've got to get you to safety. I should never have involved you in this."

Abbey shook her head. She could feel it pounding. "This is insane. What the hell's going on?"

"Somebody's looking for that hard drive. From what he said, it seems he might think we have it."

Abbey reached into her jacket and pulled out the aluminum case, duct tape dangling. "We do. This was taped to the back of the fridge."

Ford stared at her. "Did the shooter see you grab that?"

"I think so."

"Shit," said Ford quietly. "*Shit.*"

54

ABBEY SAT CROSS-LEGGED on the rucked-up bed, laptop in front of her, FireWired to the mysterious hard drive. Stenciled on the side was the information:

#785A56H6T 160Tb
CLASSIFIED: DO NOT DUPLICATE
Property of NPF
California Institute of Technology
National Aeronautics and Space Administration

The five-dollar motel clock, screwed to the Formica night table to prevent it from being stolen, glowed midnight. They had gotten into Washington-Dulles at eight and driven for an hour into the middle of nowhere in suburban Virginia to a hotel that Ford seemed to have once used as some kind of safe house. The Watergate it wasn't and Abbey didn't like it at all. There was no room service, the room smelled of old cigar smoke, and the sheets looked suspiciously dirty. Ford had registered without showing an ID and had paid in cash. The sleazy clerk had leered at them, and Abbey had a pretty good idea of the kind of vile thoughts that were going through his mind.

Ford had ordered her pizza and disappeared, refusing to say where he was going, promising to be back before dawn. He had left her with a laptop and the hard drive and told her to break into it.

Easier said than done. She'd been at it for hours with no success. The hard drive was no brand she recognized or could find on the Web; it looked proprietary, very high density. No normal drive this size could possibly hold 160Tb. An NPF special. And password protected. She'd been running through all the obvious candidates, "password," "letmein," "qwerty," "12345678" and a zillion other common combinations, taken from Web sites that listed common passwords. Then she had started in on combinations of Corso's names, birthdate, his mother's names and birthdate, various street and place names near his house, local bars, names of his high school and college teams, mascots, the top bands and hit songs of his teen years—in short, anything she could guess about him from his age and digging up information on him on the Web. But then she considered that she was going about it all wrong. The password would have been created by the mysterious professor who'd stolen it from NPF. She knew nothing about this man, not even his name. How could she possibly guess his password? Or even worse, it might still have an NPF password, which would be well-nigh uncrackable.

She downloaded several programs from the Web and tried a brute-force attack using hashes and rainbow tables, to no avail. It was starting to look hopeless. For all she knew, the drive was locked up with military-level cryptography.

Still, the drive did ask for a password and that was a good sign. There had to be another way to solve the problem. She cracked her sixth Diet Coke and guzzled it. Feeling the need for further sustenance, she rummaged in the pizza box and pried up the last cold, hard piece from the cardboard, scarfed it down, and chased it with more Coke.

She thought about her own passwords and how she chose them. Most of them were dreamed up on the spot, often curse words mingled with the first digits of π or e, two numbers she had memorized to many digits for no good reason back in junior high. Her favorites were E3a1t4s1h5i9t and F2u7c1k8y2o8u. Simple to remember, impossible to crack. For the hell of it she tried both of those, again with no result.

She sipped the Coke, imagining this professor's last day at work, what it would be like to get fired and told to clear out his desk by five. He was pissed enough to steal a hard drive with classified data. As soon as he got home, he would have changed the password on the drive to prevent anyone from NPF being able to access it.

She sighed and tossed the Coke can toward the wastebasket. It bounced off the rim and rolled across the floor, dribbling liquid on the already stained rug. "Fuck," she said out loud. If only she had a joint to relax her, help her mind drift a little, figure things out.

She picked up her earlier train of thought. He would have changed the password when he got home, first thing. She closed her eyes, trying to visualize the scene: this imaginary professor arriving back at some shabby bungalow in Southern California, stained carpeting, wife upstairs complaining about having no money. The guy pulls the hard drive out of his underwear or wherever he'd put it, plugs it into his laptop. He's furious, he's upset, he can't believe what's happened to him. He's not thinking clearly. But he has to change the password—that's essential. So he pulls a new one out of his head and types it in.

What was going through his head *at that very moment?*

Abbey typed in *fuckNPF.* No go.

She recalled the standard rules: a good password should consist of at least eight characters of mixed numbers and letters, lower and uppercase.

She typed in *fuckNPF1.*

Bingo.

55

FORD EASED HIS rented Mercedes down the curving lanes of the posh Washington neighborhood around Quebec Street NW, until he found an evening house party. He parked his car behind the other cars along the curb and stepped out into the warm night, buttoning his suit jacket. Elegant Georgian houses lined the leafy lanes, windows glowing yellow in the summer dark. The party house was more brightly lit than most, and as he walked past it he heard muted jazz trickling into the air. Ambling down the street in his suit, hands in his pockets like a neighbor out for a stroll, he made his way toward Spring Valley Park, a small ribbon of trees alongside a creek. Slipping into the park on a path, he waited until he was sure he was alone and then swiftly cut into the woods, crossed the creek, and approached the backyard of number 16 Hillbrook Lane. It was nearing midnight but he was in luck: there was only one car in the driveway. Lockwood was still at work. No doubt he was very busy these days—and nights.

Circling the property, he could see no evidence it was under active surveillance or being patrolled. The house was mostly dark, with a soft glow in an upper window—the wife, probably, reading in bed. The front stoop light had been left on. Fortunately, the president's science advisor didn't rate Secret Service protection. Still, there might be alarms or motion sensors that turned on lights, the usual suburban stuff, but by moving extremely slowly he was able to minimize the risk of setting one off. He managed to creep close to the driveway undetected.

He chose a hiding place in a grouping of yews alongside the driveway and crouched in the deepest shadow, waiting. It was possible Lockwood might remain at work all night, but he knew the man's habits well enough to know he wouldn't sleep in the office. Eventually he would come home.

Ford waited.

An hour passed. He shifted his position, trying to stretch his cramped legs. The light went out in the top of the house. Another hour passed. Then, a few minutes past two, he saw car lights down the street and a sudden rumble from the automatic garage door as it was activated and began to rise.

A moment later headlights swept into the driveway and a Toyota Highlander eased in and glided past him; Ford ducked from his hiding place and darted behind the car into the garage. He crouched behind the rear bumper, then waited. A moment passed, the left-hand door opened, a tall man got out.

Ford rose and stepped out from behind the car.

Lockwood jumped back, staring at him. "What the hell—?"

Ford smiled, held out his hand. Lockwood stared at it. "You scared the daylights out of me. What are you doing here?"

Keeping the friendly smile, Ford dropped his hand and took a step forward. "Call your man off."

"What are you talking about? What man?"

There was a note in Lockwood's voice that Ford believed. "The man who murdered Mark Corso and tried to kill me and my assistant this afternoon in Brooklyn, shot up a bar, and killed the bartender. You can read about it in the *Times* online. He was from the Agency, I'd guess. Looking for a hard drive."

"Jesus Christ, Wyman, you know I'd never be involved in anything like that. If someone's trying to kill you, it isn't us. You better tell me what the hell you've been doing to provoke this."

Ford stared at Lockwood. The man looked flustered and confused. The operative word was *looked*. After eight years in Washington, people got awfully good at deception.

"I'm still on the case."

Lockwood's lips tightened and he seemed to be collecting his wits. "If someone's after you, it isn't CIA. They're not that crude and you were one of their own. Of course, it might be one of those acronyms at DIA. A black agency. Those sons-of-bitches answer to nobody." Lockwood's face turned red. "I'll look into it immediately and if it's them, I'll take appropriate action. But Wyman, what in *God's* name are you doing? You're assignment is long over. I warned you before to leave this alone. Now I'm telling you: give it up now or I'll bust you. Is that clear?"

"Not clear. Another thing: my assistant is a twenty-year-old student who is completely innocent in this affair."

Lockwood dropped his head and shook it. "If it's one of ours, trust me, I'll find out and make a stink. If I were you, though, I'd consider who else it might be—*outside* the government." He added, "But I've got to ask you again: why the hell are you doing this? You don't have a dog in this race."

"You wouldn't understand. I'm here to get more information. I want you to tell me what's going on, what you know."

"Are you serious? I'm not telling you anything."

"Not even in exchange for the information I've got?"

"Which is?"

"The object didn't fall in the Maine ocean. It struck an island."

Lockwood took a step forward, lowered his voice. "How do you know that?"

"I've been there. I've seen the hole."

"Where?"

"That's the information you'll get—in return."

Lockwood looked at him steadily. "All right. Our physicists think the thing that went through the Earth was a chunk of strange matter. Also known as a strangelet."

"Not a miniature black hole?"

"No."

"What the hell is strange matter?"

"It's a superdense form of matter. Made entirely of quarks. And extremely dangerous. I don't really understand it—look it up if you want more. That's all we really have that's new. So—where's this island?"

"Name is Shark. In Muscongus Bay, about eight miles

offshore. It's a small, barren island—you'll find the crater at the high point."

Lockwood turned, pulled his briefcase out of the car, shut the door. As Ford turned to leave, Lockwood stuck out his hand and grasped his, surprising him. "You keep your head down, be careful. If I find out our people are after you, I swear I'll put a stop to it. But keep in mind it may not be our people . . ."

Ford turned, ducked out the garage door, and crossed the backyard into the darkness of the park. He moved toward the creek where the growth was thickest, crossed the stream, and came out on the path. He emerged on Quebec Street, straightened up, adjusted his suit, and ran his fingers through his hair. He again assumed the air of a neighbor taking the air, walking briskly, ducking into the shadows once to avoid a cruising cop car. Rounding several corners, he came to the end of the street where he'd parked his car, keeping to the shadows of a copse of trees.

Bad news. Peering through a screen of trees he could see two cop cars, light bars going, parked on either side of his rental car, obviously making the plates. Had Lockwood called the cops? Or maybe he'd left it parked too long: the house party was long over and some paranoid suburbanite had called the cops. Unfortunately, he'd rented the Mercedes in his real name—there'd been no choice.

Cursing under his breath, Ford melted back into the darkness and threaded his way through backyards and parkland toward American University and the bus stop on Massachusetts Avenue.

56

ABBEY SCANNED THE files on the 160 terabyte hard drive, sampling a few at random. There were hundreds of thousands, maybe even millions of images of Mars, spectacular, amazing, extraordinary images of craters, volcanoes, canyons, deserts, dune fields, mountains, and plains. The radar images were equally spectacular, slices through the Martian crust. But the gamma ray data were simply tables of numbers and various arcane graphs, impossible to decipher. No images there—just numbers.

One folder caught her eye, titled GAMMA ANOMALY. Inside was a single file with a pps extension—a PowerPoint presentation, and it had been created on the disk only a few weeks before.

Abbey clicked on the pps file. A screen popped up and the presentation began.

The MMO Compton Gamma Ray Scintillator:
An Analysis of Anomalous High-Energy

Gamma Ray Emission Data
Mark Corso, Senior Data Analysis Technician

This was looking good—this must be the presentation that irritated his supervisor, Derkweiler, and got him fired. His obsession. She clicked to the next page, which showed a schematic of the planet Mars with the orbital trajectories of the MMO satellite drawn around it, the multiple orbits overlaid. Then came a graph labeled *Theoretical Signature of Gamma Ray Point Source on the Surface of Mars*, showing a nice, neat square wave pattern. The next one was labeled *Actual Gamma Ray Signature*, which was hard to make out, and then both were combined for what looked to her like a pretty tenuous match, with large error bars and a lot of background noise. There were peaks and valleys, but just barely, and the theoretical and actual signatures looked out of phase.

She clicked again but that was the end.

What did it mean? It was obviously an oral presentation, no written text to go along with it.

She clicked through it again, trying to figure it out. *Theoretical Gamma Ray Point Source on the Surface of Mars.* She thought back to her freshman physics class at Princeton and what she was supposed to know about gamma rays. They were the most energetic part of the electromagnetic spectrum, higher energy than X-rays. Gamma rays, gamma rays . . . Like she told Ford, there shouldn't be any coming from Mars—or should there? She cursed herself for not studying harder.

She Googled gamma rays and read up on them. They were produced only by extremely violent events—supernovae, black holes, neutron stars, matter-antimatter annihilations. In the solar system, she read, gamma rays were naturally created in one way and one way only: when powerful cosmic rays from deep space struck the atmosphere or surface of a planet. Each cosmic ray strike tore apart atoms of matter, producing a flash of gamma radiation. As a result, all the solar system's planets, bathed in a diffuse cosmic ray bombardment from deep space, glowed faintly in gamma rays. The glow was diffuse, planetwide.

She read through several articles but it all came down to the same thing: no known natural process could create a point source of gamma rays in the solar system. No wonder Corso was interested. He'd found a point source for gamma rays on Mars—and no one at NPF believed him. Or was it all in his head? It was hard to tell.

She stared at the computer screen, rubbed her eyes, glanced at the clock. Three A.M. Where was Ford?

She sighed and got up, rummaged in the small fridge. Empty. She had drunk up all her Diet Cokes, eaten the bags of Cheetos and wolfed down the Mars Bars. Maybe she should sleep. But the thought of sleep did not appeal to her. She was too worried about Ford. She began idly looking through the data, and then Googled the Mars Mapping Orbiter. Launched a few years ago, gone into orbit around Mars a year later. An orbiter stuffed with cameras, spectrometers, subsurface radar, and a gamma ray scintillator. Purpose: to map Mars. It carried the most powerful telescope ever launched into deep space, called HiRISE, which was classified but thought to be able to see an object twelve inches across from 130 miles up. In the few months of its operation the MMO had sent more data back to Earth than all previous space missions combined.

And it looked like a lot of that data, maybe all of it, was on the hard disk.

She reordered the folders by date. At the very top was a recent one—very recent—labeled DEIMOS MACHINE.

That sounded intriguing. She opened it and saw there were more than thirty files in it, with names like DEIMOS-BIG and VOLTAIRE-ORIG to VOLTAIRE-DETAIL with a suite of files labeled VOLTAIRE1 through VOLTAIRE33.

She clicked through them all, one after another, staring at the blurry, false-color images, each one clearer than the last. They were all of a strange-looking construction, a hollow cylinder surrounded by spherical projections sitting on a five-sided base. Sunken in dust. It looked like something from a movie set or an art project of some kind.

She began clicking through all the Voltaire images, and finally the bigger files at the top, DEIMOS-BIG and VOLTAIRE-ORIG, staring at the images with growing comprehension. Her heart began to accelerate as it dawned on her just *where* this strange construction had been photographed. She could hardly breathe. This was incredible, unbelievable—

She heard a footfall outside the door, a thump, the click from the lock, and the door swung open.

She sat up. "*You won't believe*—!"

Ford cut her off with a harsh gesture. "Shut that down and pack up. We've got to get out of here. *Now.*"

57

HARRY BURR LOOKED around the lobby of the cheap hotel, smelled something, checked his shoes for dog shit. Nothing—somebody else must've tracked it in. He had had plenty of time to cool off on the trip down to Washington. He'd been *so* close: Christ, he'd even *seen* the girl rip the drive from the back of the fridge on their way out, but they'd jumped in a damn cab before he could catch up to them and finish the job.

They hadn't completely escaped him. He'd been able, with the hack number on the cab's roof and a little help from a friend on the D.C. force, to trace them here. He went up to reception and rang the little bell, and a few moments later a doughy man-boy with a belt three sizes too tight, squeezing a tight ring in his fat, shuffled out from the back. "Help you?"

Burr put on an appropriately agitated air and spoke in a rush. "I certainly hope you can. I'm looking for my daughter. She ran away with a man, a real scumbag, met her in church if you can believe it, the pervert." He paused to take a breath. "I think they spent the night here, got some pictures of them"— he fumbled in his suitcase and pulled out glossies of Ford and the girl—"here they are." He paused, gulping in breath.

Smacking his lips, the man slowly bent over the two photographs and looked. A long silence ensued. Burr resisted the impulse to poke him a twenty, which was clearly what the man was waiting for. Burr didn't like paying for information—you sometimes got bad information that way. People who gave you information from the kindness of their dumb little hearts always gave you good.

Another smacking of the lips. Mr. Phlegmatic raised his eyes and met his. "Daughter?" he asked, with a skeptical note in his voice.

"Adopted," he said. "From Nigeria. My wife couldn't conceive and we wanted to give a little girl in Africa the opportunity. Look, have you seen her? Please help me, she's my little girl. That scumbag met her at our church, he's twice her age and married, too."

The eyes dropped back to the picture and a long sigh came out, like a bag being squeezed. "I seen 'em."

"Really? Where? Are they staying here?"

"I don't want any trouble."

"There won't be, I assure you. I just want to save my daughter."

The clerk nodded, masticating a piece of gum. His face reminded Burr of a cow with its cud. "If there's trouble, I'll have to call the cops."

"Do I look like a man who'd cause trouble? I'm a professor of English literature at Yale for heaven's sake. I just want to talk to her. What room?"

No answer. Now was the time to apply a little cash. He flipped up a fifty, which the clerk pawed out of his hand. With a grunt he went into the back office and came out with the register. He opened it on the desk and turned it around, pointing with a fat finger. *Mr. and Mrs. Morton.*

"Mr. and Mrs. Morton? They took only one room? Number one-fifty-five?"

The man nodded.

Harry Burr made the face of a father thinking about something he'd rather not think about. "What about ID, didn't they have to show ID?"

"Sometimes we forget to ask," he said lamely.

Burr checked the map of the motel and noted that room 155 was in the motel's back wing, first floor. It was a cheap motel, all the rooms with separate front entrances and no back doors. So much the better.

He straightened up. "Thank you, thank you very much."

"No noise or I call the cops."

"Don't worry." Burr went out to his idling car, pulled out of the drive-through, reached in the glove compartment, and felt the reassuring grip of the Israeli Desert Eagle .44 magnum semiautomatic, his working firearm. He grasped the suppressor and affixed it to the muzzle and laid it on the seat next to him as he eased the car around to the back of the motel.

There wouldn't be any noise if Burr could help it.

58

"OUT THE WINDOW? Are you nuts?" Abbey stood in the door to the bathroom, hands on her hips.

Ford ignored her. He pulled open the cheap sliding aluminum window in the bathroom. He shoved Abbey's suitcase out, pushed out his own. "Now you."

"This is crazy." But Abbey obeyed, ducking her head out and wiggling through the window. Ford handed her the laptop and drive and then he squeezed out. They were behind the motel. There was a weedy service drive, a chainlink fence, a drainage ditch, and then a large parking lot surrounding a frowzy mall. The sky was gray and a light drizzle fell.

Abbey picked up her suitcase. "What now? Call a cab?"

"To the mall."

"It isn't open yet."

"We're not shopping. Just follow me."

"Why are we running?" Abbey asked. "What've you done?"

"Later."

Abbey followed Ford across the driveway. He tossed their suitcases and his briefcase over the fence. "Go."

"This is ridiculous." Abbey grabbed the chain links and climbed over, dropping down the other side. Ford scrambled up and over.

"Keep up."

He took off at a jog across a trash-strewn strip of grass, jumped the drainage ditch, and headed into the parking lot. Abbey heard a faint squealing of tires and turned to see a yellow New Beetle tearing down the service road behind the motel. It screeched to a halt, the door burst open, and a man jumped out, kneeling.

Ford grabbed her arm and yanked her behind a parked car. There was a *thunk* and the side windows blew out in a spray of glass.

"Jesus Christ!"

Another thunk as a round punched into the car.

"Just *stay down*. Forget the suitcases. Follow me."

Ford took off at a crouch, scuttling between the parked cars. After a moment Abbey heard another squeal of rubber and the Beetle had taken off. She could see it heading at high speed for the main road.

"He's coming around into the parking lot here," Ford said. "Run, and I mean *run*."

He sprinted toward the only section of the parking lot where there were cars, his jacket flapping behind him, still carrying his briefcase. Abbey ran to keep up. She glanced over her right shoulder and could see the yellow car whipping along the main road, then the screech of tires as it slewed into the mall parking lot and came bombing toward them.

"Get down."

They crouched behind a battered old Ford pickup and Ford immediately began to work on the lock. In a moment he had the door open. "Crawl in, stay down."

Abbey obeyed, crawling into the cab and staying below the window. Ford got in beside her, shoved the briefcase behind the seat, and popped the glove compartment. He pulled out a screwdriver, pried off the cover and panel around the ignition tumbler, exposing a panel clipped to the rear. He stuck the screwdriver into the ignition switch, turned it—and the car fired up.

Abbey lay crouching on the floor in front of the seat, head down.

"All right," said Ford. "Hold on and keep on the floor."

She heard the engine roar, the floor vibrating, and the truck shot out, rolling Abbey back. There was a screech of rubber as the truck cornered and another high-pitched roar as Ford floored it.

She heard the *pop pop* of gunfire, felt the truck swerve and go into a powerslide, then spin back in a fishtail and continue on.

"Jesus," she cried, trying to keep from being thrown about.

"Sorry."

Another distant *pop pop*.

With a tearing screech of rubber and a sickening sideways slide, the truck took a sudden bump that threw it up, airborne for a moment, then a violent bottoming out. Now the truck was pounding and shaking along what was either a bad dirt road or a field, lurching up and down, rattling hard, stuff jouncing up and around her.

"You can get up now."

Bracing herself, Abbey lurched back up and into the seat. Sure enough, the truck was tearing across an abandoned field toward a set of railroad tracks. Ford turned and raced parallel to the tracks, following an old tractor path, and after half a mile came to a raised road crossing; he gunned it up onto the roadbed, skidded sideways, crossed the tracks, and bombed down the dirt road, fifty, sixty, seventy miles an hour.

"Take a look, Abbey, make sure we lost him."

Abbey turned. There was nothing but the dirt road, the big field full of stubble, the looping tracks of the truck, and in the far distance, a broken fence and the road they had just come from. Abbey thought she could just see the yellow spot of the Beetle, by the side of the road.

"He's gone."

"Excellent." Ford slowed down and they soon came to a paved road. Ford turned onto it.

"Jesus Christ," she said, flicking an old french fry from her hair. She looked around at the truck for the first time. It was an old-model pickup and it stank of stale cigarette smoke and sour milk. She was filthy from the car floor, which was heaped with food trash and dirt. They passed a sign for the interstate and soon they were humming along.

"I don't like this," Abbey said. "I don't like this at all."

"I'm truly sorry, Abbey. I'm getting you to a safe place, right now."

"I quit. This job sucks. I want to go home."

"Not yet. I'm sorry."

"Did we just steal this truck? Or is that a stupid question?"

"Yes to both."

She shook her head and wiped her eyes, which had unaccountably teared up. "This is like a bad movie."

"Yes."

"So where are we going?"

"I haven't decided yet. I'm taking you someplace where you'll be absolutely safe and leaving you there until I can fix this problem."

Abbey sat back, rummaged in the glove compartment, found some tissue, and blew her nose. "I had my iPod in that suitcase."

"That's the least of your worries."

"But all my songs!"

"I've got to get you into a safe location. I'm thinking of a cabin in New Mexico I've used in the past . . ."

"New Mexico? In a stolen car? We'll never make it."

"You have a better idea?"

"Yes, as a matter of fact. My friend Jackie's family owns an island off the coast of Maine with a fishing shack on it. Got a solar panel, water from the roof—perfect place to go to ground."

The car hummed along the interstate. "And Jackie?"

"She'll come with us. She's cool. And she knows boats and the sea like no one else."

Ford moved over and took an exit. "So how do we get to this fishing shack?"

"Borrow my father's boat and go at night."

"That just might work," said Ford. "You understand, Abbey, I'm going to leave you there for a while until I straighten this mess out. I can't stay. You'll have to fend for yourselves."

"I'm all for hiding. Getting shot at really sucks."

"Good. Then we're going to Maine."

"I didn't have a chance to tell you," Abbey said, taking a deep breath. "I made a pretty wild discovery on that NPF drive."

Ford looked astonished. "How did you break into it?"

"I guessed the password. You aren't going to believe this—there are pictures on that drive of something on Deimos. Something unnatural. And very old. Corso labeled it the DEIMOS MACHINE."

Ford stared at her. "Come now."

" 'Come now' yourself. There are a whole suite of images of it. At the bottom of a crater called Voltaire, hidden in the shadows, barely visible. A machine of some kind. No shit."

"It could be a natural geological feature. Or a scientific prank."

"No way."

Ford gazed at her, his pale blue eyes probing. "What does it look like?"

"A round, rimlike thing, like a cylinder, or maybe the opening to a tunnel. With some spheres attached to it. Half-buried in dust."

Ford stared at her. "Wait. Are you saying this is something *alien*?"

"That's exactly what I'm saying."

59

HARRY BURR CRUISED into the mall, swinging his arms, strolling along with his face arranged into a suitable slack-jawed shopper expression. He checked a color-coded mall map and saw where he needed to go. It was a downscale mall, shabby, 20 percent of the storefronts vacant. The AC was cranked up. They needed the Siberian temperatures, Burr figured, to keep the natives cool. Wouldn't want all these fat ones to stroke out before they'd unloaded their dollars.

He finally found what he was looking for in a sign that said MALL SECURITY. The door was shut. Burr knocked, waited, then tried the knob. Locked. He looked around: not a security man in sight.

At this, irritation rose up like a hiccup of bile in the back of his throat. This was turning into a real balls-up. Surely he wasn't losing his touch. His research revealed that Ford was ex-CIA and somehow the fucker had sniffed him out back at the bar, when that damn Jap-in-the-box bartender popped up with a cannon. Lucky for him the man couldn't shoot worth a shit, probably never fired a .45 before in his life. Somehow Ford had also eluded him at the motel. Burr sure was earning his money on this one.

Burr tried to push down his anger. He prided himself on being a cheerful fellow by nature, not given to brooding or vengeful feelings. That was another of his strengths. He didn't allow himself to get emotionally involved in what was essentially the straightforward business of killing for money. Or so he told himself. He couldn't let this one become personal.

He looked around at the mall, rapidly filling with morning shoppers. Good luck finding the door shakers in this place. Instead of wasting fruitless hours searching the entire mall for security, better to have security come to him. The mountain to Mohammed, so to speak. Spying a CD World he strolled in, picked out a mark in the heavy metal section, and began browsing nearby. The mark was perfect: a pimply faced goth with purple hair, smelling like hemp, carrying a shopping bag. Burr edged toward him, plucked up a CD by a group called Spineshank, turned and walked past the goth, bumping him gently as he went by.

"Excuse me."

The goth grunted something unintelligible and went back to flipping through the CDs. Moving toward the cash registers, Burr waited for the goth to finish browsing and then followed him toward the exit. As soon as the goth hit the security gates the alarms began to whoop, and the freak stood there like a deer caught in the headlights, his kohl-rimmed eyes wide with a *who me?* expression.

And here came the mountain to Mohammad, two mountains in fact, huffing and jingling. They surrounded the goth and searched his bag, finding the Spineshank CD. Overriding his ineffectual and utterly unbelievable protests that the CD must've fallen in the bag by accident, they began to hammer him with questions like the tough guys they were, giving him the third degree.

Harry Burr walked over, flashed a shield he carried—formerly in the possession of a D.C. state police officer who had allowed himself to be pickpocketed during a traffic stop. "Officer Wilson?" he asked the door shaker in charge, reading his name off the badge.

"Yes?"

Burr folded away the shield. "They told me you were the man to ask for."

"They did?"

"It's about the car theft this morning. I'm the D.C.-Virginia liaison officer, Undercover Investigations Division, Motor Vehicles. Name's Lieutenant Moore." Offered his hand. Wilson took it.

"Talk in private, Officer?"

"Certainly." Burr moved Wilson away from the increasingly shrill protests of the kid, who was now being cuffed. Burr pulled out a little notebook, licked his finger, turned the pages. "I won't take up but a minute—just need to get a few details."

"The file's back in the office. We forwarded the information to the state police already."

Burr rolled his eyes in disgust at the bureaucracy. "We're a bit top-heavy these days. Could take a week for the file to rise to the surface—or you could help me out right now." A wink. "What say?"

"Sure thing, Lieutenant. Glad to help."

The office was just what Burr expected, a windowless cell smelling of Mennen. Wilson, the glorified door shaker, sat behind the desk, pulled open a drawer, and took out a file.

"I need the usual," said Burr, "car, license plate, witnesses . . . whatever you got."

"No witnesses, Lieutenant," said Wilson, his face firmly set as befitted the seriousness of the crime. "It was a white Ford F150 king cab pickup, 1985 model, Virginia license . . ." He reeled off the details in full-throated cop-speak, while Burr jotted it down.

"We'll recover the vehicle; we always do," said Wilson. "Some kids on a joyride. No chop shop would be interested in an old-model pickup like that."

"I have no doubt you will attain a successful conclusion, Officer," said Burr, rapping his gold pencil on the notebook and tucking it away. He held out his hand. "Don't bother contacting me, I'll keep in touch with you myself, by phone. When that pickup resurfaces, I'd sure like to know. Got a card?"

Wilson passed him his card.

"Much obliged, Officer." He hesitated. "Might be best— for diplomacy's sake, you understand—not to mention my visit to the D.C. or Virginia state police HQs. They don't like it when someone from UID makes an end run around their wall of bureaucracy." Again he flashed Wilson a knowing wink.

"Sure thing," said Wilson, with a grin.

Burr left the mall and got back into his Beetle. God, it was hot, especially after the frigid air in the mall. Ford and the girl had almost certainly gone to ground. Now he could do nothing except cool his ass waiting for the stolen vehicle to turn up. Slapping the steering wheel in frustration, Harry Burr muttered a low curse. This was one fucked-up situation. Maybe this time he would make an exception—and take pleasure in the kill.

60

A WARM SUMMER breeze was blowing off Great Salt Bay as Abbey darted up to the door to an old building in downtown Damariscotta, firescape looming above her, framed against a starry sky. She buzzed Jackie's apartment, giving the button a quatrain of long, insistent pushes. A moment later a muffled voice said, "What the fuck?"

"It's me, Abbey. Let me in."

The buzzer went off and Abbey pushed open the door and mounted the rickety stairs. They had ditched the stolen truck in the parking lot of a depressed mini-mall along Route 1, where it seemed unlikely to be noted, at least for a while, and had hiked two miles through the woods and on back roads to get to Damariscotta.

She arrived at the apartment door. "Jackie?"

She heard a querulous grunt. "Go away."

"Wake up, it's important!"

A groan. The sound of feet hitting the floor. The locks turned and Jackie opened the door. She stood squinting in a nightgown, her hair disheveled. "It's two in the frigging morning."

Abbey pushed her way in and shut the door. "I need your help."

Jackie stared at her. A sigh. "God, you in trouble again?"

"Big time."

"Why am I not surprised?"

ROUND POND HARBOR lay black under the night sky, the water lapping around the oak pylons. Abbey paused at the top of the pier. She could see *Marea II* on its mooring about fifty yards off. It was three o'clock, dark as a tomb, Moon obscured by clouds, about half an hour before the lobstermen normally began arriving. Close enough to the normal hour that a boat firing up and heading out would not be noted as anything special.

Jackie Spann and Wyman Ford stood on the dock behind her, Ford with his ubiquitous briefcase in hand. "Wait here. I'll bring the boat around to the floating dock, then you come down and get in fast."

Abbey untied her father's dinghy, unshipped the oars. As she rowed out to the waiting boat, she hoped her father wasn't up yet. She had left a short note, but there was no way of knowing how he would react to her "borrowing" his boat again for some unspecified purpose—and then asking him to lie about it.

She pulled hard. The splashing of the oars and the tapping of rigging against the masts of the sailboats at anchor were the only sounds in the quiet harbor. Even the gulls were sleeping. She arrived at the *Marea II*, boarded, and started the engine, the sudden rumble shattering the peace of the summer night. She was pretty sure no one would notice. Boat noise, even in the middle of the night, was a way of life in a working harbor.

She eased it into the floating dock, not even bothering to bring it to a full halt as it drifted along. Jackie and Ford tossed in their supplies and hopped in, and she turned the wheel and headed out of the harbor, past the blinking light on the can marking the channel, into the sound.

"So," said Jackie, settling down in a seat in the pilothouse and turning to Ford with a grin. "Who are you and what the hell's going on?"

61

MABEL FORTIER LEFT the Wand-o-Matic Laundromat with her laundry in a wire basket, wheeling it across the parking lot toward her car. At the far end of the parking lot she could see the usual group of scruffy kids that hung out there with their souped-up cars, talking on their cell phones, cursing, drinking beer, smoking cigarettes, and throwing the butts on the ground.

Once again Mabel tried to tell herself that these were nice boys letting off steam. She had even taught some of them in the first grade before she retired. They were such nice little kids then. What had happened? She shook her head; all teenagers smoked these days, and swearing today wasn't what it used to be in her time.

Trying to keep these charitable thoughts in her mind, she stacked the laundry on the backseat, folded up the basket, and put it in her trunk. In the background she heard a fresh screech of tires as another car arrived at the teen gathering. She looked up and saw a metallic blue Camaro—the Hinton boy's car—tearing into the far end of the parking lot at a high rate of speed, announcing its arrival with a blaring horn. He was driving too fast, way too fast. The car made a turn with a squeal of rubber and then she heard a *smack!* and the grinding sound of metal against metal as bits of plastic went skittering across the macadam. The fool in the Camaro had taken the corner too sharply and clipped the back end of a white pickup truck parked in front of a row of vacant storefronts at the far end.

She watched as the fellow driving the Camaro halted, got out, and bent down to examine the three-foot-long gouge in the side of his car. Didn't even bother to look at the damage to the pickup, with its taillight obliterated, the bumper pulled halfway off. She could hear his terrible curses all the way across the lot, answered by laughs and jeering from the crowd of youths. Then he got back in the Camaro and roared out of the parking lot with another screech of tires.

Mabel Fortier stared, shocked. The boy had just left the scene of an accident. And now the other boys were climbing into their cars and leaving, all of them "beating a retreat" before the police arrived.

It was outrageous. Outrageous. The Hinton boy had done thousands of dollars' worth of damage to somebody's vehicle and driven off, just like that.

This was the last straw. They wouldn't get away with it. Enough was enough. Mabel Fortier took out her cell phone and grimly dialed the police.

62

ABBEY AWOKE IN the shack to the smell of bacon and eggs on the woodstove, the sun streaming in the windows, the lapping sound of water on the cobbled beach outside. As she came into the main room, Ford was at the kitchen table, hunched over the laptop connected to the NPF drive. She could see he was paging through the pictures.

"About time!" Jackie cried from the stove. "It's the crack of noon." She pushed a coffee cup into her hands, prepared just the way she liked it, with tons of cream and sugar.

"Come outside and have breakfast."

With a glance at Ford, Abbey left the shack and walked over to a weather-beaten picnic table set up in front. A long unruly meadow sloped down to a cobbled beach. Beyond lay a scattering of spruce-clad islands with a few openings among them showing distant views of the sea horizon.

Jackie laid the breakfast in front of her and took a seat with her own cup of coffee.

"Where's the *Marea*?" Abbey asked, tucking into the bacon and fried eggs. She was starving.

"I moved her to the cove behind the island," Jackie said.

Abbey drank her coffee, letting her mind wake up, staring out to sea. Their island, Little Green, was tucked amidst a swarm of thirty islands, separated from the mainland by the Muscle Ridge Channel. To the south lay Muscongus Bay and to the north Penobscot Bay. It was a perfect hiding place, tucked in the middle, invisible from both sea and land, and extremely well protected from the weather. As far as she knew, no one had noted their departure from Round Pond, no one knew where they were going. Not even her father. Here they were safe. But safe from what? That was the question.

She mopped up the last of her eggs with a piece of bread and refilled her coffee from the pot sitting on the table. The ocean was calm, an easy swell falling on the rocks and withdrawing in a regular cadence. Seagulls cried overhead and a distant lobster boat chugged among the islands.

Ford came out, holding a coffee cup, and eased his lanky frame down.

"Morning!" said Jackie, giving him a big grin. "Sleep well, Mr. Ford?"

"Never better." He took a long sip of his coffee and stared out to sea.

Abbey said, "I see you've been looking over those images of Deimos."

"Yes."

"What do you think?"

Ford didn't answer right away, gazing at her steadily with

pale blue eyes. He spoke slowly, in a low voice. "I think this is an extraordinary discovery."

Abbey nodded.

"It's unquestionably alien and quite likely the source of those stray gamma rays. It must be old to have gotten so pitted and worn."

"I told you it was real."

He shook his head slowly. "This is the answer to one of the deepest mysteries in the cosmos. By finding that alien construction, now we know we're not alone. My mind is just reeling."

Abbey stared at him. "You don't get it, do you?"

"What do you mean?"

She shook her head. " 'Alien construction', my ass. That's a *weapon*. And it just fired on the Earth."

63

"A . . . WEAPON," Ford repeated slowly.

Abbey glanced over at Jackie, who had been listening in silence.

"Exactly."

Ford passed his hand over his curly hair. "And what makes you think this?"

" '*When you have eliminated the impossible—.*' "

"I know the quote," said Ford.

"Elementary, my dear Watson. A: the thing looks like a gun. B: it fired a miniature black hole that went through the Earth."

Ford leaned back. "That doesn't quite fit the facts. Even if it did 'fire' that thing and intended to destroy the Earth, it failed. And it hasn't tried again. If it's a weapon, it seems to have given up."

"How do you know it gave up? Maybe there's another shot coming."

Ford shook his head. "So these aggressive aliens . . . are they around somewhere? Living inside Deimos?"

Abbey snorted. "The aliens are long gone."

"Gone? How do you know?"

"Look at the picture. The thing's a derelict, all drifted up with dust and pitted. Nobody's taking care of it. Maybe the aliens left the weapon and split."

"What for?"

"Who knows? Not long before that thing took a potshot at us, the MMO made a close pass of Deimos, hitting it with radar and taking pictures. Maybe that woke it up. Maybe the aliens passed by here millions of years ago, saw a habitable planet and left a weapon to take care of any future technological civilizations that might challenge them. Hell, there could be thousands, millions of these weapons seeded throughout the galaxy."

"I hope you won't be offended if I express a candid opinion on your theories."

Abbey crossed her arms and waited.

"Great *Twilight Zone* plots."

"You think about it," Abbey said, "and see if you don't come to the same conclusion."

Ford sighed. "I will. But here's something you'll find interesting: according to my government sources, it wasn't a miniature black hole. It was a chunk of strange matter, or more precisely, an object known as a strangelet."

"What the heck's that?"

"A form of superdense matter," said Ford, "a bunch of particles called quarks all jammed together into a degenerate state . . . They think some apparent neutron stars might actually be strange stars or quark stars—made out of strange matter instead. You ever read Kurt Vonnegut?"

"Oh yeah," said Abbey, "I love his books."

"Remember that substance he called Ice-nine, from the story *Cat's Cradle*? It was a special kind of ice that when it came in contact with normal water, it converted it to ice at room temperature."

"I remember that."

"Strange matter is like that. When it comes in contact with normal matter, it starts converting it, gobbling it up, turning it into strange matter. Problem is, strange matter is so dense that whatever it touches gets crushed into almost nothing. If the Earth turned into strange matter, it would crush down to the size of an orange."

"Ouch."

"What's worse, the process is unstable. The Earth would then explode with a force so great that it would rip the outer layers off the sun and disrupt the solar system. It might even convert the sun to strange matter, resulting in a truly immense explosion. What's odd is that a tiny strangelet could blow right through the Earth pretty much unnoticed, as long as it was going fast enough. It wouldn't convert much matter and just continue merrily on its way, the Earth none the worse. If it were going slower and got caught inside the Earth, well, good-bye solar system."

"Why didn't it blow a bigger exit hole, cause a volcano or some kind of eruption?"

"Good question. A strangelet wouldn't build up a shock-wave because it's absorbing all the matter it touches. It gobbles up matter as it goes along, leaving a tunnel in a vacuum which would immediately be sealed up behind by geologic pressure as it passed through. The only evidence of its passage would be a small entrance hole, a larger exit hole, and an unusual seismic signature."

Abbey whistled. "All this just reinforces my theory. A strangelet would be the ultimate weapon—think about it."

He rose, setting down the cup. "I don't know how much they know of this in Washington but I've got to get down there with that drive. I'll have to leave you here. I don't dare put you in protective custody at the CIA or even the local police, because I don't know who's after us. There's a possibility we're dealing with a rogue agency in our own government."

"But what about you? You go to Washington, they might just send you to Guantanamo or something."

"I've no choice. Because I think you may be right—that thing could be a weapon. The fate of the Earth might be at stake."

Abbey nodded.

"This island's as safe as any place for you now. Just lie low and I'll be back in contact with you in five days or less. You'll be okay?"

"Don't worry, we'll be fine."

He turned and grasped her arms. "You'll take me to the mainland this evening, at dusk, when the boat is less likely to be spotted." He paused, murmured, "A weapon . . . that's exactly what it is."

64

HARRY BURR PARKED his New Beetle in front of the Wand-o-Matic Laundromat and stepped out of the car. It was one of those shabby mini-malls with a dozen storefronts, half of them empty, no security, a hangout for teen punks. A good place to ditch a stolen car; no security, few shoppers, and lots of empty storefronts. It might have been weeks before someone finally noticed. It was Ford's bad luck—and Burr's good—that some dumb-ass kid doing donuts had clipped the truck.

He strolled around the parking lot, getting a feel for the place. The white pickup was gone, of course, hauled off. The question was, where had Ford and the girl gone from here? Thanks to the Web he had a pretty good idea of where to find out. The girl was from these parts and her father lived nearby. Burr figured he was as good a place as any to start.

He gave a little laugh and lit up an American Spirit, inhaling deeply. Things seemed to be falling his way after all.

He finished the cigarette and tossed it on the ground,

got back in the Beetle. The town of Round Pond—what a jerkwater name!—could be found about twelve miles down the road, according to his GPS. He was pretty sure good old George Straw could tell him something useful about his daughter's whereabouts.

The road to Round Pond wound this way and that through woods and past farms until a few glimpses of a harbor appeared on the right, along with a bunch of old white houses. As he pulled into a small farmhouse set back from the harbor, the GPS informed him, in a clipped British accent, that he had arrived at his destination. He parked behind a red pickup truck. Shoving the Desert Eagle into a briefcase, he exited the car and went up on the porch, rang the doorbell.

He heard heavy footfalls and soon the door opened. You could tell this was country, he thought, when the dumb-asses opened the door without even bothering to check who it was. Burr was surprised to find a white man standing at the door, a truculent-looking fellow with a weatherbeaten face and pale blue eyes, dressed in a checked shirt, suspenders, and jeans. Girl must've been adopted—or maybe it was a mixed marriage.

"What can I do for you?" he said, in a friendly way.

He held up his shield. "Mr. George Straw?"

"Yes?"

"My name is Lieutenant Moore of D.C. police, homicide division. I wonder if I could take up a minute of your time."

The face shut down. "What's it about, Officer?"

Burr liked that "officer" bit. It showed the man had respect for the law.

"It's about your daughter, Abbey."

The shut-down look vanished and Straw's face betrayed the fear of a father for his child. Good. "What about my daughter? Is she okay?"

Burr adopted a deep, concerned tone. "May I come in?"

Straw stepped away from the door. He was already shaking. "Yes. Please."

He followed Straw into the living room and took a seat, unbidden.

"My daughter, is she all right?" Straw asked again.

Instead of answering, Burr let an excruciating amount of time pass and then said: "Mr. Straw, what I have to say is going to be difficult for you to hear, but I need your help. This is all strictly confidential, and you'll soon understand why."

Straw's face had lost all its color. But he held his composure.

"I'm in charge of a case involving a serial killer who's preyed on young women for years, mostly in the D.C. area but also in parts of New England. His name is Wyman Ford. He's very polished. He's good. He's got a lot of money and dresses well."

"Ford? *Wyman Ford*? My daughter just took a job with a man by that name!" He rose from his chair.

"I know that. Let me finish. What this particular perpetrator does is persuade young ladies to accept a job as his assistant. The employment is vague but involves some sort of government secrecy or classified work. He keeps them around for several weeks and then he kills them."

"Good God, he's got my daughter!"

"We believe she's fine. She's not in immediate danger. But we have to find her. And we have to do it quickly and quietly. When this killer has the slightest inkling someone's on to him, he kills and disappears. It's happened to me before. So we've got to be absolutely quiet and cool and move with exceeding care."

"Oh my God, my *God*!" Straw paced the room, fists clenched, knuckles white. "That man gave her a job about a week ago. She went off to Washington. Then they came back and borrowed my boat. I'll kill him, the bastard."

Pay dirt. "Borrowed your boat? Where did they go?"

"I don't know! They took it and left me a note. I didn't actually see her. Oh my God." He clutched his head in his hands.

"May I see the note?"

Straw rushed into the kitchen and came back out with a piece of paper, handing it to Burr.

Dear Dad,

I don't quite know how to write this but I've borrowed your boat. Again. I'm really sorry. I know it doesn't sound good, but believe me it's necessary. I can't tell you where we're going but I should be back in a week or two, I hope. I'll be out of cell range but if I get a chance I'll give you a call. I'm fine, everything's fine, don't worry. Please don't tell anyone we're on the boat. I'll take good care of it.

Love,
Abbey

He read the note with a furrowed brow, placed it on the side table. "That's him, all right. Do you have any guesses as to where they might have gone, or why?"

Straw's face was contorted as he tried to speak. "North.

She would have gone north. Fewer people, more islands. They have to be somewhat offshore, out in the islands, because she said they've got no cell reception. Close to shore the phones work."

"But why? What are they doing with the boat?"

"God only knows—you probably have a better idea than me!"

Burr checked himself.

"Oh my God, I can't lose my daughter!" His voice cracked. "I can't! I already lost my wife—!" He made a choking sound, coughed, trembled violently.

Burr rose and grasped his arm. "Mr. Straw, you've got to get ahold of yourself."

Straw nodded, swallowed.

"You've got to trust me that I know what I'm doing. Can you do that?"

Straw nodded dumbly.

"Here's what we're going to do. You're going to engage us another boat—a really good one. You're going to captain it, and we'll go out there and find her together."

"Bullshit! We've got to call the Coast Guard, get some spotter planes in the air—"

"*Absolutely not.*"

He paused, letting Straw master himself.

"If our man gets even the *slightest* idea we're looking for him, it's over. He'll see the Coast Guard coming a mile away, believe me, and the same goes for spotter planes flying overhead. He's smart, he's cunning, he's always got his radar on. We can't even risk telling the local police. They're not equipped to handle this. We have a much better chance of finding them, just the two of us, with your knowledge of the coast and my knowledge of criminal behavior. When we do find them, that's when we call in the cavalry. Big time. We won't go in alone. But for now, it's just you and me. You understand? And don't worry about the cost—the government will pay."

Straw nodded. The man was breathing fast. Amazing how people just about lost their minds when it came to their children's safety. Burr was awfully glad he'd never had kids.

"All right," said Burr, grasping his arm. "Let's get going."

Straw nodded, his face slick with sweat. "This is a small town," he managed to say, "rumors go around fast. I better hire the boat while you stay out of sight. We don't have a moment to lose."

"You and I are on the same wavelength now, Mr. Straw," said Burr. "Don't worry: we'll find your daughter, I promise."

65

HARRY BURR STOOD on the deck of the *Halcyon*, watching Straw at the helm, guiding the boat at full speed through the swell. Lacking time, they had had to rent a larger, slower boat than Burr wanted, but at least it had the advantage of being seaworthy. After leaving the dock at noon, they had followed weather reports over the VHF radio, broadcasting small-craft warnings about an approaching storm. Burr wasn't sure whether a thirty-eight-foot Downeaster yacht like the *Halcyon*, powered by twin diesels, qualified as a small craft, but he wasn't particularly eager to test the idea.

"Can't make the boat go any faster, can you?"

"I'm already pushing the engine more than I should," said Straw.

He raised a pair of binoculars for the millionth time and scanned the surrounding ocean and islands. Burr was surprised how many islands there were—dozens, maybe hundreds, not to mention rocks and reefs. Some of them were inhabited and a couple had commercial installations on them, but most were deserted. Burr shifted his gaze to the electronic chartplotter in the well-equipped pilothouse. Growing up in Greenwich, he'd spent a lot of time around boats and felt comfortable with them. Still, it had been a while. He carefully observed Straw at the helm so that he could be sure of operating the boat properly once the kill was over and he was heading back alone. The storm would give him a good excuse to explain the missing lobsterman.

"As soon as we round the tip of that island," said Straw, "we'll have a view across the northern reach of Muscongus Bay. Get out the binocs and be ready to look."

"We're passing a lot of islands here. How do you know they're not in a cove somewhere?"

"We don't. We search open water first, then come back looking into coves."

"Makes sense."

Straw was motivated, that was for sure. His hands gripped the wheel, knuckles white, his narrow eyes constantly darting around, seeking other boats. He looked on the verge of cracking.

"We still have plenty of time," said Burr, trying to keep his voice calm. "Don't worry. As long as they're out on the water, he won't strike. He'll need her to operate the boat."

"I know every harbor, cove, and gunkhole from here to Isle au Haut and I swear we're going to search every one of 'em until we find her."

"We'll find her."

"Damn straight we will."

Burr plucked a pack from his pocket and shook out a cigarette. The man was becoming tiresome. "Mind if I smoke?"

Straw looked at him. His eyes were haggard, bloodshot.

Poor fellow was thinking too much. "Smoke at the stern, away from the engine. Bring your binocs and keep looking."

Burr went to the taffrail and lit up. They were rounding the point of the island and soon another vast expanse of ocean appeared to the northeast, dotted with islands. The late-afternoon sun shimmered in a golden swath across the blue water. There were several lobster boats moving to and fro, hauling their traps. He raised the binoculars and examined each one in turn.

None were the *Marea II*.

He inhaled again and wondered just what Ford and the girl were up to, why they had run to sea like this. Some kind of espionage? As usual, he didn't know the real identity of his clients nor why they wanted the hard disk, which made it impossible to understand why Ford and the girl went from Brooklyn to Washington, stole a car, and drove to Maine and took a boat out on the water. All he knew was that Ford had a hard drive worth two hundred grand. And that was all he really needed to know.

66

ABBEY PULLED THE *Marea II* up to the tiny floating dock at the Owls Head Harbor. Jackie hopped off and tied up. The harbor was deserted, a few boats at their moorings, gulls watching them from the tops of the pilings. The sun had just set and the sky was suffused with wispy orange clouds of the kind her father called mare's tails, which signified bad weather. The tiny harbor was deserted, only half a dozen boats on their moorings.

Wyman Ford picked up his briefcase and stepped onto the creaking dock, smoothing down his rumpled suit and trying to comb his hair into place with his fingers.

"Forget it, you still look like you're coming off a drunk," said Abbey, with a laugh. "Are you going to steal another car?"

"I'm hoping that won't be necessary. Which way is the town?"

"Just follow the road. Can't miss it. You better get going, storm's coming."

"How do you know?"

She glanced up. "Sky."

"Stay on the island until you hear back from me. If you haven't heard anything in five days, it means I've been taken into custody. In that case, take the boat close enough to the mainland to get cell reception and call this number." He handed her a piece of paper. "He'll help you." He paused. "I've decided to go public with this information."

"The shit'll really hit the fan if you do that."

"It's the only way. The world's got to know." Ford took Abbey's shoulder in an affectionate grip, peering down at her from his massive frame, his unruly black hair sticking out every which way, his gray eyes steady. "Promise me you'll stay on the island and lie low. Don't go tooling around in the boat. You've got enough supplies to last you a week."

"Will do." He squeezed her shoulder. "Good luck, Abbey. You've been a great assistant. Sorry I got you mixed up in this."

Abbey snorted. "No problem, I enjoy stealing cars and getting shot at."

He turned and she watched him stride up the gangplank, walk up the pier, and onto the road. After a moment his tall angular figure disappeared around a bend, and she felt a certain odd and unexpected loneliness take hold.

"Well, there goes Mr. CIA," said Jackie. "You fuck him yet?"

"Jackie, cut it out. He's twice my age. You've got sex on the brain."

"Who doesn't?"

They cast off and Jackie lit up a joint as they cleared the harbor, Abbey driving the boat slowly, enjoying the evening.

The great bulk of Monroe Island loomed in front, covered with trees. A steady swell broke on Cutters Nubble, a reef beyond the southern end of the island, the cadence of the surf as regular as a slow clock. Abbey made a wide berth around the Nubble, and as they cleared it, a buttery full Moon rose over the limb of the ocean. A group of guillemots winged home low and fast across the water, like flying bullets, while an osprey, far overhead, headed back to his nest with a fish, still wiggling, clasped in its talons.

"Man, look at that," said Jackie, gazing eastward at the full Moon. "Looks like you could almost touch it."

Abbey eased the throttle forward, turning the wheel, and set the *Marea II* toward the Muscle Ridge Islands, a line of black humps on the horizon, four miles distant. It all looked so peaceful, so perfect, so timeless . . . It seemed surreal that somewhere up there, on a distant moonlet, there might be a weapon taking aim, right now, at the Earth. And that in a split second, all of this could be gone.

67

BURR TOSSED THE cigarette into the wake and looked around once more with the binoculars. The sun had set and most of the fishing boats had disappeared, but here and there he could still see the odd boat, loaded with traps, churning along toward some home port or other. From time to time he'd spied a lone motor yacht or sailboat cruising along—but no *Marea II*. He hadn't realized just how big the coast was and how many damn islands there were. And it seemed likely that they had gone to ground anyway or were doing whatever the hell it was they were doing, far from prying eyes. For the first time, he began to worry that he might not complete the assignment.

He lit up another cigarette, his eighth. Usually he paced himself, smoking no more than seven a day, but this was a bad day.

He strolled into the open pilothouse and stared at the chartplotter.

"Where are we now?"

"We're just leaving the north end of Muscongus Bay."

"Where to?"

"Penobscot Bay opens up on the far end of the channel."

Burr grunted, inhaled. "It's almost dark. I think we should find a place to hove to for the night."

"We're not going to hove to. We're going to keep looking. We got radar, we got GPS. We can cruise these islands all night, looking for boats in out-of-the-way places."

Burr grunted. "How are you going to see it in the dark?"

"Full Moon tonight. On the water under a full Moon it's almost like day."

He glanced up. "What about this storm?"

"We'll deal with it when it comes. This is a fine, sea-worthy boat."

"Good enough."

He went to the gunwale and finished up the cigarette. It was getting dark and there was no sign of the approaching storm. He tossed the butt overboard. In the distance he could see the dim outline of another lobster boat, crossing the far end of the channel—appearing from behind a large island and heading out instead of in. He quickly raised the binoculars. It was just light enough to make out the name painted on the stern.

Marea II.

Making an effort to control his excitement, he examined the boat more carefully. He could barely make out what looked like two figures in the pilothouse. Ford and the girl. This was an amazing stroke of luck. The boat was heading for a cluster of islands east of the channel.

Burr had already worked out in his head what he would do when he found his quarry. He reached into his holster and pulled out the Desert Eagle. No need for the noise suppressor, which was damned awkward, they were at least a mile offshore. He walked up behind Straw, who had just lifted the binoculars to look at the boat. A quick intake of breath.

"See that boat?" he cried. "It's the *Marea II*! They're heading for the Muscle Ridge Islands." He swung around. "All right. We did it. Your plan worked. Now we call in the cavalry and get that son of a bitch." He reached up for the VHF.

Burr gently placed the muzzle of the gun against the back of his head. "Do exactly what I say, Straw, or I'll kill you."

68

AS THE *MAREA II* slipped into the cluster of islands, Abbey throttled back to four knots. Little Green lay almost in the center of the grouping and it had only two approaches, one from the northwest and another from the east. Both were tight, with sunken rocks and reefs all around, and the approach took a high degree of caution. Twilight had descended and the first stars were appearing in the night sky.

The islands passed by, dark and silent. With her eye fixed on the chartplotter, Abbey maneuvered the boat through the winding channels until Little Green came into view, a long island forested in spruce, with a half-moon cove in the middle and a meadow above, at the far end of which stood the old fishing shack.

She carefully brought the boat into the cove and Jackie dropped anchor. It splashed into the water and the chain rattled out of the locker. As soon as the anchor was set, Abbey killed the engine.

In the ensuing silence she noticed the distant sound of

another boat, somewhere among the islands to the west of them.

They got into the dinghy and rowed to shore. Inside the shack, Jackie turned on lights while Abbey put kindling in the small stove.

"Hamburgers?" Jackie asked, rummaging in the cooler.

"Sounds good to me."

Abbey lit a fire in the woodstove and adjusted the dampers. The kindling crackled to life. She went to the door and breathed in the night air, which was heavy and still. There was the smell of damp grass, wood smoke from the stove, and the sea. A faint hiss of gentle waves lapped the strand—and, off in the distance, the persistent throbbing of a boat engine. It seemed to be coming from behind the adjacent island, moving very slowly.

Abbey turned in the door and spoke calmly to Jackie, so as not to alarm her. "I think I'll go out for a walk."

"Don't be long, these burgers are almost done."

Instead of walking along the shore, Abbey slipped into the moonlight-flecked woods and headed toward the western end of the island, toward the sound of the boat. At the tip of the island she paused at the edge of the trees, remaining in shadow, and looking out over the water in the direction of the sound. The air was humid. The tide had turned and was flowing back in, the currents curling and gurgling past the island. A mackerel sky was advancing from the northeast but it hadn't yet reached the Moon, which glowed almost painfully bright in the night sky.

The sound seemed to be coming from behind an adjacent island. It was probably just a yacht looking for an anchorage—recreational cruising of the coast was popular in the summer. She chided herself for being paranoid.

A dark shape of a boat, about four hundred yards distant, passed across a gap between two islands. She felt a sudden chill: the boat had doused its running lights. It vanished behind the next island and after a moment the sound of the engine stopped.

Abbey listened intently, but the wind was starting to come up and the sighing in the trees covered any faint sounds. She crouched in the darkness, waiting. She tried to calm herself down; she was spooked because Ford was gone. The killer could not possibly have followed them to Maine, let alone traced them to Little Green Island. It was probably some yachtsman who had had one martini too many and forgot to turn on his running lights. Or maybe they were drug smugglers. Marijuana smugglers often used this wild stretch of coast to bring boatloads of weed down from Canada.

She waited, and watched.

And then she saw, emerging from shadow into moonlight, the dark shape of a rowboat moving steadily across the narrow channel separating the other island from Little Green. As she stared, it resolved itself into a dinghy being rowed with care by a tall man, and it was heading right for their island, angling toward her end of the island in such a way that it wouldn't be visible from the fishing shack. The boat moved swiftly with the incoming tidal current. It would be landing in minutes on a beach just below the bluff at the island's tip.

Abbey backed into the woods and crept to a point where she could observe the probable landing point. The man pulled steadily, the faint splash of his oars reaching her across the water. He remained a dark silhouette, hunched over as he rowed. In a minute the boat grounded with a crunch. He hopped out, pulled the boat up the strand, and then stood quietly, looking around, his face still in shadow.

Abbey flattened herself on the mossy ground, watching. The man removed something from his waist and seemed to be checking it; she saw the faint gleam of metal and realized it was a handgun. He reholstered it and, with a quick look about, slipped into the darkness of the trees. He would be passing her way in a moment.

Abbey rose and sprinted through the woods, ducking branches and leaping fallen trees, and in a few minutes she arrived at the cabin, bursting through the door.

"Thanks to you, I burned the ham—"

"Jackie. We gotta go. Now."

"But the hamburgers—"

Abbey grabbed her hand and pulled her toward the door. "*Now*. And keep quiet—there's someone on the island with a gun."

"Oh my God."

She pulled her out into the darkness and cast about. He would probably be coming straight to the cabin.

"This way," she whispered, pulling Jackie across the meadow and into the woods stretching toward the southern end of the island. But the woods were too small and too obvious to be a good hiding place. On the other hand, the boulders and whalebacks at the southern tip of the island offered a better option, especially since it was low tide, exposing a range of giant, seaweed-covered rocks.

She motioned to Jackie to follow and they snuck through the trees to the bluff above the rocks. The Moon was still low in the sky and the tall spruces cast a shadow over the jumbled boulders, burying all in darkness. They slid down the dirt bluff and scrambled over the boulders, Abbey heading below the high-tide line to the long string of rocks jutting into the water.

"Tide's coming in," whispered Jackie, slipping and sliding over the seaweed. "We'll be drowned."

"This is only temporary."

At the far end, she found a dark hiding place between two steep-sided, seaweed-covered boulders with crawl spaces along their underside. The tide was coming in fast.

"Get in there."

"We're gonna be wet."

"That's the point."

Jackie hunkered down against the black, cold seaweed, wedging herself under the overhang of the rock. Abbey did the same, pulling and arranging the seaweed around and over her as much as possible. The strong smell of it filled her nostrils. She could see back up through the rocks to the spruces and, just barely, to the lighted cabin across the meadow five hundred yards away. Just beyond, the water lapped and gurgled among the rocks as the tide came in.

"Who is it?" Jackie whispered.

"The guy who's after us. Now shut up."

They waited. After what seemed like an eternity, Abbey saw the man's figure emerge from the forest into the moon-drenched meadow. Gun drawn, he slowly circled the cabin, crept up to a window and, flattening himself against the outside wall, peered inside. He spent some time looking, and then moved around to the door and kicked it in. The noise shattered the calm night air, echoing across the dark water.

He went into the cabin and came out a moment later, looking around. A flashlight appeared in his hand and he slowly circled the meadow, shining it into the trees.

Meanwhile, the tide came in.

The figure disappeared into the woods above their hiding place, the light flashing through the trees, back and forth.

He reappeared at the edge of the woods, on the top of the bluff above the rocks. Picking his way down, he stood on a tall rock, playing the light along the shore, the yellow beam licking about the rocks around them, probing here and there. Abbey put her hand on Jackie's arm and felt a tremor.

The figure began walking toward them, the loose cobbles dislodged by his feet making a rattling sound. The light flashed over the tops of the boulders again, probing briefly on either side of them. Meanwhile, Abbey could feel the tide crawling among the seaweed-covered rocks at their feet. What was the rate? Something like a vertical inch rise of water every two minutes, even more at the full moon.

As he got closer, she pulled her head back and down into the seaweed. She could feel the hiss of water now swirling around her feet, the gentle swell coming in and out. As the man got closer, she heard his hard breathing.

Once again, this time very deliberately, the yellow beam moved over the rocks. It passed by them with excruciating slowness. Once. Twice. Then came a grunt, and he began to move off. The beam flickered over a jumble of rocks to their right and moved on down the shore.

The water swept in around her ankles, stirring the seaweed, hissing back out. Darkness returned. Abbey waited for a minute, then two, and ventured another look. She could see him moving cautiously down the shore, a few hundred yards away, probing as he went, heading toward their dinghy.

"We've got to get off this island," Abbey whispered.

"How the hell are we going to do that with our dinghy out there in the open?"

"We're gonna take his."

Jackie was shaking. Abbey put a reassuring hand on her shoulder. "You stay here. Move up a little with the tide. I'll go steal his dinghy, get our boat, and come to you. I'll pass as close to shore as I dare. When you hear me coming, start swimming. The current'll be with you."

"Okay," Jackie whispered.

Suddenly, Abbey noticed a flash in the sky, a rapid brightening. For a moment she thought the killer had found them, suddenly turning on his flashlight beam.

"Shit!" Jackie said, ducking and covering her head in an instinctual movement.

After a moment, Abbey poked her head up and stared at the Moon. "Oh my God! Jackie!"

A huge fireball blossomed on one side of the Moon, with a jet of glowing dust shooting laterally from the opposite side, extending itself as if in slow motion, becoming so bright Abbey had to shield her eyes. It was strange, weird, a spectacularly beautiful phenomenon, like the Moon had burst, releasing a string of glittering jewels spilling out of its interior, glowing with internal fire.

Meanwhile, the fireball on the other side of the Moon also expanded in size and color, from brilliant cold blue in the center to a greenish yellow, grading to orange and red at the edges, like a wedge expanding from the surface of the Moon.

"What the *fuck*?" Jackie stared, her eyes wide.

The brightening light bathed the islands, the dark spruces, the rocks, the sea in a greenish yellow color, false and garish. The horizon came up, razor-sharp, the sky above it deep purple, the ocean below a pale green flecked with black and red.

Abbey turned her gaze back to the Moon, squinting her eyes against the brightness; a kind of halo was now developing around the disk, as if the Moon had been struck or shaken, lofting dust into space. A vast silence seemed to settle onto the seascape, the spectacle unfolding in absolute stillness which made it seem all the more surreal.

"Abbey!" came Jackie's low, panicked voice. "What is it? What's happening?"

"I believe," said Abbey slowly, "that the weapon on Deimos just took a potshot at the Moon—a much bigger one, this time."

69

HARRY BURR WALKED down the shingled beach, semiautomatic pistol in one hand, probing the woods and rocks with his flashlight, searching for a glimpse of fleeting figures, a face crouching among the trees, something. He knew they were on the island—their dinghy was still up on the beach and burgers had been burning on the stove. He was also pretty sure Ford didn't have a piece—otherwise he'd have used it in the bar or at the parking lot. So he was the only man with a gun.

He swore under his breath. Somehow they'd gotten wind of his coming. They'd probably heard the sound of his boat engine, which at night carried across the water a long distance. Still, he was holding all the cards; he'd cornered them on a small island and there was no way they could escape—except by dinghy. They couldn't swim to their boat—the tide was coming in full bore and the currents were swirling past the island at several knots. They'd be swept past before they'd ever make it.

There were two dinghies on the island: his and theirs.

It wasn't hard to see what they'd do: try to get one of them. His first job was to secure them. He walked down the beach to where their dinghy was pulled up. He thought of shoving it off into the current but decided that would be risky, leaving himself without a backup if something should go wrong. Instead, grasping the painter, he hauled it up into the woods where it was more or less hidden. Then he removed the oars and hid each one in widely separated locations, shoving them into raspberry thickets. It would take hours to find them.

Now to secure his own boat.

A sudden light above his head caused him to duck and spin around, gun at the ready, until he realized it was coming from above. The full Moon. He stared up at it as a bright jet seemed to come off its surface and extend into the night sky. Another bright spot appeared on the opposite side. What the hell was it?

Just a strange cloud passing over the Moon, creating a striking optical illusion.

Moving rapidly and silently through the trees, he worked his way toward the northern end of the island until he had reached his own dinghy. It sat peacefully in the brightening moonlight. He was about to haul it up and hide it as he'd done the other one when he had an idea: to leave it in full view as bait, hide and wait for them to come get it. When they found their own dinghy missing, they'd come after his. What other course of action did they have? They couldn't hide forever.

He took up a well-hidden position behind a jumble of rocks at the edge of the shore and waited.

The sky grew brighter by slow degrees, and he glanced

upward, wondering what the hell was going on with the Moon. The strange cloud kept getting bigger, and it really didn't look like a cloud after all.

He turned away, focusing on the problem at hand, waiting for them to come. He hardly had to wait: after only a few minutes he spied a shadow moving along the edge of the forest; he raised his Desert Eagle, switched on the internal laser sights, then thought better of it and turned them off. No reason to spook them with a dancing red dot. They would be close enough for a kill without it.

But the silhouette was alone. It was the girl. Ford was not with her.

70

DRIVING SOUTH ON Interstate 295, near Freeport, Ford noticed the sudden light in the night sky. He peered out the windscreen at the Moon and, with a sudden feeling of dread, pulled off the highway to get a better look. He stepped outside in the summer night and stared, aghast, at the jet of light rising from the Moon's surface. As he watched, more cars began pulling off the highway, people getting out to stare and take pictures.

A long trail of glowing material seemed to be shooting away from the Moon's surface, elongating across the night sky, blazing yellow. And on the opposite side was a similar puff of debris, more bulbous, material ejected as if from an impact.

It looked exactly like the Moon had been shot through by something that entered on the right and exited on the left.

Another shot from the thing on Deimos?

No question about it. And this time a much larger projectile of strange matter must have been used, big enough to create a spectacular display on Earth. Perhaps even *designed* to create a display. The last one had largely gone unnoticed; this one wouldn't. Even as he watched, the tail of debris kept extending itself, gradually elongating into a broad curve by the Moon's gravity.

This was striking confirmation that Abbey was right: that the alien artifact on Deimos was a weapon and had fired again, this time at the Moon. But why? As a demonstration of power?

There was no sense gaping by the side of the road, thought Ford. He had a plane to catch. He slipped back into his car and switched on the radio, tuning it to the local NPR station. The thunderous sounds of Bach's Passacaglia and Fugue in C Minor came out the speakers, but almost immediately a newscaster broke in, interrupting the program with a special announcement about the "extraordinary phenomenon occurring to the Moon."

"We reached Elaine Dahlquist," the announcer said, "an astronomer at the Harvard-Smithsonian Center for Astrophysics. Dr. Dahlquist, can you tell us what we're seeing up there?"

"My initial guess, Joe, would be that the Moon was struck by a major asteroid, perhaps two fragments at once, striking simultaneously on either side."

"Why didn't anyone see it coming?"

"Good question. Evidently we're dealing with an asteroid that escaped the attention of Spacewatch and other near-Earth asteroid search programs. Here at Harvard-Smithsonian we've turned our telescopes on the Moon, and I understand the Keck Observatory and the Hubble Space Telescope are also looking at

it—as well as thousands of other telescopes, amateur and professional."

"Is there any danger to us on Earth?" the announcer asked.

"There are reports of an electromagnetic pulse or a shower of charged particles causing scattered power failures and computer network problems. Other than that, I'd say we're safe here on Earth. The Moon is two hundred and forty thousand miles away."

Ford turned off the radio. As he drove down the interstate, the light in the sky continued to increase, slowly but steadily, as the debris cloud extended out. It was yellowish in color, grading off to reddish hues at the edges—hot, condensing debris from the strike. But the show would soon be curtained; the intermittent clouds that had earlier covered the sky had given way to a squall line of black weather, looming on the horizon, flickering with internal lightning.

He glanced at the clock: he was half an hour from the Portland airport; he'd catch the midnight flight to D.C. and be there by two or three A.M.

But first, he had to set up a little sting.

71

DAWN NEVER BREAKS *in a Vegas casino or the White House Sit Room*, Lockwood thought as he followed the duty officer into the windowless, cocoon-like Situation Room, already packed with people. Lockwood recognized the ferret-like demeanor of the national security advisor at the head of the conference table, Clifford Manfred, whose Italian suit and Thomas Pink tie were perhaps a touch sharp for Washington. Seated with him was the director of central intelligence, a gray man in a gray suit with alert gray eyes; several nondescript intelligence analysts and a communications specialist. A huge flat-panel video display at the far end was split into multiple screens, one with a real-time image of the Moon—now with two jets coming off it—and the others showing silent news feeds from the U.S. and foreign media. Other screens around the walls displayed images of people attending by video conference, including the chairman of the Joint Chiefs, a small, precise man with snowy hair, wearing an admiral's uniform.

Lockwood took a seat in one of the big black leather chairs. There was a low murmur of voices around him and the clank and rattle of spoons in coffee mugs as coffee was served. Everyone was awaiting the arrival of the president.

A few minutes later a hush fell in the room, almost by intuition, and the door opened. A duty officer appeared, followed by the president's chief of staff and then the president himself, dressed in an impeccable blue suit, tall and lean, his once black hair salted with gray, his roving eyes taking in everything, his jug ears sweeping the room like a radar beacon. His unflappable demeanor cast a spell over the room like oil on water, dissipating the air of tension. Everyone made to rise and the president waved his hand. "Please, please, stay seated."

They rose anyway and reseated themselves as the president himself took a seat, not at the head of the table, but in an empty chair halfway down. He turned to Lockwood. "Stan, I've got a country on the verge of panic. Every talking-head astronomer in the country is spouting off and saying something different. So start from the beginning and tell us what's really going on—and keep in mind some of us are scientific idiots. Is this just a light show or should we be worried?"

Lockwood rose, a slender manila file folder in his hand. "Mr. President, I regret to say it's more serious than anything you might imagine."

A silence. Everyone was staring at him.

"Some background. On April fourteenth, a meteor streaked over the Maine Coast. At the exact same time, our worldwide seismic system—designed to locate underground nuclear tests—registered an explosive signature in the remote mountains along the Thai–Cambodia border. We located what appeared to be an impact crater, and we sent out a man to investigate. It turns out it wasn't a crater—but an exit hole. Later, our man discovered the entrance hole—on an island off the coast of Maine."

"Wait a minute—are you saying something went *through* the Earth?"

"Correct."

"Who's this man you sent?"

"An ex-CIA officer named Wyman Ford. We're trying to find him now."

"Go on."

"We've determined the thing that passed through the Earth was probably a small lump of strange matter, also called a strangelet. This exotic form of matter is super-dense—the entire Earth, if made of it, would be the size of an orange. It has a very alarming property: it converts normal matter to strange matter on contact."

"So why's the Earth still here?"

"It was a very small piece, perhaps not much larger than an atom, and it was going fast. It blew all the way through the Earth and kept going. If it had been going slower and ended up caught inside the Earth, we'd be gone now."

"My God."

"That's just the beginning. We extrapolated the orbit back and found it originated at Mars."

"Mars?"

"We've no idea yet what the Mars connection is, if anything. As we speak, the military is flying a contingent of senior scientists from the Mars mission at NPF here to join the team, along with the director of NASA."

"Good."

"Here's the bad part, Mr. President. It appears this thing happening to the Moon is identical to what happened to the Earth in April, except a much larger lump of strange matter was involved. It appears to have gone straight through the Moon, producing the spectacular display you see on the screen."

"Is this stuff flying all through space around us? Is the Earth passing through a swarm of this stuff?"

"I don't think so. There are indications that the strike on the Moon might be . . . aimed."

"Aimed? Are you saying some country launched these things?"

"The physicists assure me it's absolutely impossible for any nation on Earth to possess the technology to make strange matter."

"Then what the hell do you mean by *aimed*?" The president was out of his seat, his legendary cool rapidly deteriorating.

"Because the shot at the Moon . . ." He paused and drew a breath. "The shot took out Tranquility Base. A direct hit. Tranquility Base is, of course, where humans first landed on the Moon. It has great significance to humankind."

"My God. Are you saying this is an *attack* of some kind?"

"That would be my guess."

"By who? You just said no one on Earth has the technology to make this strange matter!"

"It *isn't* anyone on this Earth, Mr. President."

A long, extraordinary silence followed. Nobody said a word. Finally the president spoke, his voice quiet. "Are you suggesting *aliens* did this?"

"I would not use that word, sir. I would simply say that it appears like a deliberate shot by some entity not of this world. It could also be a coincidence, but I somehow don't think so."

The president smoothed a thin hand over the top of his head, let it drop, tapped a finger on the table, and finally looked up. "Stan, I want you and General Mickelson to chair an ad hoc group. It will include a few of your most trusted associates in the Science and Technology Policy group, as well as some top NPF people, chairman of the Joint Chiefs, NASA chief, DNI, and NSA. Meet now. I want a recommendation—a plan, a strategy—on how to deal with this by seven tomorrow morning. That recommendation should include military options, a diplomatic strategy, and above all a plan to gather more information. You've got seven hours." He turned to leave the room, strode to the door, and paused. "And I want that man, Wyman Ford, found and put on that group."

72

THE GIRL MOVED cautiously among the rocks, keeping in the shadows, moving stealthily toward the dinghy. She'd pass by him within less than twenty feet. Rather than kill her, he would use her to get the other one. The increasing light from the sky was an annoyance but he was so well hidden that even if it were day she wouldn't see him.

As she came into range, he stepped out of the darkness, gun in hand. "Don't move."

She screamed, jumped back. Burr fired over her head, the massively calibered Desert Eagle roaring like a cannon. "Shut the fuck up and *don't move!*"

She quieted down pretty quick, standing there, trembling.

"Where's Ford?"

No answer.

He reached over with his left arm and grabbed her around the neck, wrenching her to one side and screwing the Eagle's muzzle in her ear. "You going to answer my question?"

She choked, swallowed. "I don't know."

"Is he on the *island*?"

"Um, yes."

"Where? What's he doing?"

"I don't know."

Burr yanked her by the hair, jamming the muzzle against her cheek so hard the sights ripped her skin. "Answer me."

"He . . . He said he was going after you."

"When? Where?"

"When you landed. Said he was going to get you."

"Is he armed?"

"He's got a knife . . ."

Jesus. And Ford was probably watching them right now. Keeping the gun to Abbey's cheek, he kept her body close to his. Damn, it was getting bright. He raised the barrel of the gun and fired into the night sky. The sound of the shot echoed and rolled across the island.

"Ford!" he cried. "I know you're out there! I'm going to count to ten, and if you aren't standing in front of me with your arms up, I'm going to put a bullet into her head. You hear me?" He fired into the air again and placed the hot muzzle against Abbey's cheek. "*You hear me, Ford*? One . . . two . . . three . . ."

"Maybe he can't hear you," Abbey cried. "He's on the other side of the island."

"—four . . . five . . . six—"

"Wait! I lied! He's not on the island!"

"—seven . . . eight . . . nine—"

"Listen to me! *He's not on the island!* Don't!"

"Ten!"

A long silence, and then Burr lowered the gun. "I guess

he isn't." He released her and then, as she stumbled back, he struck her across the face, sending her sprawling. "That's for lying." He grabbed her and hauled her back to her feet. "Where'd he go?"

A choking sound. "I dropped him on the mainland. He went . . . back to Washington."

"Where in Washington?"

"I don't know."

"Who's the other person? I saw another person on the boat."

She swallowed. He pushed the gun in harder. "Answer."

"Nobody. I'm alone."

"Liar."

"You must've seen my slicker hanging on a hook in the pilothouse, next to the window. It's got a big round rain hood—"

"Shut up." He thought fast. She must be telling the truth; nobody could have gone through the count and not broken down to tell everything. Fact was, he hadn't seen either figure well in the dusk across half a mile of water.

"Where's the hard drive?"

"He took it with him."

Son of a bitch. He felt a trembling rage. The job was a bust. Without the hard drive he wouldn't get paid.

There still might be a way to catch up to Ford. But first, he had to clean up—kill the girl, return to his boat, do the father, and get his ass back to the mainland. Then he could pursue Ford to Washington. No use wasting more time here. He shoved Abbey to the ground and, so as not to dirty himself, backed up a step.

She sprawled among the rocks, trying to rise.

"Move and you're dead."

She stopped trying to move. Bracing himself, his legs apart and the Glock Desert Eagle in both hands, he aimed at Abbey's head and squeezed the trigger.

73

FORD FOUND WHAT he was looking for in Topsham, Maine—a small strip mall open late. He pulled up to an electronics store, went in, and bought a nondescript hard drive. At the Kinko's next door he printed out the suite of images from the DEIMOS MACHINE file, after carefully removing any references to Deimos itself, and shoved them in his brief-case. Using their computers, he burned four DVDs with the relevant suite of images from the DEIMOS MACHINE file. From a department store he bought nail polish remover, white enamel paint, a roll of paint-masking tape, a black Magic Marker, a box, brown parcel paper, and bubble wrap.

Back at his car, using the nail polish remover, he stripped all the identifying labels, logos, and serial numbers from the new hard drive. He masked out a square area on the side with the tape, painted it with white enamel, and put it under the car's floor heater, cranking it full blast.

While that was drying, he fetched shipping materials from the FedEx dropoff. He wrote a note:

The password is FuckNPF1. Look at all the images in the DEIMOS MACHINE file and the series of radar images R-2756–2760. THESE ARE REAL IMAGES, NO ALTERATION. They depict an alien weapon at the bottom of Voltaire crater on Deimos, one of the moons of Mars. This weapon fired on the Earth on April 14 and then on the Moon tonight—you've seen the results. This is the biggest science story ever. Just look at the images and you'll understand. Publish right away or you'll be slapped with an injunction as this is highly classified information.

He sealed it in an envelope and taped it to the side of the original hard drive, wrapped the drive in several layers of bubble wrap and brown paper, and wrote on the outside:

IMPORTANT!
PROPERTY OF MARTIN KOLODY,
SCIENCE EDITOR, *WASHINGTON POST*.
IF LOST, PLEASE RETURN ASAP,
ALL EXPENSES WILL BE REIMBURSED.

He thought for a moment and then added: $500 REWARD FOR SAFE RETURN, GUARANTEED.

He then filled out a FedEx mailing label. For recipient he put down a completely fictitious name and address. For sender he put down a fake name but the real address of a well-run boutique hotel in D.C. not far from the *Post*'s editorial offices.

Putting the four DVDs into plain mailers, he addressed them to the science editor of *The New York Times*, the editor of *Scientific American*, the president of the National Association for the Advancement of Science, and the president of the National Academy of Sciences. He wrote a brief of the situation to include in each package and placed MEDIA MAIL stickers on them, with the requisite postage.

He slid the FedEx packages in the drop box. The original drive would take three to four days to reach Kolody: one day for the FedEx to realize the address wasn't good, one or two days to return it to the hotel, and one day for the hotel to deliver it to the *Post*'s editorial offices. The package's confusing chain of consignment while in transit would make it difficult to trace or intercept, and Kolody's name would not be in any FedEx database. The drive would be the proof; the DVDs were backup, as it were, insurance, in case the original drive was seized by the feds. Media mail wasn't traceable and would also take at least three to four days to arrive at their destinations.

He went to an ATM and withdrew five hundred dollars, wrapped it well, and placed it in another FedEx envelope, this time addressing it directly to Kolody. He included a simple note:

THIS WILL PAY FOR WHAT YOU WILL SOON RECEIVE.

That would guarantee his attention. In four days the truth would be on the front page of the *Washington Post* and the world would finally know what was going on.

He hoped to God it wouldn't be too late.

He walked back to his car after mailing the envelope. The parking lot was bathed in an eerie yellowish green light from the Moon. Ford paused a moment to look at the evolving spectacle. The jet of material had started to go into orbit around the Moon, curving into a scimitarlike shape. The entire Moon was now surrounded by a bright, diffuse halo. Even as he watched, swift dark clouds passed over the Moon, one after another, drawing shadows over the world. The air was heavy. A bolt of lightning cut the distant sky, the distant rumble coming half a minute later, the air smelling of humidity and ozone. A fast-moving summer storm was bearing down.

Back at his car, Ford checked the new hard drive and found the enamel dry. Taking out the Magic Marker, he block-printed the same information that had been on the original drive:

#785A56H6T 160Tb
CLASSIFIED: DO NOT DUPLICATE
Property of NPF
California Institute of Technology
National Aeronautics and Space Administration

Placing it in his briefcase, he headed back for the interstate, bound for the airport and Washington.

74

IN DESPERATION, ABBEY threw herself sideways and kicked out at the man's shin, striking it hard with her heel as the gun went off—and she saw simultaneously a figure leap up behind the man, clutching a rock. *Jackie.* The bullet richocheted off a stone next to her ear, the roar booming into the night. Even before the sound had echoed away, a wild shriek split the air and Jackie swung her arm around with the rock in her fist, whacking the man on the temple just as the second shot went off, *karang!* The killer staggered back, holding his head with one hand, trying to aim with the other. *Karang!* The pistol went off again, wildly, as he caught his foot and fell back among the rocks.

With the screech of a banshee Jackie fell on him while Abbey seized her own rock and lunged at him, but he was fast and strong and threw Jackie off him, lurching back to his feet, spinning on Jackie and raising his gun, but as he was bringing his hand up to shoot, Abbey hit him with the rock in the back of the head, knocking him forward to his knees.

He roared unintelligibly, still clutching the gun, reared back up, and aimed again at Jackie, who was fishing around for another rock.

"Jackie!" Abbey lunged at Jackie and yanked her over as the pistol went off again, the round snicking off a nearby rock, spraying them with chips. Still on his knees, the killer began to take more careful aim with both hands, blood streaming down his face. "*I'll kill you!*" he roared, steadying his wobbling arms.

"Run! To the dinghy!"

They ran down the cobbled beach toward the skiff, the gun thundering behind them, kicking up a groove in the beach in front of them. Abbey seized the rope and hauled the boat down the shingle, Jackie pushing from behind. They ran it into the water and jumped in, Abbey grabbing the oars and slamming them into the oarlocks.

The figure of the killer appeared on the beach, staggering like a drunk and aiming the gun. A little red dot danced and flashed around them.

"Down!"

The crash of the shot rolled across the water, and splinters of wood blasted up from the gunwale.

Another shot smacked the water next to them, covering them with spray. Abbey pulled the oars as hard as she could, the boat surging through the smooth ocean. Darkness suddenly fell as the clouds rolled over the bizarre Moon. The current was with them, streaming past the island, carrying them toward the cove where they'd moored the boat. More shots came from the shore, the great hollow boom of the gun rolling across the water like thunder. Gouts of water kicked up on either side and a round took a chunk out of the stern.

Still she rowed. Jackie huddled in the bottom of the boat, covering her head and swearing loudly with each shot.

The *Marea II* lay about a hundred yards offshore and the incoming tidal currents pushed them toward the boat. Another pair of shots boomed over the water, striking on either side of the dinghy.

She could see the killer running along the shore, keeping as close to them as he could. He took up a prone position on the rocks opposite the anchored boat, resting his gun barrel in front of him. He seemed to have recovered from the blows to his head. Abbey came up alongside the starboard side of *Marea II*, using the boat as cover, out of the line of fire. She scrambled on board, reaching around to grab Jackie. She heard a series of measured shots and one of the windows of the *Marea II* blew out.

"He's shooting at the boat!" Jackie screamed, falling back into the dinghy. Abbey grabbed her collar and dragged her up and over the gunwale. Another window blew out, scattering chips of glass over the deck.

"Stay down!" Abbey crawled along the cockpit and into the pilothouse, Jackie following. Grabbing a knife from the toolbox, she shoved it in Jackie's hands. "Be ready to run forward and cut the anchor rope—not now, but when I give the word."

Karang! A round smacked through the forepeak.

Abbey switched on the battery power, and, staying low, reached up and turned the key on the engine panel. It roared to life. *Thank God.*

Karang! Karang!

She gunned the engine, the boat straining forward against the anchor rode. For a moment Abbey thought it wasn't going to work, but she goosed the throttle and felt the anchor pull free. The boat surged forward, dragging the anchor along the bottom. If only she could get away, into deep water, they could deal with the anchor later.

But the boat only managed to go another hundred feet before the anchor fetched up hard on a rock and the boat swung around by the bow, the engine straining. They were still in range. *Karang! Karang!* came the shots, punching a pair of holes in the upper hull.

"Now! Cut the anchor!"

Jackie sprinted forward and, keeping low, using the pilot-house as cover, crawled up to the bow and sawed through the rope. The boat lurched forward and Abbey slammed the throttle to the console, eyes glued to the chartplotter, trying to keep the boat within the narrow channels among the islands. In a moment they were out of range and a few minutes later they passed the end of Little Green, swung around it, and headed down the winding channels for the open ocean.

Abbey throttled down and sagged against the wheel, suddenly feeling dizzy.

"Oh my God," said Jackie, holding her head. "Oh my God." Her face was bleeding from flying glass.

"Come here." Abbey wiped the blood off her face with a paper towel. "Hold still. You're hyperventilating."

Jackie made a visible effort to get her heart and breathing under control.

"Man, Jackie, that was some scream you let loose back there. I'll never call you a wimp again."

Jackie's shaking began to subside. "I was mad," she said.

"You're not kidding." Abbey wiped the blood off her own

face and steadied herself, her hands firmly on the wheel. She shifted her attention to the chartplotter, thinking of the best way to get into port. "Let's go straight to Owls Head," Abbey said. "Get the hell out of here and call the cops."

"You can call the cops right now," Jackie said, turning on the VHF. They waited for it to warm up. The boat swung north in the channel and, coming around a protected island, entered open water at the southern end of Penobscot Bay. A powerful swell shuddered the boat and Abbey was surprised to see the very heavy seas running out of the east, the kind of deep rolling swell that preceded a major storm. It was dark; she glanced up and realized the Moon had been obscured for some time. The wind was rising steadily and lightning flickered along the sea horizon.

She raised the mike, turned the VHF to channel 16, pressed the transmit button, and made an emergency broadcast to the Coast Guard.

75

FROM HIS SHOOTING perch behind a boulder, Harry Burr watched the boat disappear among the islands. He shoved the gun into his belt and leaned on the rock, his head pounding. He could feel the blood still trickling down from his ear and scalp. Feeling the growing lump on the side of his head, an ungovernable rage took hold, so powerful it caused stars to pop up in his field of vision. Two bitches had fucked up everything, smacked him on the head, taken his dinghy. They saw him and they could identify him. The stars swarmed about and he felt the almost physical pressure of anger behind his forehead, a humming sound, like a cloud of bees trying to escape.

It was him or them. If he didn't catch up to them and kill them, he would go down. It was as simple as that. If they got to shore, he'd be finished.

He ejected the empty magazine from his piece and reloaded it with loose rounds he carried in his pocket, smacking it back into place. He had very little time. But all was not lost. He still had the other dinghy and a more seaworthy boat—along with an ace in the hole: the father.

Ignoring the pounding in his head, Burr jogged down the strand and into the woods. He pulled the dinghy out of the bushes, retrieved the hidden oars, tossed them in, and dragged the skiff down the beach. Shoving off, he rowed toward where he'd anchored the *Halcyon*. The *Halcyon* was not a fast boat but he guessed it would be faster than the *Marea II*, which was, after all, just a fishing boat, not a yacht.

He pulled with the current, and as he did so, he noticed how dark it had become and how much the wind had risen. Even in the protected waters of the islands, whitecaps were forming, the sound of the wind moaning in the spruce trees. He could hear the distant thunder of surf on the windward islands, a mile off.

He crossed the channel and came around the edge of the adjacent island, the *Halcyon* coming into view. He could see the dark form of the fisherman, both hands shackled tightly to the stern rail.

He bumped up against the gunwale and climbed aboard, cleating off the dinghy. "Look sharp, Straw, we got business to take care of."

"You touch my daughter and I'll kill you," he said in a low voice. "I'll search you out—"

"Yeah, yeah." He went straight to the VHF radio, turned it on to channel 16. If there was one thing he had to do, it was stop the girl from calling the Coast Guard.

76

WHEN ABBEY FINISHED making the identification call and
released the transmit button, instantly a hoarse voice came
on. "Abbey? There you are!"

It was the killer's voice. He must have gotten back to his
boat and had been monitoring the emergency channel.

"You bastard, you're toast," she began.

"Ah, ah! Don't use bad language on an official government
frequency, where your father can hear it."

"My—what?"

"Your father. He's here on the boat and we're having such
a good time together."

Abbey was struck speechless for a moment. The wind
shook the pilothouse and a sudden hard rain slapped the
windows. A flash of lightning split the air above, followed by
the crackle of thunder.

"I repeat: your father, Mr. George Straw, is here on the
boat with me," he said smoothly. "Switch to channel seventy-

two and we'll chat." Channel 72, Abbey knew, was an obscure noncommercial frequency that nobody used.

Before she could respond, the radio hissed. "*This is Coast Guard Station Rockland responding—*"

Abbey cut off the dispatcher, and dialed in 72.

"Much better," came the voice. "Want to say hi to Dad?"

Abbey felt physically sick. It had to be a lie. She heard a muffled sound, a curse, the sound of a blow. "*Talk* to her." Another thud.

"Stop it!" Abbey screamed.

"Abbey," came her father's distorted voice. "Stay away. Just get the hell into port and go straight to the police—"

Another heavy blow, a grunt.

"*Stop* it, you *bastard!*"

The killer's voice came back on. "Get back on sixteen and call off the Coast Guard. Now. Or he's fish food."

With a sob, Abbey dialed back to channel 16 and told the Coast Guard that it was a false alarm. The dispatcher began to advise her to head to port immediately because of the storm. She signed off and dialed back to channel 72. She glanced over at Jackie but she was staring back in shock. The boat shuddered through a comber and the wheel jerked around, the boat yawing.

Jackie suddenly gripped the wheel, giving the throttle some fuel, and the boat yawed back around and just barely met the next wave on the starboard quarter. "I'll take the helm. You deal with him."

Abbey nodded dumbly. The wind was picking up by the second, lashing the ocean's heaving surface into honeycombs of foam.

Back on channel 72 the killer gave a low laugh and then said, "Hello? Anybody home?"

"Please don't hurt—"

Another smack, a groan. "What's your position?"

"Penobscot Bay."

"Listen carefully, here's the plan. Give me your GPS coordinates. I'm coming to you and I'll give you your father back."

"What do you want?"

"Just a promise that you'll forget all about this. Okay?"

"Abbey!" came a faint cry, "don't listen—"

Another thud.

"No, *please*! Don't hurt him!"

"Abbey," came the calm voice of the killer. "Keep in mind we're on an open channel. Understand? I'm coming to you. There won't be any problems if you follow my instructions."

Abbey tried to breathe through an involuntary spasm in her throat. After a moment she said, "I understand."

"Good. Now your GPS coordinates?"

Jackie reached over and grabbed the mike, turning off the transmit button so they couldn't be heard. "Abbey, you know he's lying. He's going to kill us."

"I know that," Abbey said ferociously. "Just let me *think*."

Even as they had been speaking, the swell was rising fast. The *Marea II*, engine grinding away, was being shoved sideways by each wave.

"Abbey? Are you there?"

Abbey took the mike back. "I'm figuring it out!" She turned to Jackie. "What do we do?"

"I . . . I don't know."

"Hello? Maybe Dad needs another beating to help you figure?"

"I'm just southwest of Devil's Limb," Abbey said.

"Devil's Limb? What the hell are you doing way out there?"

"We were heading for Rockland," she said, madly thinking.

"Bullshit! If you're out there, gimme the coordinates!"

Abbey punched the keys of the chartplotter, fixed a waypoint next to Devil's Limb, and read him back the false coordinates.

"Jesus Christ," said the killer after a moment. "I'm not going out there. You come back here."

Abbey sobbed. "We can't! We're almost out of fuel!"

"Lying bitch! Get back here now or Dad goes chumming!"

"No, please," Abbey sobbed. "All your shooting cut a fuel line. We're almost out of fuel!"

"I don't believe it!"

"We just now clamped it. It's the truth!"

Smack. "You hear that? That's for lying again!"

Abbey swallowed. She had to take the risk. "Please believe me!" she said, controlling her voice. "Why do you think I was calling the Coast Guard?"

"Fuck that, I'm not crossing open water in this sea."

A gust carrying a wallop of rain lashed the boat, water spraying in the broken windows. Another swell shoved the boat sideways and Abbey had to seize the ceiling grips to keep from falling.

"He's going to kill us!" Jackie hissed. "What the hell are you doing?"

"I'm . . . *pretending* to surrender."

"And then what?"

"I don't know."

"You hear me?" came the voice. "Get your ass back here or he's chum."

She pressed transmit. "Look, please, I don't know how to make you believe me, but I swear I'm telling the truth. You blew the shit out of this boat and a bullet nicked a fuel line. I barely got enough left to maneuver. Just bring me my father and I'll do whatever you want. You win. We surrender. *Please believe me.*"

"I'm not going out there!" the man screamed.

"You *have* to come this way to get to Rockland Harbor."

"Why the fuck would I want to go to Rockland?"

"You'll never make it anywhere else in this storm! Don't be an idiot, I know this ocean! If you think you're going to Owls Head, you'll be wrecked on the Nubble."

She heard a string of profanities. "This better not be bullshit because your father's handcuffed to the rail. My boat sinks, he's going down."

"I promise I'm not lying, just please get here and bring me my father."

"Keep channel seventy-two open and listen for my instructions, over." The transmission clicked off with a burst of static.

"What're we doing?" Jackie cried. "You have a plan after we surrender or what?"

"Take us to Devil's Limb."

"In a storm like this? It's way the fuck out there!"

"Exactly."

"Do you have a plan?"

"I will when we get there."

Jackie shook her head, gunned the engine, and sent the boat surging through the moiling sea on a course for Devil's Limb. "You better think fast."

77

RISING FROM TAKEOFF at the Portland Jetport, the plane broke through the storm clouds and was suddenly bathed in the eerie light of the full Moon. Wyman Ford peered out the window, freshly awed by the spectacle. It was no longer the familiar orb of memory and romance but a changeling Moon, new and frightening, casting a greenish light over the mountains and canyons of cloud below the plane. The plume of debris from the strike had gone into orbit, spinning into an arc. An excited murmur of voices rose in the cabin as passengers peered out the windows. After gazing at it for a while, Ford, disturbed by the sight, slid the window shade shut and leaned back in his seat, closing his eyes, and concentrating on the meeting to come.

An hour and a half later, as the plane approached Dulles, Ford roused himself and, despite his vow not to, lifted the shade to look at the Moon again. The arc of debris was still stealing around the disc of the Moon, growing into a ring.

The city of Washington lay spread out below, bathed in an eerie green-blue glow that was neither day nor night.

He was not all that surprised to be met at the gate by federal agents, who escorted him through the deserted concourse, the television screens in waiting areas blaring identical news, showing pictures of the Moon intercut with various talking heads and reports from the reactions around the world. Panic, it seemed, was taking hold—particularly in the Middle East and Africa. There were rumors of the testing of nefarious and top-secret weapons by the U.S. or Israel, panic about radiation, hysterical people being rushed to emergency rooms.

The agents walked on either side of him, stone-faced, saying nothing. The streets of Washington were virtually deserted. People in the capital were, perhaps instinctually, staying inside.

Walking through baggage claim, the agents helped him into a police-issue Crown Victoria, placing him between them in the backseat. The car blazed through the deserted streets, light bar going, until they arrived at the Office of Science and Technology Policy on Seventeenth Street, pulling up to the ugly redbrick building where Lockwood and his staff worked.

As he expected, all the lights in the building were ablaze.

78

USING THE GPS, Harry Burr fixed a waypoint on his chart and set a course for the reef labeled "Devil's Limb."

He glanced back at the father; he lay slumped in the stern, still shackled to the taffrail, semiconscious, the pouring rain and sea spray drenching him. Burr might have hit him a little too hard that last time. Fuck it, he'd revive enough to play his part for the final act.

As the boat moved from the protection of the Muscle Ridge Islands into the exposed seas of Penobscot Bay, Burr found himself struggling with the wheel. One massive swell after the other marched toward him out of the darkness, each one honeycombed with foam and chop, lashed by sheets of rain. He turned on the spotlight mounted on the hardtop and swiveled it around, peering into the stormy murk. The beam illuminated mountains upon mountains of water as far as the beam could reach. It frightened him.

This was crazy. Maybe he didn't need to do anything— they'd probably sink on their own and solve his problem for him. But there was no guarantee of that and God knows what they would say to the Coast Guard in the meantime. They might have an emergency radio beacon on board—his boat did—which would go off automatically even if they didn't call the Coast Guard. No, he could not take the chance—not even the slightest—that they would survive to tell their tale. All three had to die. And the storm provided cover.

The radar screen was awash with static return from the rain, high seas, and blowing spume. He fiddled with gain but the radar was useless. The GPS put his speed at six knots and at least the chartplotter was working perfectly. He edged the throttle up to eight knots, the boat bucking and kicking through the sea, rising precipitously on each wave, ploughing through the foaming crest, and then dropping with a sickening falloff, almost as if going over a waterfall. He clung to the wheel, trying to keep his balance and keep the bow headed right, when all the forces in the world seemed to want to shove the boat sideways to the terrifying sea. As if to underscore his fright, a comber broke over the bow, green water racing along the gunwales, slopping into the cockpit and boiling out the scuppers. Losing his nerve, Harry eased his speed back down to six knots. The girl wasn't going anywhere—and the father was his ace in the hole. The bitch would never abandon her father.

He considered the possibility that this might be some kind of ruse, an attempt to lure him out into the open ocean where the storm would sink him. But surely that wasn't her plan: he had her father on board. Beyond that, he had the bigger, more seaworthy vessel. If anyone would sink, it would be them.

Did they plan to ambush him? Maybe. If so, that was the stupidest plan of all. He had a gun and he had the father shackled to a rail, the key in his pocket. Did they plan to lure him onto the rocks? Not with the state-of-the art GPS and chartplotter he had on board.

No, Harry Burr figured they were probably telling the truth about their fuel problem. They were so freaked out that they were willing to believe his lame promises. He had run no less than five loads through the Desert Eagle, thirty .44 mag rounds in all, and it seemed quite possible that at least one would have damaged the fuel system. Devil's Limb was on the way to Rockland, and it also made sense that getting around the Nubble into Owls Head would be way too dangerous in this sea. Everything they said held up.

Hanging onto the wheel with one hand, he took the four empty magazines and laid them out on the dashboard, next to a box of rounds. Keeping one hand on the wheel, he awkwardly thumbed the bullets into each magazine until all were filled. He slipped the heavy magazines into his pants pockets, two on each side. There would be no dicking around here. His plan was simple: kill them, sink their boat, and run for Rockland Harbor. There he would tie the boat up and walk away. Nothing was in his name; Straw had rented the boat by himself and picked him up in another location later, in a nearly deserted cove up the coast. Nobody even knew he was on board. Sure, in a few days or weeks they might find Straw's fish-eaten corpse with a bullet through the brain, but by then he'd be long gone. And he'd make sure Straw received a proper sea burial, with plenty of anchor chain and rope to keep him down.

As for the girls, well, he'd give them a similar burial, and sink their boat as well.

It was probably too late to get the hard drive and make his two hundred grand, at least on this go-around. But it was never too late to clean up—nor was cleanup optional. He felt the anger boiling up again and he tried to keep a lid on it. *All in a day's work,* he said to himself. *Win some, lose some.* This wasn't the first job he'd failed, and it wouldn't be the last. *Take care of loose ends and you'll live for the next job.*

He fished the cigarettes out of his pocket and realized they were, of course, soaked. The boat bucked over a wave and dropped down the other side, the engine roaring, and he grabbed the wheel and held on. Jesus Christ, he'd be glad when those three sons of bitches were at the bottom of the Atlantic.

79

AS THE *MAREA II* moved farther out into the open ocean, the wind increased to a roar and the seas rose up in monstrous hills and valleys, the foaming crests of the combers like dim gray ridges coming at them. Abbey let Jackie remain at the wheel, grateful for her seamanship. Jackie had a trick of riding up each wave at a thirty-degree angle, gradually increasing speed, and giving the boat a turn and a goose to bust through the breaking water on top, then throttling down as they sank into the trough. It scared the hell out of her but Jackie seemed to pull it off, again and again.

"Oh shit," said Jackie, peering ahead. A line of white came rumbling toward them, higher than the others, so high it looked like something detached from the sea, a freakish low cloud. The boat sank down into the preceding trough with stomach-churning speed, falling into an eerie silence as they entered the lee of the approaching wave. Then the boat began to rise, tipping up as the face of the wave loomed above them, striped with foam.

"Ease off!" Abbey cried, losing her nerve.

Jackie ignored her, pushing the rpms up to three thousand, turning the boat more diagonally to the wave as it surged up the face. The comber suddenly appeared above them, hissing loudly, a tumbling wall of water, and the boat's prow slammed into it as Jackie gave the wheel a sudden turn. Seawater broke over the bow with a roar and raced across the deck, slamming into the pilothouse windows and jetting off into space; the boat gave a shudder, hesitated as if about to be pushed under, and broke free with a roar, tipping forward and suddenly descending. Jackie instantly throttled back almost to idle and let gravity take the boat down into the next trough.

"There's another ahead," said Abbey. "Even bigger."

"I see it," murmured Jackie. She gunned the engine and climbed the face, busting through the breaking top, the entire boat groaning from the stress, before sinking back down. They fought through the massive series of waves, one after another, mountains of water on a march to nowhere. Each time Abbey felt sure they were going under; but each time the boat shed the water and righted before plunging down to start the terrifying process all over again.

"Jesus, you learn that working on your dad's boat?"

"We used to fish beyond Monhegan in the winter. Got caught in a few northeasters, no big deal."

She was trying to keep her voice steady but Abbey wasn't fooled. She thought of her own, overprotective father, who had never let her drive his boat. She felt sick with fear for him, shackled to the rail, out in this sea with that maniac. Her plan was crazy, in fact it wasn't even a plan. Surrender? And then what? Of course he would kill them all. That was his intention. What was she thinking, that she could talk him out of it? Should she make an emergency call to the Coast Guard? He'd hear it and kill her father if she did that. And even if he didn't, the Coast Guard would never go out in this weather.

She had to think of something.

And then, over channel 72, a voice grated out: "Daddy's awake. Want to say hello?"

80

THE AGENTS ESCORTED Ford into the conference room. As soon as he came in, Lockwood leapt up from his position at the head of a large conference table, ringed by suits and uniforms, surrounded by flat-panel screens. By the dark and serious looks on their faces he knew they must be at least partially aware of what was going on.

"Good God, Wyman, we've been trying to reach you for hours! We've got an extraordinary situation on our hands. The president needs a recommendation by seven."

"I have some information for you of critical value," Ford said, laying the briefcase on the table and gazing around, assessing his audience. Lockwood was flanked by Gen. Mickelson, his grizzled hair roughly combed, his casual uniform rumpled, the athletic frame uncharacteristically tense. A contingency of NPF people occupied one side of the table, among which he recognized Chaudry and Derkweiler, along with an Asian woman with a badge that said Leung. A smattering of OSTP scientists and national security officials sat at the far end; conferenced in on flat-panel screens were the chairman of the Joint Chiefs, the national security advisor Manfred, the head of NASA, and the director of national intelligence. The long cherry-wood table was littered with legal pads, paper, and laptops. Various secretaries and assistants sat in chairs along the walls, taking notes. The atmosphere was one of tension, verging on desperation.

Ford opened his briefcase and took out the fake hard drive, setting it down gently on the table like it was a piece of Baccarat crystal. Then he took out the large print of Voltaire33, the clearest one of the batch which he had blown up at Kinko's, and unrolled it. "This, ladies and gentlemen," he said. "This is an image taken by the Mars Mapping Orbiter back on March twenty-third."

He let a beat pass and he showed it around. "It depicts an object on the surface of Mars. I believe this object fired on the Earth in April, and fired at the Moon tonight."

Another moment of shocked stasis, and then the table erupted with talk, questions, expostulations. Ford waited for the hubbub to die down and said, "The image came from that classified hard drive there."

"Where on Mars is it?" the woman named Leung spoke up.

"It's all on the drive," said Ford. "Everything." He added, lying, "I don't know the exact coordinates offhand."

"Impossible!" cried Derkweiler. "We would have seen that in our general reviews long ago!"

"You didn't see it before because it was hidden in the shadow of a crater, almost invisible. The image here required enormous processing time and skill to tease it out of the darkness."

Chaudry rose from the table and, giving Ford a suspicious glance, reached out and picked up the drive. He turned it over in his mahogany hands, his black eyes examining it intensely, his California ponytail out of place among the suited Washington crowd.

"This isn't an NPF drive." He looked at Ford, his eyes narrowing. "Where'd you get this drive?"

"From the late Mark Corso," said Ford.

Chaudry paled slightly. "No one can copy or remove a drive like this from NPF. Our data encryption and security procedures are fail-safe."

"Is anything really impossible to a skillful computer technician? If you doubt it, check the serial number on the side."

Chaudry examined it further. "It does seem to be an NPF serial number. But this . . . this *image* of yours. I'd like to see the original. This could be Photoshopped for all we know."

"Proof of it is right there on the drive, in the original binary data from the MRO." Ford removed a piece of paper from his suit pocket and held it up to the group. "Problem is, the NPF password on this drive has been changed. I have the new password to unlock it—without which the drive is useless." He gave the paper a little shake. "Trust me, it's *real.*"

The woman named Marjory Leung had risen from her seat. "Excuse me, did you say the *late* Mark Corso?"

"Yes. Mark Corso was murdered two days ago."

Leung swayed, like she might collapse. "*Murdered?*"

"That's right. And it seems his predecessor, Dr. Freeman, was also murdered—and not by a homeless man. Both he and Corso were killed by a professional—someone looking for that very drive on the table."

A deep silence settled over the room.

"So you see," said Ford, "we have a big job ahead of us. Because not only is the world apparently under attack, but someone on our side has betrayed us."

81

BURR HANDED THE VHF mike to the lobsterman, placing it in his manacled hands. It didn't matter what he said now; Burr just wanted to remind the girl her father was alive and in desperate straits, keep her terrified, panicked, easier to handle.

"Dad? *Dad*? Are you okay?"

"Abbey! Get the hell off the water! Your boat can't take it! Go!"

"Dad." There was a choking silence. "We're out of fuel."

"Good God, Abbey, he's got a gun. Call the Coast Guard! Don't be fooled—"

Burr snatched back the mike. It was an obscure, unused channel and they were broadcasting at a quarter watt, a range that wouldn't reach the mainland, especially in this weather—but why take chances?

"You hear that?" he said into the mike. "Everything's going to be okay, you'll get your father back. I need you alive, I can't get the drive otherwise. Think about it—you're more useful to me alive than dead. We need to figure this out, but let's do it in a place where we're not going to drown. You hear me?"

"I hear you," Abbey said tersely.

He clicked off, thinking that they probably didn't believe it but what could they do? He was holding all the cards. Sure, they might have some stupid plan but it wasn't going to work.

The boat rose on a wave and lurched to starboard. Christ, he hadn't been paying attention. A rogue wave was approaching, a two-story wall of water, black as Guinness with a breaking crest. He turned the wheel toward the wave, the boat lifting fast. But he couldn't get it all the way around before the roaring crest slammed into the hull, knocking the boat sideways, and it fell back as ebony water burst over the gunwale, pushing the boat down and heeling it over.

The boat tipped into the trough, the water boiling out the scuppers, the deck tilting thirty degrees from the horizontal, while he clung to the wheel, speechless with fear. He tried to turn the wheel, but it was as if a huge weight was pushing back, pressing the boat down. He shoved the throttle forward but heard no answering rumble from the engine, just the creaking strain of thousands of pounds of water roaring over the boat. And then the wheel began to loosen up and the boat shuddered as the weight of the sea lessened, the water pouring off the bow and gunwales. Gradually it righted itself.

Burr had never been so frightened in his life. He looked at the chartplotter; they were halfway to Devil's Limb. Behind the reef they could at least get into the lee of this crazy sea. They were going six knots—how much longer would it take? Ten minutes. Ten more minutes of hell.

"Let me take the helm," said the fisherman. "You're going to sink this boat."

"Fuck off." Burr braced himself as another whitecapped comber came at them, the boat rising swiftly to meet the boiling mountain of water, which slammed into it, the pilothouse shuddering and groaning as if about to come apart at the seams. If it fried the electronics . . . he'd be helpless.

He clung to the wheel, the boat sinking precipitously down the backside into another bottomless trough of the wave, the water swirling around his feet and rushing for the scuppers.

"Unlock me," said Straw. "Otherwise we're both going to the bottom."

Burr fished in his pocket and pulled out the key. He stretched out his hand. "Unlock yourself, bring the cuffs."

Keeping one hand on the wheel, he pulled out his gun and watched as Straw unlocked his cuffs and came forward, holding the rail for stability.

The boat wallowed for a moment in the trough, eerily quiet, and began to mount up. It was turning broadside again.

"Gimme the helm!" Straw cried, seizing it.

Burr stepped back, pointing the gun at him. "Lock yourself to the wheel."

The fisherman ignored him, struggling with the wheel and throttling up as the boat tipped up the face of the wave, steeper and steeper, and suddenly the wind was howling around them, the air full of water, all confusion and noise. The boat rammed through the crest and fell back down, righting itself and subsiding into the churning trough.

"I said lock your wrist to the wheel!" Burr fired a round through the roof to underscore the demand.

The fisherman locked his left wrist to the steeling wheel. Burr stepped over, tested it, making sure it was really locked, took the key and tossed it into the sea.

"You follow the course straight to the reef. Any tricks and I'll kill you. And then I'll kill your daughter."

The boat rose on another wave and a lightning bolt split the sky with a terrific roar, briefly illuminating a wilderness of water.

Burr braced himself as the next wave bore down on them. The fisherman said nothing, hanging grimly onto the wheel, his face set toward darkness.

82

IN THE SILENCE, there was a faint squeaking of wheels and a duty officer came in pushing a cart, serving coffee all around.

"You said you were to make a recommendation to the president at seven," Ford said. "What are the options?"

Lockwood spread his hands. "Dr. Chaudry?"

Chaudry rubbed a hand over his finely sculpted cheek. "We've got half a dozen satellites orbiting Mars. We had planned to reassign all to a new mission—to locate the source of these attacks. But now you seem to have those coordinates."

"Yes," said Mickelson, "and with those coordinates we could use one or more of those satellites as a weapon, send it crashing into the alien weapon at high speed."

Chaudry shook his head. "That would be about as effective as throwing an egg at a tank."

"Option two," said Mickelson, ploughing ahead, "is to launch a nuke at it."

"The launch window wouldn't be for another six months

minimum," said Chaudry, "and the travel time to Mars would be well over a year."

"The nuclear option is our only effective means of attack," said the chairman of the Joint Chiefs from a screen.

Chaudry turned to him. "Admiral, I doubt the alien weapon is going to sit there and allow itself to be nuked."

"May I remind you again that the operative word here is 'machine.' We don't know for a fact that it is a weapon," said Lockwood.

"It's a Goddamned *weapon*," said Mickelson. "Just look at it!"

Chaudry spoke quietly. "That artifact comes from a civilization of tremendous technological sophistication. I'm truly aghast that you people think we can kill it with a nuke. We're like a cockroach committee debating how to kill the exterminator. Any military option is futile—and exceedingly dangerous—and the sooner we recognize it the better."

A tense silence built. The conference room had grown hot. Ford took the opportunity to remove his jacket and casually draped it over the back of his chair. *The bait*, he thought. Now to hook the fish. Or the mole, as it were.

83

THE *MAREA II* crested another terrifying wave and Abbey caught a glimpse, through the lashing rain, of a smudge of white-water ahead. The chartplotter placed them a few hundred yards from the first of the three great rocks.

"There! Ahead!"

"I see it," said Jackie calmly, easing the wheel over. "I'm heading into the lee."

The sea calmed as they entered the protected area of water behind the rocks. A huge swell still warped through, but the chop and wind dropped considerably. As the boat rose and fell, Abbey could see immense seas thundering along the base of the rocks, some of the curlers reaching twenty feet or more, rearing into the rock and exploding upward as if in slow motion, great spumes of atomized water.

"All right," said Jackie, as she brought the boat into a slow, tight circle. "What's the plan?"

"I—" Abbey hesitated. "We pretend to surrender. He'll

take us aboard his boat and then we'll look for our opportunity."

Jackie stared. "You call that a plan?"

"What else can we do?"

"He's going to kill us, *boom boom*. And that's it. There won't be time to 'look for an opportunity.' And don't fool yourself, he ain't giving up your father. Abbey, I want to save your father but I don't want to throw away my own life. You understand?"

"I'm thinking," Abbey gasped.

Jackie brought the boat around in a slow circle, staying close to the lee shore. "Stop hyperventilating, he's going to be here any minute. Focus. You're smart. You can do it."

Abbey turned to the radar to see if she could get a fix on the approaching boat. She fiddled with the gain, trying to tune out the rain and sea return. The screen was a wash of static. Slowly, as she manipulated the various parameters, she began to get an image of the huge exposed reefs to starboard, big green blobs on the screen. And then she saw another blob, smaller, washing in and out—moving toward them.

"That's it," she said. "They're here. Back the boat in that channel between the two rocks."

"You crazy? That's a narrow channel with surf on both sides!"

"Give me the helm then."

"No. *I'll* do it."

"Get the boat in there so he can't see us on his radar."

Jackie stared at her, face pale. "And then?"

"We need weapons." Abbey threw open the cabin door and scrambled down the shuddering steps—hanging onto the rails. With a hideous feeling of déjà vu, she threw open the cabin, hauled out the toolbox, and removed a small pair of marine bolt cutters, standard onboard equipment for dealing with frozen bolts, clamps, and rods. She also took out a fish knife and a long Phillips-head screwdriver. She came back up and slammed the tools on the dash.

Abbey grabbed Jackie by both shoulders and leaned into her face. "You want a plan? Here it is. Ram. Board. Kill him. Cut Dad free."

"We ram them and we're both gonna sink."

"Not if you hit them broadside, aft of the pilothouse. The skeg'll just ride up on the gunwale, I'll jump off, and then you reverse like hell and pull back off before the boat breaks its spine. The *Marea II*'s built like a brick shithouse."

"Ram, board, and kill? He's armed! What've we got—a fish knife?"

"You got a better plan?"

"No."

"Then we go with what we've got."

The green blob on the radar screen was creeping closer. Abbey glanced out at the dark water and could see a glimmer of light.

"He's got his spotlights on! Get going!"

Jackie throttled the boat up and moved it behind the rock, backing and turning furiously, fighting the wind, sea, and a powerful current running between the rocks. The roaring noise of the surf was deafening, the wind blowing tatters of spume over their boat. Jackie struggled to keep the boat in the middle of the channel, beyond the rearing breakers that thundered into the spires of rock.

"How am I going to know when to come out and ram him?"

"He'll enter the lee," said Abbey, "just like we did. He'll be looking for us, shining the light around. A slow target. When he doesn't see us he'll call. That's our signal. Wait for him to get broadside, then you come out full-speed ahead and t-bone him. Here, take a knife."

Jackie took the long fish knife and stuck it into her belt.

Abbey stuck a long thin screwdriver in one pocket and pushed the boltcutters through a belt loop. "I'll be at the bow rail, ready to jump on board."

The sea pushed the boat toward the rocks and Jackie struggled to control it, reversing, trying to keep it out of the sucking surf. "It isn't going to work—"

"*Don't* say it."

84

THE CLOCKS IN the room approached 3 A.M. as the discussion crawled along, going nowhere. From the flat-panel at the end of the room, the chairman of the Joint Chiefs finally said a few words, addressing them to Chaudry. His voice was mild, courteous. "If you wish to take the military option off the table, Dr. Chaudry, what do you propose to replace it with?"

Chaudry stared at him. "Study. Research. Now that we know where it is—assuming that image is of the thing responsible for the strangelet missiles—we can redirect all our moveable satellite resources toward it. We just need to get the coordinates off that disk."

"And then?" the chairman asked.

"We attempt communication."

"And what, exactly, would we say?"

"Explain that we want peace—that we're a peaceful people. We aren't a threat to them."

"A peaceful people?" Mickelson said, with a snort. "Let's

hope that 'machine' has been sound asleep over the past few bloody centuries."

"That may in fact *be* the problem," said Chaudry, "the reason it's threatening us. Because of our aggressive behavior. Who knows how long it's been monitoring us, listening in on all our radio and television broadcasts which have been pouring into space for the past century. Its computers would decipher them, of course. Anyone looking at all our news broadcasts over the past hundred years would take a dim view of humanity."

"How the hell would it know English?" Mickelson asked.

"If it was built to keep tabs on intelligent life," said Chaudry, "it's probably got exceedingly powerful artificial intelligence capabilities; one would assume it could decipher any language."

"How old is it? When was it built?"

Ford spoke up. "The image shows erosion and pitting by micrometeoroids as well as blanketing by regolith thrown up by ancient impacts. That machine's at least a few hundred million years old."

Mickelson turned to Chaudry. "You agree?"

Chaudry scrutinized the image. "Yes, I do. This is very old."

"So you think it's real?"

Chaudry hesitated. "I'd like to see the original images and its location before I answer that question."

"We don't have time right now for verification," said Lockwood. "We have four hours to report to the president. Let's pass by the military option and move on to communication. Assuming it can interpret English, do we communicate with it?"

"We've got to reassure them we mean no harm," said Chaudry.

"You start pleading peace with them," Mickelson said, "that's advertising your weakness."

"We *are* weak," said Chaudry, "and that machine knows it."

Silence followed.

Derkweiler raised a hand. "The Spacewatch group at NPF has been studying ways to divert killer asteroids. Maybe we could use one of their techniques to nudge a large asteroid from the Asteroid Belt and send it plunging into the machine. Like a dinosaur-extinction-size asteroid."

Chaudry shook his head. "It would take years to plan such a mission, launch it, and get it to Mars. And we don't even have the technology yet to do it. We've got to tell the president the truth: *we have no options.*" He glared around the room.

This was followed by another long silence, which Lockwood finally broke. "We're still hung up on the military option. Forget the military option and let's talk about something else—what the hell *is* this machine, who put it there, and what's it trying to do?"

Ford cleared his throat. "It might be defective."

"Defective?" Chaudry looked surprised.

"It's old. It's been sitting for a long time," said Ford. "If it's damaged, maybe there's a way to mislead it. Fool it. Trick it in some way. Its behavior up to this point has been erratic, unpredictable. That may not be deliberate—it may be a sign of malfunctioning."

"How?" asked Mickelson.

At this a silence fell. Lockwood glanced at his watch. "It's almost dawn. I ordered a quick breakfast at five in the private dining room. We'll patch over the others and continue the discussion there."

Ford rose, deliberately leaving his jacket draped on the back of the chair. He exited the room and waited in the hall for the room to empty, the stragglers emerging and making their way to the dining room at the far end of the hall. Ford lingered near the door, watching everyone leave. The second to last to leave was Marjory Leung. She looked like hell. Ford had been sure she was the mole, but she hadn't taken his bait.

Chaudry was the last to emerge from the conference room.

The mission director came out, his hand just withdrawing from his suitcoat pocket. Ford stepped up quickly as if to speak to him confidentially, shot his hand into the pocket, and pulled out a piece of paper.

"What the hell—?" Chaudry cried, his wiry body moving like lightning, his arm shooting out to snatch back the paper, but Ford sprang back out of reach.

He held the paper up before a group of astonished witnesses. "This is the password to the hard drive. Dr. Chaudry here just lifted it out of my jacket pocket. I said there was a mole in your group. And we just caught him."

85

BURR STOOD IN the pilothouse, swiveling the spotlight around, peering into the storm. The beam stabbed into the raging murk, showing nothing but boiling water and rocks. Where were they? Had they drifted out of the lee? He fiddled with the dials of the radar, trying to tune in a coherent image beyond the limited range of the light, but all he could get was static.

A bolt of lightning flashed, illuminating the towering rocks on his right. The roar of surf was almost deafening and the water around him was webbed with spindrift, the sea heaving.

"Son of a bitch!" Burr pulled down the VHF mike and pressed transmit. "Where are you?"

No answer.

"Respond or he's dead!"

Still no answer. Was it a trap? He hollered into the VHF, "I got the gun at his head and the next one's for him!"

With a sudden roar the boat surged forward, throwing

Burr off balance. He seized the passenger seat and arrested his fall, trying to pull himself up as the boat accelerated. "What the hell are you doing?" he cried, struggling to brace himself and get the gun back over on the fisherman. He stared through the pilothouse windows: the son of a bitch was accelerating the boat straight for the reef, a wall of rock rising from a hell of boiling surf, rain streaming from its ramparts.

"No!" He lunged for the wheel with his left hand while bringing the gun up with his right and firing it almost point-blank at Straw. But the fisherman anticipated the move and jerked the wheel, causing the boat to careen sideways, throwing him off balance. The shot went wide and Burr fell hard, crashing through the flimsy wheelhouse door to end up sprawled in the rear cockpit.

"Motherfucker!" He struggled to rise, grasping the gunwale railing and pulling himself up into the teeth of the storm. The boat had swung ninety degrees and was still tilting to one side, coming broadside to the sea. Straw jerked the wheel back again, trying to keep Burr off balance. But he seized the rail and hauled himself to his feet despite the tilting deck, bucking and heaving, and braced himself while bringing the gun up and aiming it into the pilothouse at Straw. He was about to fire when he heard a new sound—a full-throated roar of an engine—and turned to see a terrifying sight. A boat suddenly materialized out of the storm, bulling straight at him at full speed, gleaming steel keel splitting the black sea, throwing water to either side. And standing in the forepeak, gripping the rails, like a figurehead from hell, was the girl. He scrambled backward, trying desperately to get out of the way, but at that very moment

Straw threw the *Halcyon* into reverse, guaranteeing a collision and throwing him sideways again. Off-balance, one arm wrapped around the rail, Burr could do nothing but point the weapon and unload it, pulling the trigger one, two, three, four times—

With a deafening crash of pulverized fiberglass, the bow slammed into the gunwale, bursting through it and riding up on the deck; Burr made one final effort to throw himself out of the way but he still didn't have his footing on the bucking deck. The bow struck him square in the chest with a massive bone-crunching blow. It felt like his rib cage had been shoved into his spinal cord and he hurtled through the air, plummeted into the raging waters, sinking helplessly down into the black, cold, crushing depths.

86

WITH A SICKENING smack, Abbey saw the body fly head over heels into the sea and disappear. The force of the collision threw her forward into the curved rail and she almost went over. With a roar Jackie reversed the *Marea II*'s engines, the water boiling around the stern, and Abbey clung for dear life while the *Marea II* ground to a halt, heeling to one side and almost capsizing; after a moment of terror the boat backed off and righted itself. Abbey hadn't had a chance to board. Her boat's momentum pushed the other into the breaking seas, where a large incoming comber caught it and carried it onto the rocks with a shuddering crash. Abbey, horrified, could see her father in the pilothouse, struggling to free himself from the handcuffs on the wheel.

Without waiting for orders, Jackie slammed the *Marea II* into forward and brought it up to the crippled stern of the other boat.

"Dad!" Bolt cutters in hand, Abbey took a flying leap off the bow, landing in the sinking stern. An incoming wave heaved the boat up against the rocks a second time with an enormous crunching sound, throwing her down. Gripping the bolt cutters, she grabbed a broken rail and struggled to her feet, trying to maintain her balance on the buckling, splitting deck. A bolt of lightning blasted the scene with spectral light, followed by a thunder crack. She staggered toward the pilothouse. Her father was inside, still shackled to the wheel.

"Dad!"

"Abbey!"

A vertiginous comber materialized out of the dimness, rising like a mountain above the boat. Abbey braced herself, wrapping her arms around the rail as the wave came crashing down, throwing the boat full against the wall of rock and crushing the pilothouse like a Styrofoam cup. Buried in roiling water, Abbey clung on for dear life, trying to keep from being ripped from the boat by the withdrawing surge. After what seemed like an eternity, her lungs almost bursting, the swirl of water subsided and she surfaced, gasping for breath. The boat was a sudden wreck, lying on its side, the hull split, the ribs sprung, the pilothouse in pieces—and the helm underwater. Her father, gone.

With a superhuman effort she grabbed the railing, hauling herself to the shattered pilothouse. The boat was sinking fast and everything was underwater.

"Dad!" she screamed. "Dad!"

Another wave slammed the boat, throwing her so violently into the smashed wall of the pilothouse that it tore the bolt cutters from her hands, and they vanished into the black water.

She held her breath and dove down, her eyes open

underwater in the dim turbulence. She saw a thrashing leg, an arm—her father. Handcuffed to the wheel. Underwater.

The bolt cutters.

With a scissor kick she propelled herself to the bottom of the overturned pilothouse, frantically feeling around for the cutters. The dim light from the *Marea II*'s spotlight filtered down and gave her enough light to see. Jagged underwater rocks were cutting and sawing through the lower part of the pilothouse where it had caught on the reef, but below that was yawning black space—the cutters had sunk into the abyss. The current was swirling and the water was full of debris and oil streaming up from the shattered engine, making it almost impossible to see. That was it; with the cutters gone, her father didn't stand a chance. She couldn't hold her breath any longer and surfaced, gulped air, then dove again, with the crazy hope she could dive to the bottom and find them.

Suddenly there they were: the bolt cutters had hung up on a broken window frame, dangling over the ocean depths. She snatched them and swam up to the wheel. Her father was no longer thrashing, floating silently. She grabbed the wheel to steady herself, fixed the cutters around the handcuff chain, and slammed the handles shut. The chain parted and she dropped the cutters and grabbed her father's hair, dragging him up. They broke the surface inside the pilot-house, just as another wave slammed the boat again, rolling it upside down. They were suddenly underwater, Abbey still grasping her father's hair, and a moment later she pulled him back up. This time they surfaced underneath the cabin hull, in an air pocket.

"Dad, Dad!" she screamed, shaking him, trying to keep

his head above water, her voice ringing hollow in the small air space under the hull. "Dad!"

He coughed, gasped.

Abbey shook him. "Dad!"

"Abbey . . . Oh my God . . . What?"

"We're trapped under the hull—!"

A tremendous crash jarred the space and the hull shuddered, rolling sideways; a moment later a second booming crash ripped open the hull and it parted with a tearing screech, water surging in as air rushed out.

"Abbey! *Out!*"

In the confusion of water she felt herself given a great shove and they were in the raging surf just outside the rocks, being drawn toward the killing surf by an undertow.

"Abbeeeey!" She saw the *Marea II*, thirty feet off, Jackie standing at the rail with a life ring. She flung it in their direction, but the rope wasn't quite long enough and it fell short. A moment later her father surfaced. Grabbing a fistful of his hair, scissor-kicking and stroking one-handed as hard as she could, she dragged him to the ring. Jackie reversed the boat and pulled them out of the sucking breakers and then hauled them in, hoisting them over the side, one after the other, where they fell sprawling on the deck.

87

CHAUDRY STARED AT Ford with a pair of cold eyes. "I was protecting that crucial piece of classified information that you so carelessly left in your jacket pocket."

The others were looking on, startled.

"Really?" Ford said quietly. "Then why not say something to me directly? Why wait until everyone was out of the room and then steal it? Sorry, Dr. Chaudry: that paper was bait and you're the fish that took it."

"Come now," said Chaudry, abruptly relaxing. "This is absurd. You can't possibly believe what you're saying. We're all under a strain. What in the world would I want with that password? I'm mission director—I have access to all the classified data."

"But not to the location, which is on that drive. That's what your clients have been after all along—the location." Ford glanced at the group, which hadn't yet reacted. He could read skepticism in their eyes. "It all started with Freeman. He was murdered by a professional assassin specifically for that hard drive."

"Absurd," said Chaudry. "The killing was thoroughly investigated. It was a homeless man."

"Who was in charge of the investigation? The FBI—with the heavy involvement of NPF security and you, personally."

"This is a blood libel on my reputation!" said Chaudry angrily.

"One can speculate how this worked," said Ford. "You didn't do this for money. This was too big for money. You realized long ago that Freeman had discovered an alien machine on Mars, although Freeman himself hadn't quite gotten that far with his conclusions. So you fired him to keep the knowledge to yourself. And then you learned he'd stolen a classified hard drive. Somehow decrypted it, copied it, gotten it out. Something even you couldn't do. What an opportunity for your clients to get all the crucial information. And then you learned that Corso continued the work. Not only that, he built on it. *He discovered the location of the machine.* And it was on that hard drive. So you told your handlers, and they went to get it, killed Corso and his mother. But they didn't get the drive—because I found it first."

Chaudry faced the stupefied group. "This man has no proof, no evidence, just a crazy conspiracy story. We have work to do."

Ford glanced around at the group, and saw skepticism, even hostility, in their eyes.

"Freeman was killed by a piano-wire garrote," said Ford. "No homeless drug addict would kill that way. No: the killer wanted *information*—the hard disk. That's what the garrote was for. You wrap that around someone's neck, they're gonna talk. Except Freeman."

"What a fairy tale," said Chaudry with an easy laugh. "Why are you listening to him?"

Suddenly Marjory Leung spoke up. "I believe it. I *believe* Dr. Chaudry is guilty."

"Marjory, have you lost your mind?"

She turned to him. "I'll never forget what you said about Pakistan, India, and China. That evening?" She flushed. "That evening we spent together? You said that Pakistan's destiny was to become a world technological power. That the U.S. was finished, that it was spoiled by wealth and materialism and easy living, that we'd lost our work ethic, that our educational system was collapsing. And I'll never forget when you said that China and India were too corrupt and would eventually lose out to Pakistan."

"Pakistan?" Lockwood said. "But I thought Dr. Chaudry was from India."

Leung turned. "He's *Kashmiri*. Big difference."

Chaudry remained grimly silent.

"I know how it works," said Leung. "I've experienced it myself. A few of my Chinese colleagues, they drop a hint here, a hint there. They think that because I'm ethnic Chinese that I should naturally pass on information to help their space program. It burns me up. Because I'm an American. I'd never do that. But *you*—I know what you said that night. I know how you think. That's what this is all about: you were passing information to Pakistan."

"It wasn't about money," said Ford. "But something a lot deeper. Patriotism, perhaps, or religion. This is the greatest discovery of all time. Very, very tempting to get your hands on it, to own it. Who knows what technological advances could be gleaned from an alien machine—a weapon no less. And then when a hard drive with all the information on it miraculously escaped from NPF, there was the opportunity."

"What rubbish," said Chaudry.

"I knew the mole was probably in this room. So I set up a little sting operation. With the password. And look who we caught."

"You finished?" said Chaudry coolly.

Ford glanced around, meeting a mass of skeptical faces.

"Well, well, that's quite a story," said Chaudry. "There's only one problem with it: it's all supposition. It's true I had a little thing with Marjory, like so many others at NPF. Bad judgment. But I'm no spy."

"Oh yeah?" said Leung. "Then why did Freeman tell me, right before he was fired, that you wanted his entire analysis of the gamma ray data? Only to get it and tell him the next day you'd fire him if he kept working on it? Why did you go to such great lengths to discourage anyone at NPF from looking too closely at the gamma ray data? You got Derkweiler here to fire Corso—because *he* got interested in gamma rays."

Comprehension blossomed on Derkweiler's face. "That's right. And then you asked me for all of Corso's gamma ray analysis. I wondered why you were suddenly so interested."

Chaudry said, "What utter nonsense. I have no recollection of that."

"That was just a week ago."

"I won't stand for these ridiculous accusations."

Ford held up the slip with the password on it. "You could have asked me for this. But you didn't. You *stole* it. Why?"

"I told you, it was for security reasons. You just left it in your coat pocket."

Leung said, "You asked me repeatedly, that night: '*What did Freeman tell you about the gamma rays?*'" She paused, then pointed a trembling finger at him. "You . . . are a *murderer.*"

"Pakistan?" said Lockwood, finally speaking up. "But that's a backward country. What in hell would they want with information like this? They have no space program, no science, nothing."

"I beg to differ," said Chaudry, his voice icy. "We are the country of A. Q. Khan, one of the greatest scientists who ever lived. We have the bomb, long-range missiles, uranium enrichment. But most importantly, we have God on our side. Everything that happens is Fate, which is another word for God's plan. The die was cast long ago. Those who think they can affect the true course of things are delusional. Einstein called it Block Time. We call it Fate. Who, I ask you, is more powerful than Allah?"

Ford turned to one of the duty officers standing dumbly in the hall. "I think you better take this man into custody."

Nobody moved. The duty guard seemed frozen into place. All that could be heard was Chaudry's hard breathing.

Mickelson removed his sidearm and pointed it at Chaudry. "You heard the man. Cuff him."

Chaudry held his hands out, crossed his wrists. His face twisted into a smile. "Please."

As the cuffs went on, Chaudry went on quietly, "It doesn't matter now. You're finished as a country and you know it. We are pure and we have God's favor. In the long run, we will prevail. Mark my words: the future belongs to Pakistan.

We will defeat India, God willing, and usher in an era of Pakistani science that will dazzle the world."

Tucking the gun back into his rumpled uniform, Mickelson spoke sharply to the duty officer. "Get him out of here." He turned to the group. "We've got ninety minutes before we brief the president, so pull yourselves together."

Ford said, "Now that we've exposed the mole, I can give you the location of the machine. Because it's not on Mars at all."

The group, shaken up, fell silent.

"It's on Deimos."

88

JACKIE KEPT THE boat in a slow circle in the lee behind Devil's Limb while Abbey and her father examined it for damage. He leaned into the main hatch, scrutinizing the engine compartment, while Abbey held a light for him. She could see black, oily bilgewater sloshing around in the well; the boat was leaking.

"How bad is it?"

Straw emerged, straightened up, and wiped his hands on a paper towel. He was soaked and his light brown hair was plastered to his forehead. He had a black eye and a cut on his cheekbone. "There're some nasty cracks in the hull that could get worse in a heavy sea. Nothing the bilge pumps can't handle now."

He came back up the companionway stairs into the pilot-house. Jackie had tuned the VHF to the marine weather channel, and the computerized voice droned out the ugly statistics: wave heights to fifteen feet, winds thirty knots gusting to sixty, heavy rain, a tidal surge five feet higher than mean, small craft warnings . . . The storm was going to get worse before it got better.

Jackie stood at the helm, peering at the paper chart spread on the dashboard tray. "I think we should go around Sheep Island and take the inside passage to Rockland."

Straw shook his head. "Put us in a beam sea. We'd be better off making a straight shot across the bay—in a following sea."

A flash of lightning lit up the sky, followed by a boom. Abbey caught a glimpse of the wreckage of the other boat, now just a tangled mass of shattered fiberglass being pounded into nothing by the relentless breakers on the reef.

"We could always head to Vinalhaven," said Jackie. "That would put us in a heading sea."

"That's a possibility."

Abbey finally said, "We're not going to Rockland or Vinalhaven."

Her father turned to her. "What do you mean?"

She faced him and Jackie. "We've got something more important to do."

They stared at her.

"This is going to sound crazy but Jackie will back me up. Last year, the U.S. put a satellite in orbit around Mars. The goal was to map the planet and its moons. One of the things it did was take pictures of Mars's moon, Deimos, with ground-penetrating radar."

"Abbey, please, this is *not* the time—"

"*Listen* to me, Dad! The radar woke up something on Deimos. A very ancient, very dangerous alien machine. Probably a weapon."

"Of all the crazy—"

"*Dad!*"

He fell silent.

"An *alien* weapon. Which fired on the Earth. That meteor we saw a few months ago was the first shot. That show on the Moon was the second shot."

She briefly explained how she and Jackie went looking for the meteorite and found the hole, how she'd met Wyman Ford, and what they had discovered.

The expression on her father's face suddenly changed from disbelief to skepticism. He looked at her intently. "And?"

"That shot at the Moon was a demonstration. A warning."

"So what's this thing you want to do?" asked Jackie.

A gust of wind buffeted the pilothouse, spray hitting the windows. "I know this sounds crazy, but I think we can stop it."

Jackie looked incredulous. "Three wet people huddled in a boat in a storm off the coast of Maine, without cell reception, are gonna save the world? Are you nuts?"

"I have an idea."

"Oh no, not one of your ideas." Jackie groaned.

"You know the Earth Station, that big white bubble on Crow Island? Remember going there on field trips in high school? Inside that bubble there's a dish that AT&T built to send telephone calls to Europe. Now it's used for satellite communications, uplink and downlink of television shows, Internet and cell phone calls, shit like that."

"Well?" Jackie swiped her wet hair out of her face.

"We point it at Deimos and use it to send that motherfucker a message."

Jackie stared at Abbey. "Like what kind of message? 'My big brother's gonna beat you up'?"

"I haven't quite figured that out yet."

89

JACKIE LAUGHED. "You really are crazy, you know that? We'll be lucky just to get our ass into port in this storm. But you want us to cross Muscongus Bay to send a message? Can't this wait until tomorrow?"

"We have no idea when the weapon might fire again. And something tells me the next shot might be the end."

"How's that alien machine gonna know English?"

"It's highly advanced and it's been listening to our radio chatter for at least two months now, since it was awakened."

"If it's so advanced, call it on the VHF."

"Come on, Jackie, be serious. Even if it could distinguish our radio call from a billion other signals, it wouldn't take it as official. What's required is a big, strong, powerful signal hitting it with a clear message. Something that looks like an official communication from the Earth."

Her father turned to her. "Why can't the government deal with it?"

"You trust the *government* to handle this? First of all,

they're in denial. Either they'll hold endless meetings or they'll take a potshot at it. Either way, we're dead. On top of that, I think the CIA, among others, have been trying to kill us. Even Ford was afraid of them. We're on our own—*and we must do something, now.*"

"Getting to Crow means traversing the Ripp Island tidal bore and then three miles of open water," said her father. "We'll never make it in this storm."

"We've *got* to make it."

"And once we're there," Jackie continued, "we're going to waltz in there and say, 'Hey, can we borrow your Earth Station to make a call to aliens on Mars?'"

"We'll force them, if need be."

"With what? A boat hook?"

Abbey stared at her. "Jackie, you don't get it, do you? *The Earth is under attack.* We may be the only ones who know it."

"Hell with this," said Jackie. "Let's take a vote." She glanced at Straw. "What do you say? I'm for going to Vinalhaven."

Abbey looked at her father, his pale eyes red, his beard dripping water. He stared back at her. "Abbey, you sure about this?"

"Not completely."

"It's more like an educated guess, then?"

"Yes."

"It sounds crazy."

"I know it does. But it isn't. Please, Dad, trust me—just this once."

He was silent for a long time, and then he nodded and turned to Jackie. "We're going to Crow Island. Jackie, I want you as spotter. Abbey, you navigate. I'll take the helm."

90

WITHOUT A MOMENT'S hesitation, Straw thrust the throttle forward, spun the helm, and headed the boat into the storm. "Hold on," he said.

As soon as they came out of the lee of Devil's Limb, the boat was enveloped in the roar of breaking water, sheets of rain slamming into the windows, spume flying through the air. The waves mounted up, violent chop riding bigger waves which themselves rode on deep and terrifying swells that marched along in a regular cadence, their breaking crests swept back by the hurricane-force winds.

The wind had shifted from the east and now the waves were coming on their stern quarter, pushing the boat forward and sideways. Her father fought the screw-turn motion of it, speeding up and slowing down. Each comber rose under the boat, throwing its nose forward, steeper and steeper, as her father gunned the engine and tried to keep the breaking water from pushing the stern under. As soon as the wave passed, the boat would tip back, bow rising into the air, and it would subside into the trough of the following wave. The air would fall into eerie silence for a moment in the lee of the trough, and then a wave would tilt them up again, lifting them into the gale. Under her father's expert seamanship the boat seemed to fall into a rhythm, its predictability bringing a small sense of reassurance. Abbey watched their progress across the bay, and finally, when they entered the protected waters of the Muscle Ridge channel, the sea subsided dramatically.

"Abbey," said her father, "check the forward bilge. I'm getting almost continuous bilge pump action here."

"Right."

She climbed down the stairs into the cabin and undogged the hatch, peering in with a flashlight. She could see water sloshing about. Probing with the light, she saw the water was well above the automatic bilge pump switch.

Leaning in farther, she shone the beam into the murky water, then reached down into it, feeling along the inside curve of the hull. Her fingers located a crack and she could feel the flow of water coming in. It wasn't a wide crack but it was long, and what was worse, the corkscrew motion of the boat was moving the two pieces on either side, grinding them against each other, slowly but surely opening it up. The water level was increasing in the bilge, despite the pump working full time.

She came back up. "The water's coming in faster than the pump can pump it out," she said.

"You and Jackie form a bucket brigade."

Abbey pulled a plastic bucket out from under the sink. Jackie positioned herself at the cabin door, while Abbey dipped it into the bilge and handed it to Jackie, who tossed the water overboard. It was exhausting, cramped work. The bilgewater had engine oil and diesel fuel in it, and soon they were both covered and stinking with it. But they seemed to have turned the corner: slowly but surely the water level was dropping. Soon the long crack came into view.

"Get me some of that waterproof marine gaffing tape," Abbey said.

Jackie handed her the roll and she pulled off a strip. Leaning into the rocking bilge, stinking with fuel and oil, Abbey wiped the fiberglass clean with a rag. Then she taped the crack, horizontally and vertically, adding several layers and pressing down. It seemed to hold. The bilge pump, going full bore, now was able to draw down the water on its own, without the help of their bucket brigade.

Jackie called down to her, "Abbey, your father wants you on deck. We're heading into the rip."

Abbey climbed up the stairs into the pilothouse. They were out of the channel and the seas were mounting up again. Ahead, Abbey could see a stretch of whitecaps where the rip current began that gave Ripp Island its name, churning along the northern reefs. It was a classic cross tide, the flow running against the prevailing wind and seas, creating massive standing waves, whirlpools, and a brutal chop.

"Hang on," said her father, increasing speed. As the boat hit the current, it slowed down and her father continued to throttle up to counteract the current. The sea was pushing the stern and the current wanted to turn the *Marea II* by the bow, giving the boat a fierce and unpredictable motion which her father struggled to control, throwing the wheel from one side to the other, heavy chop bursting over the bow and washing hard across the foredeck, while swells battered the stern, sending water boiling in through the scuppers. The boat shuddered under the twisting strain, the booming sound of water hammering the hull in two directions.

Silently, her father remained at the wheel, the faint light from the electronics bathing his tense face in a ghastly greenish glow, his muscular arms working the wheel. It was a losing battle. The water erupting into the stern couldn't clear out of the scuppers, each wave breaking over the foredeck piling more water into the stern cockpit.

"Jesus, I think we're swamping," Jackie said, heading for the stern with a bucket.

"Get back in here!" Straw said. "You'll be washed overboard!"

The engine roared, straining against the increase in weight, the boat shuddering and struggling in the sea. Abbey could hear the grinding and scraping of the cracked hull. It didn't sound good.

She ducked down the stairs into the cabin.

Undogging the hatch, she saw the crack had opened up again, worse than ever, seawater pouring in. She grabbed the tape and peeled off a strip, trying to affix it to the crack, but it was underwater again and the previous piece had pulled loose. The heavy flow of water coming in prevented any attempt to cover it.

"Get the bucket brigade going!" her father cried.

"It's coming in too fast!"

"Then shift the forward bilge pump aft! Jackie! Get to it!"

Jackie ducked down into the forward hatch and emerged a moment later with the pump, a roll of hose, and some wires.

"Cut the hose and wires," said her father. "Hardwire it

straight to a battery and reclamp, run the hose out a port-hole."

"Right."

The boat boomed and groaned through the seas while they worked furiously. In five minutes they were done, the outflow hose pushed out a porthole.

The pumps hummed. The rising water in the bilge held steady and even began to drop.

"It's working!" Jackie yelled, giving Abbey a high five.

At that moment a huge wave slammed the hull with a deep thunderous boom and Abbey heard a *crack!* Suddenly the water in the bilge was boiling in, a cascade of air bubbles coming up.

"Oh my God."

Abbey watched in horror as the water gushed and swirled up, within moments spilling over the hatch and flooding the cabin.

"Dog the hatch!" Jackie screamed.

Abbey slammed the hatch into place and jerked around the levers as water came squirting up around the edges, and in a moment it was sealed. But the remedy was only tempo-rary. The bulkheads, run through by cables and hoses, were not watertight and Abbey could hear the roar of water com-ing into the engine compartment.

"On deck!" she heard her father yell.

They scrambled up.

"Dad!" She scrambled up. "We're sinking—"

"Get on your life preservers. Now. As soon as that water tops the forward bulkheads, we're DIW."

Trying to build as much forward momentum as possible, he shoved the throttle to the console. The boat roared past

Ripp Island and Abbey got a glimpse of the lights in the admiral's house flickering dimly through massive curtains of rain. Even with the engine at peak rpms the boat was slowing rapidly and beginning to list. The engine struggled, roaring.

"We're sinking!" Jackie cried.

A wave broke over the side, tilting the boat, and it remained cockeyed, dragging itself along, the heaviness of the incoming water straining the engine. Abbey glanced at the raging currents beyond, the massive breakers thundering on the rocky shore; they would not survive a sinking.

Her father spun the wheel and pointed the boat straight toward the rocks of Ripp Island. Now the seas were bashing the boat on the beam, water erupting over the gunwales. A lash of sparks arced across the engine panel. With a loud *pop* the electronics went dark and the smell of fried insulation filled the wheelhouse. Simultaneously the engine coughed, jerked, and died. Steam came rushing up from the engine compartment, bringing with it the stench of oil and diesel. The boat slid along, propelled more by current than momentum, the waves breaking over the sides. Lightning flashed and there was a roar of thunder.

The boat swung toward the pounding surf, the combers pushing it toward the line of white.

"You two, get in the bow and get ready to jump!" her father cried.

The boat, now dead in the water, swung past the tail of the rip current and another rising breaker caught it by the stern and carried it toward the maelstrom.

"Go!"

Clinging to handholds and the rail, Abbey and Jackie

went forward. The surf in front of them roared like a hundred lions, a great boiling mass of white, with great jets of spray leaping ten, twenty feet into the air. Her father stayed in the wheelhouse, at the wheel, trying to keep the boat aligned.

"I can't do it," Jackie said, staring forward.

"No choice."

Another massive, breaking wave caught the stern and carried the boat forward, forward; as the curler thundered down upon them, the boat was propelled into the frothing surf. A massive, jarring crunch, almost like an explosion, shook the boat as they struck the rocks. But the deck held and the next wave lifted the boat and carried it past the worst of the breaking sea. It came down with another hideous crash, breaking its back, the deck suddenly askew.

"Now!" came the roar of her father's voice.

They both leapt into the swirling water, scrambled for a footing. A wave came blasting over the *Marea II*, but the boat itself absorbed the brunt of the force, giving them just enough time to pull themselves up.

"Dad!" Abbey screamed. It was pitch black and she couldn't see anything except the vague gray shape of the boat. "Dad!"

"Get up here!" Jackie cried.

Abbey scrambled up through the boulders, half-swimming, half-slipping in the surf, and in a moment she made it to the top of a sloping rock. She saw a shape in the water, an arm, and her father rose from the breakers, his arm wrapped around a rock.

"Dad!" Abbey scrambled down and seized his arm, helping to pull him to safety. They retreated up the rocks and into a small meadow at the shoreline, breathing hard from the effort. For a moment they watched in shocked silence as the *Marea II*, lifted high on the rocks, virtually split in half. The two pieces were sucked back out, wallowing and turning in the boiling sea, cushions and trash dancing on the waves. She glanced at her father's face, turned toward his wrecked boat, but the expression was unreadable.

He glanced away. "Everyone okay?"

They nodded. It was a miracle they had all survived.

"Now what?" said Jackie, wringing out her hair.

Abbey looked around. The shingled mansion stood above the trees, upper-story windows glowing with light. Across the meadow, through a screen of trees, she could see the jetty and the island's cove, where a large white yacht was moored in a sheltered corner.

Jackie followed her eye. "Oh, no," she said. "No way."

"We've got to do it," said Abbey. "We've got to try. That alien machine is trying to get our attention, it wants to hear from us, and God knows what it'll do if it doesn't."

Her father rose to his feet. "All right then. We're taking the yacht."

Rising, they crossed the meadow to the cove. The wind was lashing the treetops and the house stood, gaunt and tall, in the gusting rain. They walked to the end of the pier. A dinghy had been pulled up on the floating dock; they pushed it back in the water and climbed in. Her father took the oars and rowed, putting all his weight into it. The dinghy ploughed across the choppy cove, and in a moment they'd drawn up to the yacht's swim platform. He jumped out and held the dinghy, hauling the others out. The pilothouse was unlocked.

The keys were not in the ignition slots. They began searching and Jackie picked up a canvas bag and dumped it on the chart table. Money, tools, a whisky flask, and keys tumbled out.

"Look here," said Jackie with a grin.

Her father took the helm, ran his hand down the engine panel turning on circuit breakers; he checked the fuel and oil levels and stuck the keys into the ignition slots, firing up each engine in turn.

The engines answered with a deep-throated rumble.

Abbey saw the flicker of lights out on the pier. A hundred yards away, people were running down the pier, shouting and gesturing. The dock lights blazed on, turning the harbor as bright as day. A gunshot sounded.

"Cast off!" Straw cried.

91

THE YACHT WAS longer and heavier than the *Marea II*, which made it considerably more seaworthy. The boat rounded the jetty, her father at the helm, doggedly ploughing into the heavy seas. Lightning flickered in the heavy rain and the roll of thunder mingled with the roar of the wind and rumble of the waves. The VHF radio sputtered to life and an unintelligible but clearly enraged voice crackled over it.

Her father turned it off.

The boat slammed through a wave, plunging down into the next trough. Abbey felt her heart up in her throat.

"Jackie, get the electronics working," said Straw, gesturing at the wall of dark screens.

Abbey said, "I'll search the boat for weapons."

"Weapons?" Jackie asked.

"We want to take over the Earth Station," said Abbey. "We're going to need a weapon."

"Can't we just explain?"

"I doubt it."

Abbey tried to open the door to the cabin but it was locked. She raised her foot and gave it a kick, then another. The flimsy door popped open. She felt her way down the stairs, hanging on to the rails, and turned on the lights.

Acres of mahogany and teak greeted her eye, a sleek galley filled with gadgets, a dining room beyond dominated by a huge flat-panel TV on the far wall, and a door into a stateroom. She went into the kitchen and began opening drawers, taking out the longest kitchen knives. Then she went into the stateroom forward. It was paneled in mahogany, with plush carpeting, recessed lighting, another big-screen television, and a mirror on the ceiling. She searched the bureau drawers, which seemed mostly stuffed with sex toys and erotic apparatus, and moved on to the bedside table.

A revolver.

She hesitated and took it.

The boat shuddered, bashed by a wave, and various bric-a-brac shifted, some being flung to the floor. Another hollow *boom* and a light fixture was jarred loose, hanging by a wire. Abbey clung to the bedpost while the boat rose and rose, seemingly forever. It was far more terrifying being below, where you couldn't see what was coming. But as the boat continued to rise, she realized this was a big one: the biggest of all.

She heard the muffled roar of the breaking comber and braced herself. It was as if a bomb went off; the boat was slammed sideways with a jarring crash, the sound magnified in the hollow room, glass breaking and objects flying. The room tilted more and more, heeling over, with bureau drawers opening, pictures falling from the walls, objects careening about, and for a moment Abbey felt the boat was going to roll. But the tilting finally came to a halt and with a groan of stress the boat began to right itself while dropping with a sickening plummet into the next trough. There was a terrifying moment of silence, and then it mounted again, up, up. Another muffled explosion, followed by the jarring, twisting motion. A popping sound resounded and the television screen shattered, the fragments cascading to the floor and rattling around like pebbles.

She waited for the pause in the next trough and bolted for the stairs, making it up into the wheelhouse. One hand on the wheel, her father snatched the gun and popped open the cylinder. "It's loaded." He snapped it back into place, and shoved it in his belt.

"You're . . . not going to use it, are you?" asked Jackie.

"I hope not."

92

A HALF-HOUR LATER, with a huge relief, Abbey could begin to make out the lights of the Earth Station, winking on and off through curtains of rain. The yacht, its superstructure battered but still seaworthy, ploughed into the calmer waters of the well-protected anchorage that served Crow Island. The big white bubble itself loomed into view, illuminated by spotlights, rising from a cluster of buildings on the barren, windswept crown of the island.

From a long-ago school trip Abbey vaguely remembered a couple of nerdy technicians lecturing them about what the Earth Station did and how they lived on the island and kept it running. Inside the huge white bubble was a huge, motorized parabolic antenna that she remembered could be rotated to point at any number of telecommunications satellites or even used for deep-space communications with spacecraft. But its primary function was to handle overseas telephone calls—or at least that was what she remembered.

She hoped it could be moved to point at Deimos—and

that Deimos, in its orbit around Mars, hadn't gone around the backside of the planet where it would be cut off from radio contact with Earth.

The yacht slowed as it came into the harbor. It was well sheltered by two high, rocky arms of land that encircled the harbor like an embrace. A pair of concrete piers, old and cracking, jutted into the water below the Earth Station. A few boats were moored in the harbor but the ferry slip was empty.

Her father throttled down and brought the yacht into the ferry berth, easing it toward the landing.

Abbey checked her watch: four o'clock. She gazed up at the huge dome.

"So what's the message?" Jackie asked.

"I'm working on it." How could she even begin to understand the purpose of the alien weapon—if it even was a weapon—and what it wanted?

"If it's a weapon," Jackie said, "why didn't it destroy the Earth already?"

"Perhaps habitable planets like Earth are hard to find. Or maybe it didn't want to destroy the human race but instead do something else with us. Warn us, kick a little ass, intimidate with its power, enslave us."

"Enslave?"

"Who knows? Perhaps their psychology is so unreachable that we'll never hope to understand it."

The engines backed as the yacht shuddered to a halt against the platform.

"Tie up," her father ordered tersely.

Abbey and Jackie hopped out and secured the boat. They stood on the dock in the howling storm, the rain lashing down. Abbey was so wet and cold that she hardly felt it. Looking at her father and Jackie, she realized they looked a fright, faces smeared with engine oil, clothes smelling of diesel.

Abbey glanced up at the dome and felt incipient panic; what should she say? What *could* she say that would save the Earth? Suddenly her plan seemed half-baked, even idiotic. What was she thinking—that she could talk this alien machine out of destroying the Earth? On top of that the machine might not even be able to interpret English— although she felt certain an artifact that advanced would surely be capable of listening in on communications, translating and interpreting what it picked up.

Whatever. It was worth a try—if she could only think what to say.

Her father tucked the gun into his belt. "Follow my lead, stay cool—and be nice."

93

storm, they made their way to the end of the pier and up the asphalt road leading to the complex of buildings on the crown of the island. The wind howled, lightning flashed, and the thunder mingled with the crashing of surf on the shore to create an continuous roar of sound.

As the road ascended the island, the Earth Station came into full view, occupying the highest ground, a big white geodesic dome rising over a cluster of drab cinder block buildings, with a radio tower and cluster of microwave antennas. Far from being a high-tech wonder, the Earth Station had a sad, neglected air about it, a feeling of desuetude and abandonment. The dome was streaked with damp, the houses shabby, the road potholed and weedy. Once whitewashed, the buildings had been so scoured and battered by storms that they had been partly stripped back to raw concrete. A large Quonset hut, open on one end, was filled with rusting equipment, stacks of I-beams, sand piles, and graying lumber. Below the station, in a protected hollow, stood several houses and what appeared to be a recreation hall. A scattering of gaunt, gnarled spruces—the only trees on the island—surrounded the houses, providing little shelter and less cheer. The rest of the island was barren, covered with grass, scrub, and knobs of glacially polished granite.

The road split and they took the fork leading to the Earth Station. A rusty metal door stood in a concrete entryway, the word TRANCE on it, the first part effaced by weather, and was illuminated by a harsh fluorescent light that cast a pall over the dismal islandscape. Abbey reached out and tried the handle. Locked. She rang a doorbell set into a rusted plate.

Nothing.

She pushed the button harder but heard no ring inside, and finally resorted to knocking. A crackle of static sounded from a rusted grate next to the door, and a tinny voice came out. "What's the matter, Mike, forget your key again?"

Abbey spoke into the grate. "This isn't Mike. We made an emergency landing in your harbor. We need help."

"What? Who's that?"

"WE'VE BEEN SHIPWRECKED," Jackie yelled into the grate, enunciating each word.

"Holy crap." The door opened immediately. A balding, cadaverous man of about fifty stood in the doorway, the sad fringe of hair around his pate tied back in a long, thin ponytail. "Good God! Shipwrecked? Come in, come in!"

They filed into a stuffy annex, grateful for the warmth. An old bulbous television stood in the corner, screen filled with silent snow. On the table were scattered the remains of a midnight snack, candy bar wrappers, several Coke cans,

and a coffee mug, along with several well-worn books—
Eliot's *The Waste Land*, Kerouac's *On the Road*, Joyce's
Finnegans Wake.

"Are you all right?" the guard said, staring at them and
almost babbling. "Did your boat sink? Sit down, sit down!
Can I get you some coffee?"

"We're fine now," said her father, extending his hand. "My
name's Straw. Our boat's in the harbor."

"Coffee would be great," said Jackie loudly.

"Right, hey, coming up."

They sat down at the metal table and the man bustled
over to a coffeepot warming on a hot plate and poured out
coffee, bringing the steaming mugs to the table with jars
of cream and sugar. Gratefully, Abbey dumped in huge
amounts of cream and sugar, stirred, and drank.

"What the heck were you doing out there in that storm?"
asked the man.

"It's a long story," said Abbey's father, stirring his coffee.

"Do you want me to call the Coast Guard?"

"No, we're safe now. Please don't. They wouldn't come out
here anyway, until the storm's blown over."

"Of the northeasters I've seen out here," said the fellow,
"this is one of the bigger ones—especially for summer. You're
damn lucky to be alive."

"Who else is on the island?" her father asked casually.

"There's me and three others—two technicians and a
communications specialist. We live in the houses down
below."

"With your families?"

"No families out here. We come for a three-month rotation, three on, three off. This is my fourth year. The pay's

great and you get a chance to unwind from the world. Read. Think. By the way, name's Fuller. Jordan Fuller." He stuck out a lanky hand and they introduced themselves all around.

Her father nursed his coffee. Rain battered the windows. Even at the top of the island, Abbey could hear the muffled thunder of surf on the rocks below.

"So you're up here in this station all by yourself tonight?" her father asked, stirring.

"No, there's a technician in the station. I'm sort of just security. Dr. Simic's in the station now."

"And when does he get relieved?"

"She. Not til seven."

"We'd like to meet Dr. Simic," Abbey said.

Fuller shook his head. "Sorry. Can't go in there. Off limits."

"Come on," Abbey said, with a laugh. "I've been in there twice before. On school field trips."

"Well, that's different. We get a lot of school groups. But normally no one's allowed in. Door's kept locked at all times."

"But you can open it, right?" her father asked, rising.

"Sure I can. Why do you ask?"

Her father removed the revolver from his pocket and laid it carefully on the table, keeping his hand on it. "Then please do it."

94

THE PRESIDENT WAS already standing impatiently at the far end of the Sit Room. The wall monitors were ablaze with CNN, MSNBC, FOX, and Bloomberg.com, the sound turned off, flashing images of the Moon, various talking-head astronomers, and the growing chaos caused by widespread power outages and computer failures.

Ford filed in with the rest and they all remained standing, waiting for the president to sit. But he did not sit down. The flat-panels switched over to videoconferencing mode, the images of generals, cabinet officers, and others popping up.

"All right," said the president, "let's have it."

Lockwood nodded to an assistant and an image of the Deimos Machine flashed on the biggest screen at the end of the room.

"What you're looking at, Mr. President, is a photograph taken by the Mars Mapping Orbiter on March twenty-third of this year of an object hidden in a deep crater on Mars's moon, Deimos. Voltaire crater. Some background first: Mars has two tiny moons, Phobos and Deimos, named after the Greek gods of Dread and Terror. Both appear to be recently captured asteroids—recent as in half a billion years. Their almost perfectly circular orbits in the ecliptic have long puzzled astronomers, who've never been able to figure out how Mars could have captured these two asteroids into coincidentally perfect orbits unless a third body were involved, which removed some of the angular momentum from the other two and was flung away, never to be seen again. This has always seemed to astronomers to be a highly unlikely event."

"What does this have to do with anything?"

"Mr. President, the idea has been raised that both Phobos and Deimos may have been placed in orbit artificially."

"All right. Go on."

Lockwood cleared his throat. "The object you see in this picture—which we're calling the Deimos Machine—is clearly not natural. We believe it was built by an unknown, extraterrestrial intelligence. We believe it is the source of the gamma rays which the MMO has picked up. And we also believe it lobbed a lump of strange matter at the Earth on April fourteenth, and a larger piece at the Moon tonight, which as you know destroyed Tranquility Base. In this sense, it appears to be a weapon.

"A rough analysis of surface erosion from micrometeo-roids and the accumulation of regolith around it indicates an age of between one hundred and two hundred million years old. All the satellites we have in orbit around Mars which can be redirected to Deimos are being redirected.

"Deimos is like a misshapen potato—it doesn't rotate like a normal planet. It sort of tumbles. Obviously the Deimos

Machine can't fire unless Voltaire crater is oriented toward the Earth. And since it's a deep crater, the orientation has to be fairly close. That doesn't happen very often and not on a regular schedule."

"And?"

"It was aligned in April, the night the strange particle struck. The next alignment was tonight. You saw what happened to the Moon."

"When's the next alignment?"

"Three days from now."

"When will the satellites be in position around Deimos?" asked the president.

"Over the next few weeks," said Lockwood.

"Why so long?"

"Most require gravitational and orbital assists. They don't have the fuel to go jetting anywhere at a moment's notice."

"Isn't it possible," asked the president, "that repositioning our satellites around Deimos might be seen as an aggressive maneuver?"

"The satellites are small, fragile, and clearly unarmed," said Lockwood. "But, yes, there's a danger that anything we do—anything—might be misinterpreted. We're dealing with alien thinking, even if it is alien A.I. It also might be defective. Malfunctioning."

The DIA asked, "This 'strange matter' that you say was fired at the Earth—I don't understand why it's so dangerous. Just what does it do?"

Lockwood spoke. "It's a form of matter that converts regular matter into strange matter on contact, like Midas turning everything he touched to gold."

"How would that be dangerous?"

"For one thing, the Earth would shrink to the size of a baseball. And then, because strange matter is unstable, it would explode with force so great it would blow apart the solar system, driving strange matter into the sun, which would then explode, affecting our corner of the galaxy." His deep, pebbly voice seemed to echo ominously in the room.

"So why did the last one go *through* the Earth without destroying it?"

"It was very small and moving fast. It converted some matter, but that matter accreted onto it and all of it exited the Earth on the way out. That's why there wasn't a huge explosion of ejecta, magma, and so forth when it emerged. No shock wave developed. It was like a hot knife through butter, essentially. Our geologists tell us the vacuumed-out hole sealed up behind it. The Moon, on the other hand, was a much bigger chunk. It was too fast to convert the Moon, but it was big enough to generate a huge shock wave that rang the Moon like a bell and ejected a stream of debris."

"So all this alien artifact has to do," the DIA said, "is lob another strangelet at the Earth and we're dead."

"That's right. The key is speed. If it's tossed at us at a slow enough speed to be trapped inside the Earth, we're finished."

A long silence settled in the room. "Any other questions?"

No one spoke. Finally the president said, "Why? *Why* is it attacking us?"

"We don't know. We don't even know if this is an attack. Maybe it's a mistake. Bad programming. It's been suggested . . ." he paused, "that the Deimos Machine might have been monitoring our planet for some time, picking up radio and television broadcasts and analyzing them. Perhaps it concluded we were a dangerous species that needed to be eliminated. Or it may have been placed there by a hyper-aggressive alien species which wanted to eliminate any intelligent life that might develop in our solar system, nip a challenge in the bud so to speak. It might also have just been woken up. The first shot on April fourteenth occurred only three weeks after Deimos was illuminated with radar from the Mars Mapping Orbiter."

The president paced in front of the screen showing the Deimos Machine. "Any idea what these globes are, this tube?"

"We can't begin to analyze it."

Another round of pacing. "All right, what's the recommendation of the OSTP? What the hell are we going to do?"

"Mr. President, we have no recommendation."

A short, shocked silence. "That's not what I asked you to do," said the president, exasperation in his voice. "I asked for actionable advice."

Lockwood cleared his throat. "Some problems are so far beyond our experience, so intractable, that it would be irresponsible to 'recommend' anything. This is one of those problems."

"Surely you could come up with a plan to attack it—nuke it, whatever. General Mickelson?"

"Mr. President, I'm a military man. My instincts are to fight. I started off arguing for a military solution. But I've been persuaded by Dr. Lockwood that any aggressive move would be dangerous. Even the *discussion* of aggression might provoke another attack. The Deimos Machine might somehow be able to monitor our communications."

"I don't accept that."

"That machine could destroy us in a heartbeat. We're

sitting ducks. Powerless. Any military response would take years to plan and launch and would be obvious, even if conducted under the tightest secrecy. Eventually we would have to loft something into space and it would take nine months to get to Mars. We can't imagine that machine just sitting there waiting to be hit."

The president looked at the director of NASA. "Nine months? Is that right?"

"At least. And the next window of opportunity for a major Mars launch is nearly two years off."

"Sweet Jesus."

"All we can do," said Mickelson, "is gather more information about the artifact in a careful, nonaggressive fashion."

"We don't have time," the president said. "You said it might fire again in three days. That thing's like the sword of Damocles hanging over our damn heads!"

Mickelson spread his hands.

The president swore loudly, his cool blown. "Anyone else got a bright idea?"

Ford rose.

"Who are you?"

"Wyman Ford, ex-CIA. I was sent undercover to Cambodia to investigate the impact crater—or rather the exit hole."

"Right. You're the guy who blew up the mine."

"Mr. President, this isn't a problem just for the United States. The whole world has to confront it. We've got to put aside our differences. We need a massive mobilization of the world's technological resources, the best and the brightest minds, a full court press. And in order to do this, everyone must know what we face here. The world *must* know."

There was an immediate hubbub of protest. The president waved them all silent. "So, you think people aren't panicked enough, is that it? Haven't you been watching the television?"

"Yes."

"A massive electromagnetic pulse from that strike is causing much of the world's power grids and computer networks to crash. We're receiving reports of suicide bombings across the Middle East and a massacre of Christians in Indonesia. We've got some people right in this country gathering in churches, waiting for the Rapture. And you want to panic them more?"

"Without panic nothing will get done."

"We could be looking at nuclear war."

"It's a risk we've got to take."

"That's not a risk *I'm* prepared to take," the president said, his voice clipped. "Going public is not an option."

"It's not only an option," said Ford, "it will soon be a fact. And all of you in this room need to be ready."

And he began to explain what he had done with the real hard drive.

95

FULLER ROSE SLOWLY from his chair, staring at the gun, his face a mask of confusion and shock. "What the hell—?"

"Easy now," Straw said. "Nobody's going to get hurt. Please raise your hands and stand up. No heroics."

The guard raised his hands.

"Abbey, take his weapon."

Abbey tried to control her hammering heart. This was even more frightening than being on the boat in the storm. She reached around the guard, unsnapped a keeper, and removed a revolver from a holster around his waist. Then she removed a nightstick from the belt and what seemed to be a can of Mace.

"What in hell do you think you're doing?" Fuller asked, his voice low.

"I'm really sorry, but it'll all be clear in a moment." Straw remained seated, his hand resting on the pistol. "Right now, you do what we say, nice and easy. It's for a good cause. Believe it or not, we're nice people."

The guard scowled, looking around at the three of them in turn. "Nice? You people are fucking nuts."

"Now please open the door and introduce us to Dr. Simic. From now on, Fuller, *I won't be repeating myself,* so listen carefully and hop to."

Abbey was taken aback. She had never seen her father like this: so calm, determined—and scary.

"Right." The guard turned, punched a code into a set of buttons on a panel, and opened the door. They stepped into a cinder block corridor that ended in a vast, hangar-like space under the dome. In the middle stood a giant parabolic dish on a rusty scaffolding of iron struts. The drumming of the rain and the buffeting of the wind filled the space with a muffled moaning noise that sounded eerie, like they were in the belly of some great beast.

A woman was sitting on a rolling chair before a bank of old-fashioned-looking consoles, dials, knobs, and oscilloscopes. She wasn't paying attention to them; instead, she was playing a computer game on an iMac sitting to one side.

"Jordan!" she said, rising in astonishment "What's this? Visitors?" Simic was a slender, surprisingly young woman with a cascade of brown hair, no makeup, and a pair of deep gray eyes. She wore tight black jeans and a striped cotton shirt, which somehow gave her the look of a college student.

"Uh, Sarah? He's got a gun," said Fuller.

"A what?"

Her father wagged the revolver. "A gun."

"What the *hell*?" Simic jumped back.

"Take it easy," said Straw. "You're Dr. Simic, the station manager?"

"Yes, yes I am," she stammered.

"You know how to operate this dish?"

"Yes."

"I apologize for the intrusion, but it can't be helped." He turned to Abbey. "Tell Dr. Simic what you would like her to do."

96

SIMIC STARED AT Abbey, her gray eyes settling down into a steady gaze. "Is this some kind of joke?"

"We're quite serious," said Abbey. "I need you to reposition this dish."

After a moment, Simic said, "All right."

"You're going to point it at Deimos. You know Deimos, one of the moons of Mars? You can do that, right?"

Simic recrossed her arms. The look of surprise on her face ebbed away, replaced by hostility. "Maybe."

"Yes or no? I imagine you can get the coordinates of Deimos's current position off the Internet."

"Maybe if you tell me what's going on—"

Straw raised the gun, pointing it up. "Dr. Simic? Please answer her questions and do exactly what she says. Understood?"

"Yes." Simic's face remained steady, unintimidated. "I can point the dish at Deimos. If you could just tell me what it is you want, it would help me help you."

Abbey considered this. It was at least worth a try.

"You saw what happened to the Moon tonight?"

"The asteroid strike?"

"That was not an asteroid strike. It wasn't natural at all. It was a warning shot. A demonstration of power."

"But . . . of whose power?"

"A while ago, the Mars Mapping Orbiter satellite imaged a device on Mars's smallest moon, Deimos. A device that had been there a long time, maybe long before Homo sapiens appeared on Earth. Built by an alien race. This device appears to be a weapon, and it fired that shot at the Moon. It wasn't a normal asteroid—it was a chunk of strange matter, a strangelet. You saw what it looked like—the projectile passed right through the Moon and came out the other side."

Simic looked at her and swallowed hard, her gray eyes full of skepticism.

"Two months ago," Abbey went on, "the device on Deimos also fired a shot at the Earth. It passed right over here and struck Shark Island, went through the Earth, and emerged in Cambodia."

"Where have you gotten all this . . . information?"

"We have access to classified government data from the National Propulsion Facility."

Simic blinked. "Frankly, this story of yours is crazy and absurd, and I have grave doubts about your sanity."

"Be that as it may," said Abbey. "What you're going to do is point this dish at Deimos and I'm going to send a message to that alien device."

Simic's mouth worked. "A message? As in a *telephone* call?"

"More or less."

"What message?"

The moment of truth had arrived. A feeling of weary panic overwhelmed her. What *would* she say? The long, long night flashed before her mind, the attack on the island, the chase, the terrifying fight at Devil's Limb, the meat-smack of the bow striking the killer and sending him to his death in the roiling ocean.

And suddenly she knew exactly what message to send. The answer lay in what had happened that night. So simple, so logical—so perfect. Or . . . perhaps disastrous.

97

ABBEY STOOD BEHIND Simic as she went online with her Mac and searched various databases, looking for real-time orbital data on Deimos.

"Mars is in the sky and Deimos is in front of it," she said. "Ideal conditions to make the, ah, call." More typing, and then Simic scratched out some calculations by hand on a scrap of paper. She copied down the celestial coordinates and brought the piece of paper over to an old computer keyboard with a bulbous monitor.

"What's the procedure?" Abbey asked.

"It's simple. I just type in the celestial coordinates and the computer calculates the actual position in the sky and aims the dish at it." She rapped away on the keyboard with her long fingers; the screen called for a password, she typed it in. Finally she stood up, went over to a gray panel festooned with switches, and flicked several. For a moment, nothing happened. And then, with a screech of metal and a humming of electric motors, the huge dish began to turn on greased gears, tilting slowly upward, moving almost imperceptibly. The meshing gears and creaking metal sounds filled the interior of the dome, temporarily drowning out the sounds of the storm. Several minutes passed and, with a *clunk*, the dish stopped. Simic rapped on the keyboard, read off a string of numbers, and sat back.

"All right. It's pointed."

"So how do I send a message?"

Simic thought for a moment. "We use a special frequency to communicate directly with commsats. Mostly for calibration purposes, although we did use it back when we were one of the Earth Stations in contact with the Saturn mission. I suppose we could use that channel."

She paused. Abbey thought she detected perhaps a faint glimmer of sympathy, if not interest, among the skepticism stamped on the woman's face.

"Do you want to send a voice message . . . or, ah, send it in written form?"

"Written. If it responds, will you be able to capture it?"

"If it responds . . ." She paused. "I would think that the 'alien artifact' would be smart enough to respond on the same frequency, using the same ASCII coding scheme. Assuming, of course, it can read and write English." She cleared her throat ostentatiously. "If you don't mind me asking . . . are you some kind of religious cult?"

Abbey returned the look. "No, although I can see why you might think that."

Simic shook her head. "Just asking."

"Can you capture a reply?"

"I'll set it up for duplex transmission. If a message comes back, it'll print on that printer there. We'll need paper." She turned to Fuller. "Hand me a stack from that cabinet over there, will you, Jordy?"

"Right," said Fuller.

"I'll get it," said Jackie, stepping past Fuller and opening the drawer. She pulled out a thick stack of paper, handing it to Simic.

"That should be enough for an alien *War and Peace*," Simic said dryly, loading it into the tray.

"When you send the message," said Abbey, "make sure it's at full power. Mars is a lot farther away than a commsat in geostationary orbit."

"I understand," said Simic. Her fingers rattled over the keyboard, she checked the switches and knobs on the old metal console, adjusted a few dials, then sat back. "It's all set up."

"Good." Abbey took a piece of paper and scribbled two words on it. "Here's the message."

Simic picked it up and examined it for a long time. She raised her gray eyes and locked on Abbey's. "Are you sure this is wise? Assuming what you say is true, this strikes me as an exceedingly dangerous, or perhaps unfortunate, message to send."

"I have my reasons," said Abbey.

"All right." She swiveled around in her chair and poised her fingers over the keyboard, pausing. And then, with a nod, she typed the two-word message into the keyboard and hit return. Then she stood up, adjusted a few dials, examined an oscilloscope, and threw another switch.

"Message sent." She leaned back in the chair.

The seconds went by. The sound of the storm filled the

room. "Well," said Fuller, his voice laden with sarcasm, "the phone's ringing at the other end but no one's answering."

"Mars is ten light-minutes away," said Abbey. "It's going to take twenty minutes for a response."

She found Simic looking at her curiously, and with a faint glimmer of respect.

Abbey kept her eyes on an old clock ticking away above the console. Everyone stood unmoving: her father, Jackie, Fuller. The storm shook the old dome. If anything it sounded worse, like a monster pawing and batting the dome, trying to get in. As she watched the clock sweeping around the dial, doubts came crowding back. The message was all wrong, maybe even dangerous. God knows what it might trigger. And now they would be in trouble for what would surely be described as an armed takeover of a government facility. Her father's new boat was at the bottom of the ocean and he was going to be charged as the ringleader, the man carrying the weapon—a felony. She'd ruined her life, her friend's, and her father's. For a message that wouldn't work or might have some horrible, unintended effect.

The second hand of the clock swept its way endlessly around the dial.

Maybe Jackie was right. They should have let the government take care of the problem. Ford was in Washington, no doubt straightening everything out. On top of that, the message was idiotic, the plan was too simple, it'd never work. *This is some crazy-ass message, all right.* What had she been thinking?

"It's been twenty minutes," said Fuller, examining his watch. "And E.T. ain't phoning home."

Just then the dusty old printer began to clatter away.

98

FORD EXPLAINED EVERYTHING, from start to finish—except where he'd sent the hard drive. "All of you here are treating this like a national-security emergency," he said. "It isn't. It's a *planetary*-security emergency. You need new thinking. That's why I sent the hard drive—the *real* one—to the press, as well as backup DVDs of the same information to a number of news outlets and organizations. You can't stop it. But you can prepare for it. I set it up so that you have about three days before the news breaks. You have seventy-two hours to prepare for it, to contact heads of state, figure out a coherent response. Yes, the world will panic. You're going to need that panic. Nothing big ever gets done except in crisis mode. Now you have your crisis: use it."

The national security advisor, Manfred, rose, his face drawn, his eyes icy, his lips drawn back to expose small white teeth. "To clarify: you distributed this classified material to the press?"

"Yes. And not just the press."

Manfred made a sharp gesture to the two duty officers standing at the door. "Take this man into custody. I want you to find out from him who's got the information and I want its release prevented."

Ford looked at the president but he wasn't going to stop it. As the duty officers stepped forward, Lockwood suddenly spoke. "I think we should discuss what Ford is saying. Don't dismiss it out of hand. We're in uncharted territory here."

The NSA turned on him. In a cold, clipped voice, Manfred said: "Dr. Lockwood, you of all people should understand the meaning of the word 'classified.'" He emphasized it with a tug on the knot of his tie.

The duty officers took Ford, one by each arm. "Come with us, sir."

"You're falling into the old game," said Ford quietly. "Listen, people: *the Earth is under attack.* That weapon can destroy us in the blink of an eye. In three more days Deimos will be oriented to fire at us again—and this time it may be for keeps. Everyone dies. Extinction. Gone."

"Spare us the lecture and take him out!" the NSA yelled.

Ford looked at the president, and saw with dismay that his face was a mask of vacillation. Lockwood, intimidated, had fallen silent. Nobody was going to defend him. Nobody. Still, what was done was done. In three days, the world would know.

The two officers pulled him toward the door, Manfred following. As they exited the door and passed through the cell-phone block curtain, Ford's phone began to ring.

He answered it.

"Take that away from him," said Manfred, in the doorway.

"Sir, the phone?" asked the duty officer, holding out his hand.

"Wyman?" came the voice over the phone. "It's Abbey. We're at the Earth Station on Crow Island. We sent a message to Deimos—and got a reply."

"Sir, the phone, *now*." The officer reached for it.

"Wait!" Ford cried, but the duty officer grabbed it, wrestled it away, shut it. The other officer shoved Ford toward the elevator.

"Wait!" Ford cried, turning to Manfred. "They've received a message from the Deimos Machine!"

Manfred slammed the door to the Situation Room. The duty officers, now joined by several Secret Service agents, dragged Ford toward the elevator.

"You're making a grave mistake," Ford began, but realized from their stolid faces that any talk was hopeless.

The elevator door opened and he was manhandled inside. It rose to the State Floor and then they led him out, through the entrance hall, and outside, where a Paddy Wagon was waiting for him. At that moment one of the Secret Service officers paused, touched his earpiece, and listened.

Then he turned to Ford, face as imperturbable as ever.

"They want you back upstairs, sir."

BACK IN THE meeting, the president was standing at the end of the table, Manfred next to him, his face almost purple with rage.

"What's this about a message? I want to know what the hell you were talking about."

"It seems," said Ford, "my assistant sent a message to the alien machine on Deimos and received a reply."

"How?"

"Using the Earth Station in Muscongus Bay, the one on Crow Island."

A silence. "And what was the message?" the president asked.

"I don't know. They took away my phone. May I suggest that we call them and find out?"

"This is preposterous—" said Manfred, but he was silenced by an irritated gesture from the president.

The president pointed at the phone by his elbow. "Call them. We'll put it on speaker."

The guards released him. An assistant handed him a paper with the Earth Station telephone number on it. Ford approached, picked up the receiver, and punched it in.

What in hell, he thought as the phone began to ring, *had Abbey done now?*

99

THE DISTANT, TINNY sound of a ringing phone sounded on the speakers in the Sit Room, one, two rings, and then a hasty answer.

"Crow Island Earth Station."

"This is Wyman Ford," he said. "In the White House Situation Room."

A silence. "This is Dr. Sarah Simic, technical director for the Crow Island Earth Station. I have some . . . truly astonishing news to report." Her voice was steady, but with a slight tremble in it.

"Let's have it," said Ford. "We're listening."

"Let me put on Abbey Straw, who made the contact. She'll explain. But let me just say this is legitimate. We've checked and double-checked it."

A moment and then Abbey's voice came on, high and nervous, "Hello?"

"Abbey?"

"Wyman? You won't fucking believe—"

Ford quickly interrupted, "I'm here in the White House Situation Room, Abbey, with the president, and we're all listening to you on speakerphone."

"Oh." A silence. "Excuse my salty language."

"What is it?"

"We sent a message to Deimos, using the Earth Station."

"Why?"

"You know why! With those shots, the alien thing was trying to send us a message. Tell us something. It obviously wanted a response, it was trying to solicit a response. Otherwise, why not just destroy us with the first shot? No— that was a classic shot across the bow, to use naval parlance." She paused. "I figured we better respond—or the next shot might be the end."

"What was the message?"

"Let me explain first. Think about it. A shot across the bow. Why does a ship do that? To get another ship to stop, to surrender, to permit boarding. Right? So I figured that's what the thing wanted. So I sent it the message it wanted to hear."

A pause.

"Which was?" asked Ford.

"Just what I said. What do you do with a shot across the bow? You surrender. So I sent it a message: '*WE SURREN-DER.*'"

A long, shocked silence. "Oh my God," said the national security advisor. Mickelson's face turned white.

"And the response?"

"I'll read it verbatim. It was a little confused. '*SURREN-DER ACCEPT. WAIT. WE COME.*'"

"You surrendered?" thundered the president. "You *surrendered* on behalf of the United States of America?"

"Who's that yelling?"

"I am the president."

"Oh. Sorry. No, sir. You don't understand. No way are we surrendering! Heck, this is what ships did all the time in naval warfare in the past. They *pretended* to surrender and then blew the hell out of the boarding party when they least expected it. What we're doing is buying time, that's all. Unless God just repealed the speed of light, it's going to take many years for that alien outpost on Deimos to communicate with its home planet. It'll *have* to do that if they're going to come. It'll be twenty, thirty years, maybe even centuries before they come, depending on how many light-years away those scumbags are. That message just bought us time to get ready, arm ourselves, and prepare for the invasion."

"Did you say '*invasion*'?" Mickelson asked.

"Yeah. *Invasion.*"

A thunderous silence.

"You didn't think we were really going to *surrender*, did you?" Abbey said. "The hell with that: we're gonna *fight.*"

Epilogue

THE SUN HAD set, the sea was calm, the sky airbrushed with stars. Abbey stood at the end of the pier in Round Pond, looking out over the dark harbor, the white fishing boats at anchor all swung in the same direction by the tide, as if carefully arranged by some invisible being. A faint breeze ruffled the water and was slapping the rigging of a large sailboat against the mast, a rhythmic clanking that echoed across the water, like a clock marking time.

Wyman Ford stood at her side.

"This is where I had set up my camera," Abbey said, "when that thing passed overhead."

Ford nodded, his arms folded, staring out to sea.

"It started as a bright light behind the church, totally silent, and then came flashing overhead with a bunch of sonic booms before disappearing behind Louds Island, there."

"So that's how it began," said Ford. "Incredible what's happened since." He unfolded his arms and turned. "I came up to see you because we wanted to offer you a job. We need you, your insight. Your intelligence. For what is to come."

Abbey felt herself flushing.

"Thanks to you," Ford continued, "we have time to prepare. Time for you to become more useful by getting educated. You go back and finish your degree and we'll hire you."

"I was kicked out of Princeton. Who's going to give me a scholarship now? I'm broke."

Ford's hand went into his pocket and emerged with a white envelope. "Princeton. Full scholarship."

"How—?"

"A few well-pulled strings." He held out the envelope. She hesitated.

"Take it. We need all the bright people we can get. We've got a big job ahead of us."

She took it. "Thank you."

He smiled and held up something else: a key on a chain. He gave it a shake.

"What's that?"

"The keys to the *Marea III*."

Speechless, she took them.

"It only seemed right," he said, "after what happened. Compliments of the president. It's a new one this time, a thirty-eight-foot Stanley, moored in Boothbay Harbor. You'll have to go down there and drive it back up. Surprise your father."

"Thank . . . thank you." Abbey felt her throat closing up.

"You already sank two of your father's boats—you think you can keep this one afloat?"

She nodded.

He fell silent, looking out to sea. Then he spoke again.

"The world's a changed place. Sure, we're seeing riots, suicide bombings, crazy religious revivals. The Muslim world is on fire. But it looks like the rest of the world's turning the corner. China and India are both on board, bringing together their best and brightest with ours, the Russians, and the Europeans. The Japanese, Israelis, and Koreans have been amazing. It looks like a period of openness and cooperation—at least in most of the world—is at hand. You could be part of it . . . you *will* be part of it."

Abbey nodded.

"And now I've a little piece of classified information to give you. *Extremely* classified. Want to hear it?"

Abbey glanced at Ford. He was still looking out to sea—or rather, to the stars.

"What's the catch?"

"The catch is it's hard to keep secrets and this one must be kept. You'll understand why when you hear it."

"You know I can keep a secret."

"Last week, one of the satellites in place around Deimos by chance intercepted a powerful burst of radio noise from the artifact. Evidently a communication of sorts."

"Did you decipher it?"

"No. And we never will—it appears highly encrypted. The important thing wasn't what was in the message, but *where* it was headed."

"Where?"

"It was aimed at a stellar remnant in the constellation Corona Australis—the Southern Crown—known as RXJ. Astronomers have known about RXJ for decades. Very mysterious. It's an intense gamma ray source surrounded by a vast cloud of expanding dust—all that remains of a gigantic supernova that occurred about twelve million years ago."

"What's mysterious about it?"

"RXJ has been the leading candidate of what astronomers call a 'quark star' or 'strange star.' "

"Strange star?"

"That's right. A ball of strange matter, the core remnant of the supernova. The supernova vaporized whatever solar system might have been present around the original RXJ sun. It also sterilized the entire stellar neighborhood with an intense flux of gamma rays. It could have happened naturally. But then, it might have been . . . *unnatural.*"

Abbey's mind reeled at the implications. "Are you saying that there couldn't possibly be any life where the message was sent?"

"Exactly. Not within ten light-years, at least. The artifact sent a message to one of the most dead and irradiated corners in the galaxy."

"But . . . why? What does it mean?"

Even in the dimness, Abbey could see a gleam in Ford's eyes as he gazed intently into her own. He said nothing and merely waited for her to understand. And suddenly, Abbey did understand—completely.

"So the alien artifact sent a message back to its home world," she said slowly. "But it ain't never gonna get a reply."

Ford nodded. "Whoever they were, they're long beyond replying."